Buffy the Vampire Slayer™

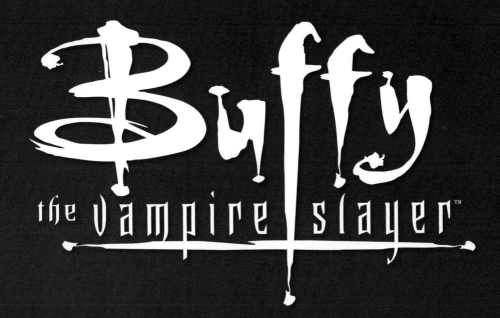

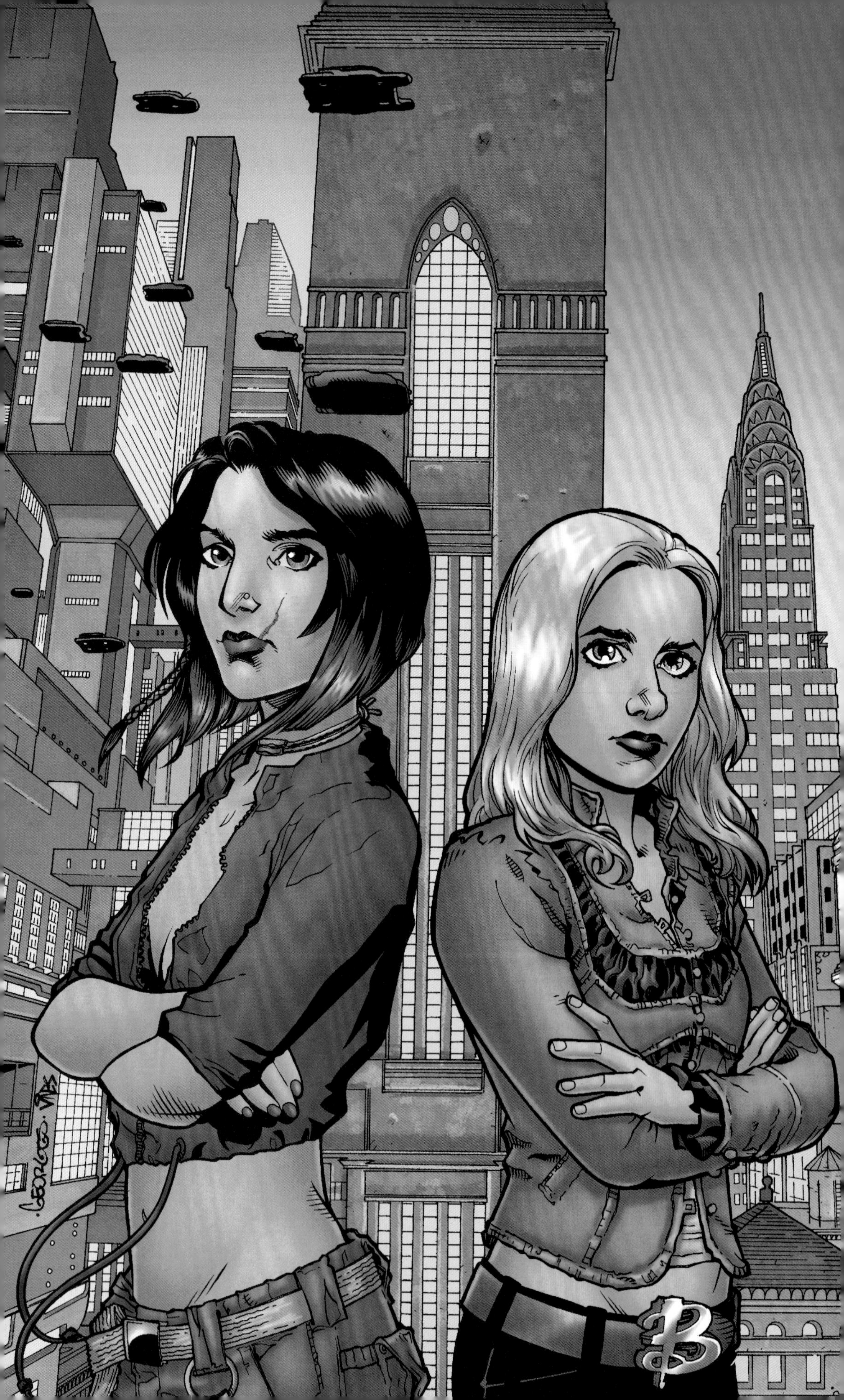

Buffy the Vampire Slayer™

SEASON EIGHT VOLUME 4

TIME OF YOUR LIFE

Script JOSS WHEDON

Pencils KARL MOLINE

Inks ANDY OWENS

Colors MICHELLE MADSEN

"After These Messages . . . We'll Be Right Back!"

Script JEPH LOEB

Pencils GEORGES JEANTY

Inks ANDY OWENS

Animation ERIC WIGHT, ETHEN BEAVERS & ADAM VAN WYK

Colors LEE LOUGHRIDGE

Letters RICHARD STARKINGS & COMICRAFT'S JIMMY

Cover Art JO CHEN

Executive Producer JOSS WHEDON

Dark Horse Books®

Publisher MIKE RICHARDSON

Editor SCOTT ALLIE

Associate Editor SIERRA HAHN

Assistant Editor FREDDYE LINS

Collection Designer HEIDI WHITCOMB

This story takes place after the end of the
television series *Buffy the Vampire Slayer*
created by Joss Whedon.

Special thanks to Debbie Olshan at Twentieth Century Fox, Julia Dalzell, and Natalie Farrell.

EXECUTIVE VICE PRESIDENT Neil Hankerson · CHIEF FINANCIAL OFFICER Tom Weddle · VICE PRESIDENT OF PUBLISHING
Randy Stradley · VICE PRESIDENT OF BUSINESS DEVELOPMENT Michael Martens · VICE PRESIDENT OF MARKETING,
SALES, AND LICENSING Anita Nelson · VICE PRESIDENT OF PRODUCT DEVELOPMENT David Scroggy · VICE PRESIDENT OF
INFORMATION TECHNOLOGY Dale LaFountain · DIRECTOR OF PURCHASING Darlene Vogel · GENERAL COUNSEL Ken Lizzi
EDITORIAL DIRECTOR Davey Estrada · SENIOR MANAGING EDITOR Scott Allie · SENIOR BOOKS EDITOR, DARK HORSE BOOKS
Chris Warner · SENIOR BOOKS EDITOR, M PRESS/DH PRESS Robert Simpson · EXECUTIVE EDITOR Diana Schutz
DIRECTOR OF DESIGN AND PRODUCTION Cary Grazzini · ART DIRECTOR Lia Ribacchi · DIRECTOR OF SCHEDULING Cara Niece

This volume reprints the comic-book series *Buffy the
Vampire Slayer* Season Eight #16–#20 from Dark Horse Comics.

Published by
Dark Horse Books
A division of
Dark Horse Comics, Inc.
10956 SE Main Street
Milwaukie OR 97222

darkhorse.com

To find a comics shop in your area,
call the Comic Shop Locator Service toll-free at (888) 266-4226.

First edition: May 2009
ISBN 978-1-59582-310-6

1 3 5 7 9 10 8 6 4 2

Printed in Canada

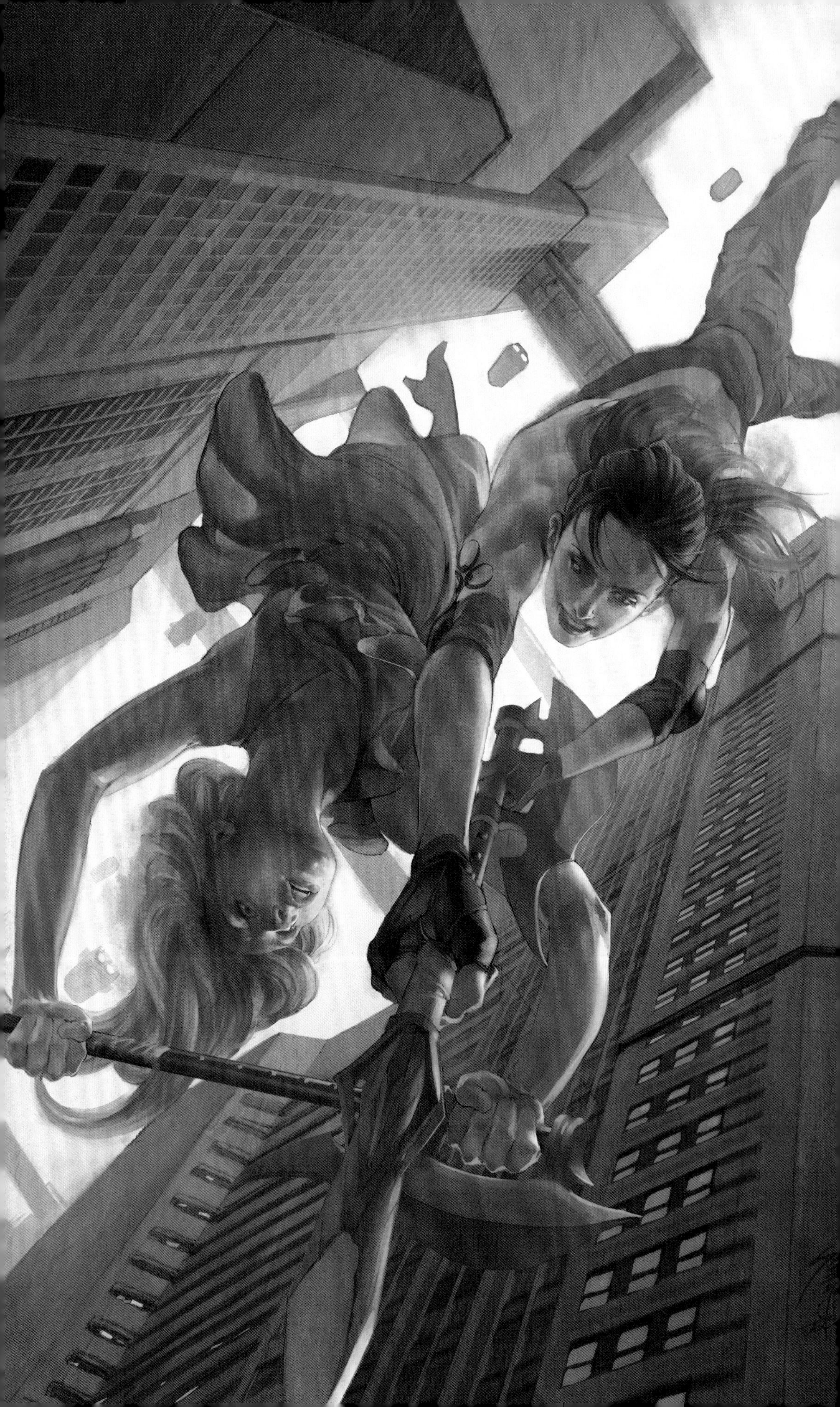

TIME OF YOUR LIFE
PART ONE

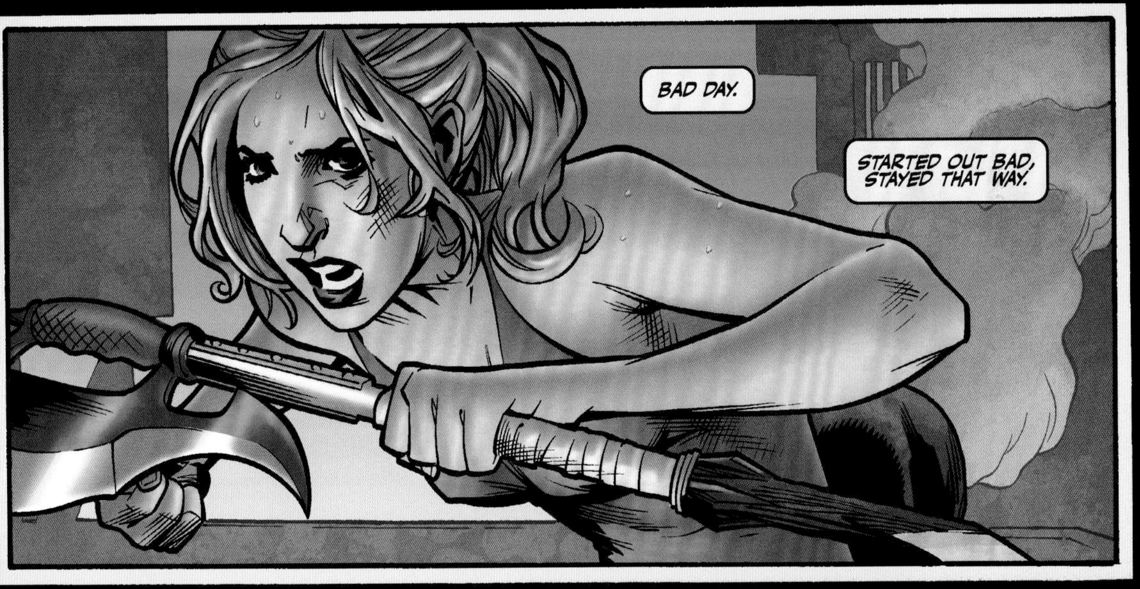
BAD DAY.
STARTED OUT BAD, STAYED THAT WAY.

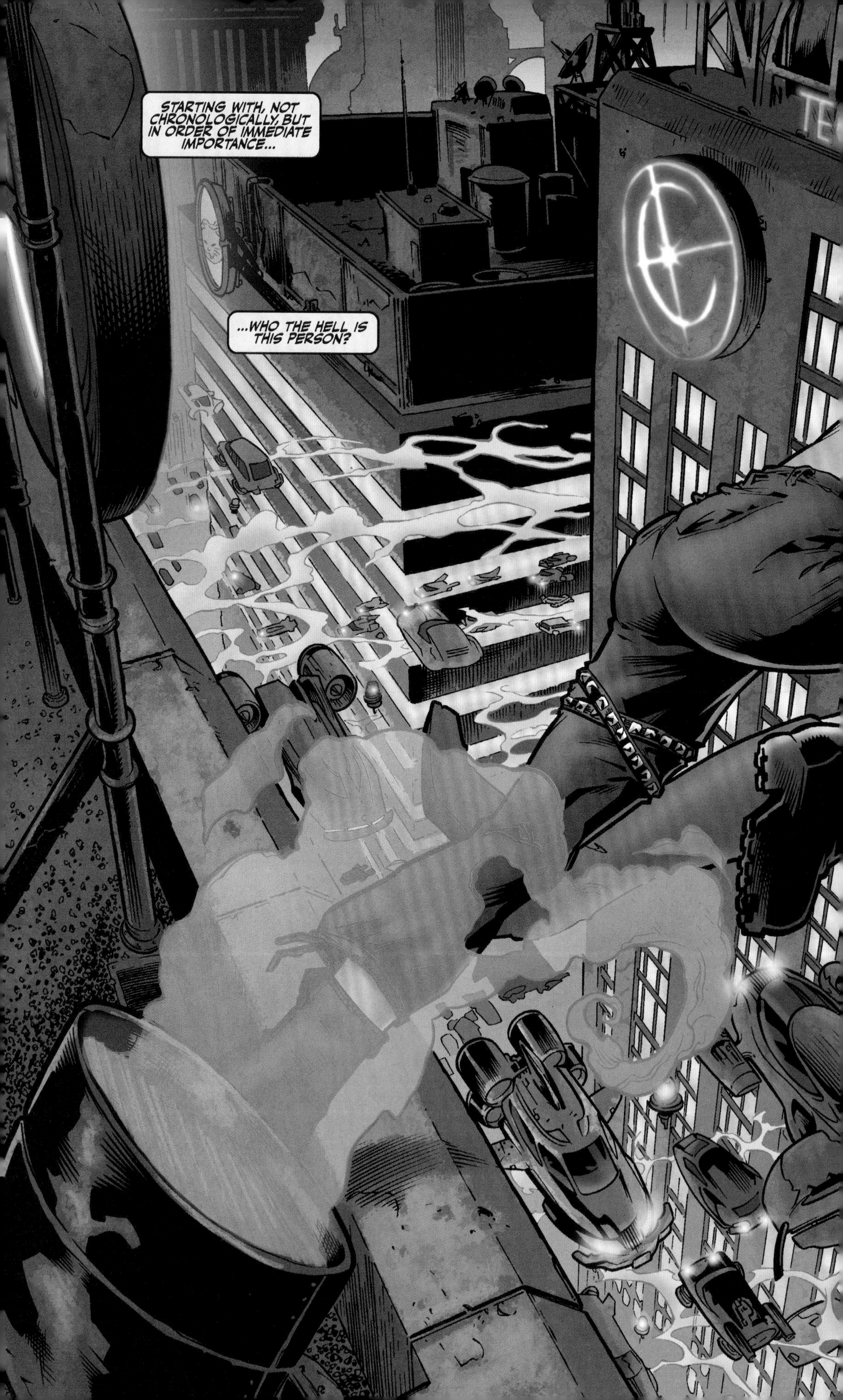
STARTING WITH, NOT CHRONOLOGICALLY, BUT IN ORDER OF IMMEDIATE IMPORTANCE...
...WHO THE HELL IS THIS PERSON?

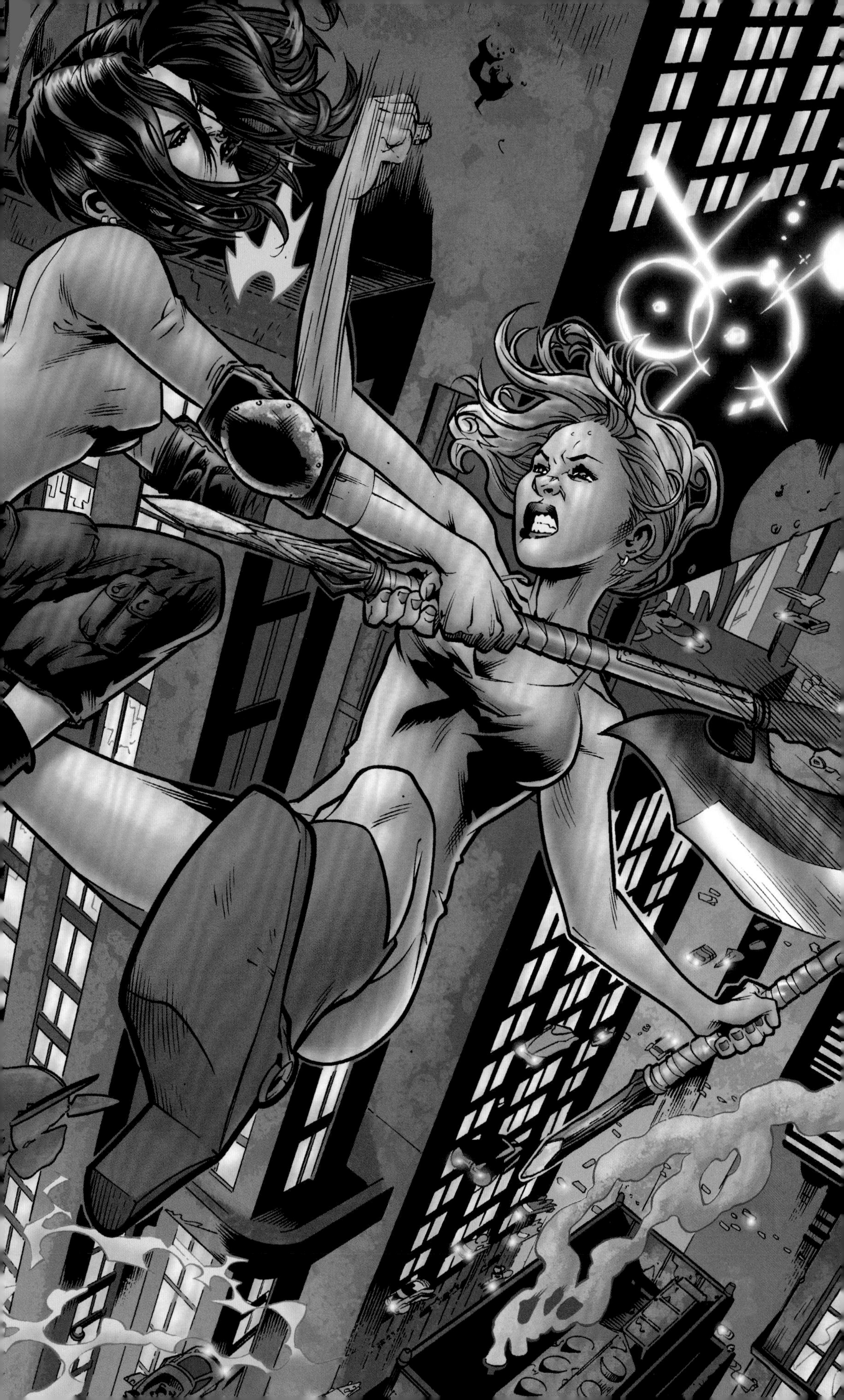

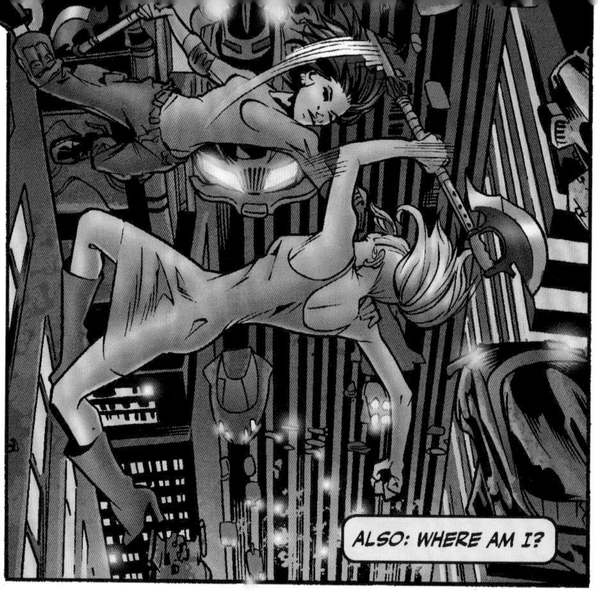
ALSO: WHERE AM I?

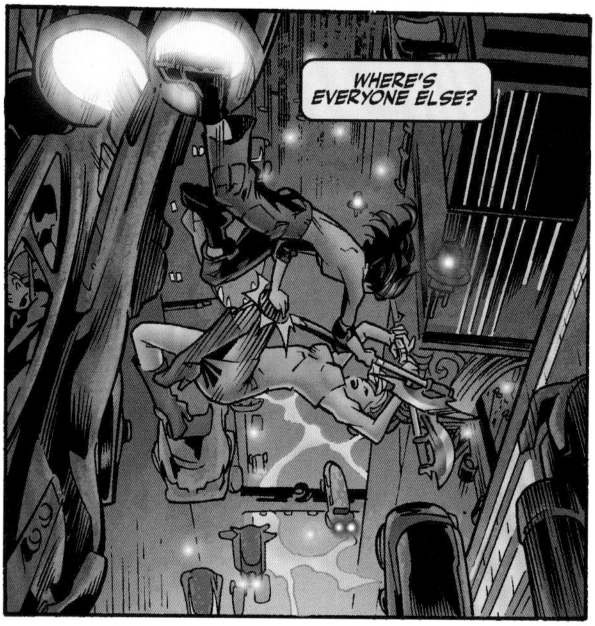
WHERE'S EVERYONE ELSE?

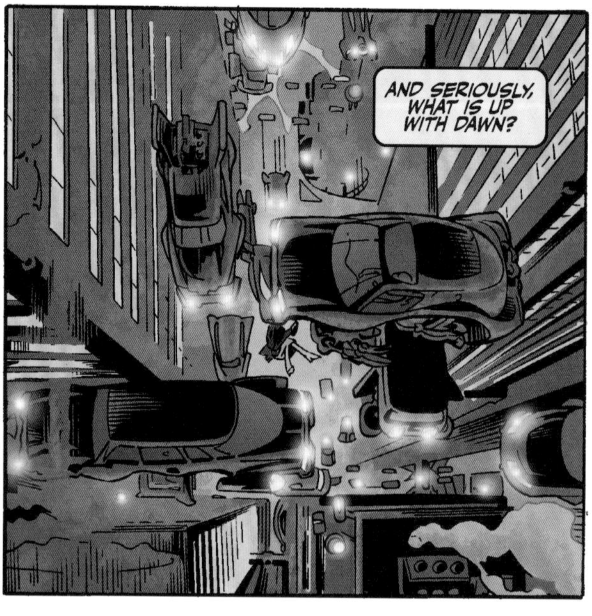
AND SERIOUSLY, WHAT IS UP WITH DAWN?

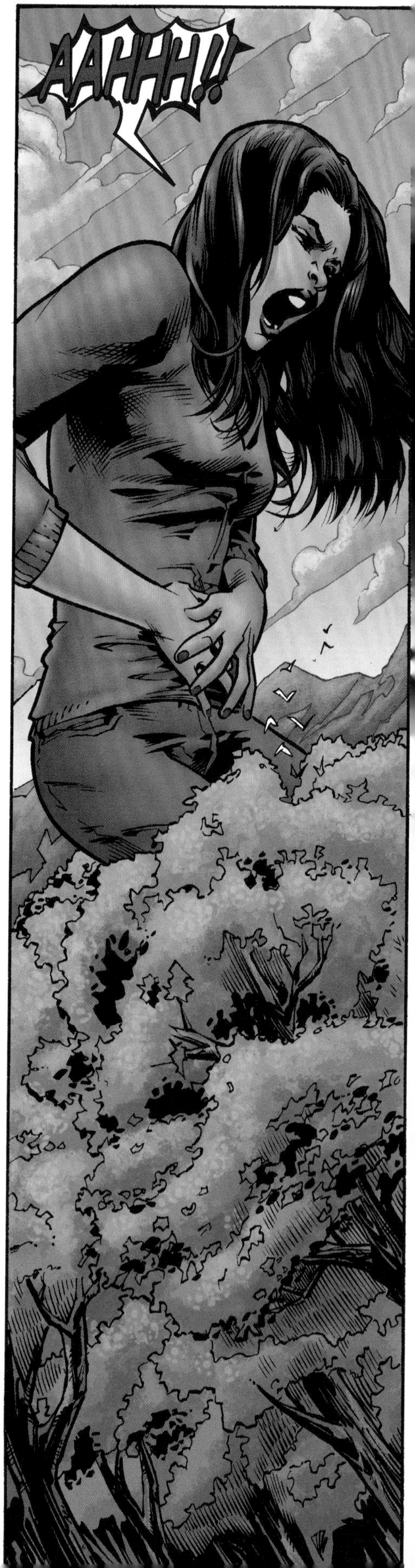
AAHHH!!

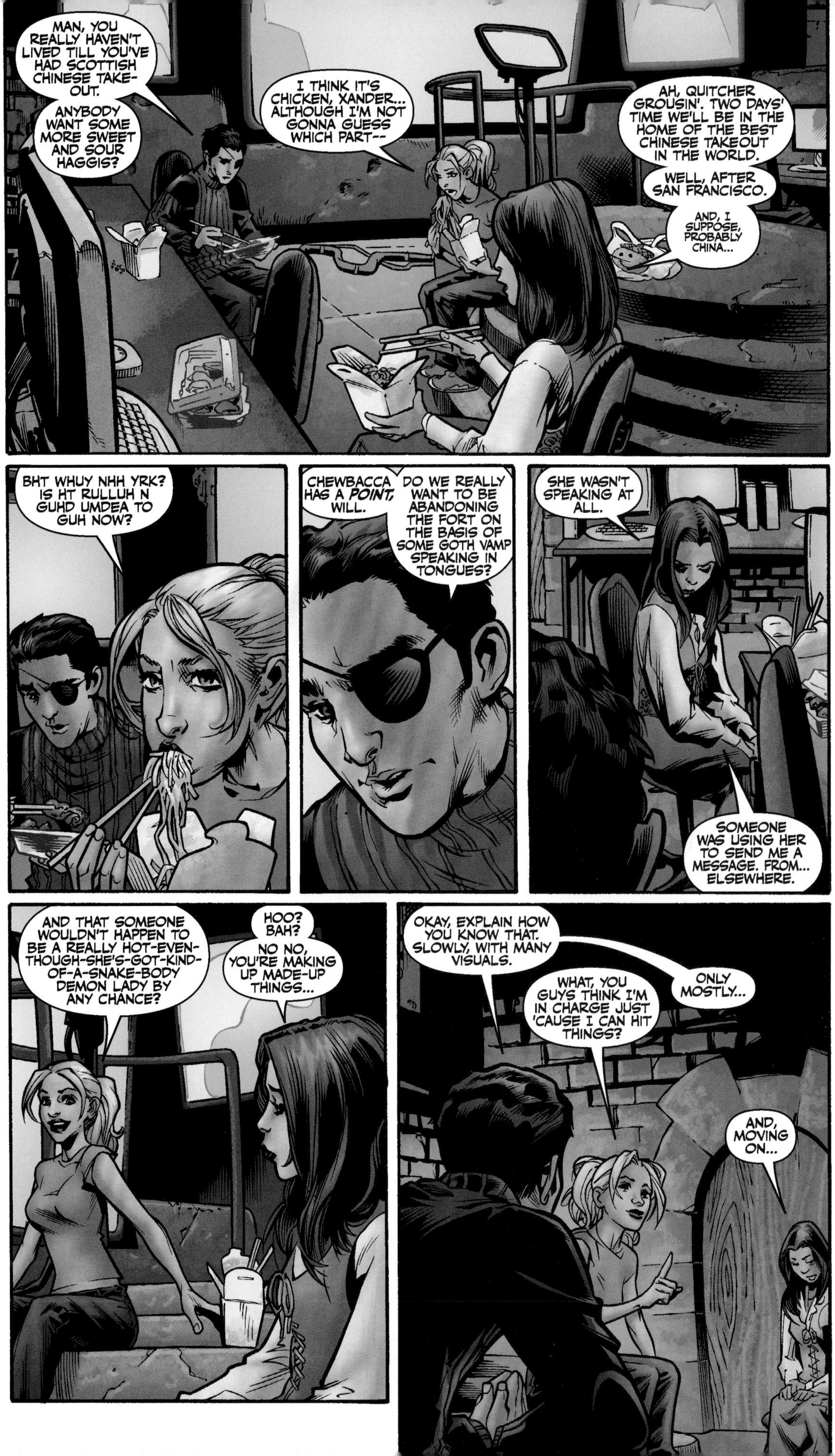

MAN, YOU REALLY HAVEN'T LIVED TILL YOU'VE HAD SCOTTISH CHINESE TAKE-OUT.
ANYBODY WANT SOME MORE SWEET AND SOUR HAGGIS?
I THINK IT'S CHICKEN, XANDER... ALTHOUGH I'M NOT GONNA GUESS WHICH PART--
AH, QUITCHER GROUSIN'. TWO DAYS' TIME WE'LL BE IN THE HOME OF THE BEST CHINESE TAKEOUT IN THE WORLD.
WELL, AFTER SAN FRANCISCO.
AND, I SUPPOSE, PROBABLY CHINA...
BHT WHUY NHH YRK? IS HT RULLUH N GUHD UMDEA TO GUH NOW?
CHEWBACCA HAS A POINT, WILL.
DO WE REALLY WANT TO BE ABANDONING THE FORT ON THE BASIS OF SOME GOTH VAMP SPEAKING IN TONGUES?
SHE WASN'T SPEAKING AT ALL.
SOMEONE WAS USING HER TO SEND ME A MESSAGE. FROM... ELSEWHERE.
AND THAT SOMEONE WOULDN'T HAPPEN TO BE A REALLY HOT-EVEN-THOUGH-SHE'S-GOT-KIND-OF-A-SNAKE-BODY DEMON LADY BY ANY CHANCE?
HOO? BAH?
NO NO, YOU'RE MAKING UP MADE-UP THINGS...
OKAY, EXPLAIN HOW YOU KNOW THAT. SLOWLY, WITH MANY VISUALS.
WHAT, YOU GUYS THINK I'M IN CHARGE JUST 'CAUSE I CAN HIT THINGS?
ONLY MOSTLY...
AND, MOVING ON...

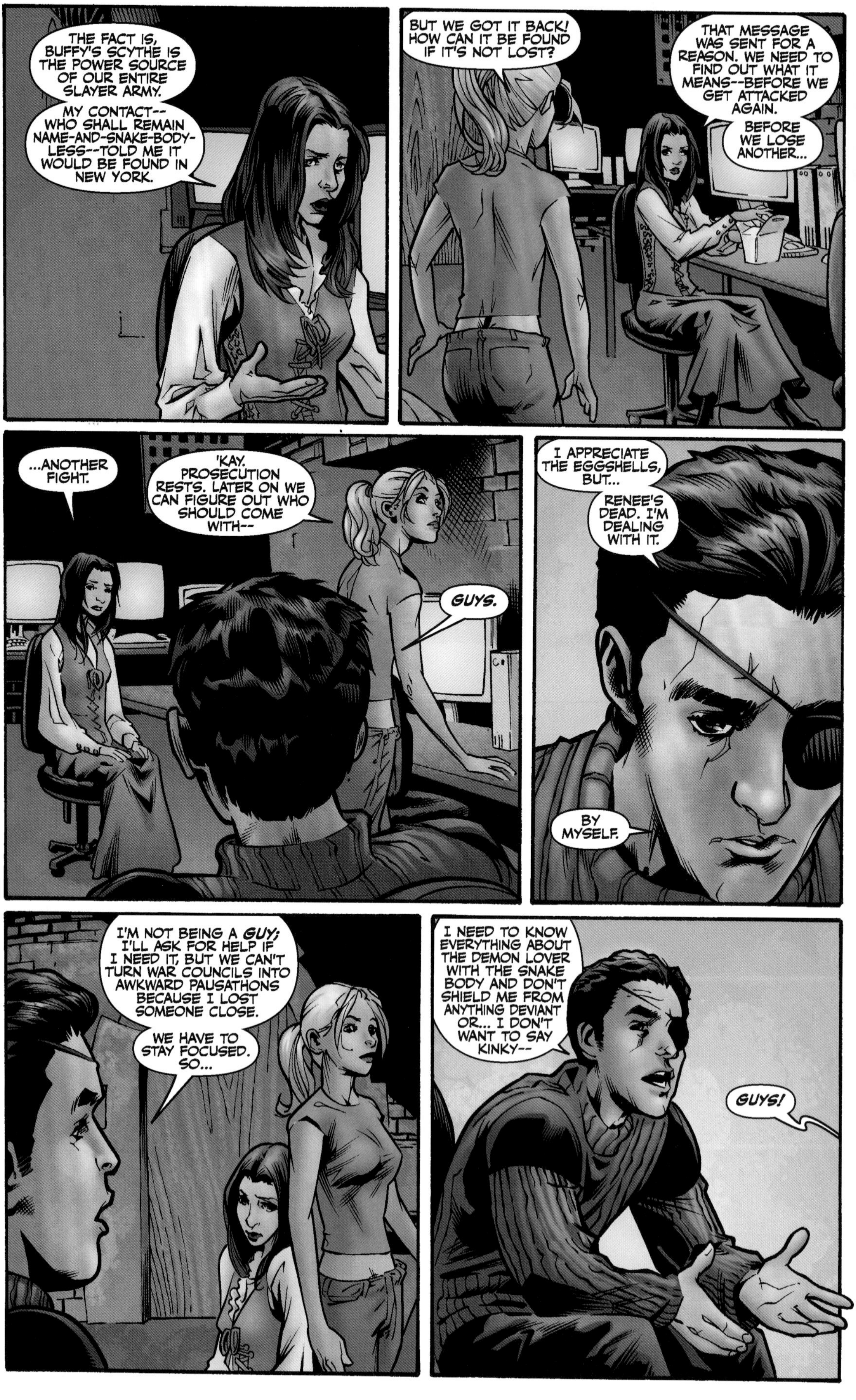
THE FACT IS, BUFFY'S SCYTHE IS THE POWER SOURCE OF OUR ENTIRE SLAYER ARMY.
MY CONTACT-- WHO SHALL REMAIN NAME-AND-SNAKE-BODY-LESS--TOLD ME IT WOULD BE FOUND IN NEW YORK.
BUT WE GOT IT BACK! HOW CAN IT BE FOUND IF IT'S NOT LOST?
THAT MESSAGE WAS SENT FOR A REASON. WE NEED TO FIND OUT WHAT IT MEANS--BEFORE WE GET ATTACKED AGAIN.
BEFORE WE LOSE ANOTHER...
...ANOTHER FIGHT.
'KAY. PROSECUTION RESTS. LATER ON WE CAN FIGURE OUT WHO SHOULD COME WITH--
GUYS.
I APPRECIATE THE EGGSHELLS, BUT...
RENEE'S DEAD. I'M DEALING WITH IT.
BY MYSELF.
I'M NOT BEING A GUY; I'LL ASK FOR HELP IF I NEED IT, BUT WE CAN'T TURN WAR COUNCILS INTO AWKWARD PAUSATHONS BECAUSE I LOST SOMEONE CLOSE.
WE HAVE TO STAY FOCUSED. SO...
I NEED TO KNOW EVERYTHING ABOUT THE DEMON LOVER WITH THE SNAKE BODY AND DON'T SHIELD ME FROM ANYTHING DEVIANT OR... I DON'T WANT TO SAY KINKY--
GUYS!

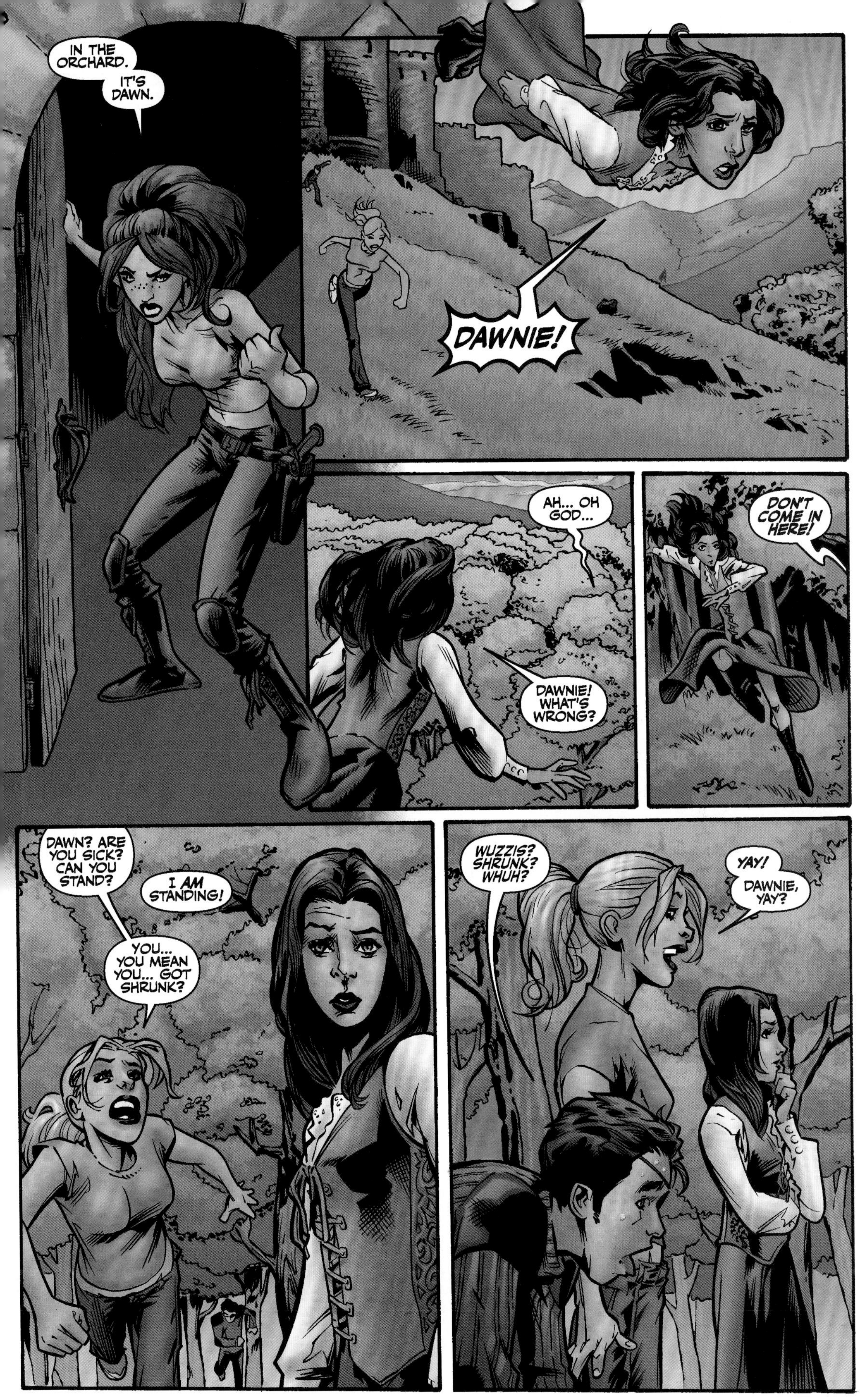
IN THE ORCHARD.
IT'S DAWN.
DAWNIE!
AH... OH GOD...
DAWNIE! WHAT'S WRONG?
DON'T COME IN HERE!
DAWN? ARE YOU SICK? CAN YOU STAND?
I AM STANDING!
YOU... YOU MEAN YOU... GOT SHRUNK?
WUZZIS? SHRUNK? WHUH?
YAY!
DAWNIE, YAY?

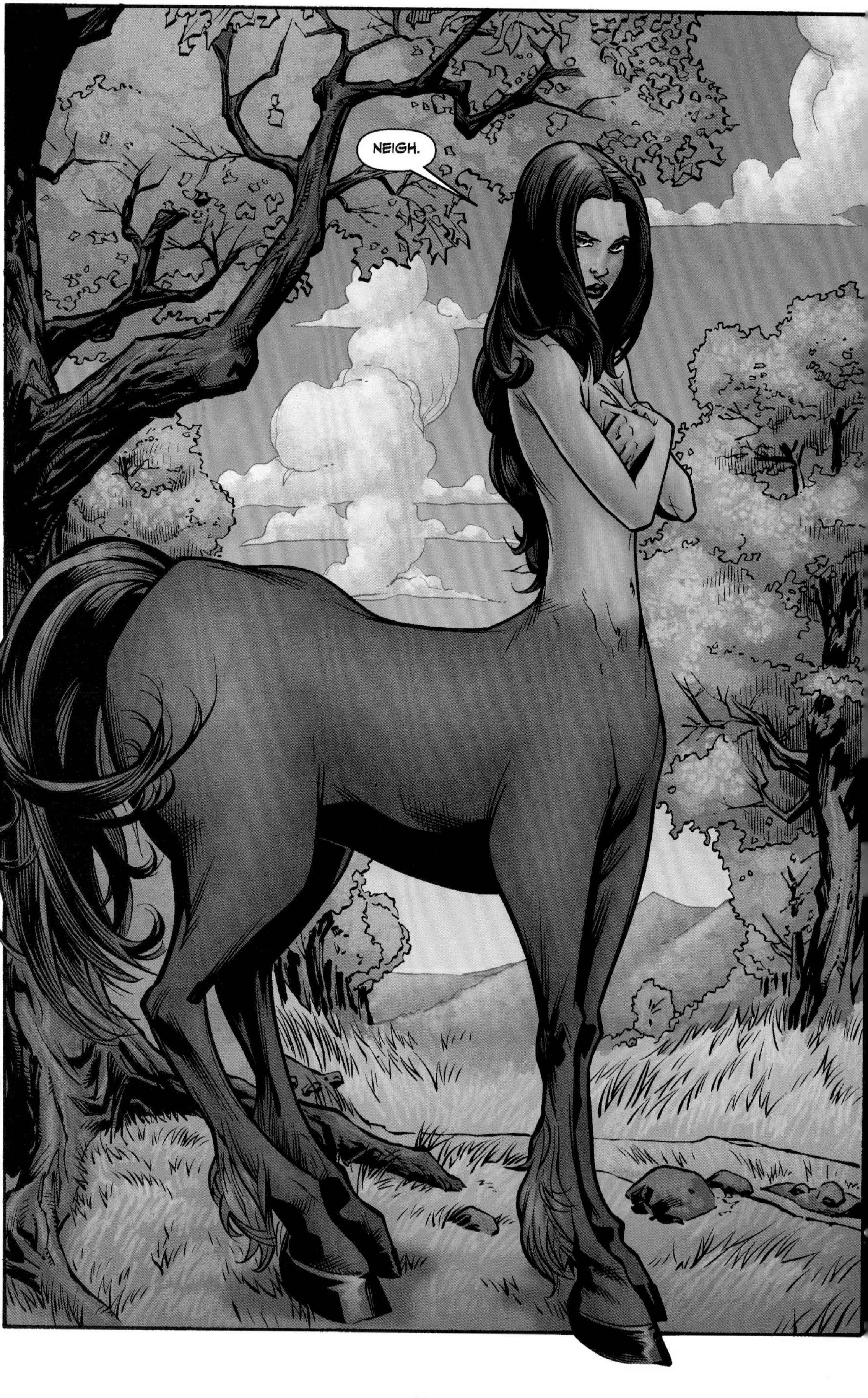
NEIGH.

HMM.

"HMM"? F$&@ YOU, "HMM." THIS IS *PRIMO*.

SWEETIE...

LOOK, COPPERHEAD, WE BUSTED OUR ASSES ON THIS BABY. AND IT WILL DO THE JOB.

YES.

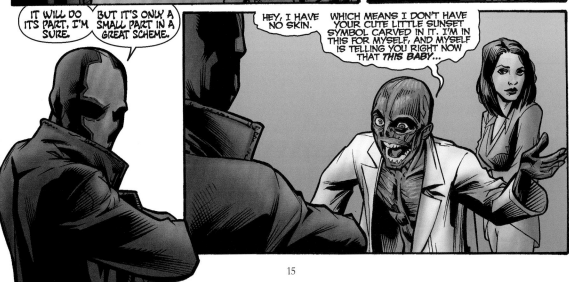

IT WILL DO ITS PART, I'M SURE. BUT IT'S ONLY A SMALL PART IN A GREAT SCHEME.

HEY, I HAVE NO SKIN.

WHICH MEANS I DON'T HAVE YOUR CUTE LITTLE SUNSET SYMBOL CARVED IN IT. I'M IN THIS FOR MYSELF, AND MYSELF IS TELLING YOU RIGHT NOW THAT *THIS BABY*...

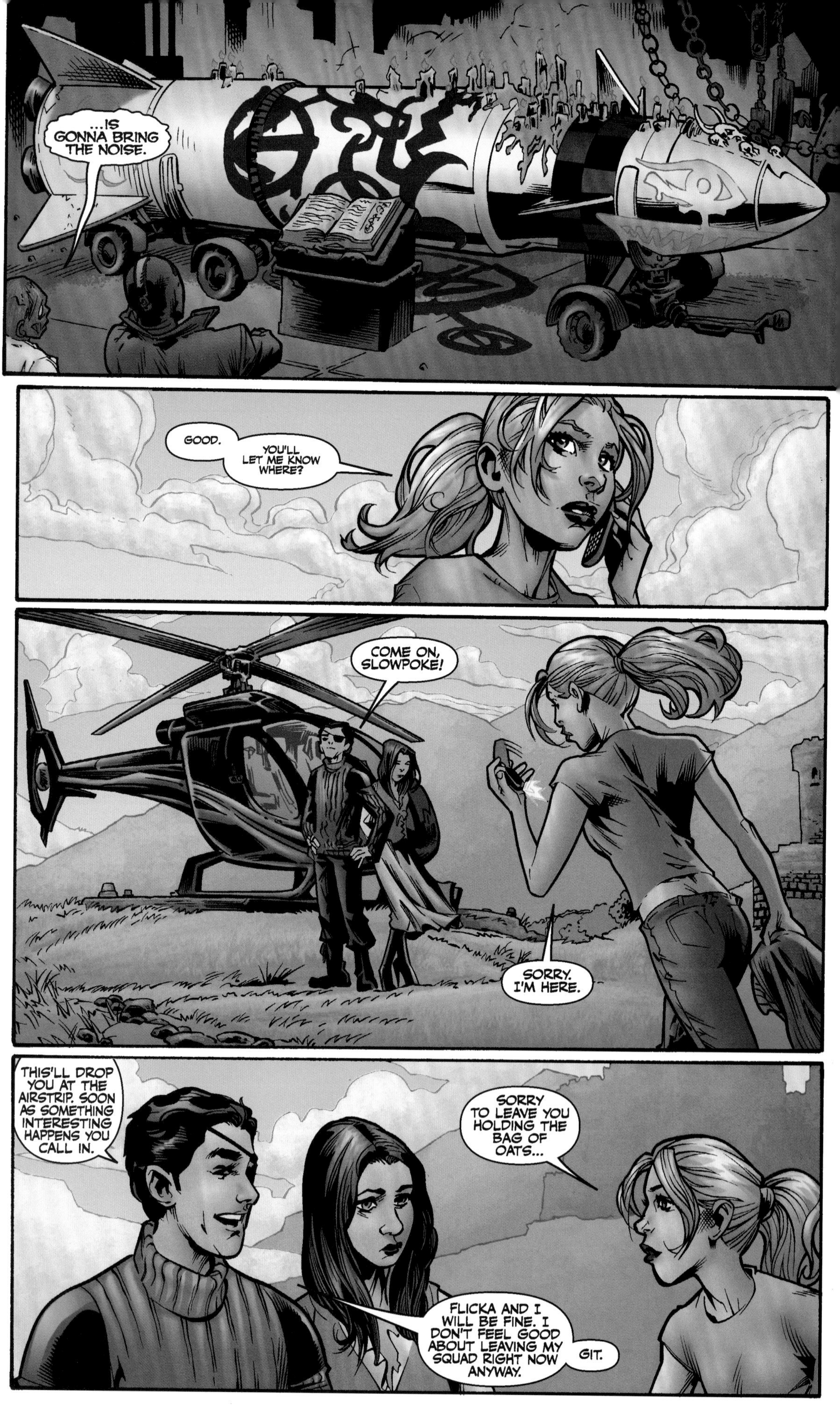

...IS GONNA BRING THE NOISE.
GOOD.
YOU'LL LET ME KNOW WHERE?
COME ON, SLOWPOKE!
SORRY. I'M HERE.
THIS'LL DROP YOU AT THE AIRSTRIP. SOON AS SOMETHING INTERESTING HAPPENS YOU CALL IN.
SORRY TO LEAVE YOU HOLDING THE BAG OF OATS...
FLICKA AND I WILL BE FINE. I DON'T FEEL GOOD ABOUT LEAVING MY SQUAD RIGHT NOW ANYWAY.
GIT.

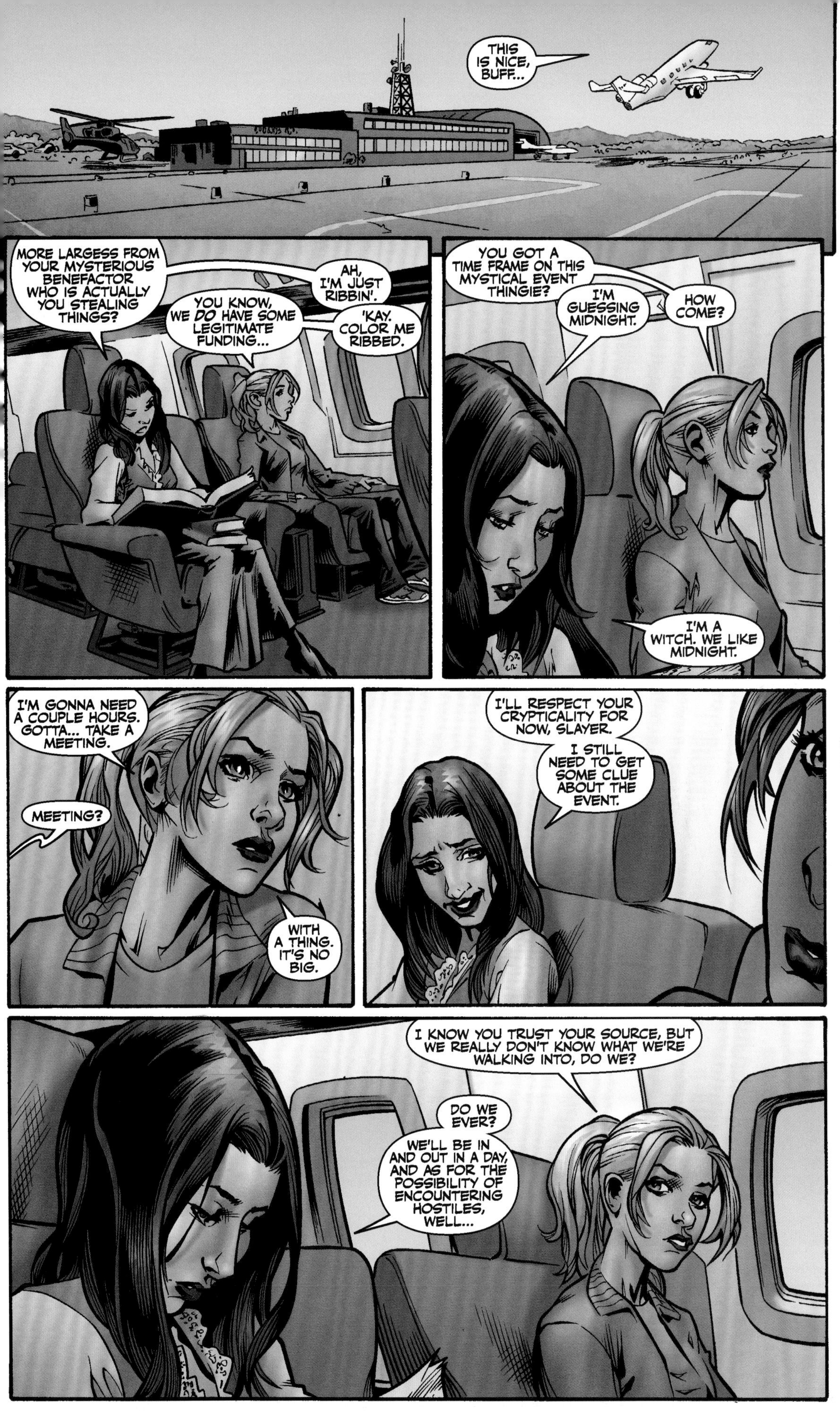
THIS IS NICE, BUFF...
MORE LARGESS FROM YOUR MYSTERIOUS BENEFACTOR WHO IS ACTUALLY YOU STEALING THINGS?
AH, I'M JUST RIBBIN'.
YOU KNOW, WE *DO* HAVE SOME LEGITIMATE FUNDING...
'KAY. COLOR ME RIBBED.
YOU GOT A TIME FRAME ON THIS MYSTICAL EVENT THINGIE?
I'M GUESSING MIDNIGHT.
HOW COME?
I'M A WITCH. WE LIKE MIDNIGHT.
I'M GONNA NEED A COUPLE HOURS. GOTTA... TAKE A MEETING.
MEETING?
WITH A THING. IT'S NO BIG.
I'LL RESPECT YOUR CRYPTICALITY FOR NOW, SLAYER.
I STILL NEED TO GET SOME CLUE ABOUT THE EVENT.
I KNOW YOU TRUST YOUR SOURCE, BUT WE REALLY DON'T KNOW WHAT WE'RE WALKING INTO, DO WE?
DO WE EVER?
WE'LL BE IN AND OUT IN A DAY, AND AS FOR THE POSSIBILITY OF ENCOUNTERING HOSTILES, WELL...

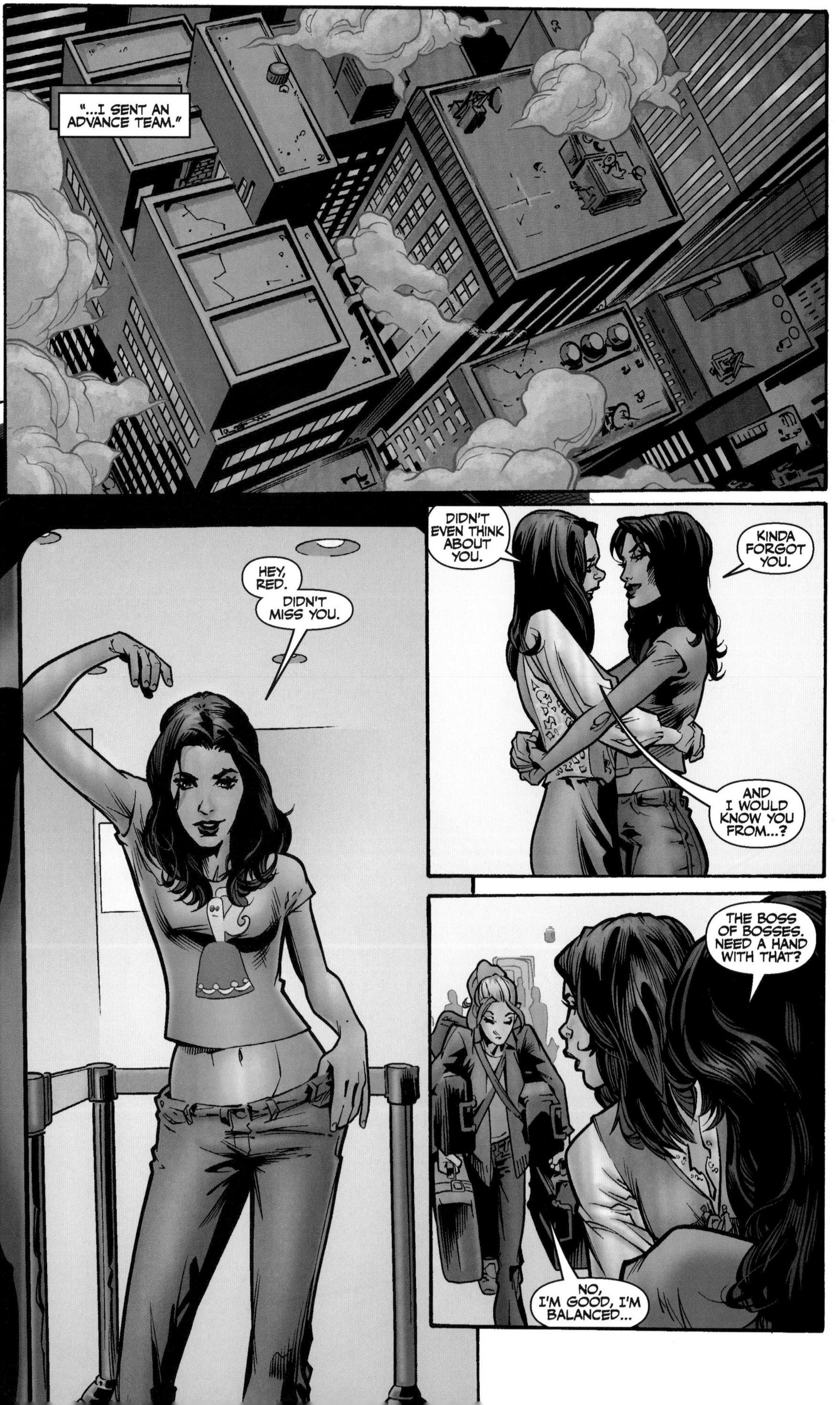
"...I SENT AN ADVANCE TEAM."
HEY, RED.
DIDN'T MISS YOU.
DIDN'T EVEN THINK ABOUT YOU.
KINDA FORGOT YOU.
AND I WOULD KNOW YOU FROM...?
THE BOSS OF BOSSES. NEED A HAND WITH THAT?
NO, I'M GOOD, I'M BALANCED...

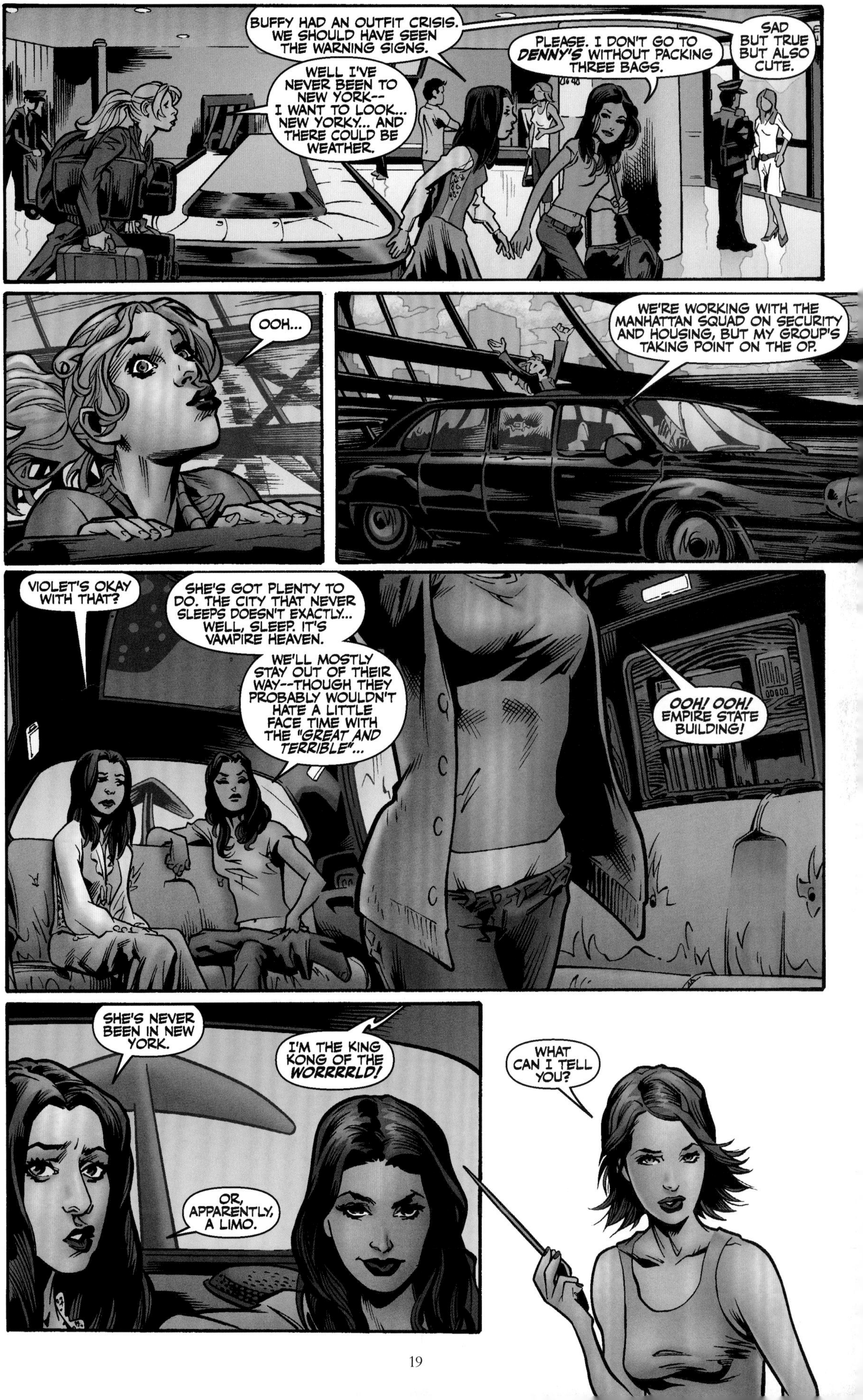
BUFFY HAD AN OUTFIT CRISIS. WE SHOULD HAVE SEEN THE WARNING SIGNS.
WELL I'VE NEVER BEEN TO NEW YORK-- I WANT TO LOOK... NEW YORKY... AND THERE COULD BE WEATHER.
PLEASE. I DON'T GO TO *DENNY'S* WITHOUT PACKING THREE BAGS.
SAD BUT TRUE BUT ALSO CUTE.
OOH...
WE'RE WORKING WITH THE MANHATTAN SQUAD ON SECURITY AND HOUSING, BUT MY GROUP'S TAKING POINT ON THE OP.
VIOLET'S OKAY WITH THAT?
SHE'S GOT PLENTY TO DO. THE CITY THAT NEVER SLEEPS DOESN'T EXACTLY... WELL, SLEEP. IT'S VAMPIRE HEAVEN.
WE'LL MOSTLY STAY OUT OF THEIR WAY--THOUGH THEY PROBABLY WOULDN'T HATE A LITTLE FACE TIME WITH THE *"GREAT AND TERRIBLE"*...
OOH! OOH! EMPIRE STATE BUILDING!
SHE'S NEVER BEEN IN NEW YORK.
I'M THE KING KONG OF THE *WORRRRLD!*
OR, APPARENTLY, A LIMO.
WHAT CAN I TELL YOU?

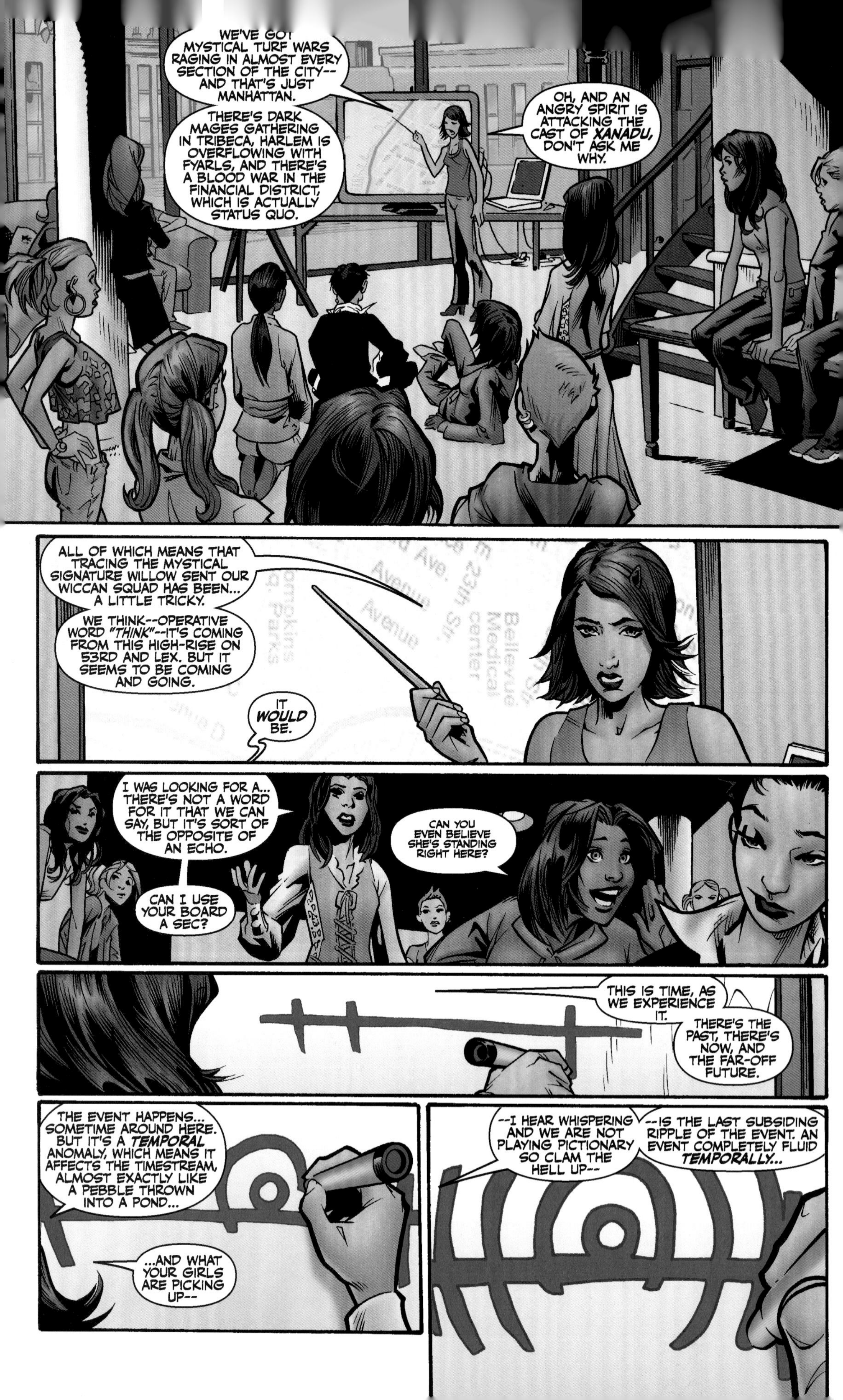
WE'VE GOT MYSTICAL TURF WARS RAGING IN ALMOST EVERY SECTION OF THE CITY-- AND THAT'S JUST MANHATTAN.
THERE'S DARK MAGES GATHERING IN TRIBECA, HARLEM IS OVERFLOWING WITH FYARLS, AND THERE'S A BLOOD WAR IN THE FINANCIAL DISTRICT, WHICH IS ACTUALLY STATUS QUO.
OH, AND AN ANGRY SPIRIT IS ATTACKING THE CAST OF XANADU, DON'T ASK ME WHY.
ALL OF WHICH MEANS THAT TRACING THE MYSTICAL SIGNATURE WILLOW SENT OUR WICCAN SQUAD HAS BEEN... A LITTLE TRICKY.
WE THINK--OPERATIVE WORD "THINK"--IT'S COMING FROM THIS HIGH-RISE ON 53RD AND LEX. BUT IT SEEMS TO BE COMING AND GOING.
IT WOULD BE.
I WAS LOOKING FOR A... THERE'S NOT A WORD FOR IT THAT WE CAN SAY, BUT IT'S SORT OF THE OPPOSITE OF AN ECHO.
CAN I USE YOUR BOARD A SEC?
CAN YOU EVEN BELIEVE SHE'S STANDING RIGHT HERE?
THIS IS TIME, AS WE EXPERIENCE IT.
THERE'S THE PAST, THERE'S NOW, AND THE FAR-OFF FUTURE.
THE EVENT HAPPENS... SOMETIME AROUND HERE. BUT IT'S A TEMPORAL ANOMALY, WHICH MEANS IT AFFECTS THE TIMESTREAM, ALMOST EXACTLY LIKE A PEBBLE THROWN INTO A POND...
...AND WHAT YOUR GIRLS ARE PICKING UP--
--I HEAR WHISPERING AND WE ARE NOT PLAYING PICTIONARY SO CLAM THE HELL UP--
--IS THE LAST SUBSIDING RIPPLE OF THE EVENT. AN EVENT COMPLETELY FLUID TEMPORALLY...

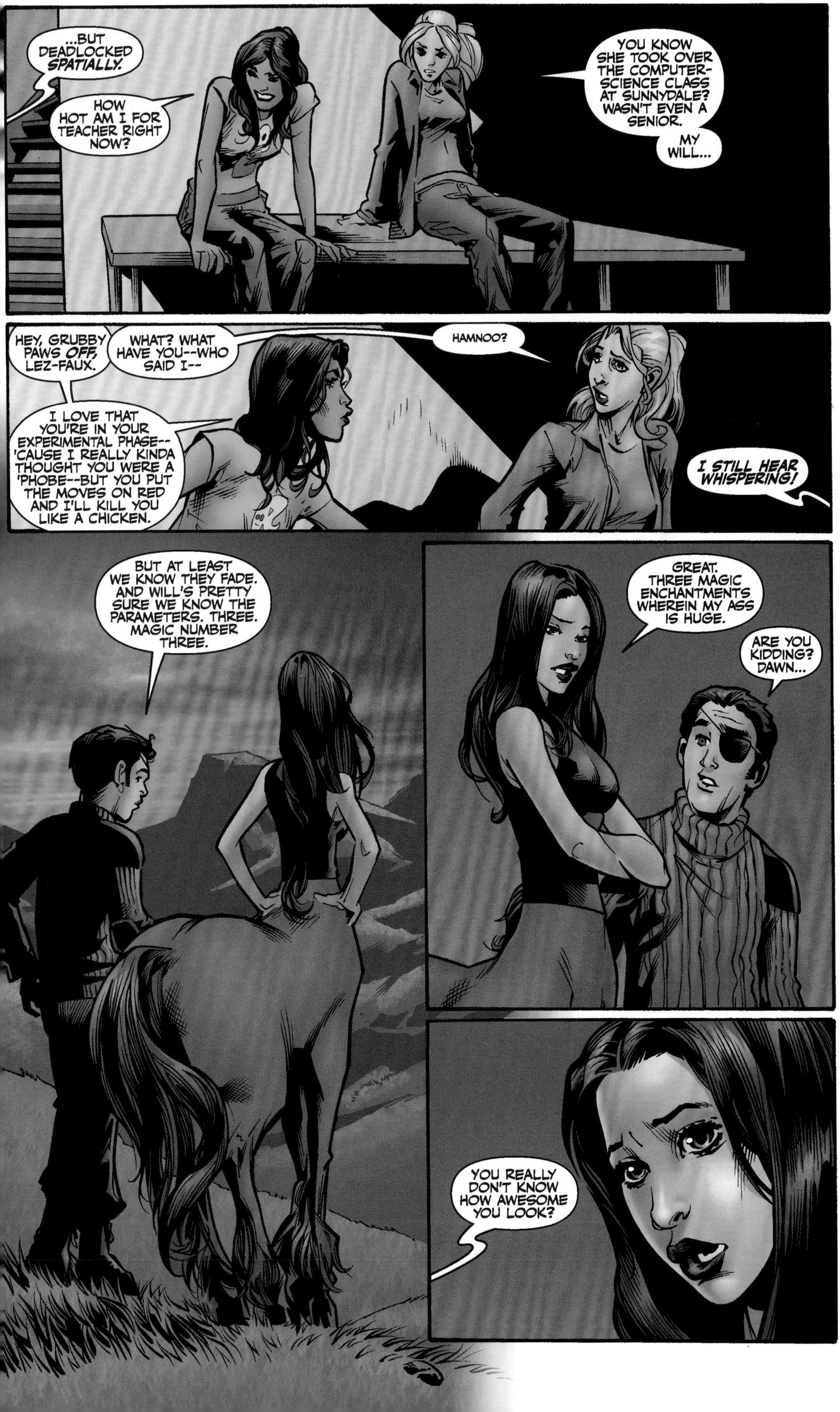
...BUT DEADLOCKED SPATIALLY.
HOW HOT AM I FOR TEACHER RIGHT NOW?
YOU KNOW SHE TOOK OVER THE COMPUTER-SCIENCE CLASS AT SUNNYDALE? WASN'T EVEN A SENIOR.
MY WILL...
HEY, GRUBBY PAWS OFF, LEZ-FAUX.
WHAT? WHAT HAVE YOU--WHO SAID I--
HAMNOO?
I LOVE THAT YOU'RE IN YOUR EXPERIMENTAL PHASE--'CAUSE I REALLY KINDA THOUGHT YOU WERE A 'PHOBE--BUT YOU PUT THE MOVES ON RED AND I'LL KILL YOU LIKE A CHICKEN.
I STILL HEAR WHISPERING!
BUT AT LEAST WE KNOW THEY FADE. AND WILL'S PRETTY SURE WE KNOW THE PARAMETERS. THREE. MAGIC NUMBER THREE.
GREAT. THREE MAGIC ENCHANTMENTS WHEREIN MY ASS IS HUGE.
ARE YOU KIDDING? DAWN...
YOU REALLY DON'T KNOW HOW AWESOME YOU LOOK?

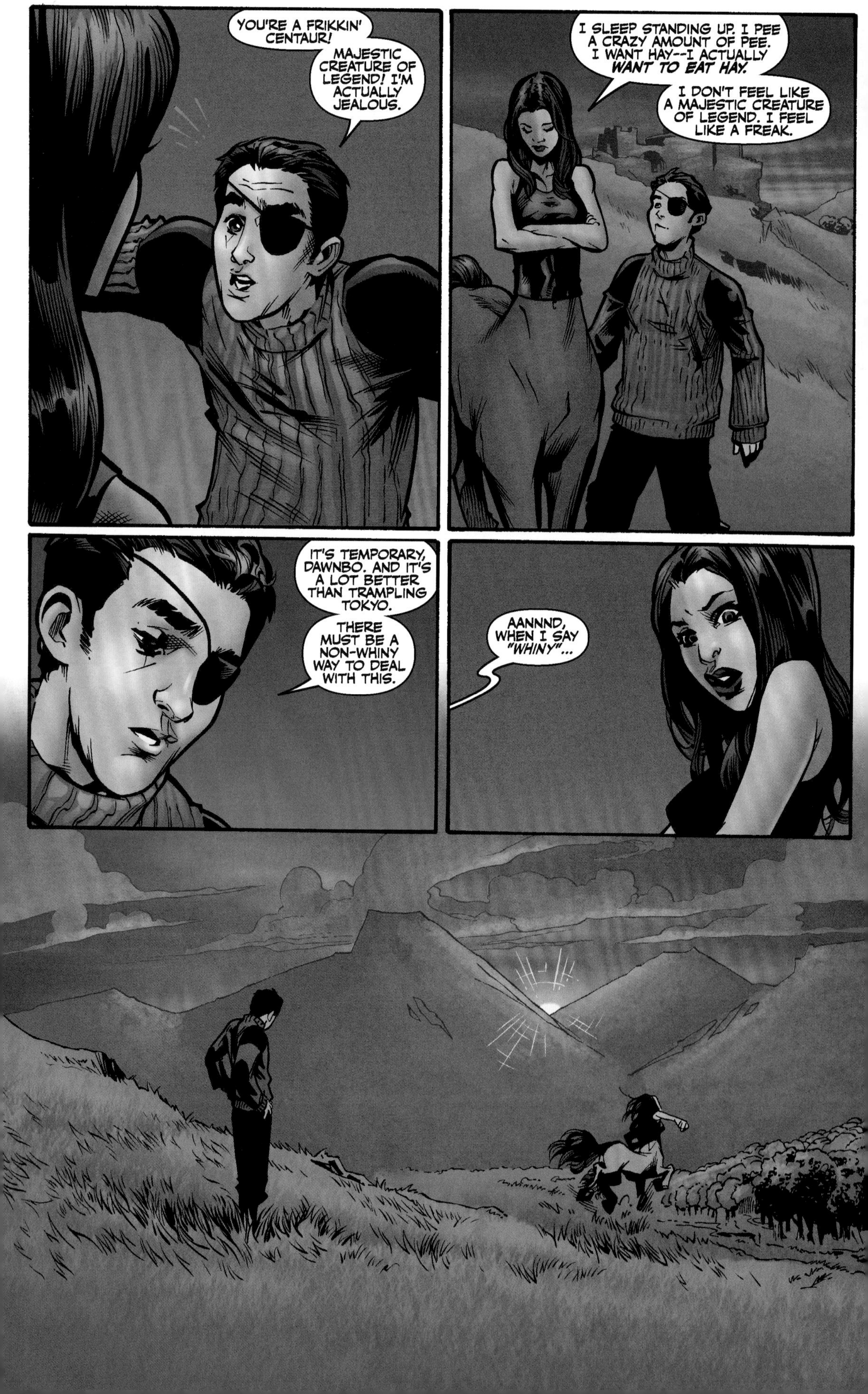
YOU'RE A FRIKKIN' CENTAUR!
MAJESTIC CREATURE OF LEGEND! I'M ACTUALLY JEALOUS.
I SLEEP STANDING UP. I PEE A CRAZY AMOUNT OF PEE. I WANT HAY--I ACTUALLY *WANT TO EAT HAY.*
I DON'T FEEL LIKE A MAJESTIC CREATURE OF LEGEND. I FEEL LIKE A FREAK.
IT'S TEMPORARY, DAWNBO. AND IT'S A LOT BETTER THAN TRAMPLING TOKYO.
THERE MUST BE A NON-WHINY WAY TO DEAL WITH THIS.
AANNND, WHEN I SAY *"WHINY"*...

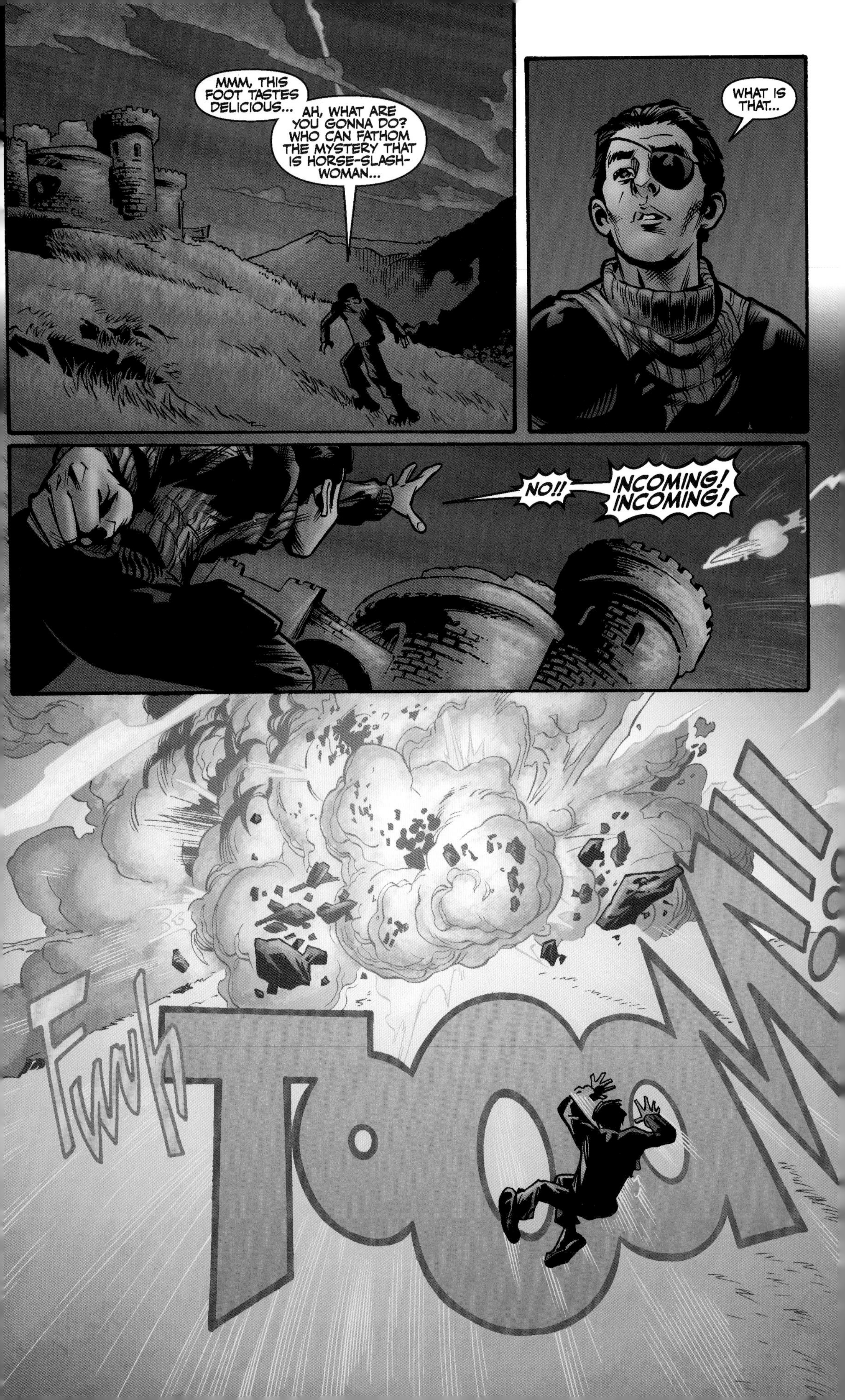
MMM, THIS FOOT TASTES DELICIOUS...
AH, WHAT ARE YOU GONNA DO? WHO CAN FATHOM THE MYSTERY THAT IS HORSE-SLASH-WOMAN...
WHAT IS THAT...
NO!!
INCOMING! INCOMING!
FWUH TOOM!!...

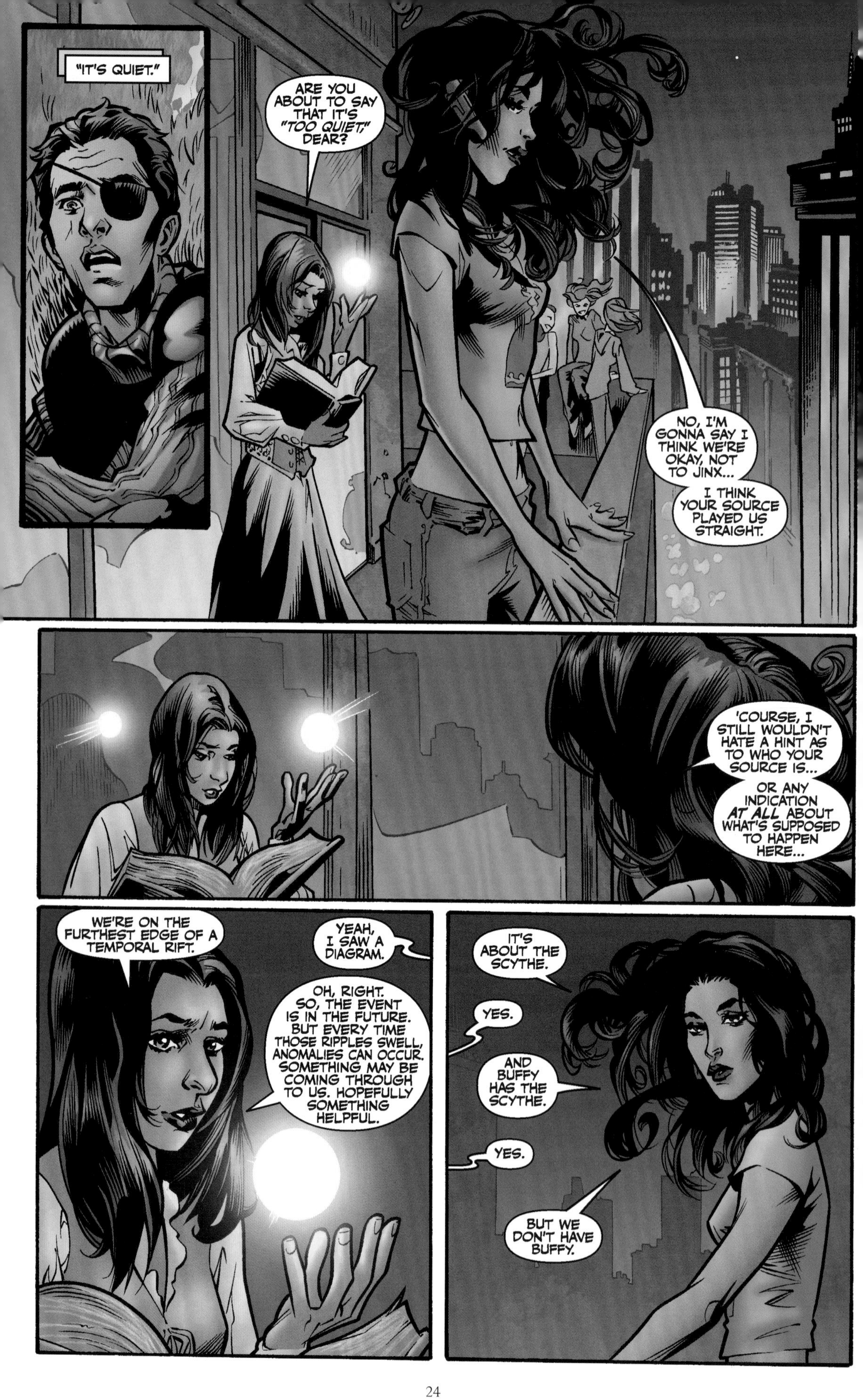

"IT'S QUIET."
ARE YOU ABOUT TO SAY THAT IT'S "TOO QUIET," DEAR?
NO, I'M GONNA SAY I THINK WE'RE OKAY, NOT TO JINX...
I THINK YOUR SOURCE PLAYED US STRAIGHT.
'COURSE, I STILL WOULDN'T HATE A HINT AS TO WHO YOUR SOURCE IS...
OR ANY INDICATION *AT ALL* ABOUT WHAT'S SUPPOSED TO HAPPEN HERE...
WE'RE ON THE FURTHEST EDGE OF A TEMPORAL RIFT.
YEAH, I SAW A DIAGRAM.
OH, RIGHT. SO, THE EVENT IS IN THE FUTURE. BUT EVERY TIME THOSE RIPPLES SWELL, ANOMALIES CAN OCCUR. SOMETHING MAY BE COMING THROUGH TO US. HOPEFULLY SOMETHING HELPFUL.
IT'S ABOUT THE SCYTHE.
YES.
AND BUFFY HAS THE SCYTHE.
YES.
BUT WE DON'T HAVE BUFFY.

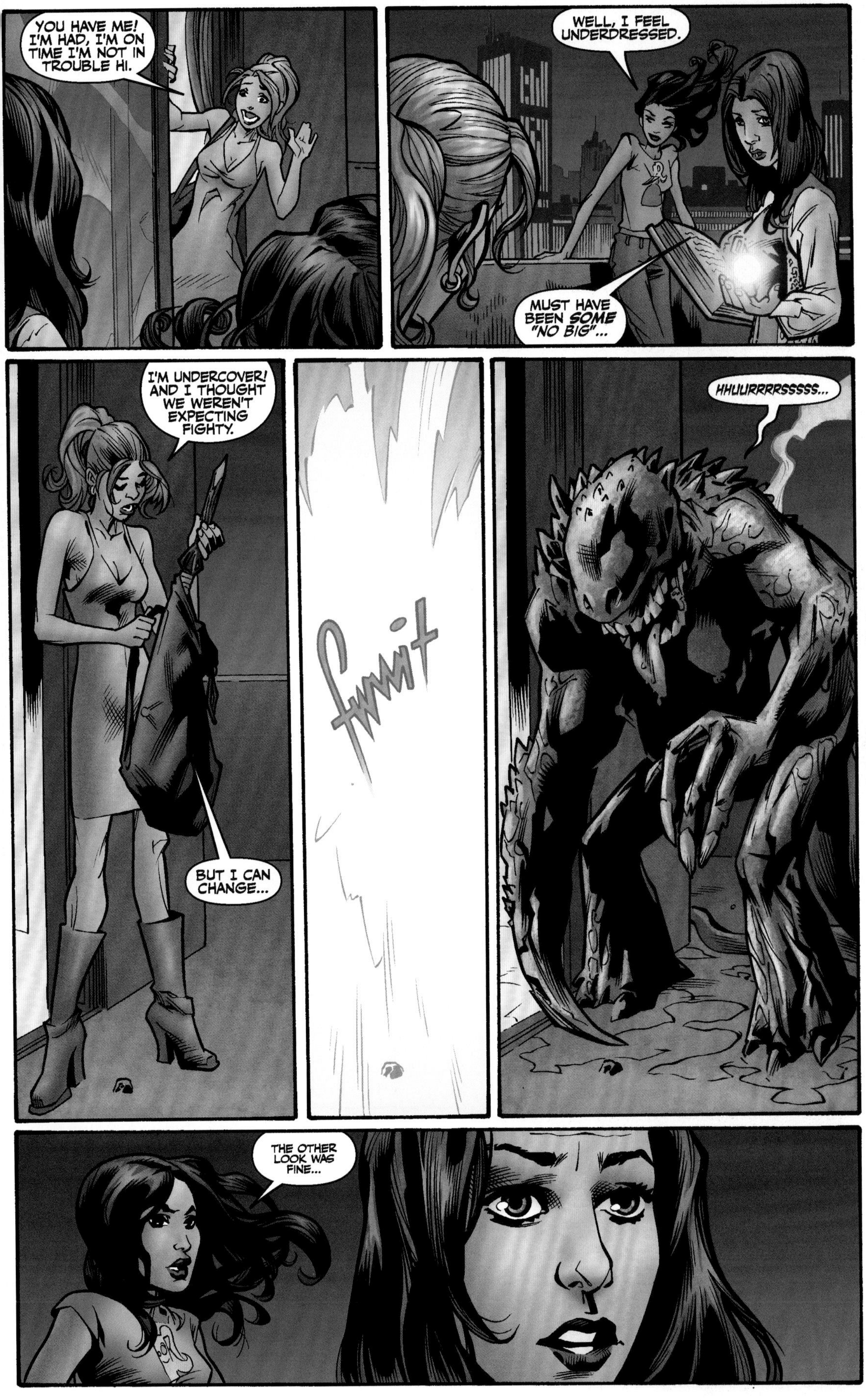
YOU HAVE ME! I'M HAD, I'M ON TIME I'M NOT IN TROUBLE HI.
WELL, I FEEL UNDERDRESSED.
MUST HAVE BEEN SOME "NO BIG"...
I'M UNDERCOVER! AND I THOUGHT WE WEREN'T EXPECTING FIGHTY.
BUT I CAN CHANGE...
fwwit
HHUURRRRSSSSS...
THE OTHER LOOK WAS FINE...

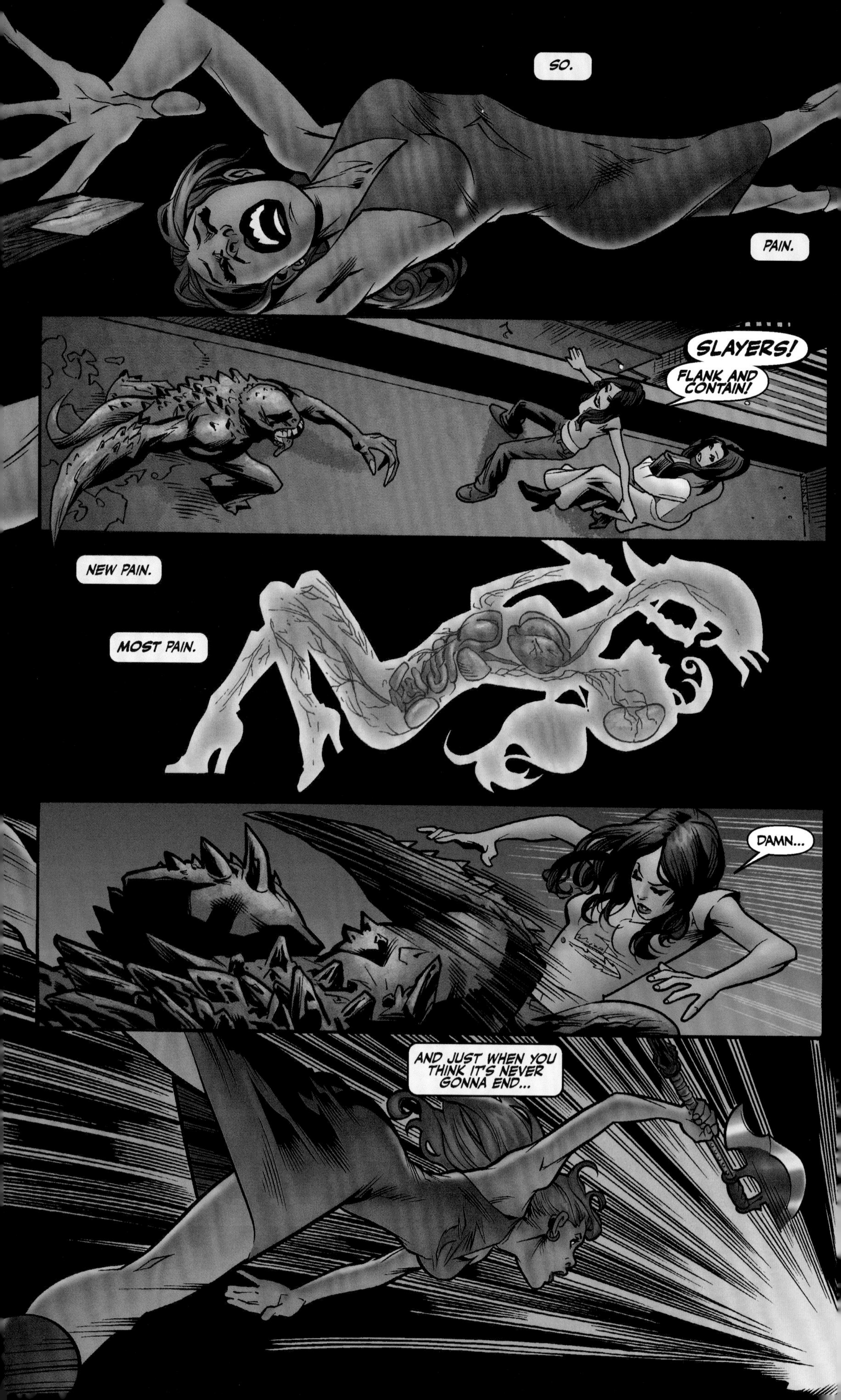
SO.
PAIN.
SLAYERS!
FLANK AND CONTAIN!
NEW PAIN.
MOST PAIN.
DAMN...
AND JUST WHEN YOU THINK IT'S NEVER GONNA END...

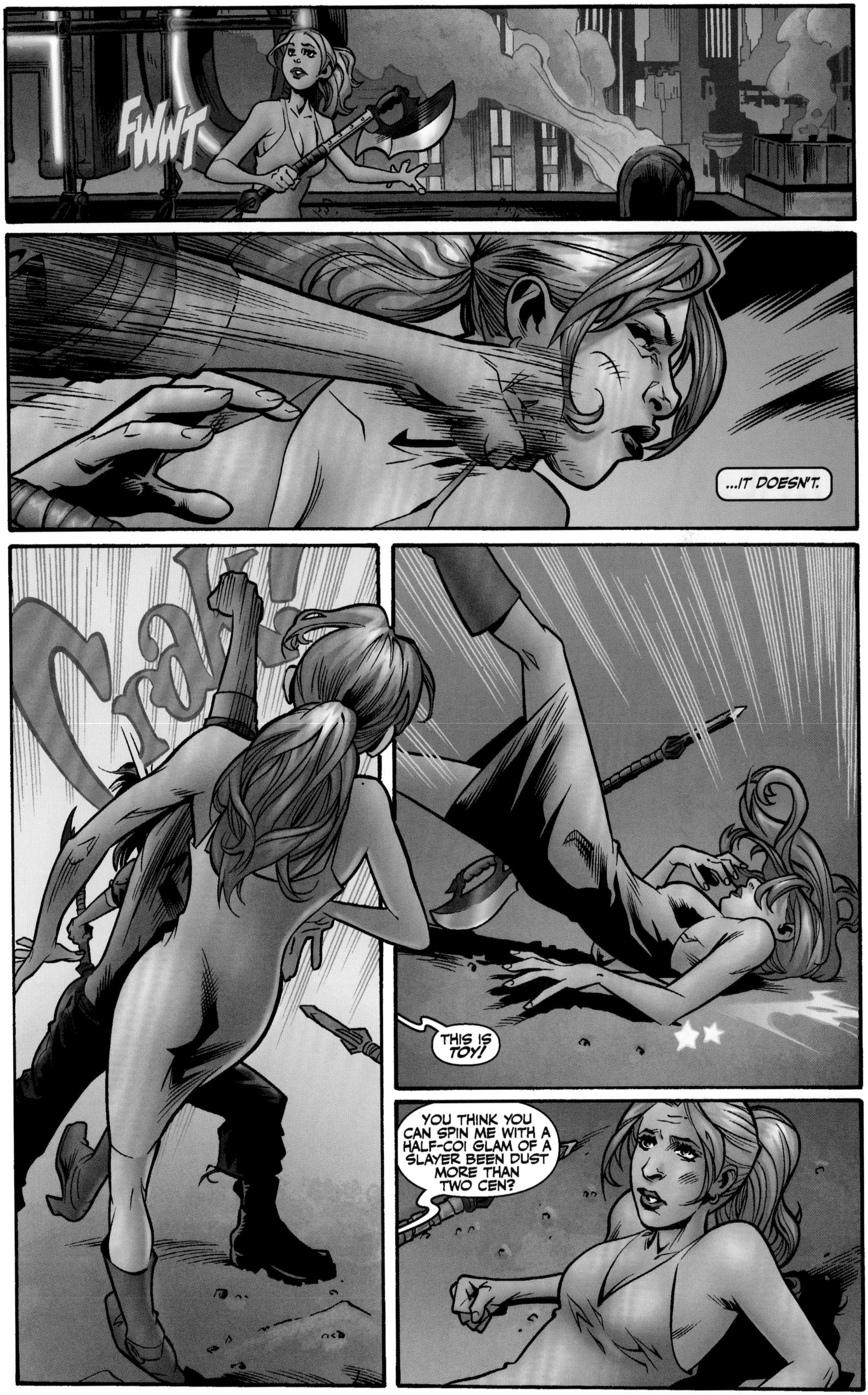
FWWT
...IT DOESN'T.
Crak!
THIS IS TOY!
YOU THINK YOU CAN SPIN ME WITH A HALF-COI GLAM OF A SLAYER BEEN DUST MORE THAN TWO CEN?

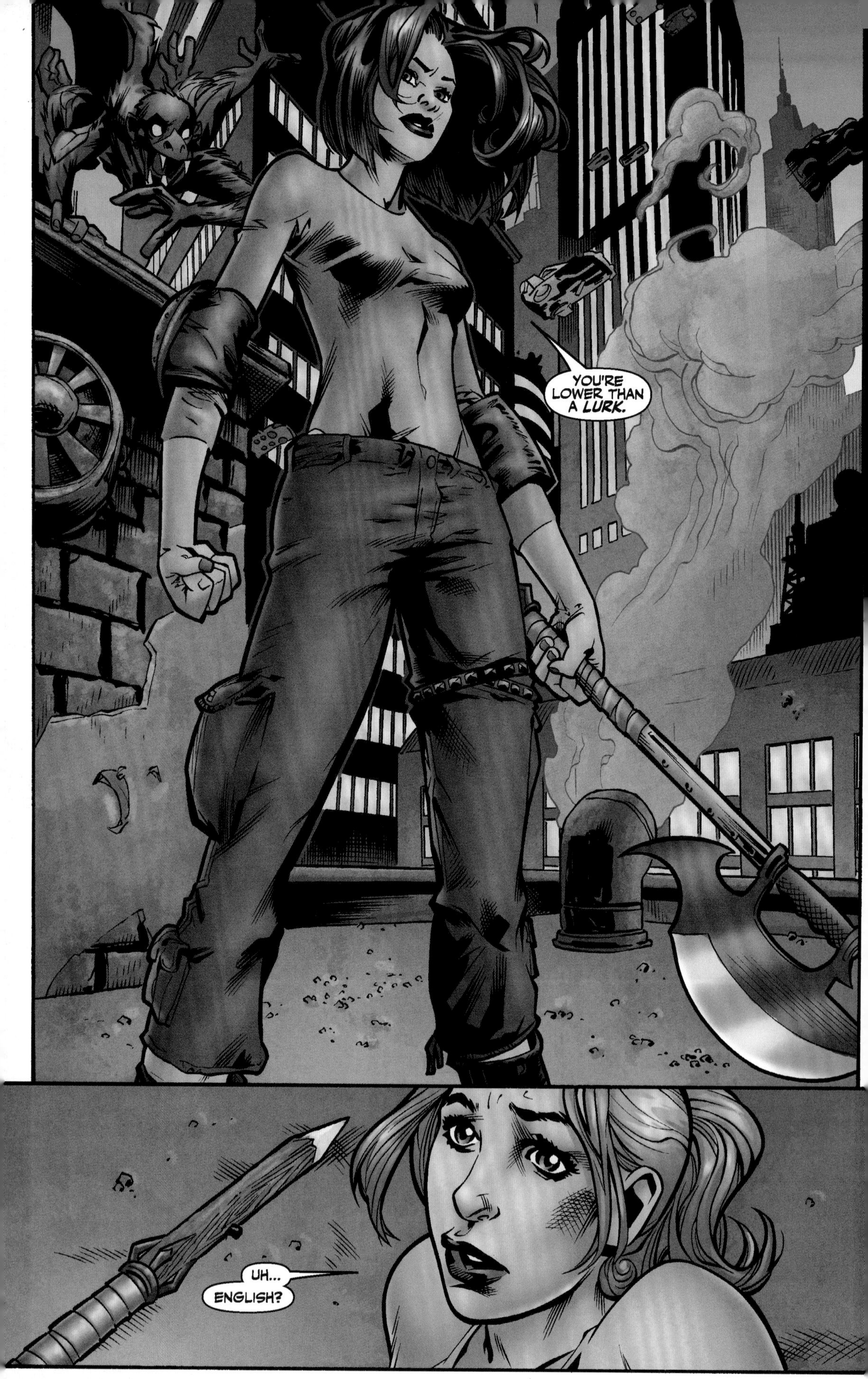
YOU'RE LOWER THAN A LURK.
UH... ENGLISH?

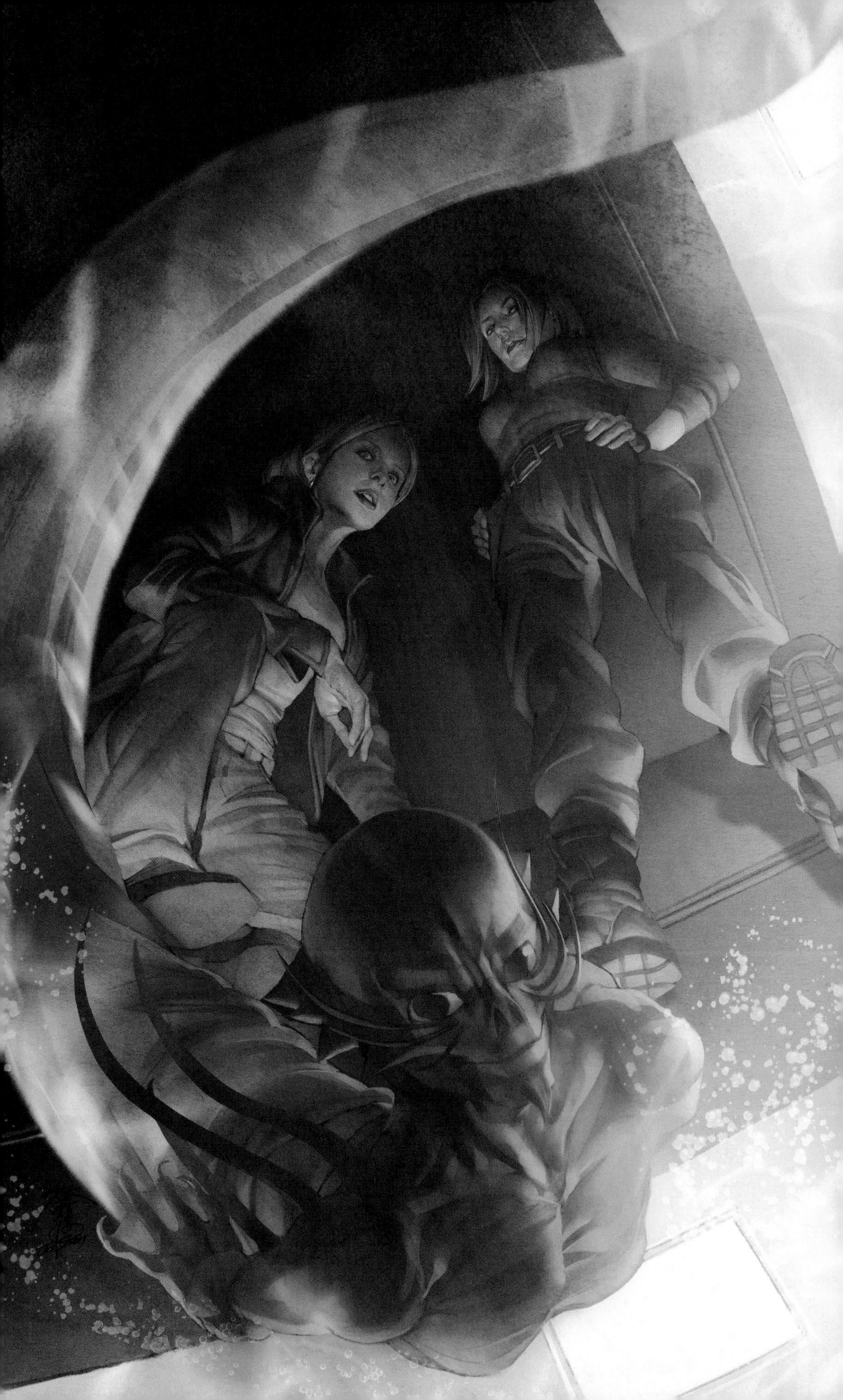

TIME OF YOUR LIFE
PART TWO

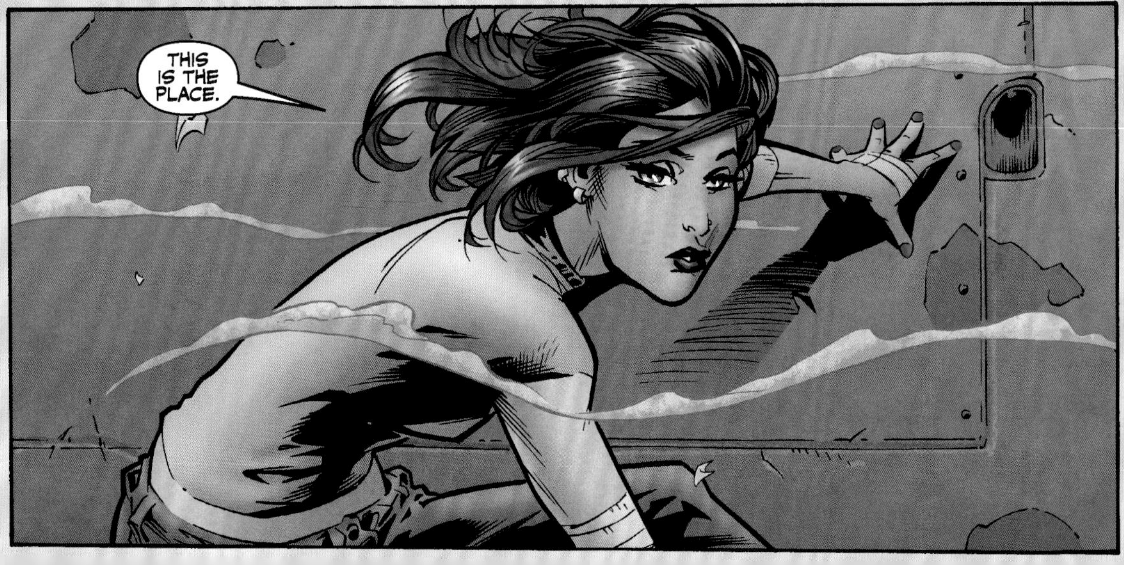
THIS IS THE PLACE.

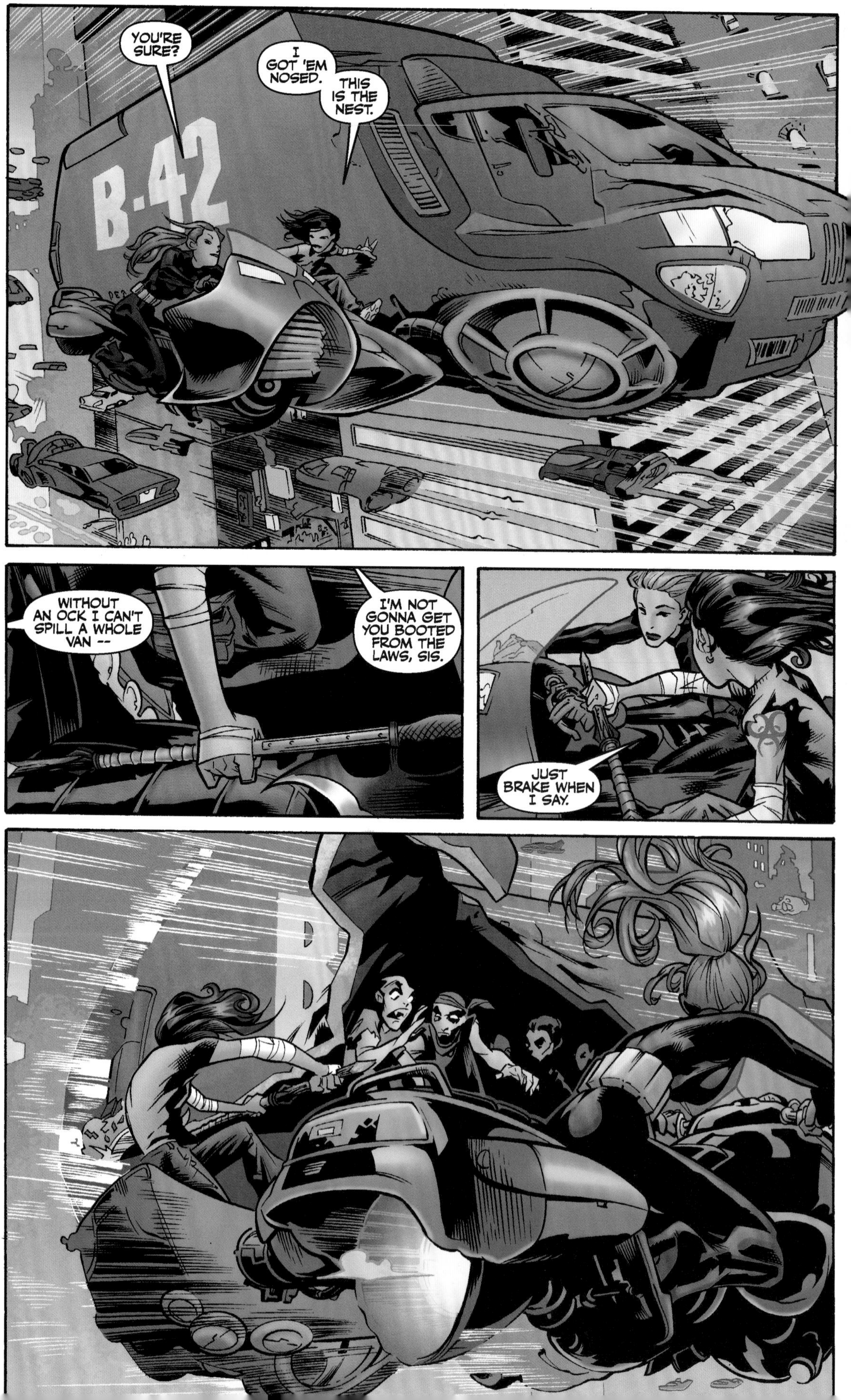

YOU'RE SURE?
I GOT 'EM NOSED.
THIS IS THE NEST.
B-42
WITHOUT AN OCK I CAN'T SPILL A WHOLE VAN --
I'M NOT GONNA GET YOU BOOTED FROM THE LAWS, SIS.
JUST BRAKE WHEN I SAY.

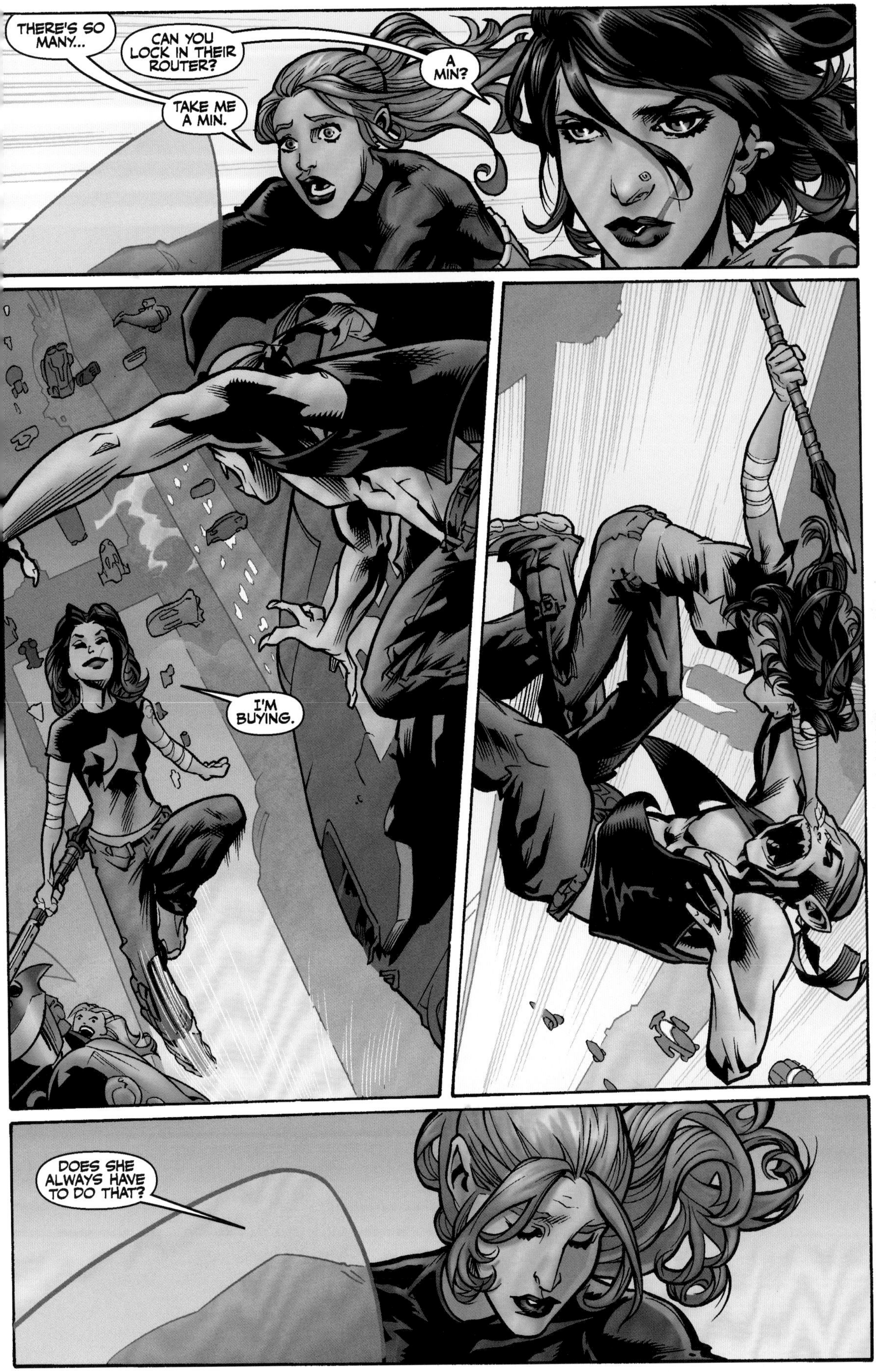
THERE'S SO MANY...
CAN YOU LOCK IN THEIR ROUTER?
TAKE ME A MIN.
A MIN?
I'M BUYING.
DOES SHE ALWAYS HAVE TO DO THAT?

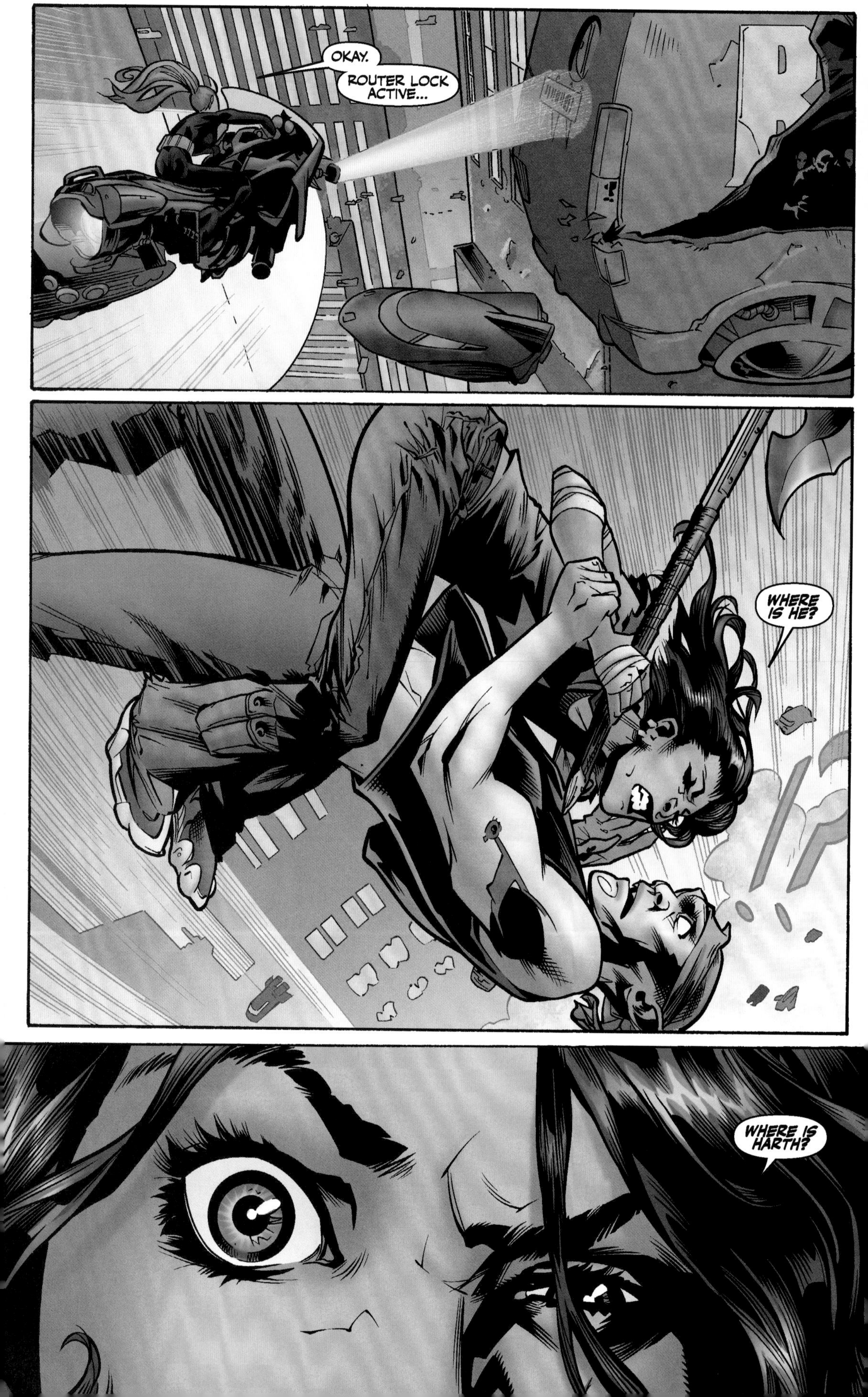
OKAY.
ROUTER LOCK ACTIVE...
WHERE IS HE?
WHERE IS HARTH?

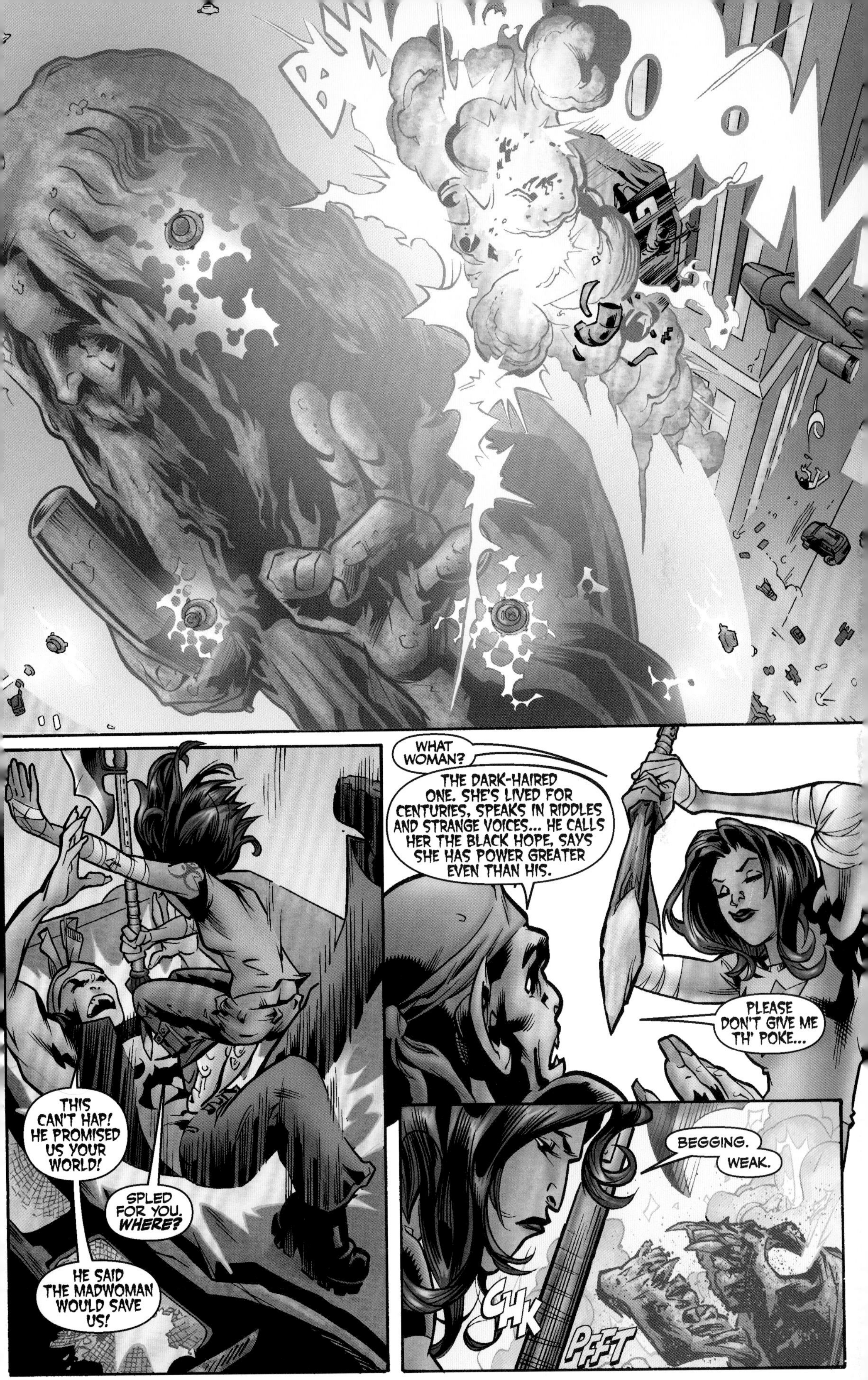
THIS CAN'T HAP! HE PROMISED US YOUR WORLD!
SPLED FOR YOU. *WHERE?*
HE SAID THE MADWOMAN WOULD SAVE US!
WHAT WOMAN?
THE DARK-HAIRED ONE. SHE'S LIVED FOR CENTURIES, SPEAKS IN RIDDLES AND STRANGE VOICES... HE CALLS HER THE BLACK HOPE, SAYS SHE HAS POWER GREATER EVEN THAN HIS.
PLEASE DON'T GIVE ME TH' POKE...
BEGGING.
WEAK.
CHK
PFFT

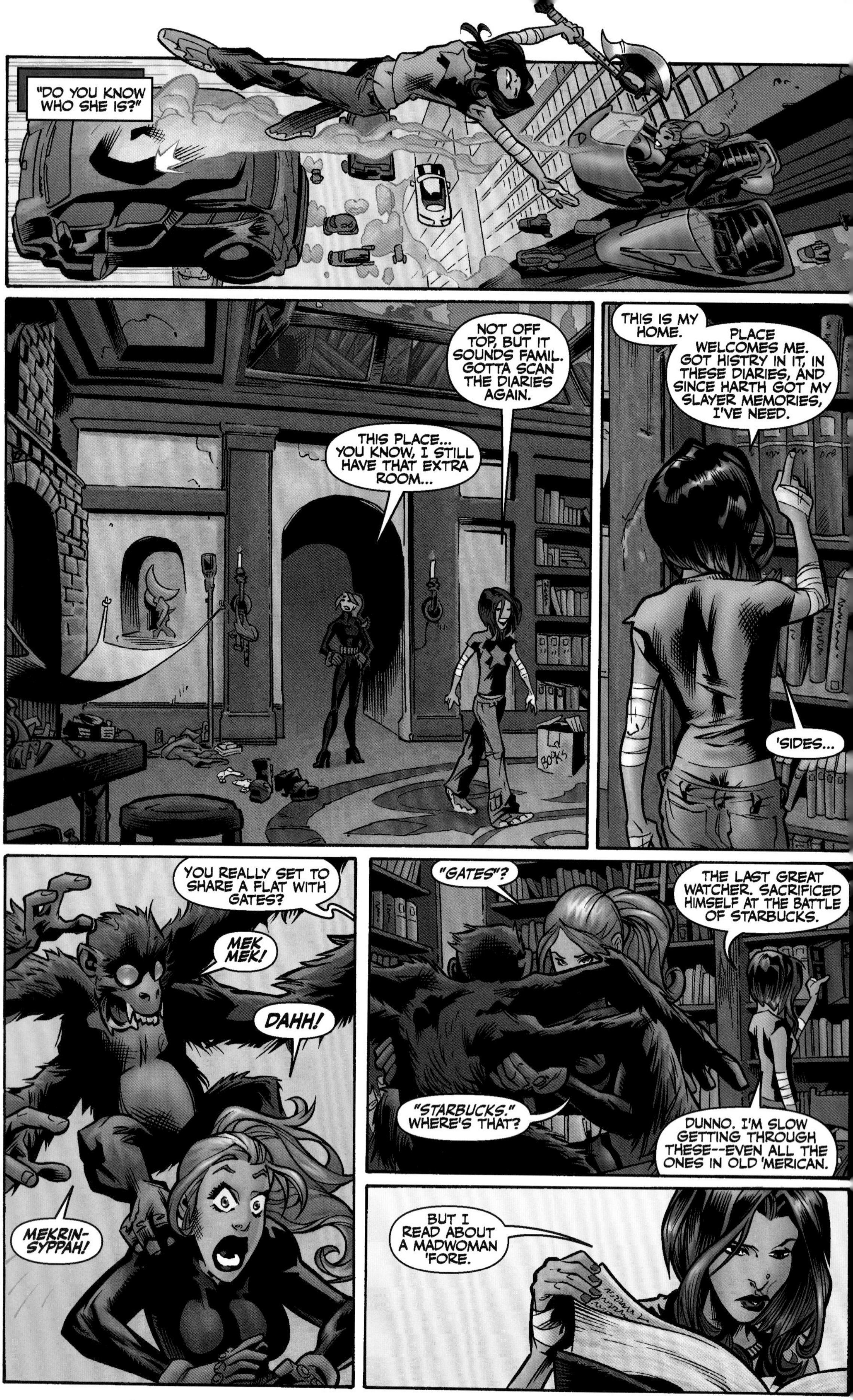
"DO YOU KNOW WHO SHE IS?"
NOT OFF TOP, BUT IT SOUNDS FAMIL. GOTTA SCAN THE DIARIES AGAIN.
THIS PLACE... YOU KNOW, I STILL HAVE THAT EXTRA ROOM...
BOOKS
THIS IS MY HOME.
PLACE WELCOMES ME. GOT HISTRY IN IT, IN THESE DIARIES, AND SINCE HARTH GOT MY SLAYER MEMORIES, I'VE NEED.
'SIDES...
YOU REALLY SET TO SHARE A FLAT WITH GATES?
MEK MEK!
DAHH!
MEKRIN-SYPPAH!
"GATES"?
THE LAST GREAT WATCHER. SACRIFICED HIMSELF AT THE BATTLE OF STARBUCKS.
"STARBUCKS." WHERE'S THAT?
DUNNO. I'M SLOW GETTING THROUGH THESE--EVEN ALL THE ONES IN OLD 'MERICAN.
BUT I READ ABOUT A MADWOMAN 'FORE.

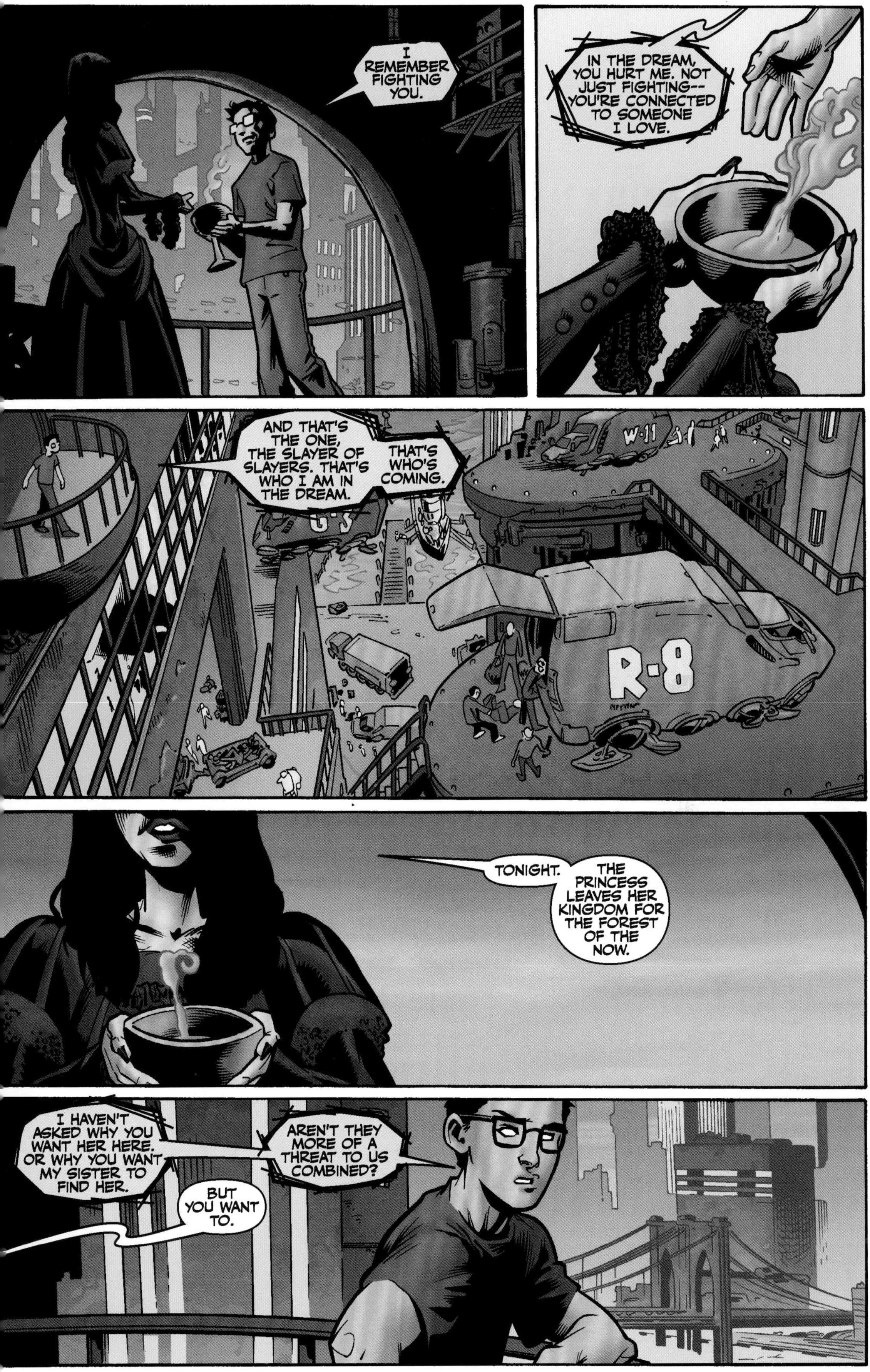
I REMEMBER FIGHTING YOU.
IN THE DREAM, YOU HURT ME. NOT JUST FIGHTING-- YOU'RE CONNECTED TO SOMEONE I LOVE.
AND THAT'S THE ONE, THE SLAYER OF SLAYERS. THAT'S WHO I AM IN THE DREAM.
THAT'S WHO'S COMING.
W-11
R-8
TONIGHT.
THE PRINCESS LEAVES HER KINGDOM FOR THE FOREST OF THE NOW.
I HAVEN'T ASKED WHY YOU WANT HER HERE. OR WHY YOU WANT MY SISTER TO FIND HER.
AREN'T THEY MORE OF A THREAT TO US COMBINED?
BUT YOU WANT TO.

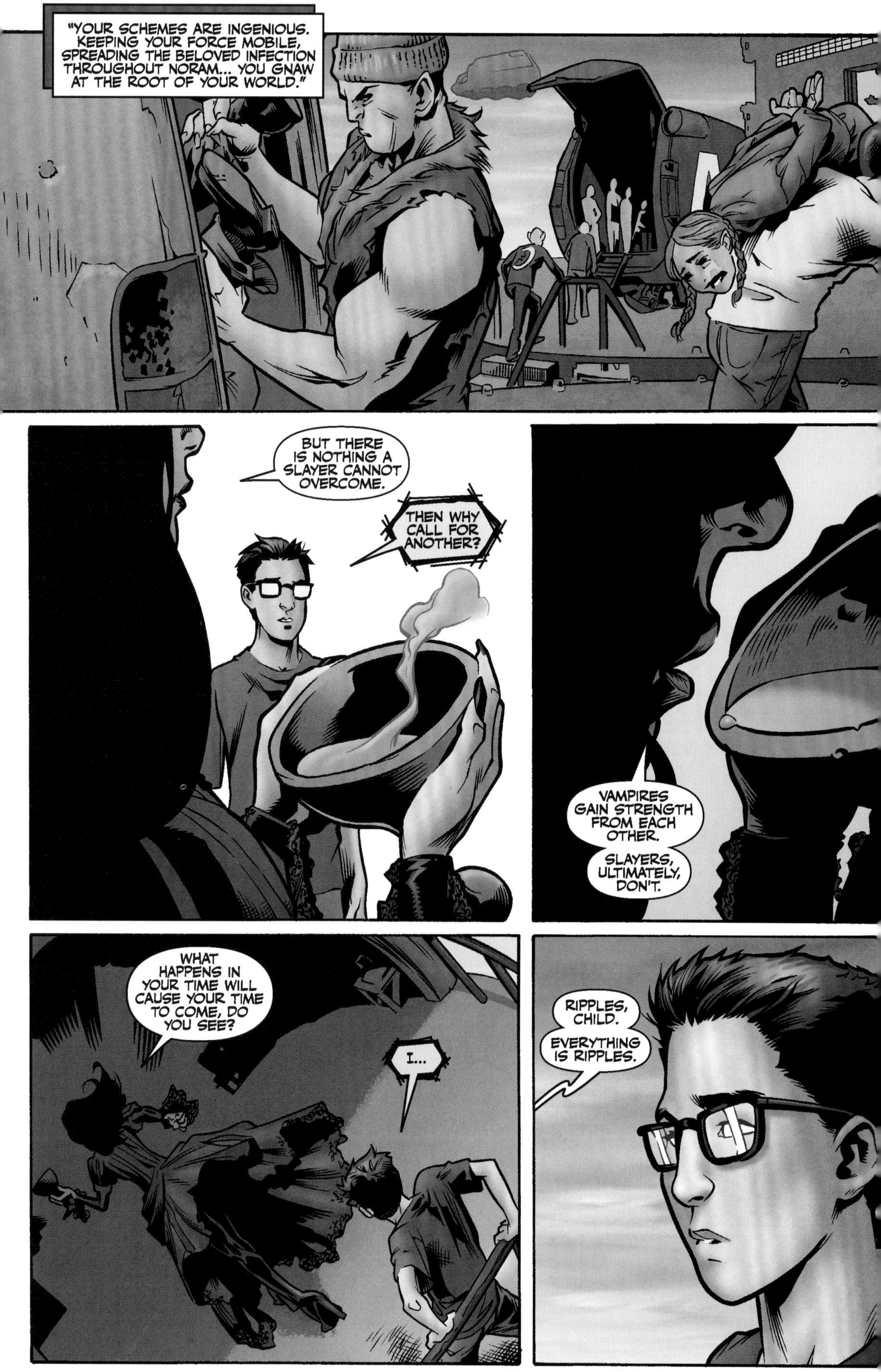
"YOUR SCHEMES ARE INGENIOUS. KEEPING YOUR FORCE MOBILE, SPREADING THE BELOVED INFECTION THROUGHOUT NORAM... YOU GNAW AT THE ROOT OF YOUR WORLD."
BUT THERE IS NOTHING A SLAYER CANNOT OVERCOME.
THEN WHY CALL FOR ANOTHER?
VAMPIRES GAIN STRENGTH FROM EACH OTHER.
SLAYERS, ULTIMATELY, DON'T.
WHAT HAPPENS IN YOUR TIME WILL CAUSE YOUR TIME TO COME, DO YOU SEE?
I...
RIPPLES, CHILD.
EVERYTHING IS RIPPLES.

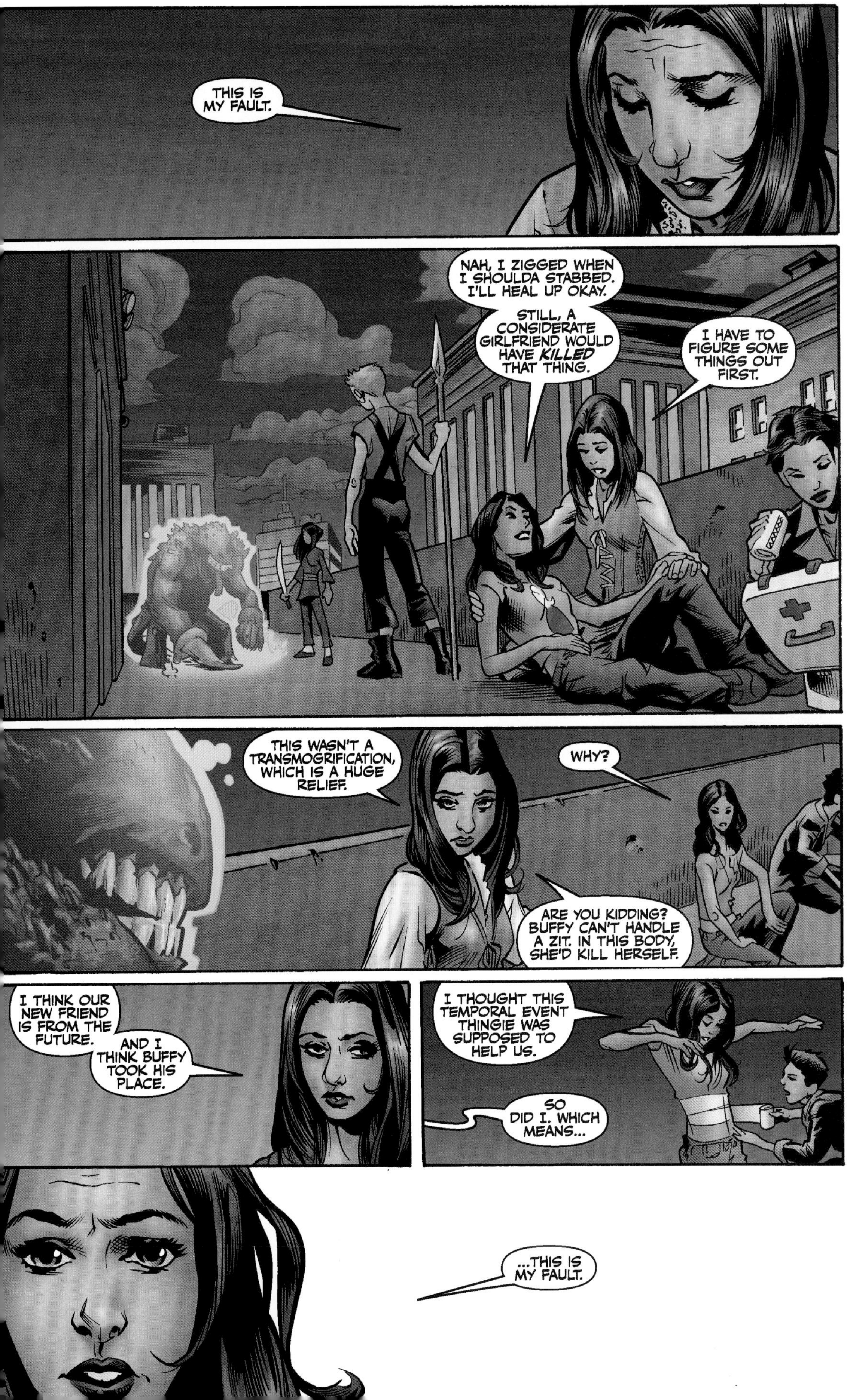
THIS IS MY FAULT.
NAH, I ZIGGED WHEN I SHOULDA STABBED. I'LL HEAL UP OKAY.
STILL, A CONSIDERATE GIRLFRIEND WOULD HAVE *KILLED* THAT THING.
I HAVE TO FIGURE SOME THINGS OUT FIRST.
THIS WASN'T A TRANSMOGRIFICATION, WHICH IS A HUGE RELIEF.
WHY?
ARE YOU KIDDING? BUFFY CAN'T HANDLE A ZIT. IN THIS BODY, SHE'D KILL HERSELF.
I THINK OUR NEW FRIEND IS FROM THE FUTURE.
AND I THINK BUFFY TOOK HIS PLACE.
I THOUGHT THIS TEMPORAL EVENT THINGIE WAS SUPPOSED TO HELP US.
SO DID I. WHICH MEANS...
...THIS IS MY FAULT.

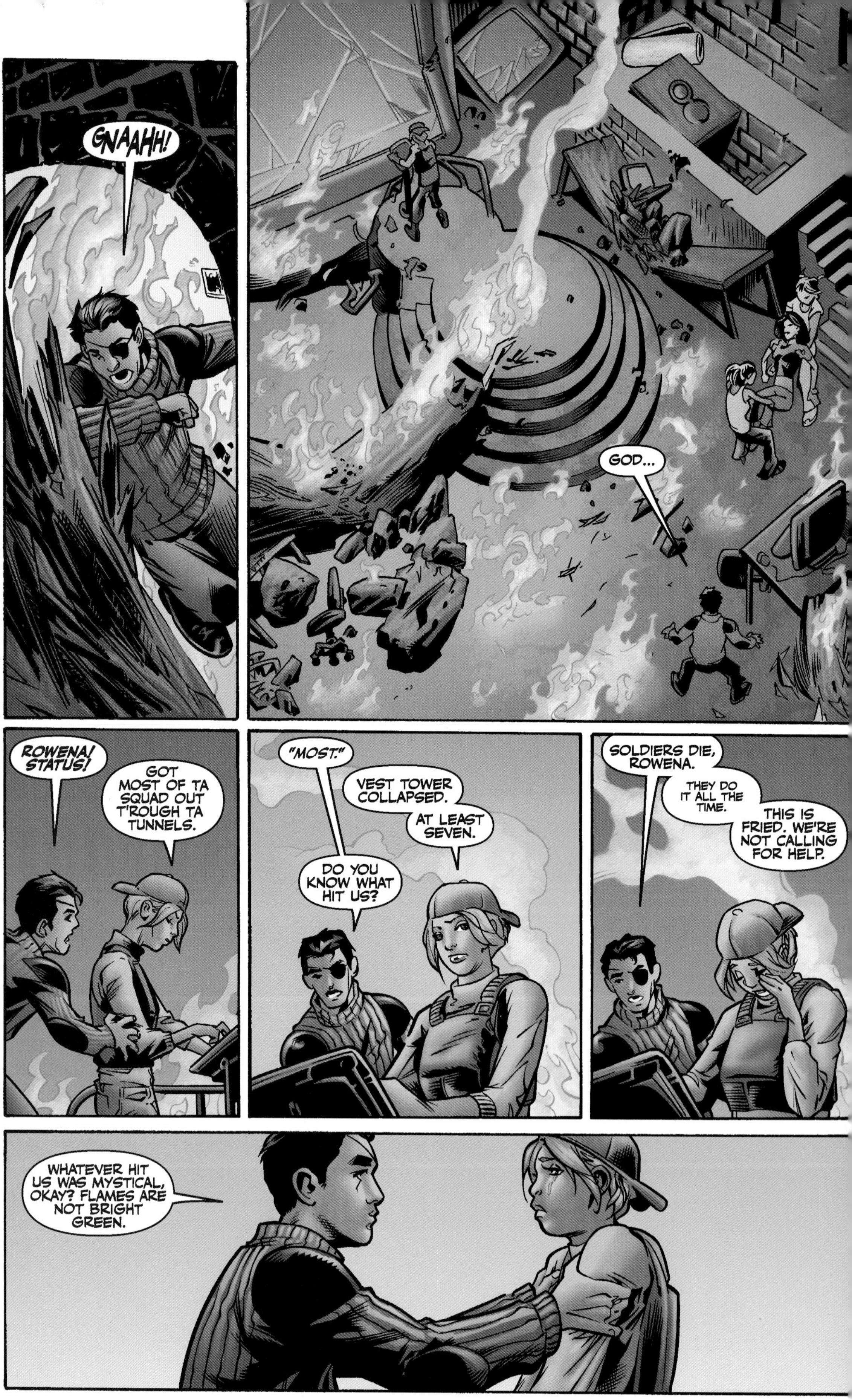
GNAAHH!
GOD...
ROWENA! STATUS!
GOT MOST OF TA SQUAD OUT T'ROUGH TA TUNNELS.
"MOST."
VEST TOWER COLLAPSED.
AT LEAST SEVEN.
DO YOU KNOW WHAT HIT US?
SOLDIERS DIE, ROWENA.
THEY DO IT ALL THE TIME.
THIS IS FRIED. WE'RE NOT CALLING FOR HELP.
WHATEVER HIT US WAS MYSTICAL, OKAY? FLAMES ARE NOT BRIGHT GREEN.

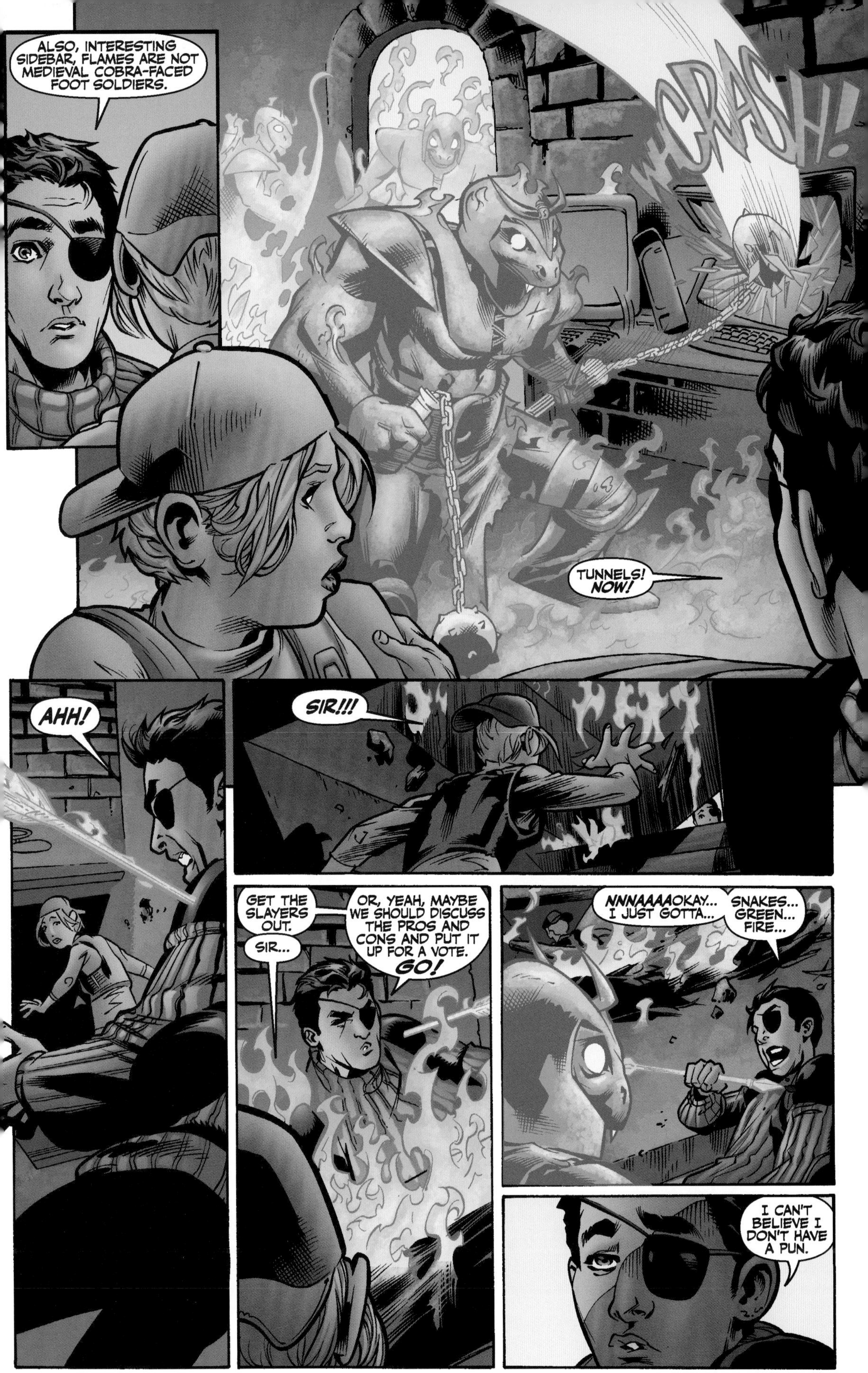
ALSO, INTERESTING SIDEBAR, FLAMES ARE NOT MEDIEVAL COBRA-FACED FOOT SOLDIERS.
CRASH!
TUNNELS! NOW!
AHH!
SIR!!!
GET THE SLAYERS OUT.
SIR...
OR, YEAH, MAYBE WE SHOULD DISCUSS THE PROS AND CONS AND PUT IT UP FOR A VOTE. GO!
NNNAAAAOKAY... I JUST GOTTA...
SNAKES... GREEN... FIRE...
I CAN'T BELIEVE I DON'T HAVE A PUN.

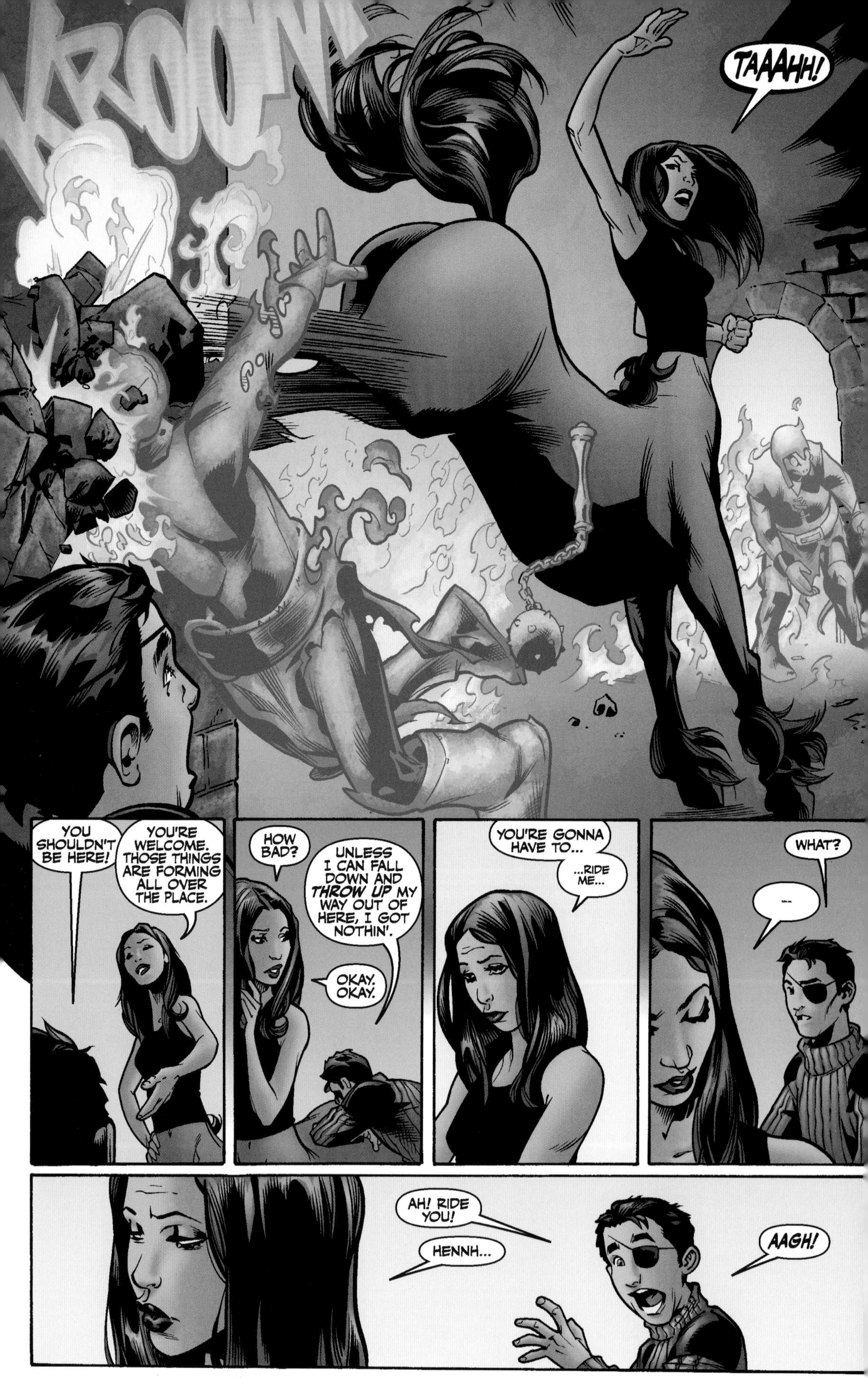
KROOM
TAAAHH!
YOU SHOULDN'T BE HERE!
YOU'RE WELCOME. THOSE THINGS ARE FORMING ALL OVER THE PLACE.
HOW BAD?
UNLESS I CAN FALL DOWN AND THROW UP MY WAY OUT OF HERE, I GOT NOTHIN'.
OKAY. OKAY.
YOU'RE GONNA HAVE TO...
...RIDE ME...
WHAT?
AH! RIDE YOU!
HENNH...
AAGH!

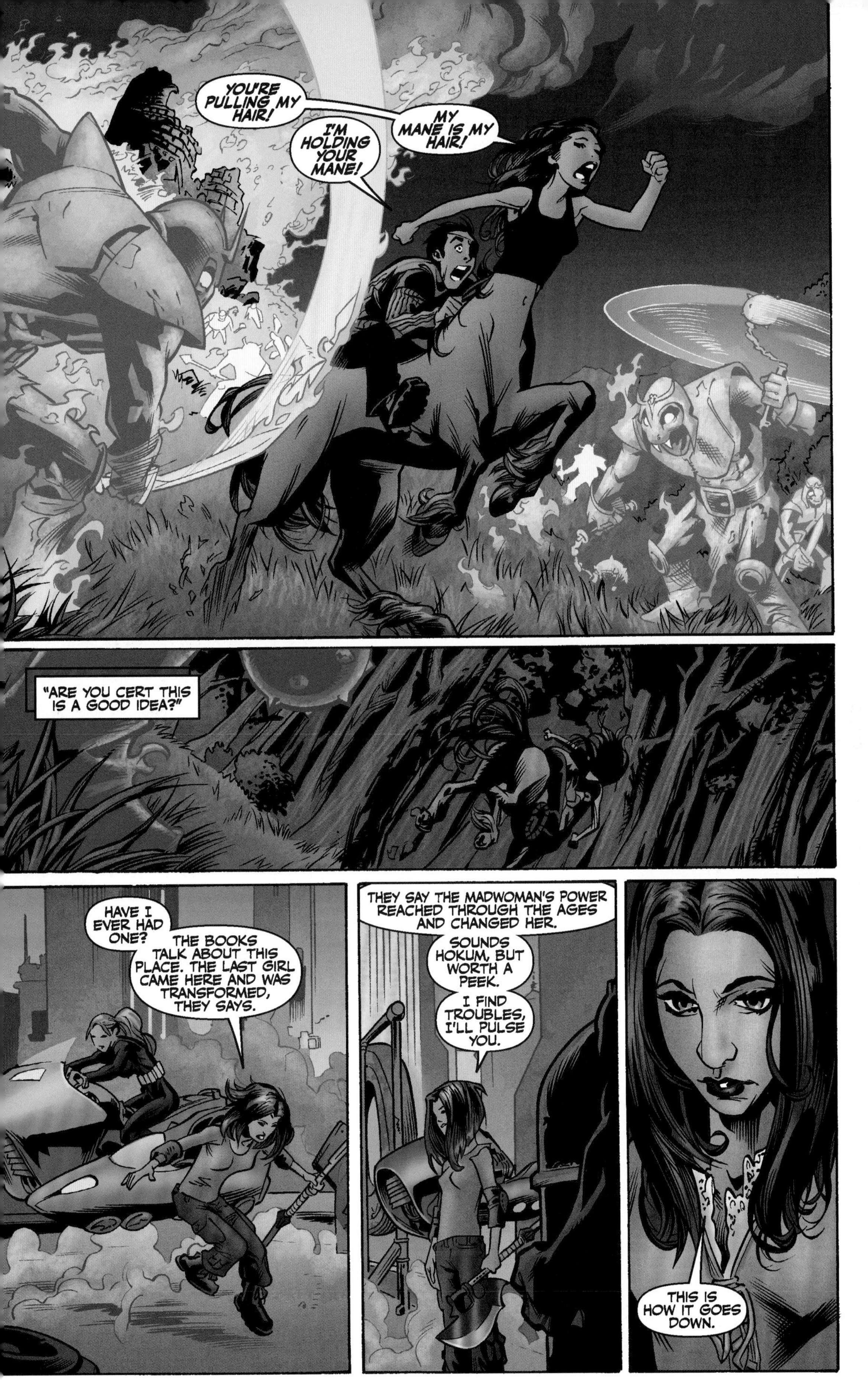
YOU'RE PULLING MY HAIR!
I'M HOLDING YOUR MANE!
MY MANE IS MY HAIR!
"ARE YOU CERT THIS IS A GOOD IDEA?"
HAVE I EVER HAD ONE?
THE BOOKS TALK ABOUT THIS PLACE. THE LAST GIRL CAME HERE AND WAS TRANSFORMED, THEY SAYS.
THEY SAY THE MADWOMAN'S POWER REACHED THROUGH THE AGES AND CHANGED HER.
SOUNDS HOKUM, BUT WORTH A PEEK.
I FIND TROUBLES, I'LL PULSE YOU.
THIS IS HOW IT GOES DOWN.

"YEARS FROM NOW, SOMEONE ENLISTS OUR BIG UGLY DEMON FRIEND TO TAKE DOWN THE SLAYER.

"I'M GUESSING THIS WAS MEANT TO DRAW HER OUT.

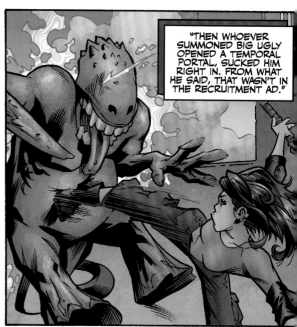

"THEN WHOEVER SUMMONED BIG UGLY OPENED A TEMPORAL PORTAL, SUCKED HIM RIGHT IN. FROM WHAT HE SAID, THAT WASN'T IN THE RECRUITMENT AD."

WHOEVER DID THIS HAS WAY MORE POWER THAN I DO. AND THEY MADE VERY SURE WORD WOULD GET OUT. TO THE MAGIC COMMUNITY, TO MY ALLIES, TO ME. WE WERE PLAYED.

WE'RE ALL PASTIES.

OR POSSIBLY "PATSIES"?

"OOH! I SUCK AT TOUGH-GUY TALK. BUT THE POINT IS, WE DON'T KNOW ANYTHING ABOUT THIS PERSON--OR ABOUT THIS FUTURE SLAYER, FOR THAT MATTER.

"SO THE QUESTION IS, WHAT'S WAITING FOR BUFFY IN THE FUTURE?

"AND HOW DO WE GET HER BACK-- BEFORE SOMETHING BAD HAPPENS?"

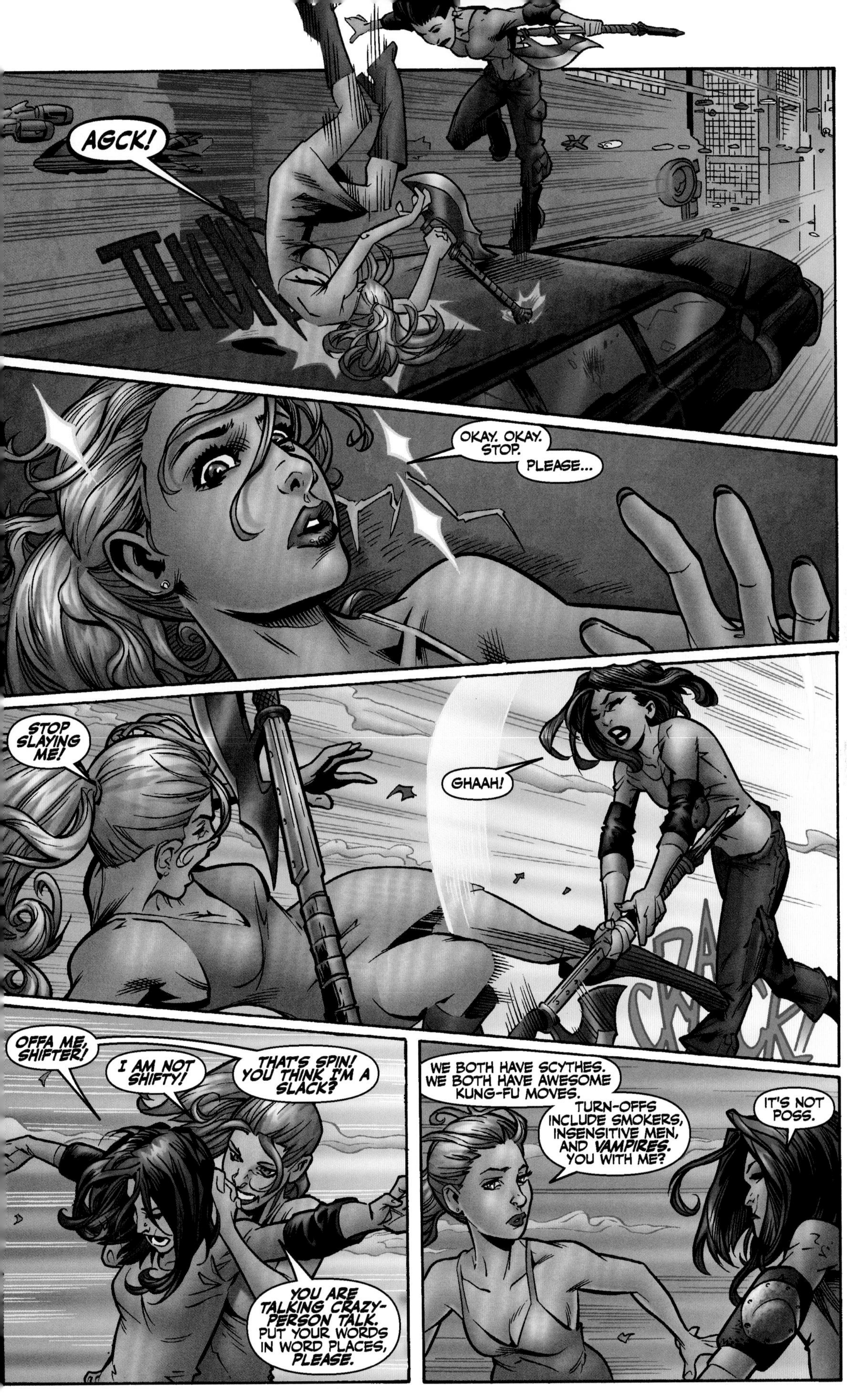
AGCK!
THUNK
OKAY. OKAY. STOP.
PLEASE...
STOP SLAYING ME!
GHAAH!
CRACK!
OFFA ME, SHIFTER!
I AM NOT SHIFTY!
THAT'S SPIN! YOU THINK I'M A SLACK?
YOU ARE TALKING CRAZY-PERSON TALK. PUT YOUR WORDS IN WORD PLACES, PLEASE.
WE BOTH HAVE SCYTHES. WE BOTH HAVE AWESOME KUNG-FU MOVES.
TURN-OFFS INCLUDE SMOKERS, INSENSITIVE MEN, AND VAMPIRES. YOU WITH ME?
IT'S NOT POSS.

WE'RE STANDING ON A FLYING CAR. "POSS" IS A PRETTY SKETCHY CONCEPT RIGHT NOW.

SO, WHAT: FUTURE? ALTERNATE, MUCH COOLER UNIVERSE?

BUFFY SUMMERS.

PRESENT.

BUFFY SUMMERS IS DEAD.

OCCASIONALLY.

NO, YEAH, WILLOW GAVE THAT LECTURE--THIS IS A FUTURE THING.

I'M ALL THE TIME GOING OFF HIGH BUILDINGS LATELY.

BOY, THAT JUST KEEPS GOING DOWN, DOESN'T IT?

BUFFY SUMMERS IS *LONG* DEAD. TWO CEN, MAYBE MORE.

WHAT'S YOUR NAME?

MELAKA.

CUTE. I TIME-TRAVELED.

WHY?

KINDA HOPING YOU WERE GONNA TELL ME. IS THERE SOMEWHERE WE CAN TALK? SOMEWHERE LESS MOTION-SICKNESSY?

FOLLOW.

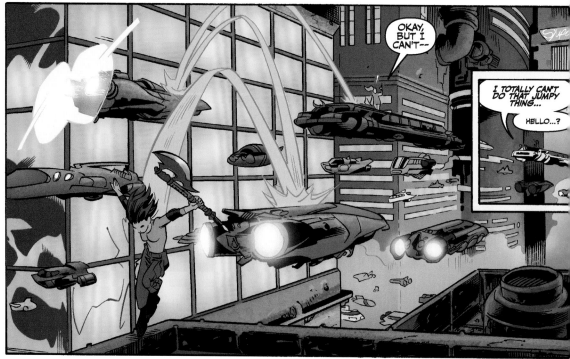

OKAY, BUT I CAN'T--

I TOTALLY CAN'T DO THAT JUMPY THING...

HELLO...?

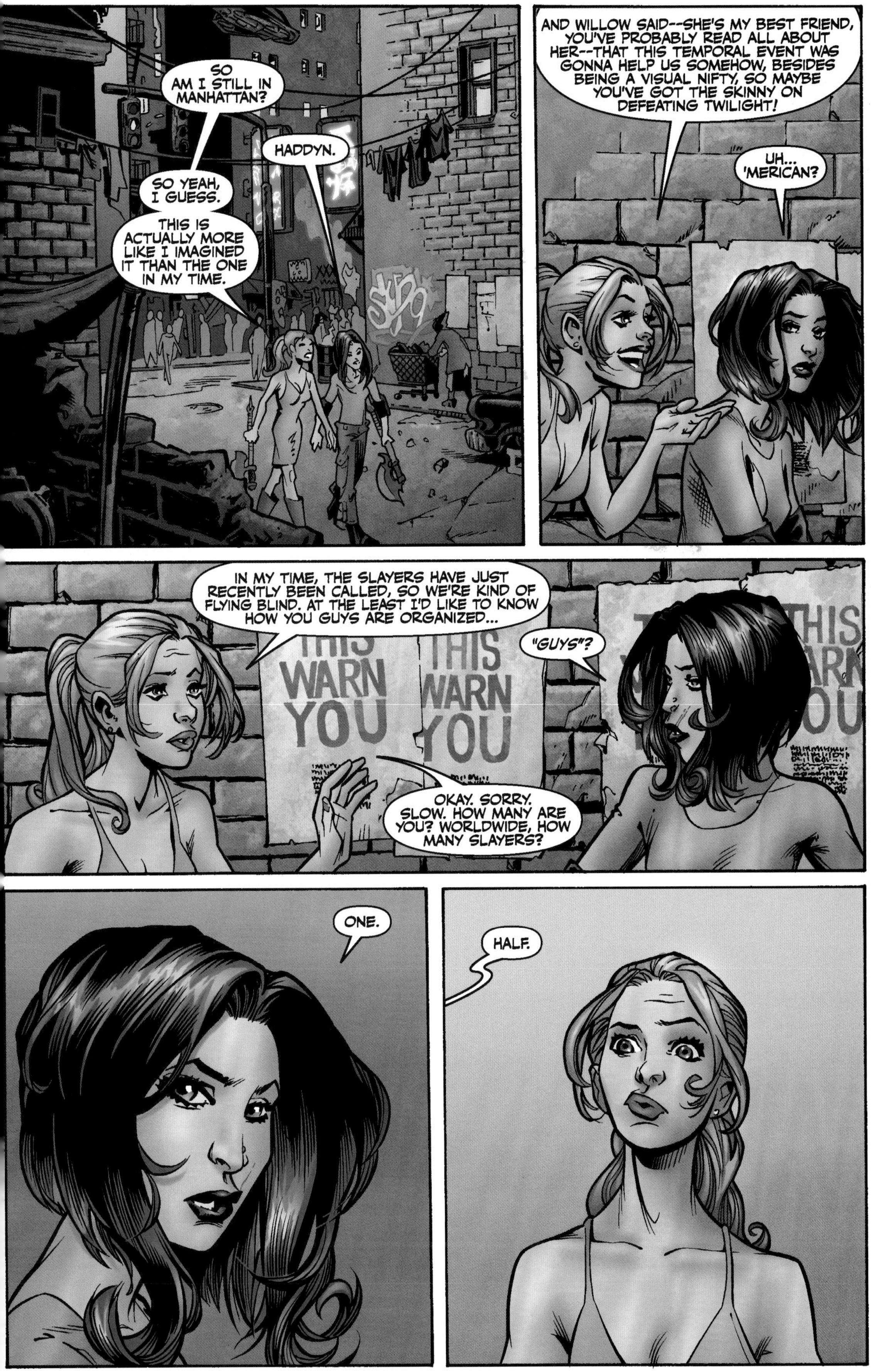
SO AM I STILL IN MANHATTAN?
HADDYN.
SO YEAH, I GUESS.
THIS IS ACTUALLY MORE LIKE I IMAGINED IT THAN THE ONE IN MY TIME.
AND WILLOW SAID--SHE'S MY BEST FRIEND, YOU'VE PROBABLY READ ALL ABOUT HER--THAT THIS TEMPORAL EVENT WAS GONNA HELP US SOMEHOW, BESIDES BEING A VISUAL NIFTY, SO MAYBE YOU'VE GOT THE SKINNY ON DEFEATING TWILIGHT!
UH... 'MERICAN?
IN MY TIME, THE SLAYERS HAVE JUST RECENTLY BEEN CALLED, SO WE'RE KIND OF FLYING BLIND. AT THE LEAST I'D LIKE TO KNOW HOW YOU GUYS ARE ORGANIZED...
THIS WARN YOU
THIS WARN YOU
"GUYS"?
OKAY. SORRY. SLOW. HOW MANY ARE YOU? WORLDWIDE, HOW MANY SLAYERS?
ONE.
HALF.

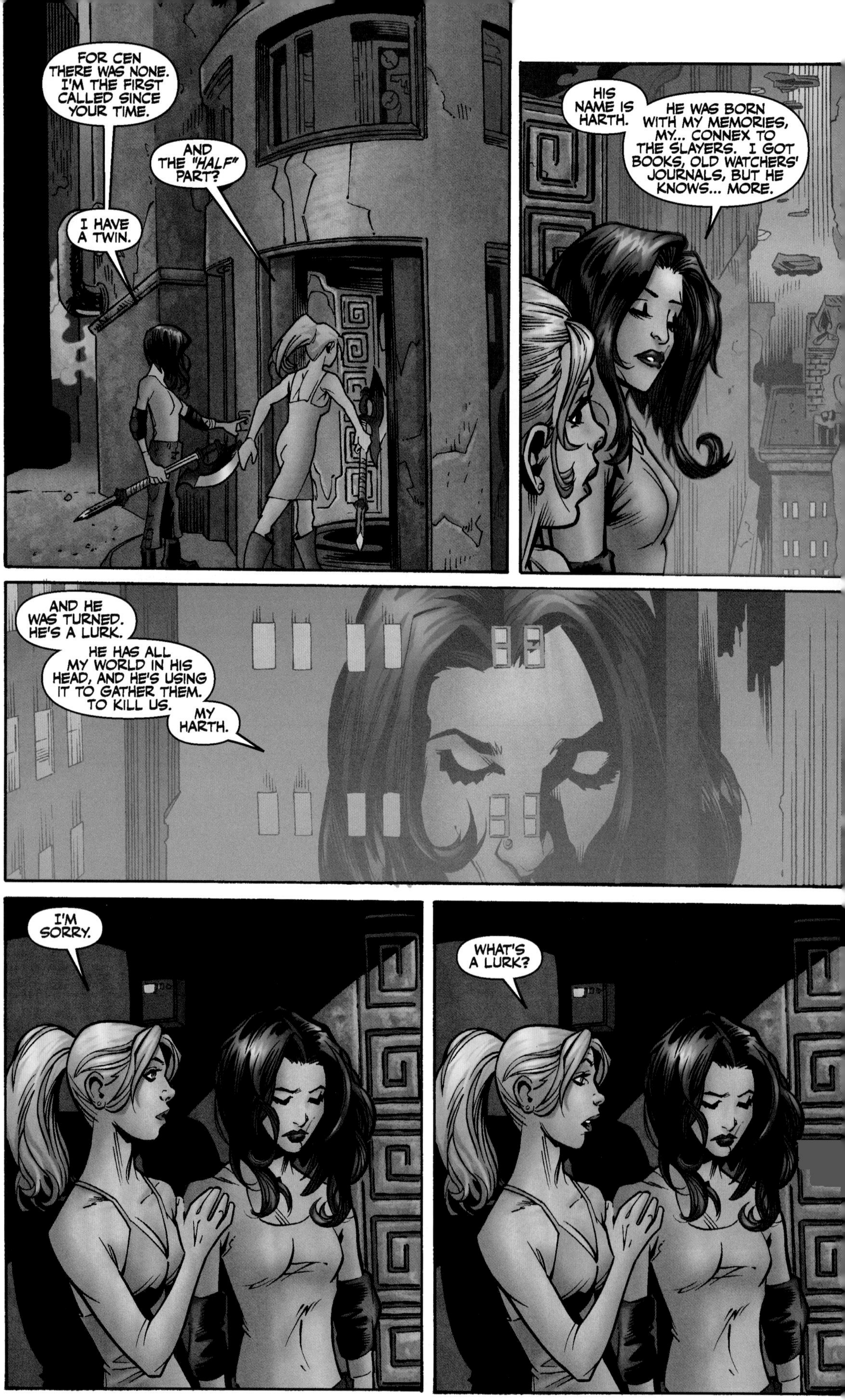
FOR CEN THERE WAS NONE. I'M THE FIRST CALLED SINCE YOUR TIME.
AND THE "HALF" PART?
I HAVE A TWIN.
HIS NAME IS HARTH.
HE WAS BORN WITH MY MEMORIES, MY... CONNEX TO THE SLAYERS. I GOT BOOKS, OLD WATCHERS' JOURNALS, BUT HE KNOWS... MORE.
AND HE WAS TURNED. HE'S A LURK.
HE HAS ALL MY WORLD IN HIS HEAD, AND HE'S USING IT TO GATHER THEM. TO KILL US.
MY HARTH.
I'M SORRY.
WHAT'S A LURK?

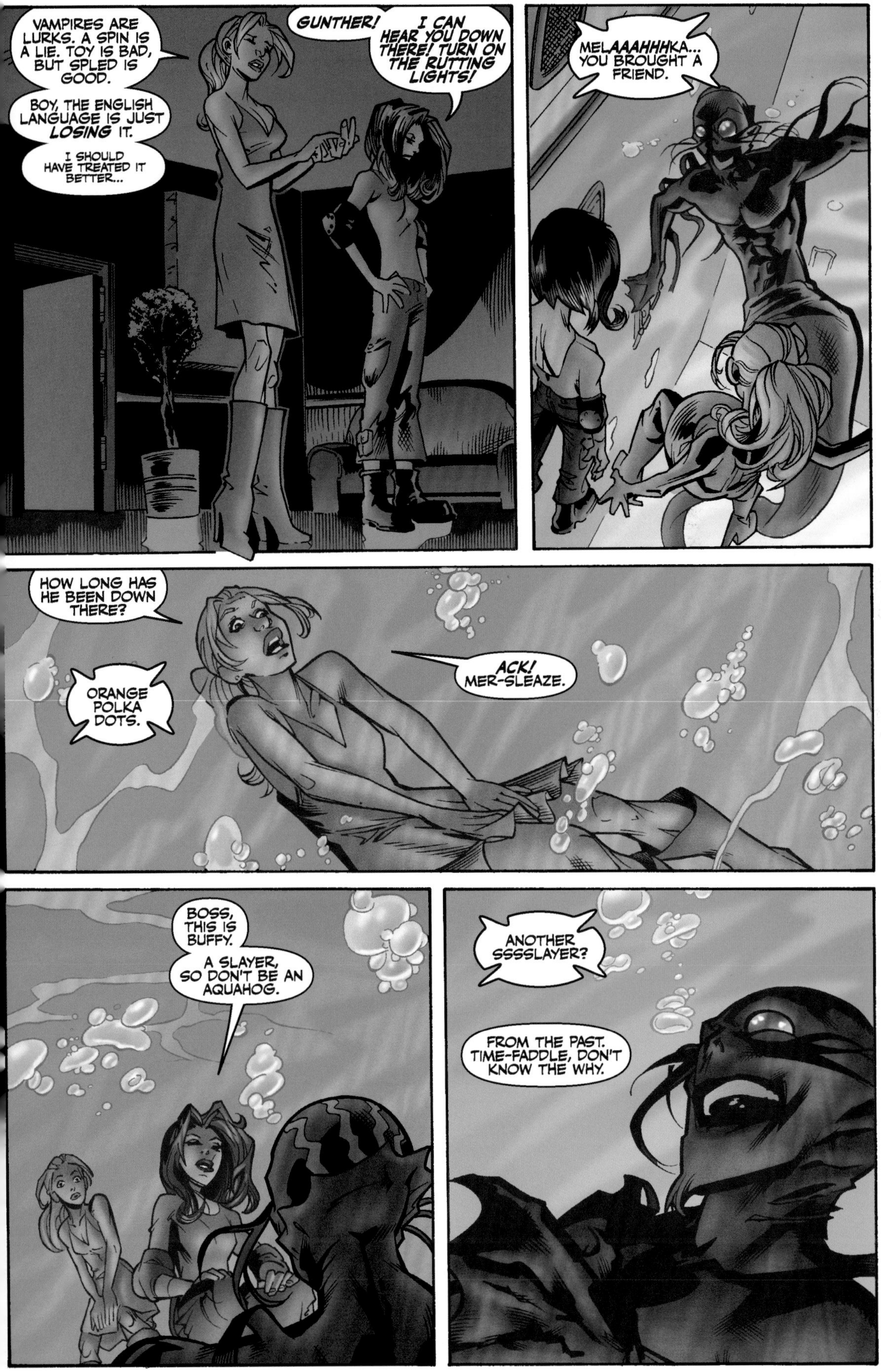
VAMPIRES ARE LURKS. A SPIN IS A LIE. TOY IS BAD, BUT SPLED IS GOOD.
BOY, THE ENGLISH LANGUAGE IS JUST LOSING IT.
I SHOULD HAVE TREATED IT BETTER...
GUNTHER!
I CAN HEAR YOU DOWN THERE! TURN ON THE RUTTING LIGHTS!
MELAAAHHHKA... YOU BROUGHT A FRIEND.
HOW LONG HAS HE BEEN DOWN THERE?
ORANGE POLKA DOTS.
ACK! MER-SLEAZE.
BOSS, THIS IS BUFFY.
A SLAYER, SO DON'T BE AN AQUAHOG.
ANOTHER SSSSLAYER?
FROM THE PAST. TIME-FADDLE, DON'T KNOW THE WHY.

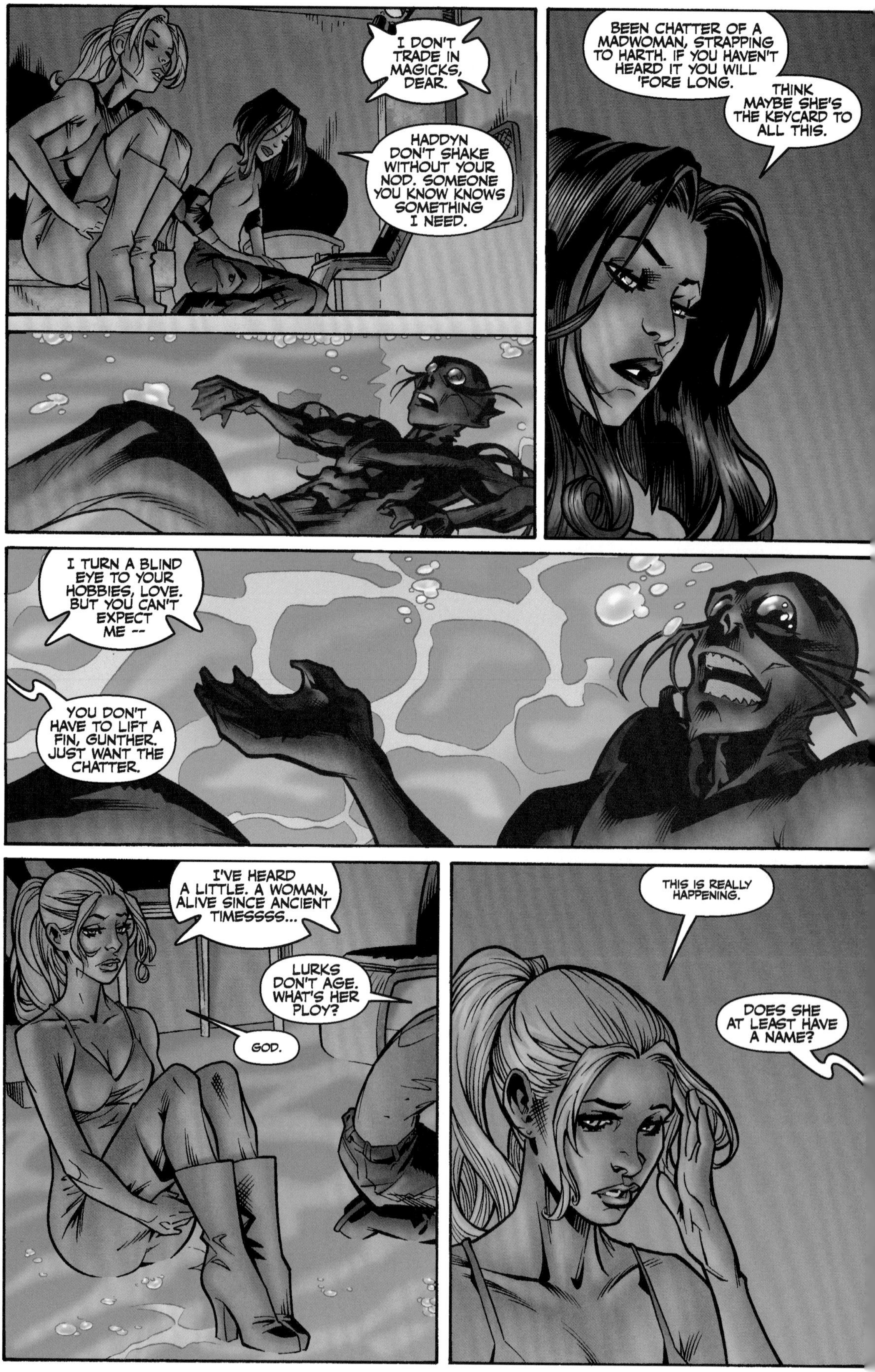
I DON'T TRADE IN MAGICKS, DEAR.
HADDYN DON'T SHAKE WITHOUT YOUR NOD. SOMEONE YOU KNOW KNOWS SOMETHING I NEED.
BEEN CHATTER OF A MADWOMAN, STRAPPING TO HARTH. IF YOU HAVEN'T HEARD IT YOU WILL 'FORE LONG.
THINK MAYBE SHE'S THE KEYCARD TO ALL THIS.
I TURN A BLIND EYE TO YOUR HOBBIES, LOVE. BUT YOU CAN'T EXPECT ME --
YOU DON'T HAVE TO LIFT A FIN, GUNTHER. JUST WANT THE CHATTER.
I'VE HEARD A LITTLE. A WOMAN, ALIVE SINCE ANCIENT TIMESSSS...
LURKS DON'T AGE. WHAT'S HER PLOY?
GOD.
THIS IS REALLY HAPPENING.
DOES SHE AT LEAST HAVE A NAME?

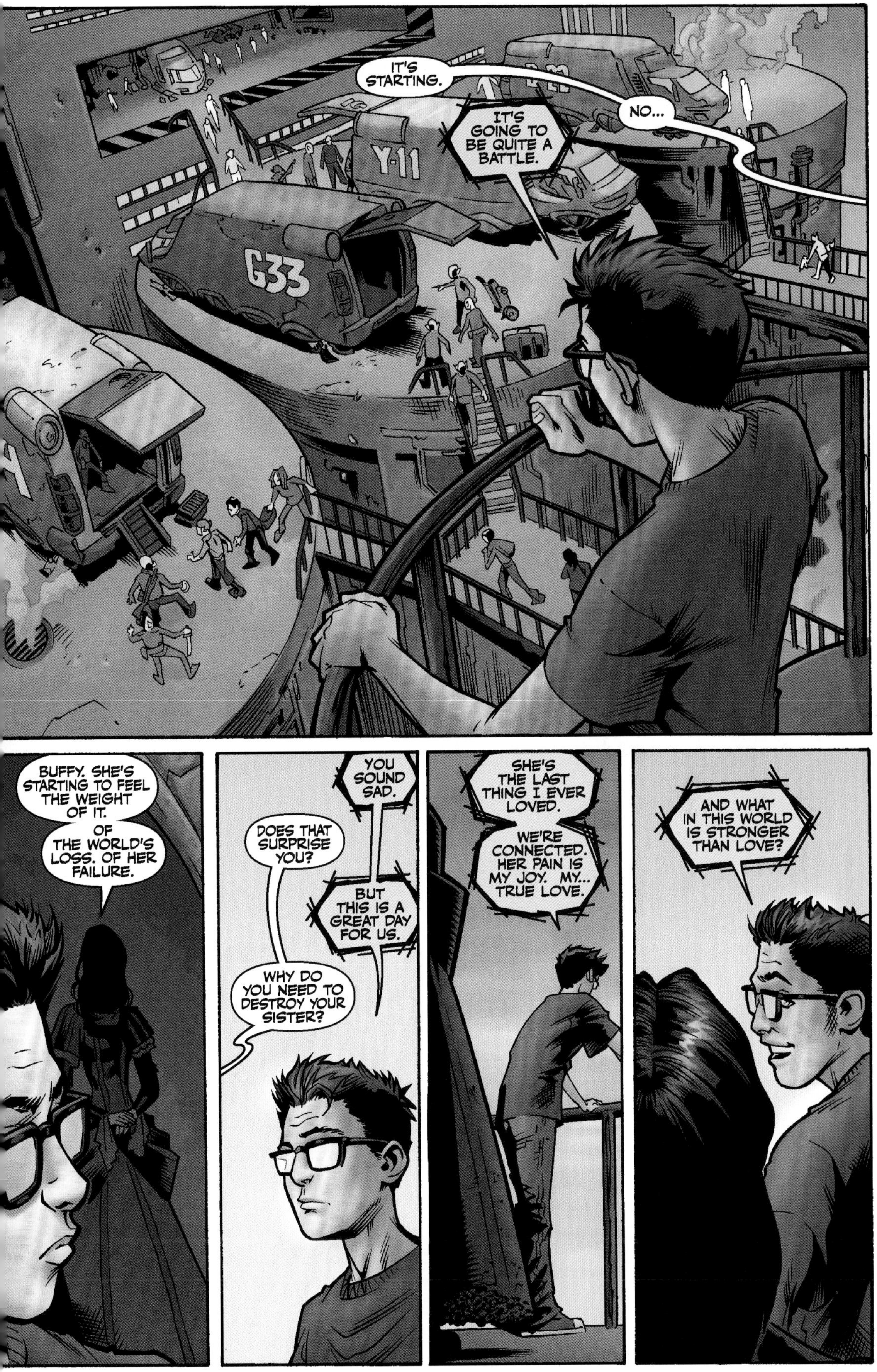
IT'S STARTING.
NO...
IT'S GOING TO BE QUITE A BATTLE.
BUFFY. SHE'S STARTING TO FEEL THE WEIGHT OF IT.
OF THE WORLD'S LOSS. OF HER FAILURE.
YOU SOUND SAD.
DOES THAT SURPRISE YOU?
BUT THIS IS A GREAT DAY FOR US.
WHY DO YOU NEED TO DESTROY YOUR SISTER?
SHE'S THE LAST THING I EVER LOVED.
WE'RE CONNECTED. HER PAIN IS MY JOY. MY... TRUE LOVE.
AND WHAT IN THIS WORLD IS STRONGER THAN LOVE?

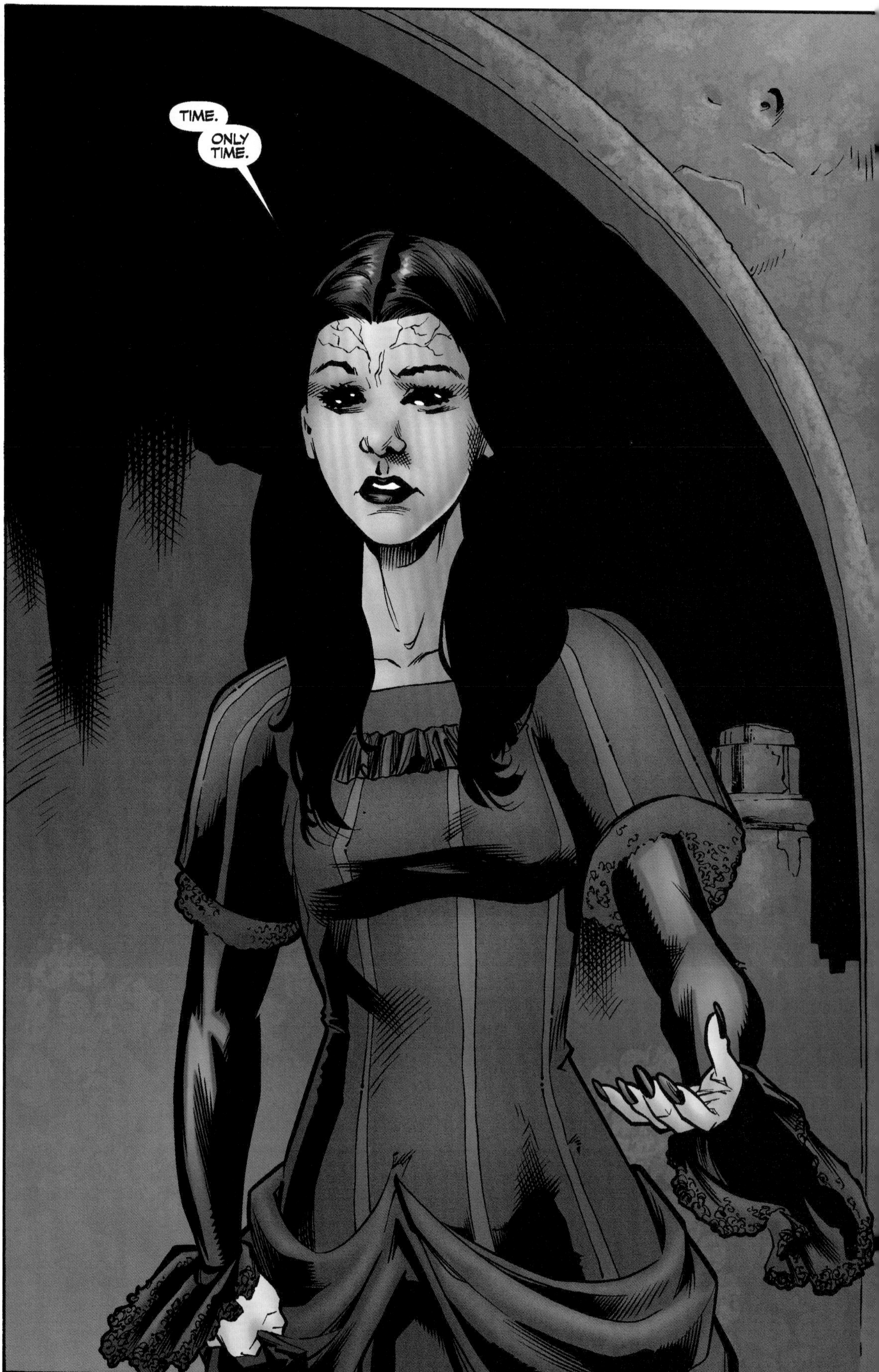
TIME.
ONLY TIME.

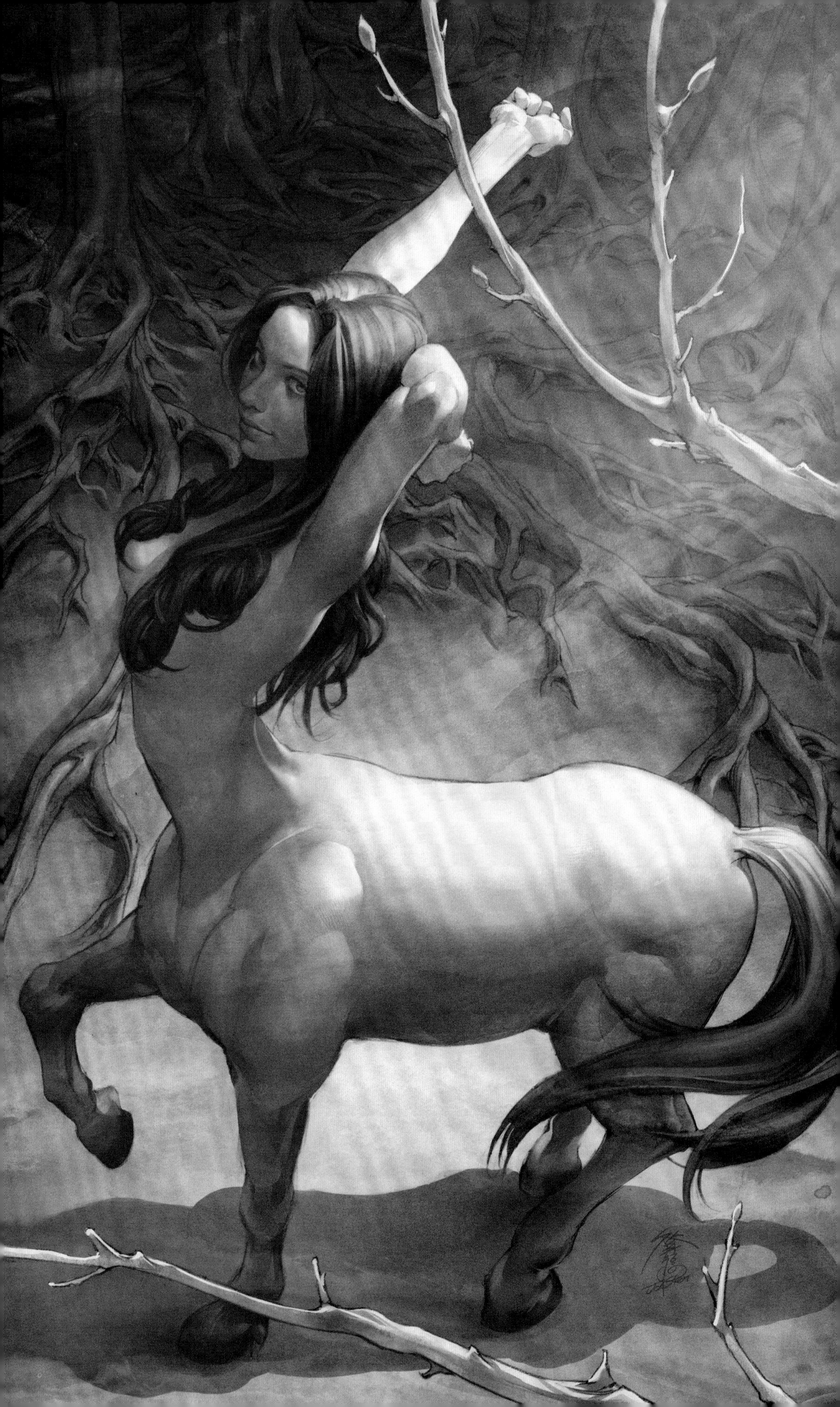

TIME OF YOUR LIFE

PART THREE

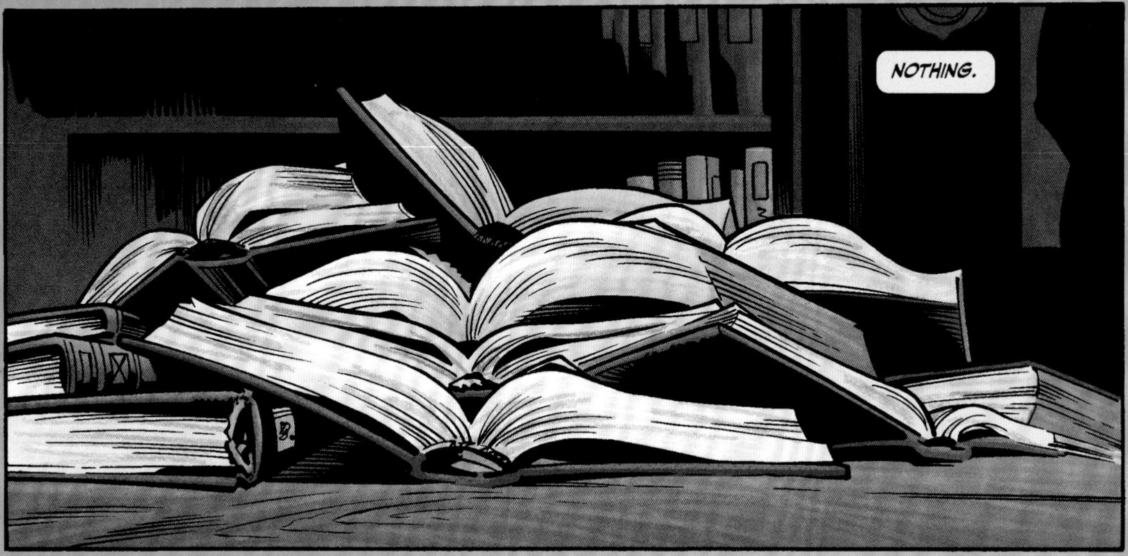
NOTHING.

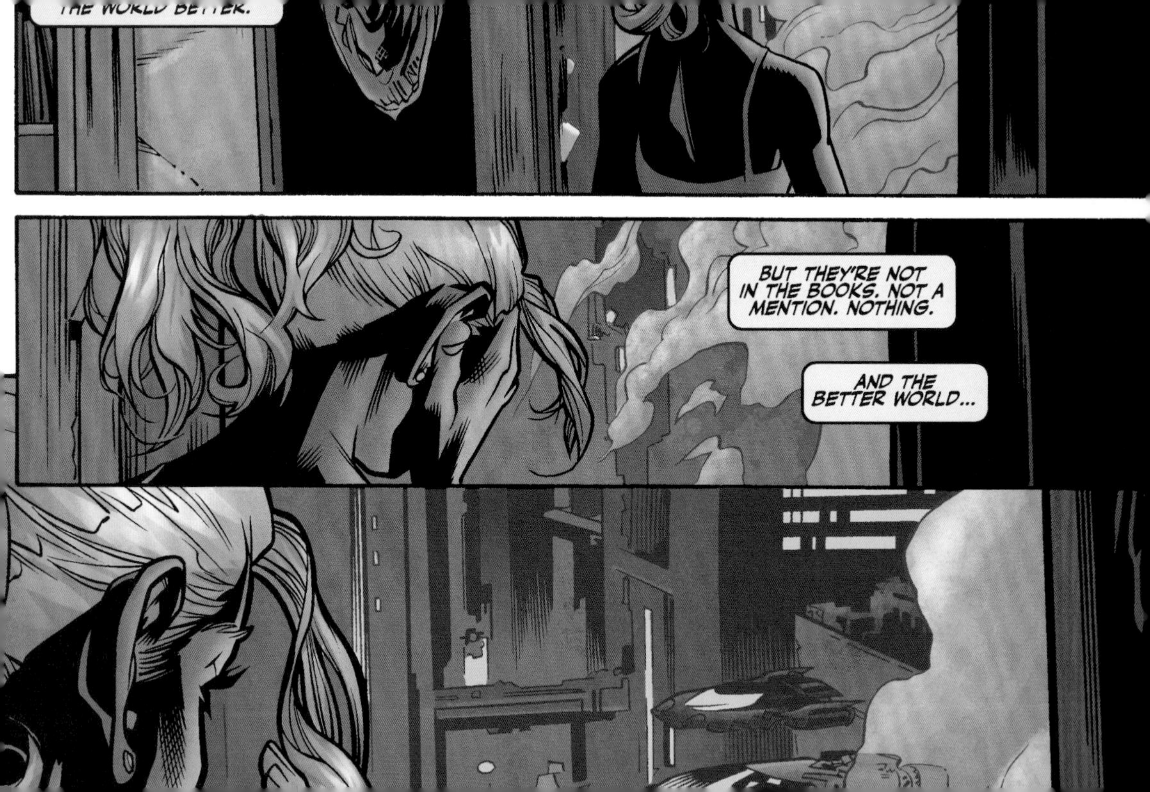
THE WORLD BETTER.
BUT THEY'RE NOT IN THE BOOKS. NOT A MENTION. NOTHING.
AND THE BETTER WORLD...

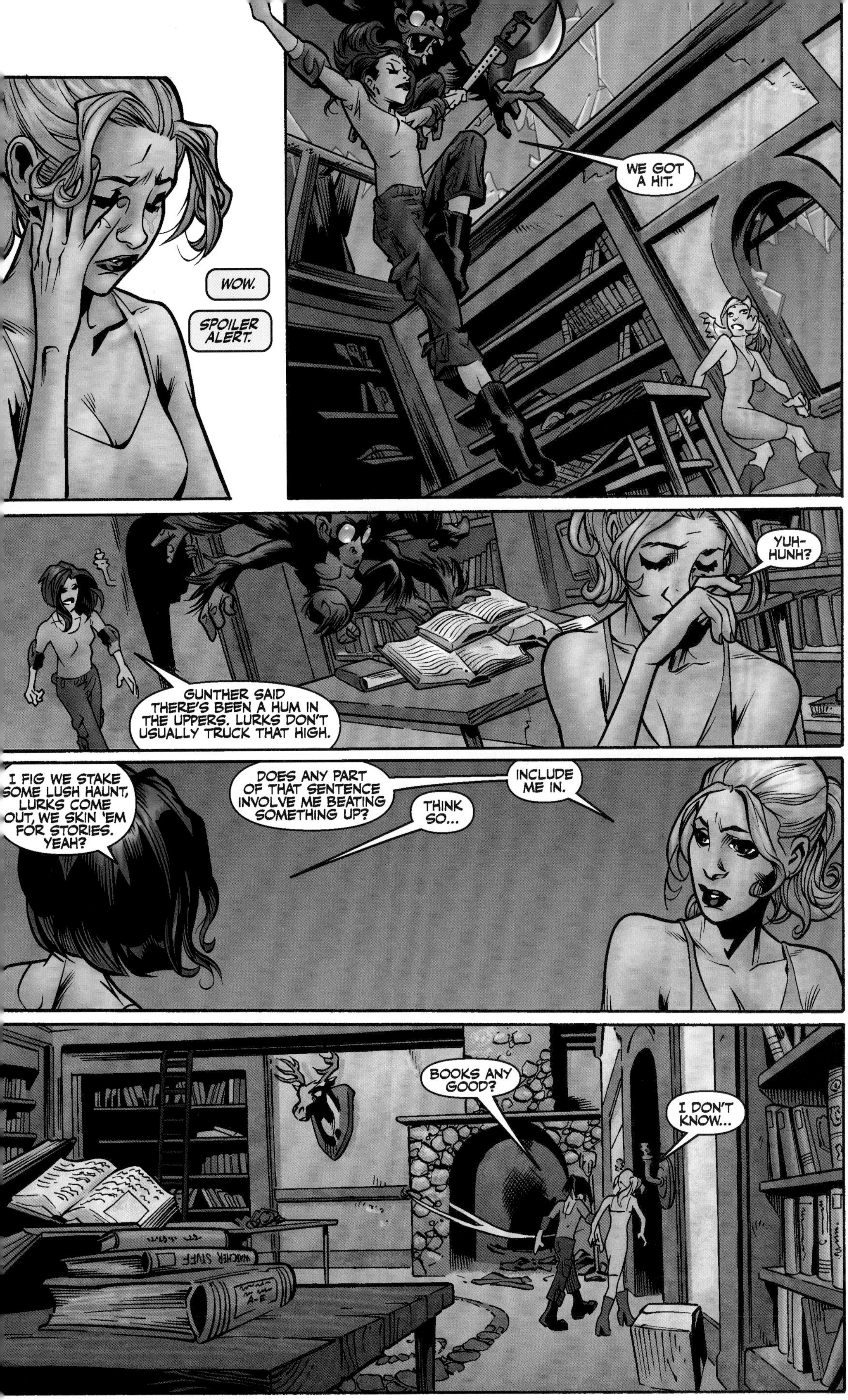
WOW.
SPOILER ALERT.
WE GOT A HIT.
GUNTHER SAID THERE'S BEEN A HUM IN THE UPPERS. LURKS DON'T USUALLY TRUCK THAT HIGH.
YUH-HUNH?
I FIG WE STAKE SOME LUSH HAUNT, LURKS COME OUT, WE SKIN 'EM FOR STORIES. YEAH?
DOES ANY PART OF THAT SENTENCE INVOLVE ME BEATING SOMETHING UP?
THINK SO...
INCLUDE ME IN.
BOOKS ANY GOOD?
I DON'T KNOW...
WATCHER STUFF
A-E

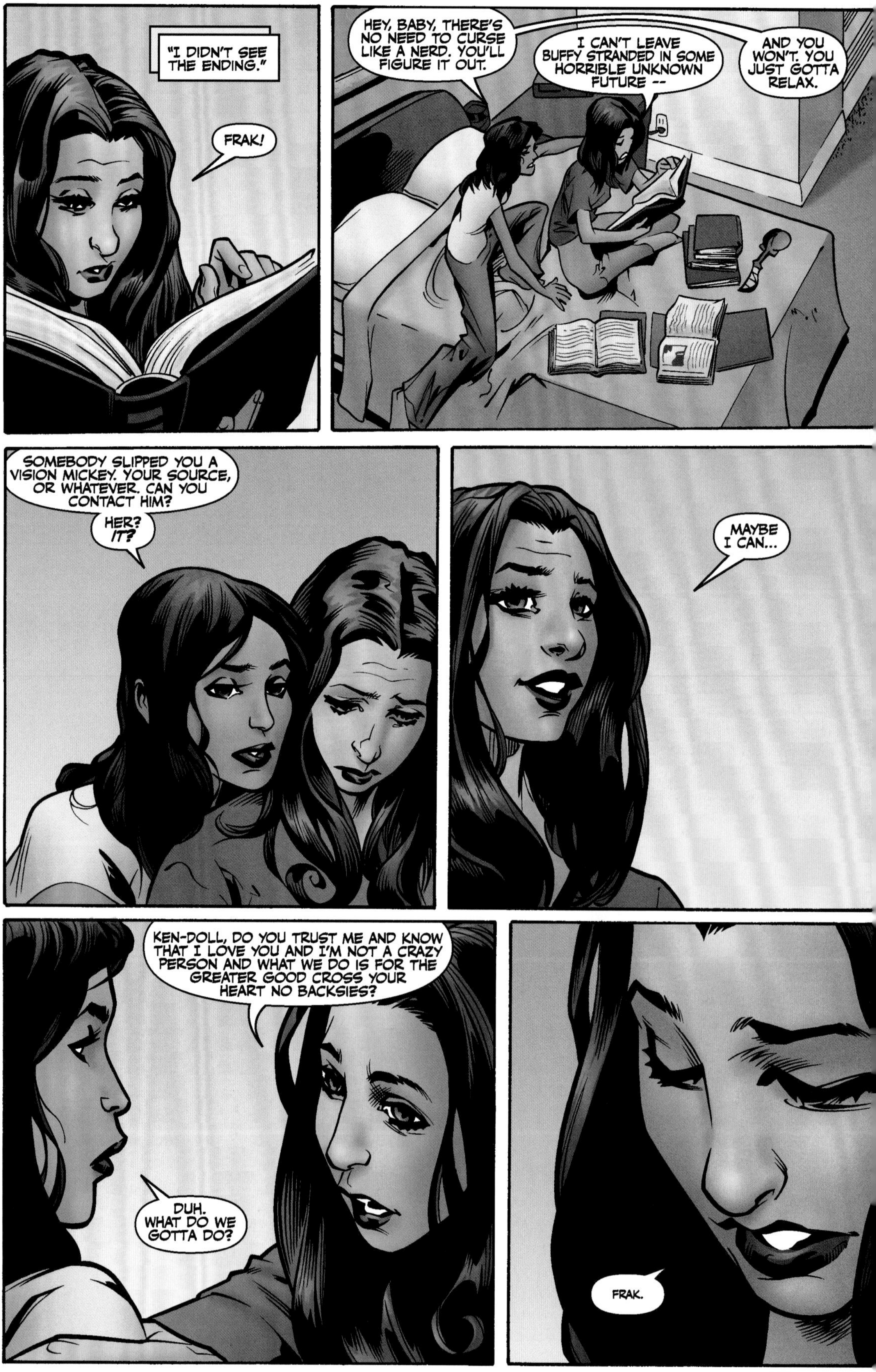
"I DIDN'T SEE THE ENDING."
FRAK!
HEY, BABY, THERE'S NO NEED TO CURSE LIKE A NERD. YOU'LL FIGURE IT OUT.
I CAN'T LEAVE BUFFY STRANDED IN SOME HORRIBLE UNKNOWN FUTURE --
AND YOU WON'T. YOU JUST GOTTA RELAX.
SOMEBODY SLIPPED YOU A VISION MICKEY. YOUR SOURCE, OR WHATEVER. CAN YOU CONTACT HIM?
HER? IT?
MAYBE I CAN...
KEN-DOLL, DO YOU TRUST ME AND KNOW THAT I LOVE YOU AND I'M NOT A CRAZY PERSON AND WHAT WE DO IS FOR THE GREATER GOOD CROSS YOUR HEART NO BACKSIES?
DUH. WHAT DO WE GOTTA DO?
FRAK.

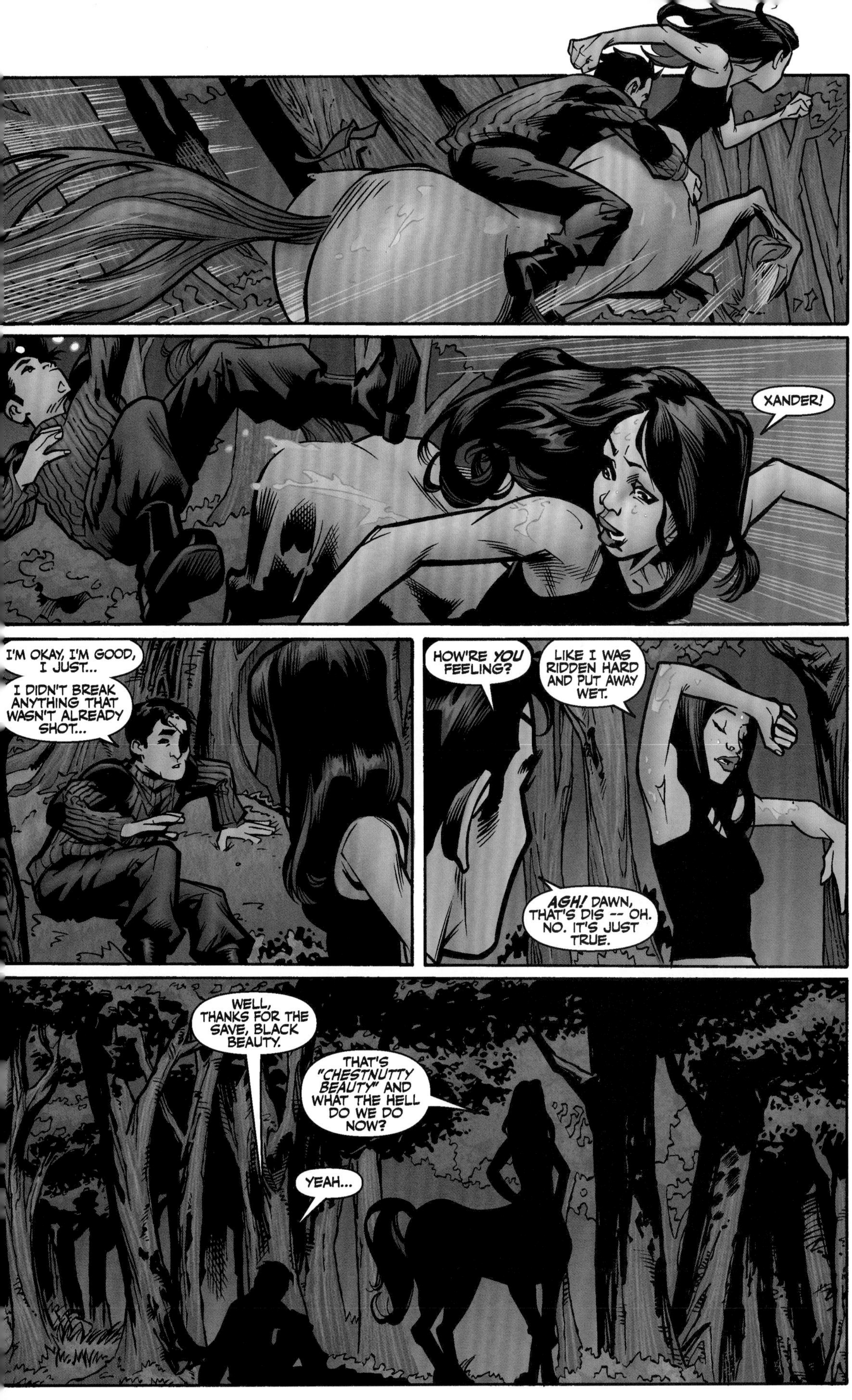
XANDER!
I'M OKAY, I'M GOOD, I JUST...
I DIDN'T BREAK ANYTHING THAT WASN'T ALREADY SHOT...
HOW'RE YOU FEELING?
LIKE I WAS RIDDEN HARD AND PUT AWAY WET.
AGH! DAWN, THAT'S DIS -- OH. NO. IT'S JUST TRUE.
WELL, THANKS FOR THE SAVE, BLACK BEAUTY.
THAT'S "CHESTNUTTY BEAUTY" AND WHAT THE HELL DO WE DO NOW?
YEAH...

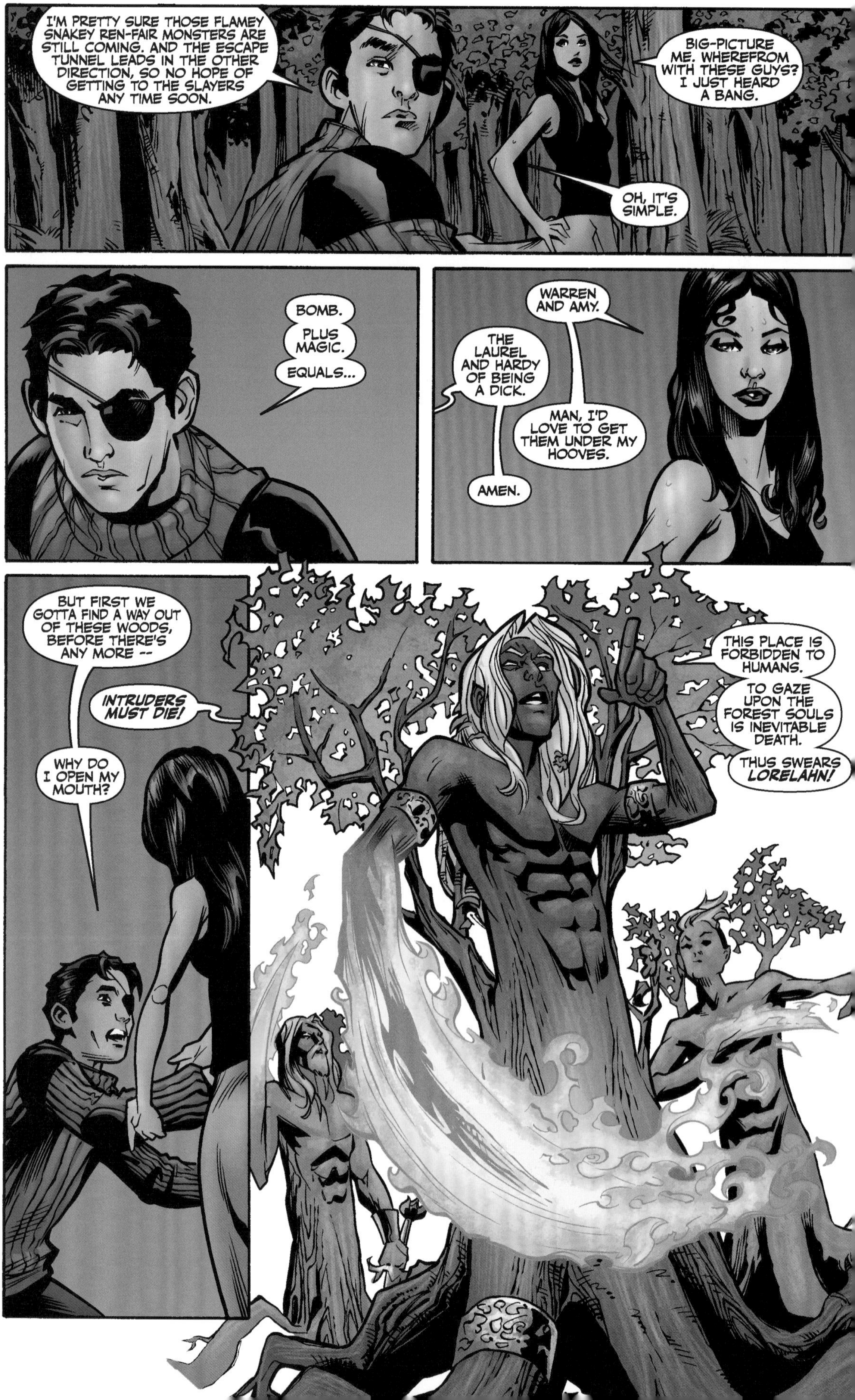

I'M PRETTY SURE THOSE FLAMEY SNAKEY REN-FAIR MONSTERS ARE STILL COMING. AND THE ESCAPE TUNNEL LEADS IN THE OTHER DIRECTION, SO NO HOPE OF GETTING TO THE SLAYERS ANY TIME SOON.
BIG-PICTURE ME. WHEREFROM WITH THESE GUYS? I JUST HEARD A BANG.
OH, IT'S SIMPLE.
BOMB.
PLUS MAGIC.
EQUALS...
WARREN AND AMY.
THE LAUREL AND HARDY OF BEING A DICK.
MAN, I'D LOVE TO GET THEM UNDER MY HOOVES.
AMEN.
BUT FIRST WE GOTTA FIND A WAY OUT OF THESE WOODS, BEFORE THERE'S ANY MORE --
INTRUDERS MUST DIE!
WHY DO I OPEN MY MOUTH?
THIS PLACE IS FORBIDDEN TO HUMANS.
TO GAZE UPON THE FOREST SOULS IS INEVITABLE DEATH.
THUS SWEARS LORELAHN!

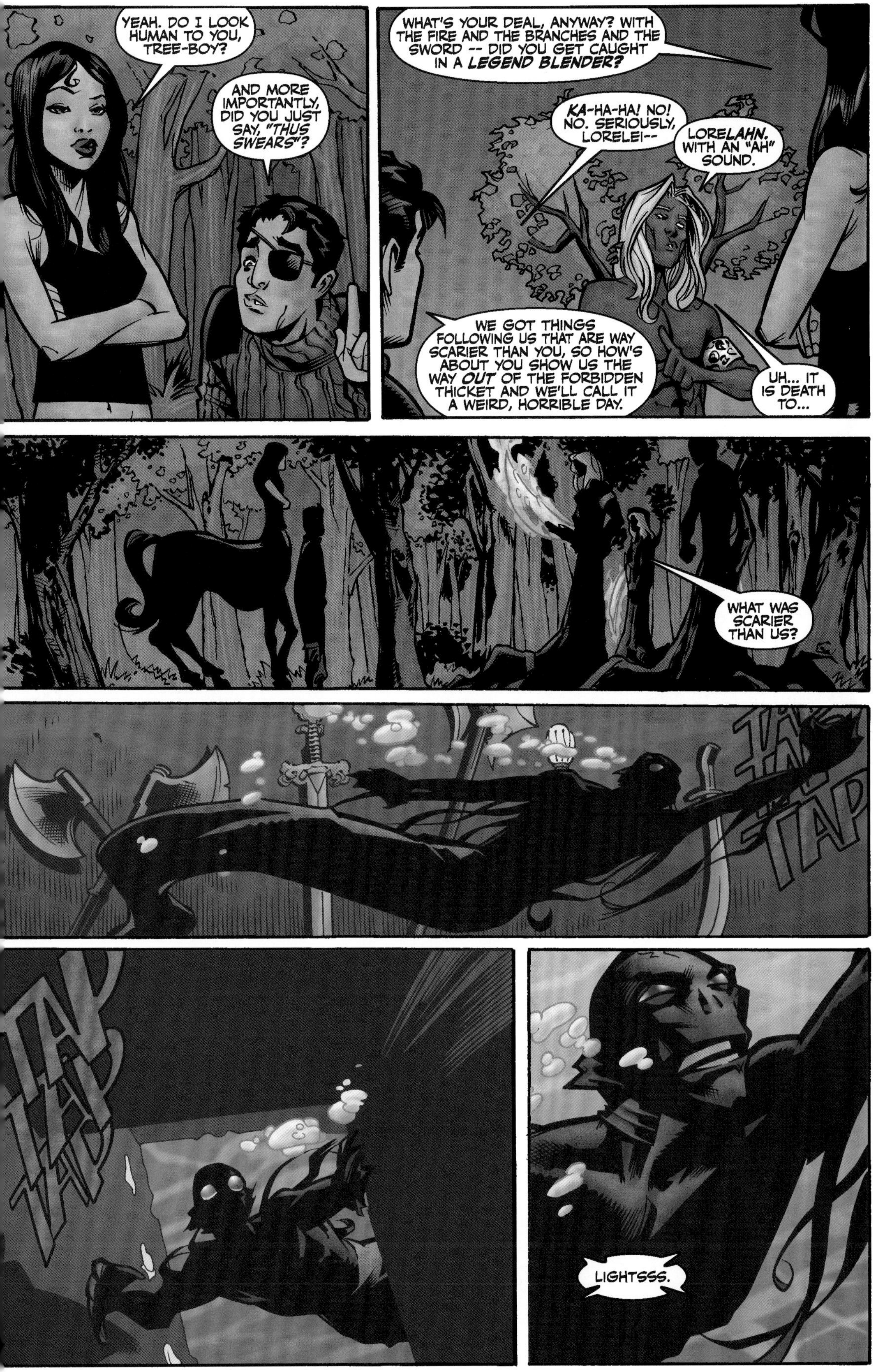

YEAH. DO I LOOK HUMAN TO YOU, TREE-BOY?
AND MORE IMPORTANTLY, DID YOU JUST SAY, "THUS SWEARS"?
WHAT'S YOUR DEAL, ANYWAY? WITH THE FIRE AND THE BRANCHES AND THE SWORD -- DID YOU GET CAUGHT IN A LEGEND BLENDER?
KA-HA-HA! NO! NO. SERIOUSLY, LORELEI--
LORELAHN. WITH AN "AH" SOUND.
WE GOT THINGS FOLLOWING US THAT ARE WAY SCARIER THAN YOU, SO HOW'S ABOUT YOU SHOW US THE WAY OUT OF THE FORBIDDEN THICKET AND WE'LL CALL IT A WEIRD, HORRIBLE DAY.
UH... IT IS DEATH TO...
WHAT WAS SCARIER THAN US?
TAP TAP TAP
TAP TAP TAP
LIGHTSSS.

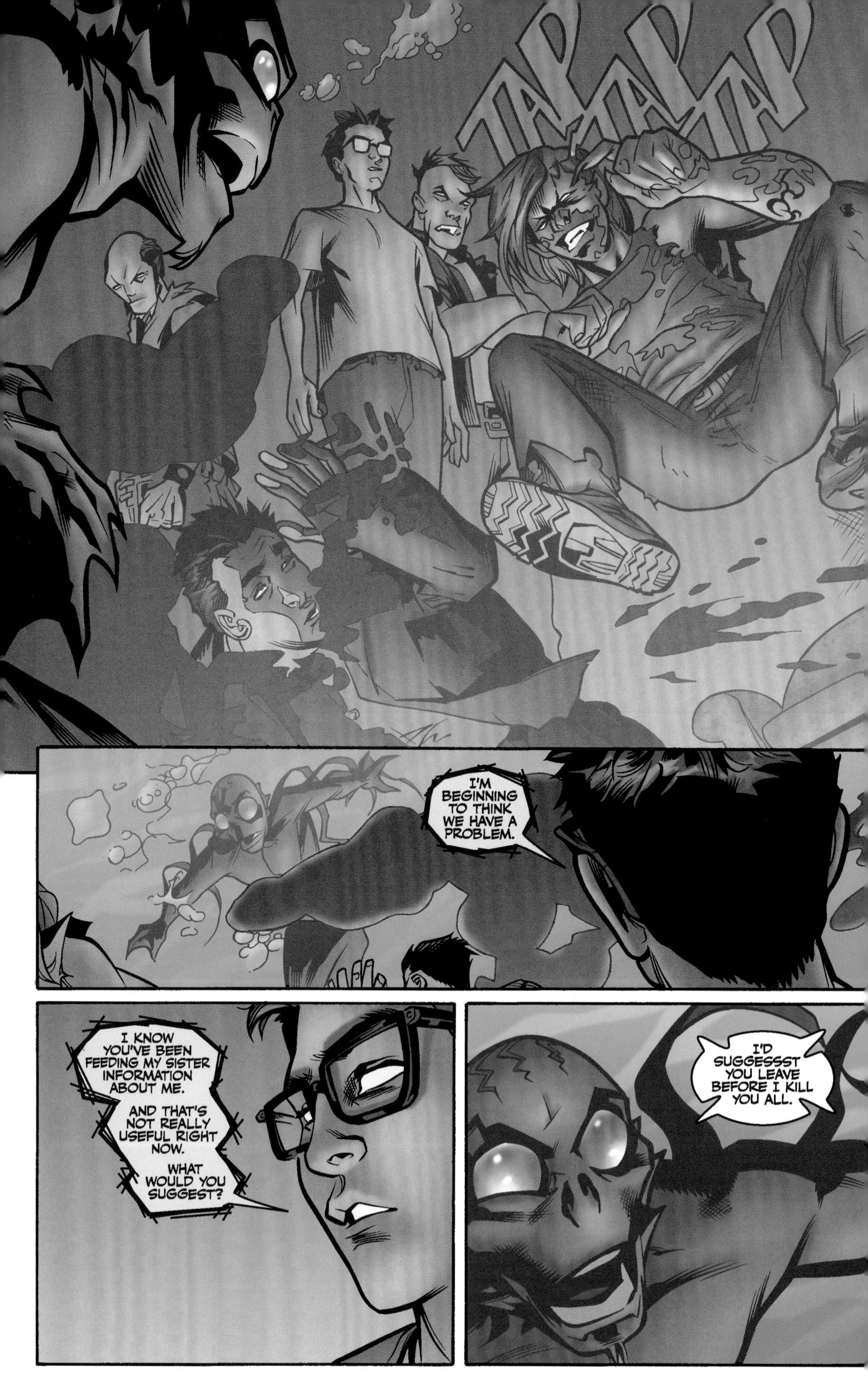
TAP TAP TAP
I'M BEGINNING TO THINK WE HAVE A PROBLEM.
I KNOW YOU'VE BEEN FEEDING MY SISTER INFORMATION ABOUT ME.
AND THAT'S NOT REALLY USEFUL RIGHT NOW.
WHAT WOULD YOU SUGGEST?
I'D SUGGESSST YOU LEAVE BEFORE I KILL YOU ALL.

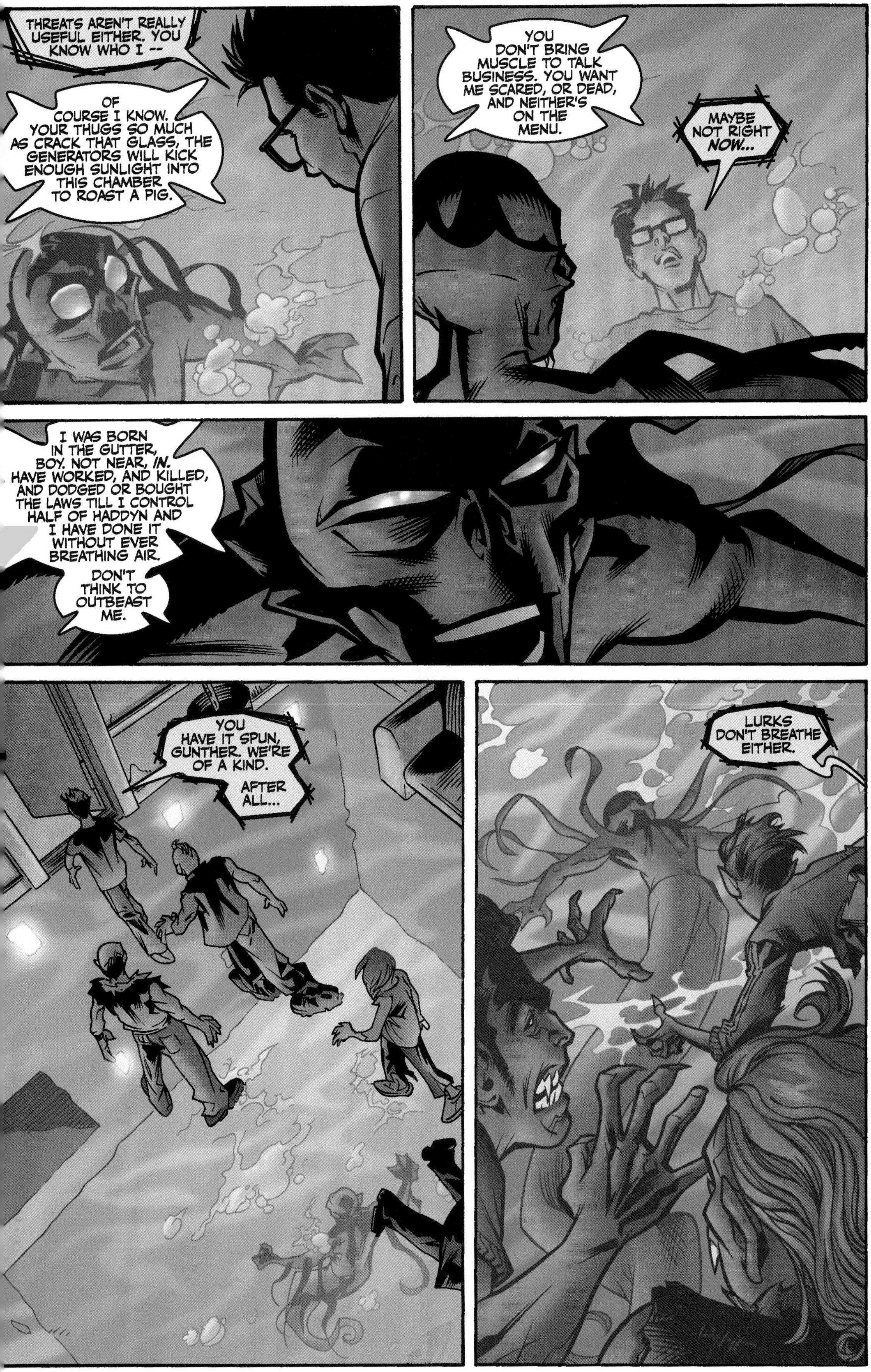
THREATS AREN'T REALLY USEFUL EITHER. YOU KNOW WHO I --
OF COURSE I KNOW. YOUR THUGS SO MUCH AS CRACK THAT GLASS, THE GENERATORS WILL KICK ENOUGH SUNLIGHT INTO THIS CHAMBER TO ROAST A PIG.
YOU DON'T BRING MUSCLE TO TALK BUSINESS. YOU WANT ME SCARED, OR DEAD, AND NEITHER'S ON THE MENU.
MAYBE NOT RIGHT NOW...
I WAS BORN IN THE GUTTER, BOY. NOT NEAR, IN. HAVE WORKED, AND KILLED, AND DODGED OR BOUGHT THE LAWS TILL I CONTROL HALF OF HADDYN AND I HAVE DONE IT WITHOUT EVER BREATHING AIR.
DON'T THINK TO OUTBEAST ME.
YOU HAVE IT SPUN, GUNTHER. WE'RE OF A KIND.
AFTER ALL...
LURKS DON'T BREATHE EITHER.

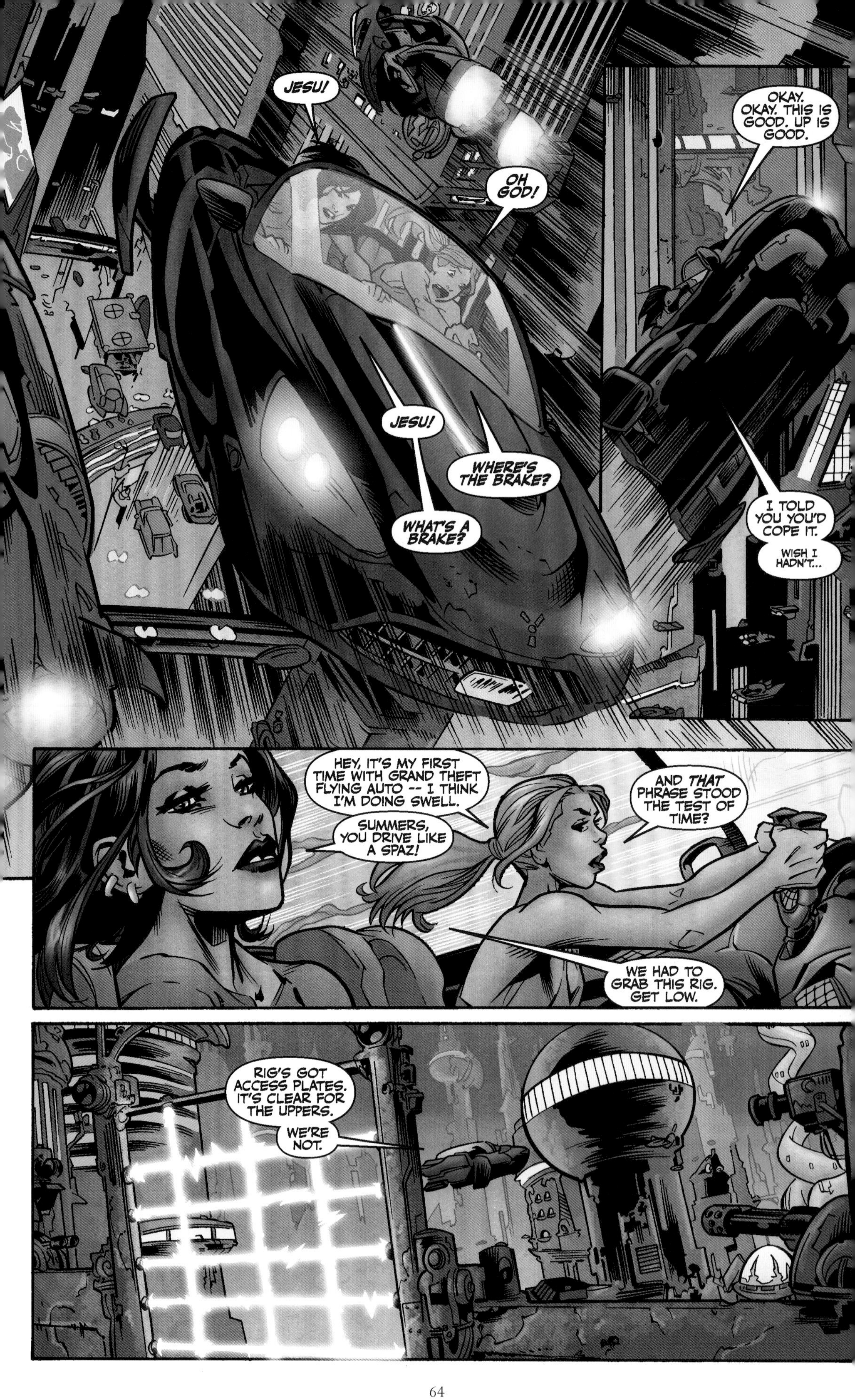
JESU!
OH GOD!
OKAY. OKAY. THIS IS GOOD. UP IS GOOD.
JESU!
WHERE'S THE BRAKE?
WHAT'S A BRAKE?
I TOLD YOU YOU'D COPE IT.
WISH I HADN'T...
HEY, IT'S MY FIRST TIME WITH GRAND THEFT FLYING AUTO -- I THINK I'M DOING SWELL.
SUMMERS, YOU DRIVE LIKE A SPAZ!
AND *THAT* PHRASE STOOD THE TEST OF TIME?
WE HAD TO GRAB THIS RIG. GET LOW.
RIG'S GOT ACCESS PLATES. IT'S CLEAR FOR THE UPPERS.
WE'RE NOT.

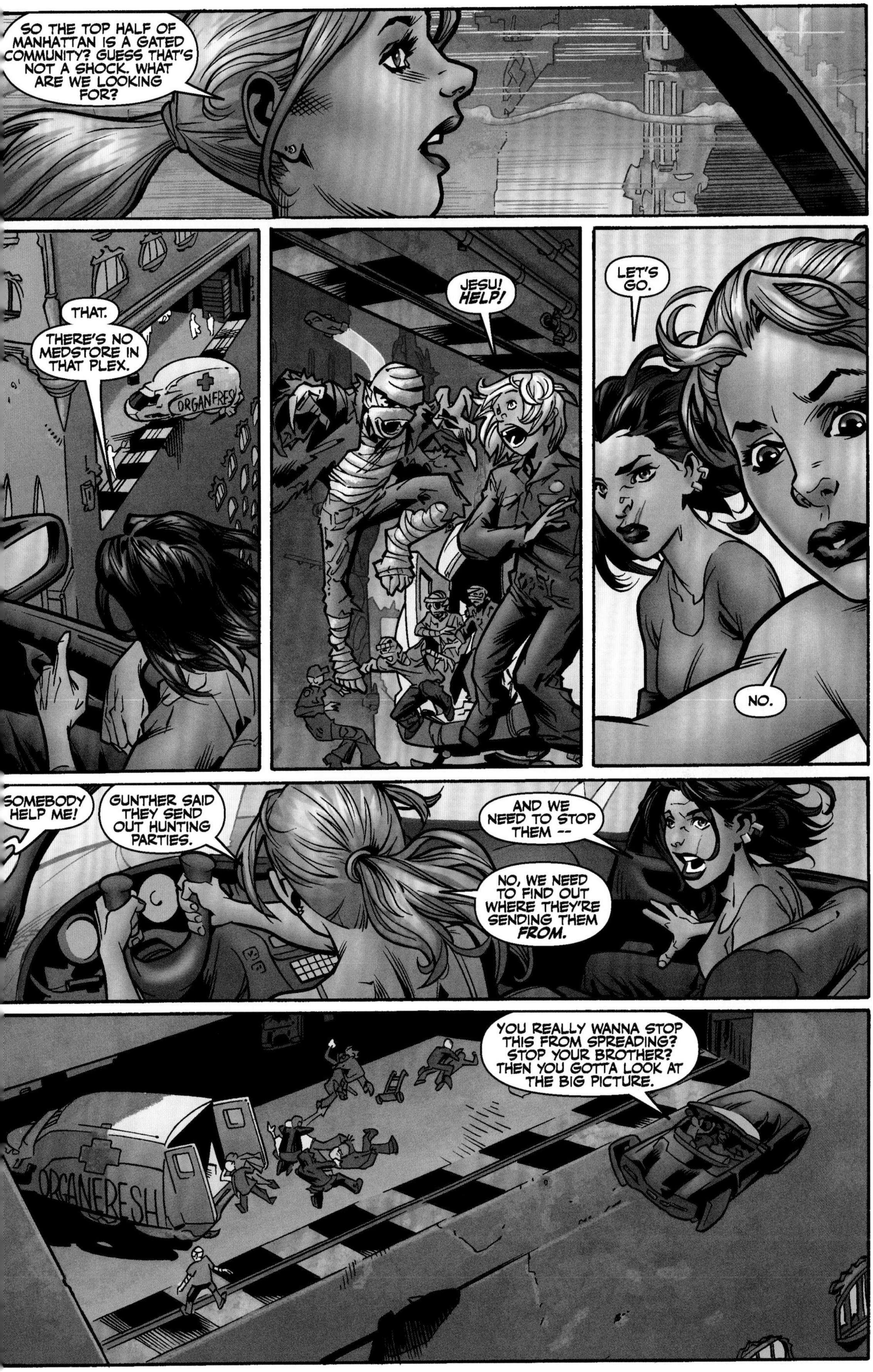
SO THE TOP HALF OF MANHATTAN IS A GATED COMMUNITY? GUESS THAT'S NOT A SHOCK. WHAT ARE WE LOOKING FOR?
THAT.
THERE'S NO MEDSTORE IN THAT PLEX.
ORGANFRESH
JESU! *HELP!*
LET'S GO.
NO.
SOMEBODY HELP ME!
GUNTHER SAID THEY SEND OUT HUNTING PARTIES.
AND WE NEED TO STOP THEM --
NO, WE NEED TO FIND OUT WHERE THEY'RE SENDING THEM *FROM.*
YOU REALLY WANNA STOP THIS FROM SPREADING? STOP YOUR BROTHER? THEN YOU GOTTA LOOK AT THE BIG PICTURE.
ORGANFRESH

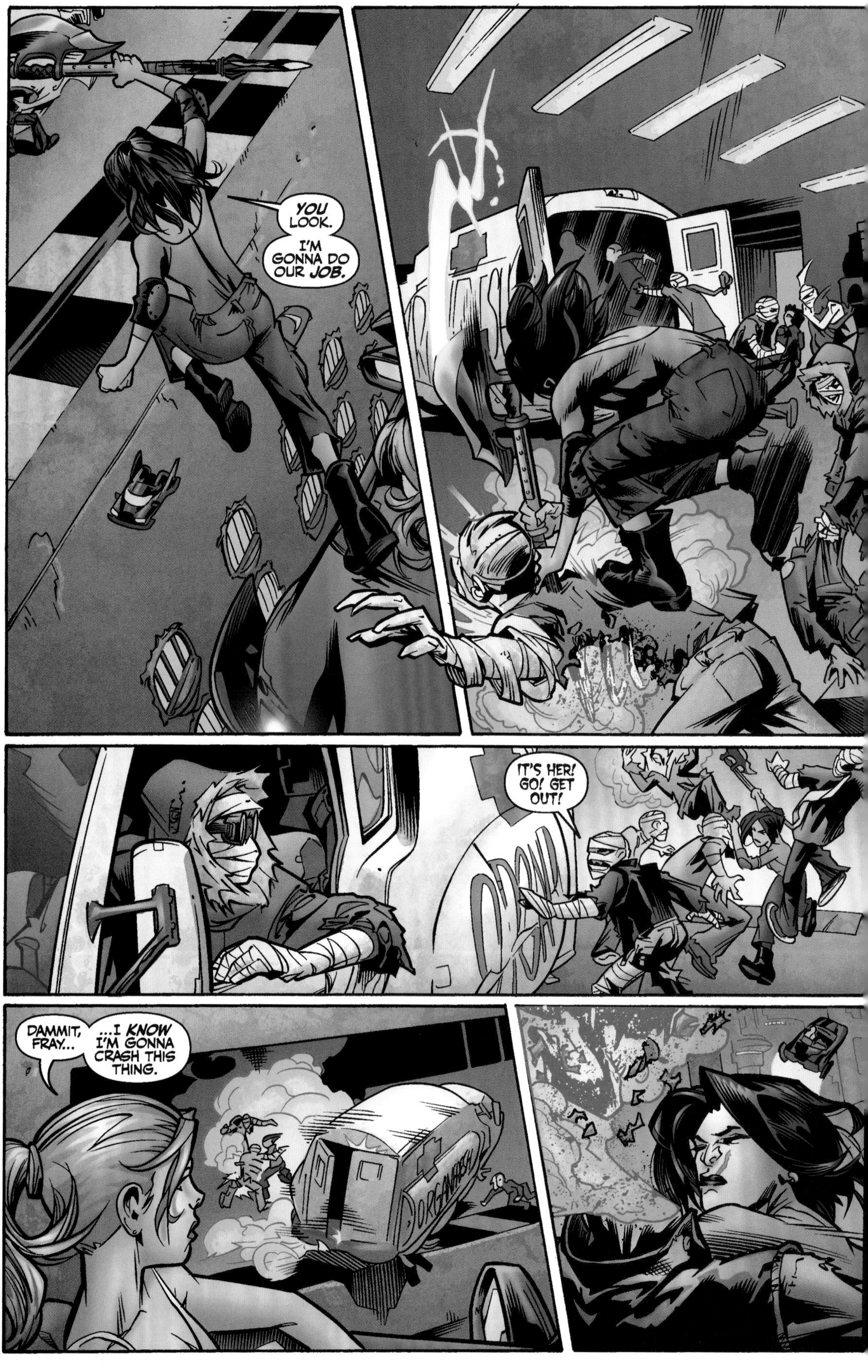
YOU LOOK. I'M GONNA DO OUR JOB.
IT'S HER! GO! GET OUT!
DAMMIT, FRAY...
...I KNOW I'M GONNA CRASH THIS THING.

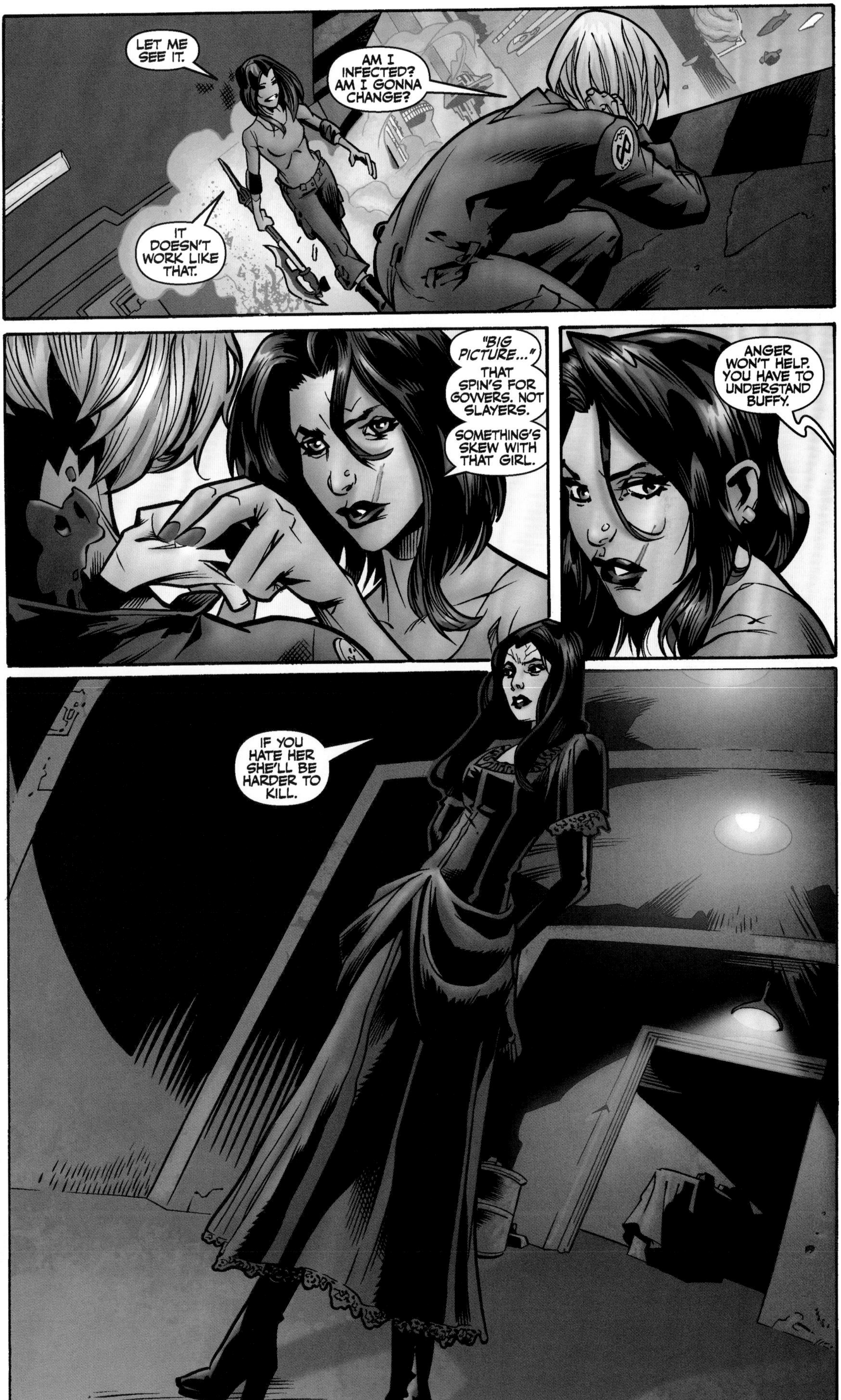
LET ME SEE IT.
AM I INFECTED? AM I GONNA CHANGE?
IT DOESN'T WORK LIKE THAT.
"BIG PICTURE..." THAT SPIN'S FOR GOVVERS. NOT SLAYERS.
SOMETHING'S SKEW WITH THAT GIRL.
ANGER WON'T HELP. YOU HAVE TO UNDERSTAND BUFFY.
IF YOU HATE HER SHE'LL BE HARDER TO KILL.

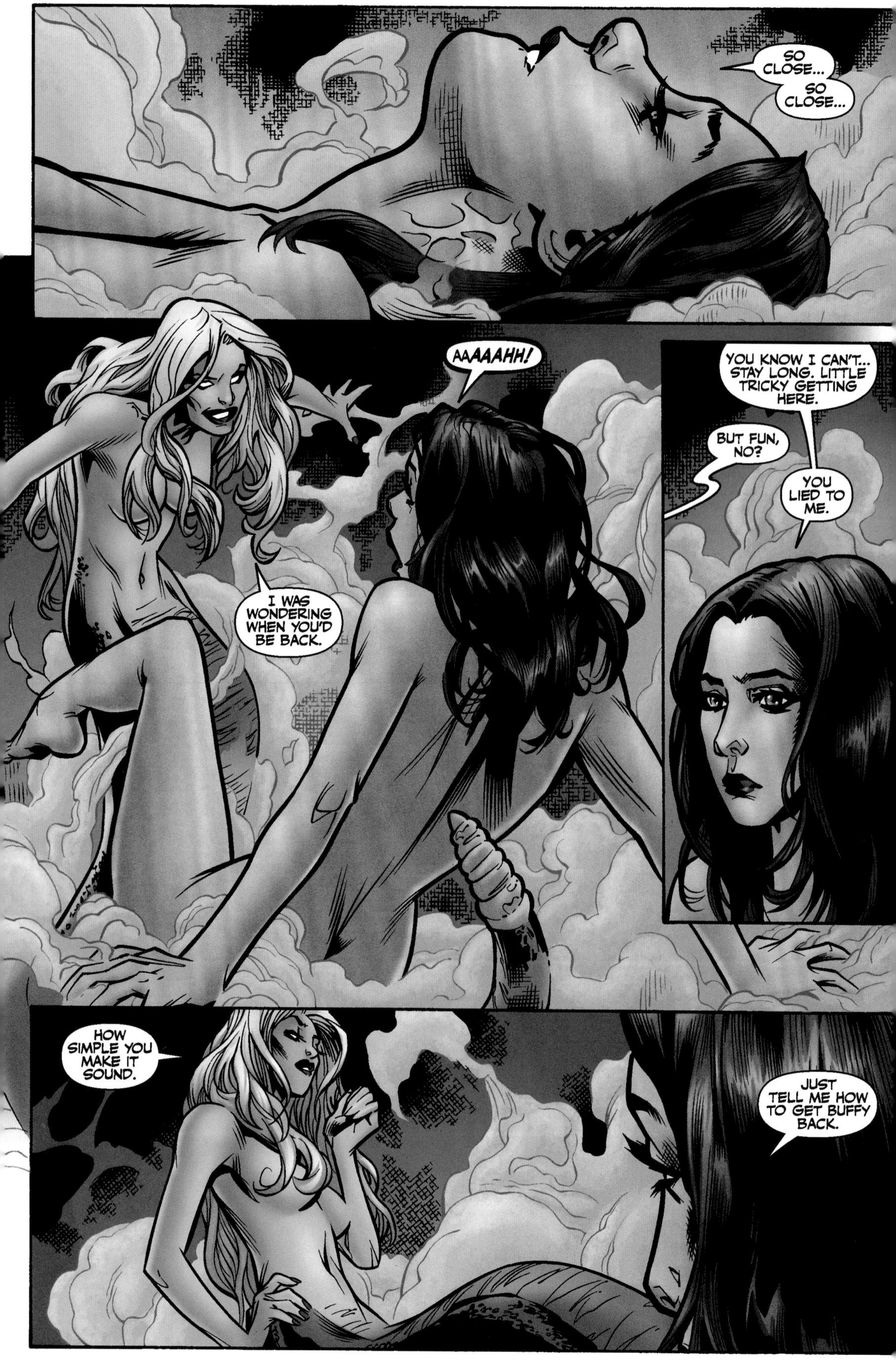

SO CLOSE... SO CLOSE...
AAAAAHH!
I WAS WONDERING WHEN YOU'D BE BACK.
YOU KNOW I CAN'T... STAY LONG. LITTLE TRICKY GETTING HERE.
BUT FUN, NO?
YOU LIED TO ME.
HOW SIMPLE YOU MAKE IT SOUND.
JUST TELL ME HOW TO GET BUFFY BACK.

YOU CANNOT DO IT YOURSELF?

I DON'T HAVE THAT KIND OF POWER.

IS THAT SO?

TIME-BENDING ISN'T SOME CROSS-DIMENSIONAL JAUNT. AND IT'S DANGEROUS. ONLY SOMEONE ON THE DEEP DARK WOULD MESS WITH THAT.

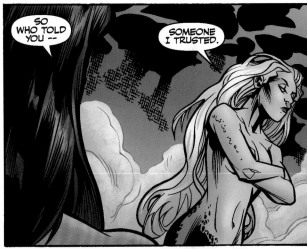

SO WHO TOLD YOU --

SOMEONE I TRUSTED.

I'M SORRY. YOU KNOW HOW GRATEFUL I AM FOR WHAT WE... WHAT YOU TAUGHT ME.

BUT THIS IS BUFFY. I NEED HER BACK.

WE ALL DO.

THE RIFT WILL REOPEN. THIS NIGHT.

REALLY? HOW DO I --

YOU WILL FIGURE IT OUT. OR YOU WON'T.

BUT I DEMAND A PROMISE.

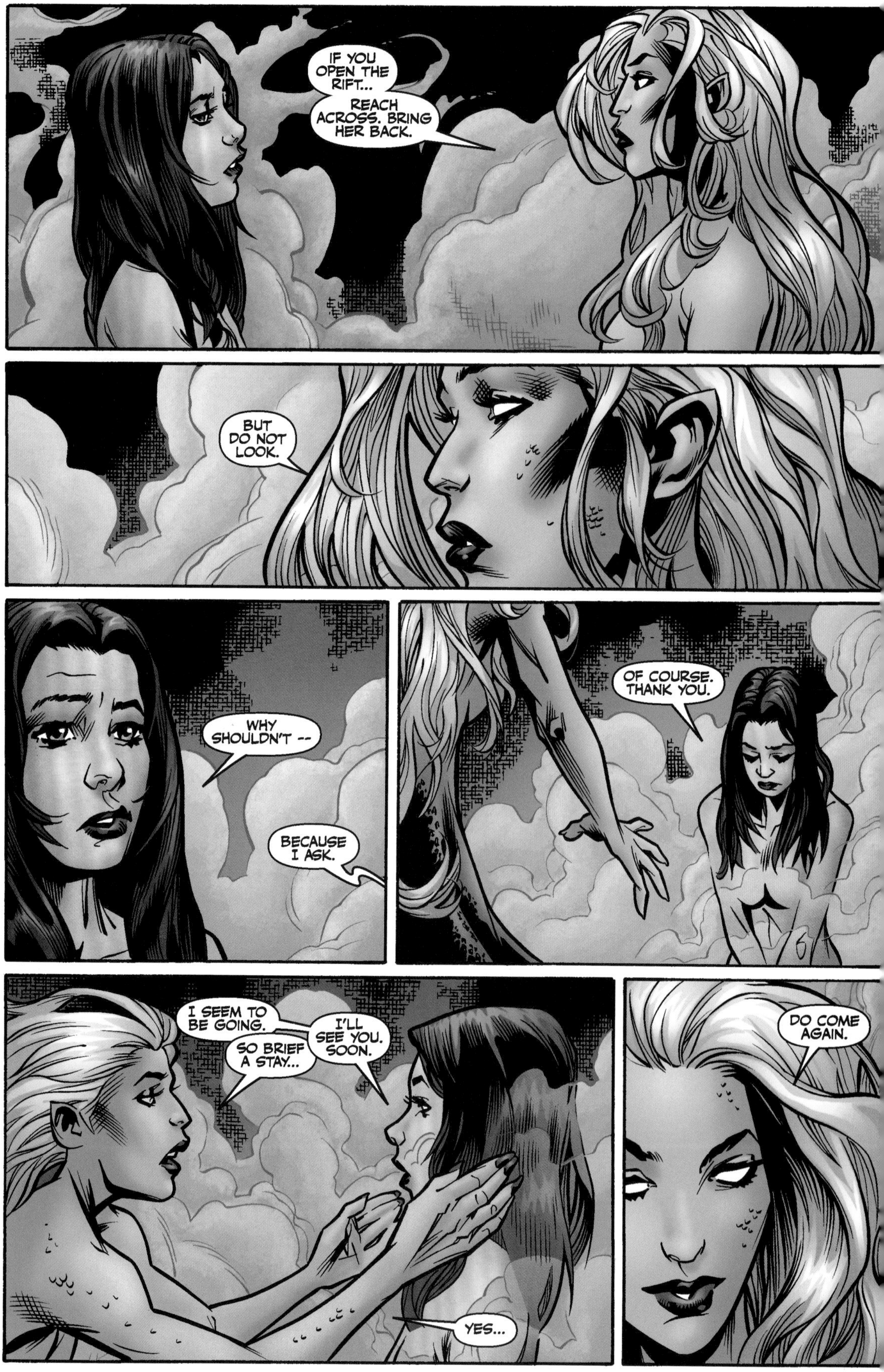

IF YOU OPEN THE RIFT...
REACH ACROSS. BRING HER BACK.
BUT DO NOT LOOK.
WHY SHOULDN'T --
BECAUSE I ASK.
OF COURSE. THANK YOU.
I SEEM TO BE GOING.
SO BRIEF A STAY...
I'LL SEE YOU. SOON.
YES...
DO COME AGAIN.

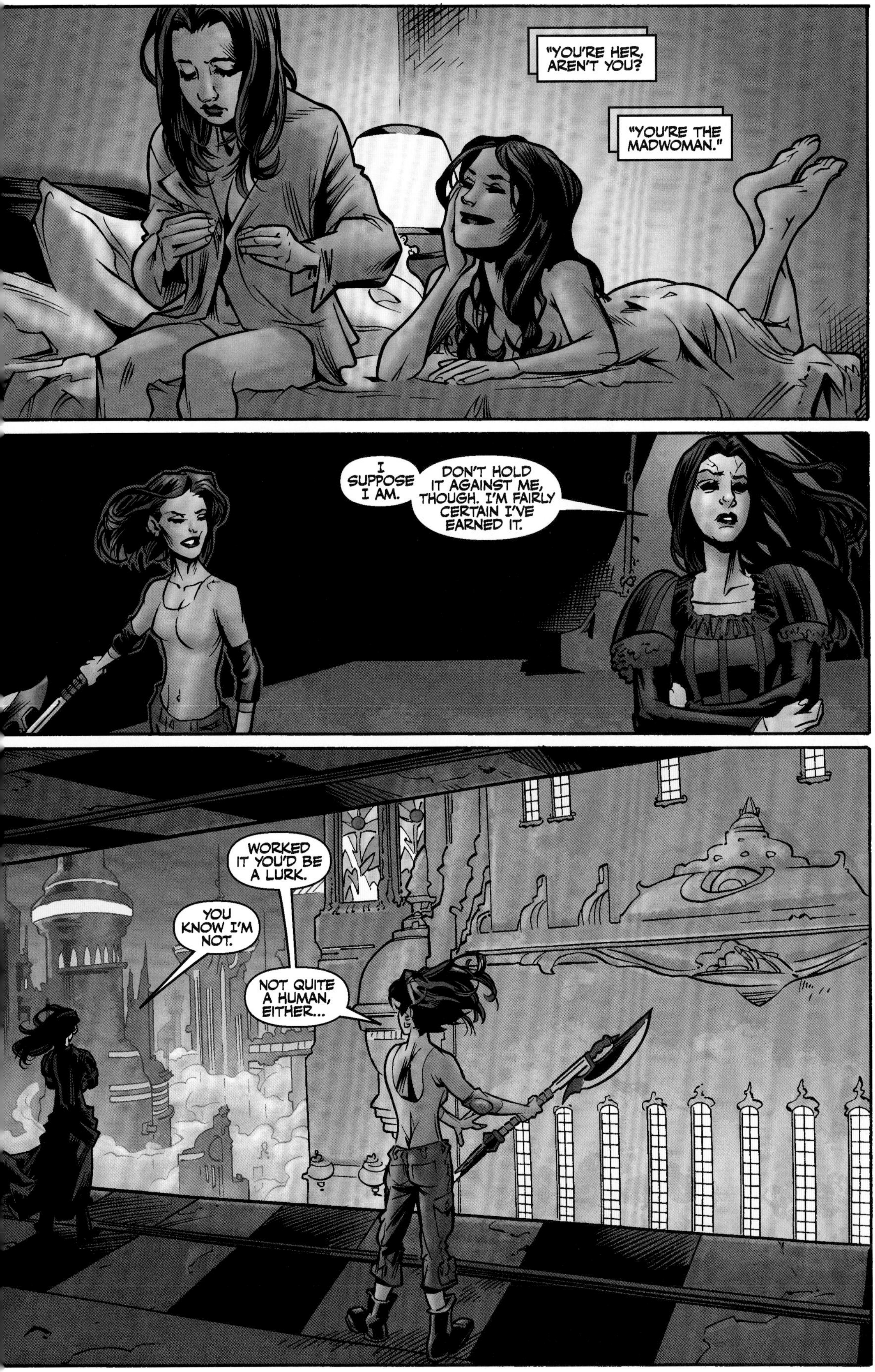
"YOU'RE HER, AREN'T YOU?
"YOU'RE THE MADWOMAN."
I SUPPOSE I AM.
DON'T HOLD IT AGAINST ME, THOUGH. I'M FAIRLY CERTAIN I'VE EARNED IT.
WORKED IT YOU'D BE A LURK.
YOU KNOW I'M NOT.
NOT QUITE A HUMAN, EITHER...

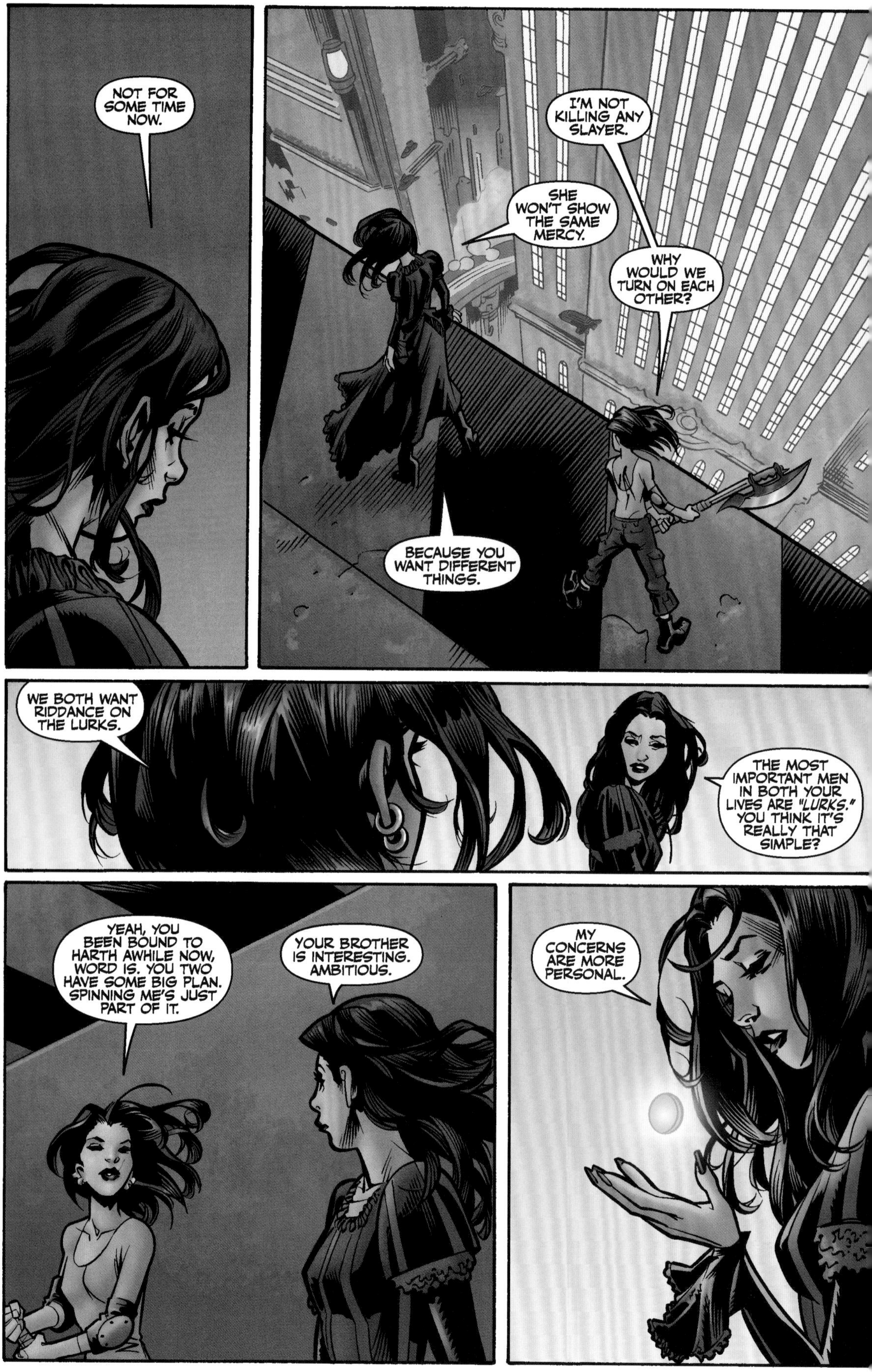

NOT FOR SOME TIME NOW.
I'M NOT KILLING ANY SLAYER.
SHE WON'T SHOW THE SAME MERCY.
WHY WOULD WE TURN ON EACH OTHER?
BECAUSE YOU WANT DIFFERENT THINGS.
WE BOTH WANT RIDDANCE ON THE LURKS.
THE MOST IMPORTANT MEN IN BOTH YOUR LIVES ARE "LURKS." YOU THINK IT'S REALLY THAT SIMPLE?
YEAH, YOU BEEN BOUND TO HARTH AWHILE NOW, WORD IS. YOU TWO HAVE SOME BIG PLAN. SPINNING ME'S JUST PART OF IT.
YOUR BROTHER IS INTERESTING. AMBITIOUS.
MY CONCERNS ARE MORE PERSONAL.

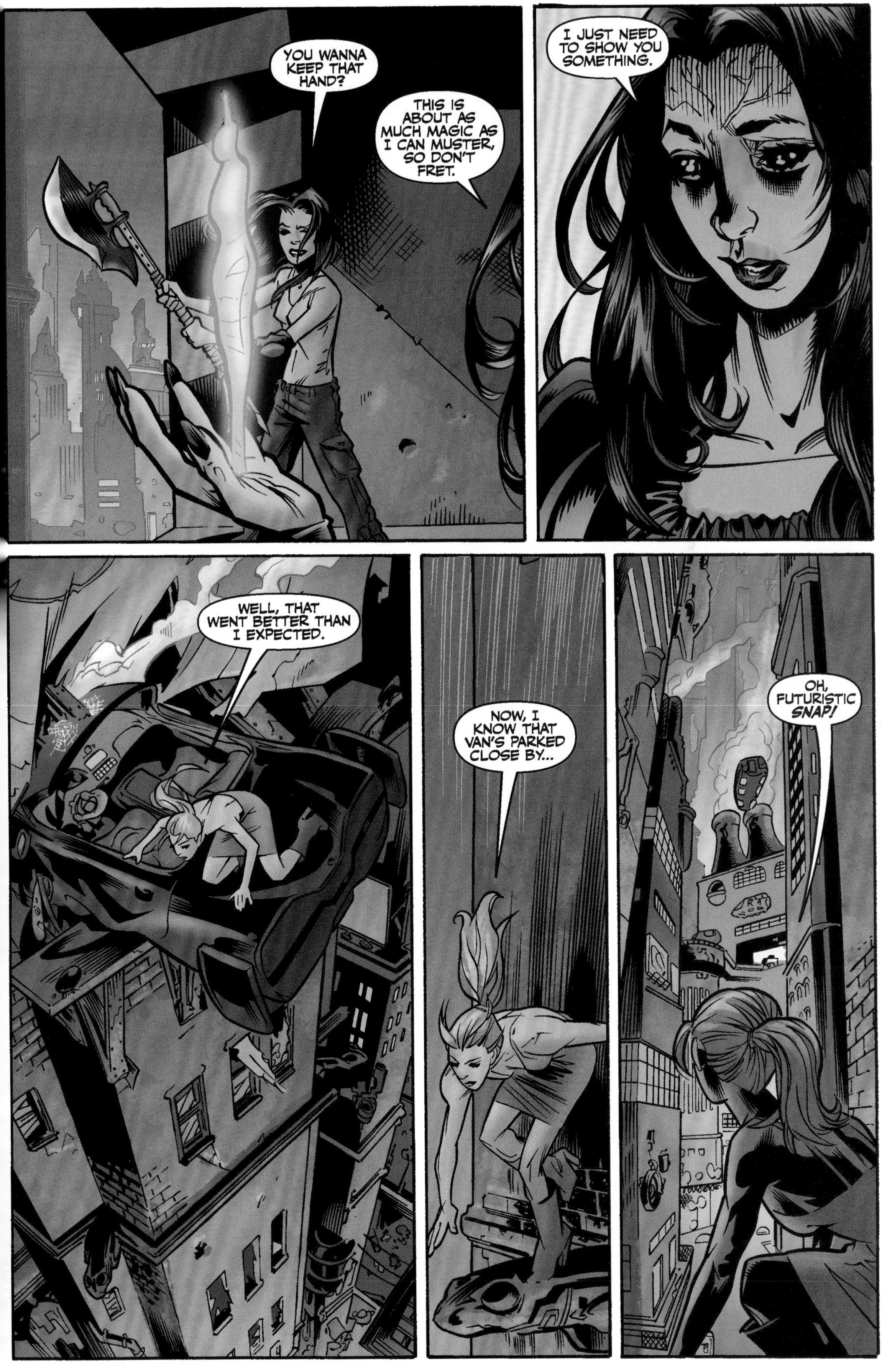
YOU WANNA KEEP THAT HAND?
THIS IS ABOUT AS MUCH MAGIC AS I CAN MUSTER, SO DON'T FRET.
I JUST NEED TO SHOW YOU SOMETHING.
WELL, THAT WENT BETTER THAN I EXPECTED.
NOW, I KNOW THAT VAN'S PARKED CLOSE BY...
OH, FUTURISTIC *SNAP!*

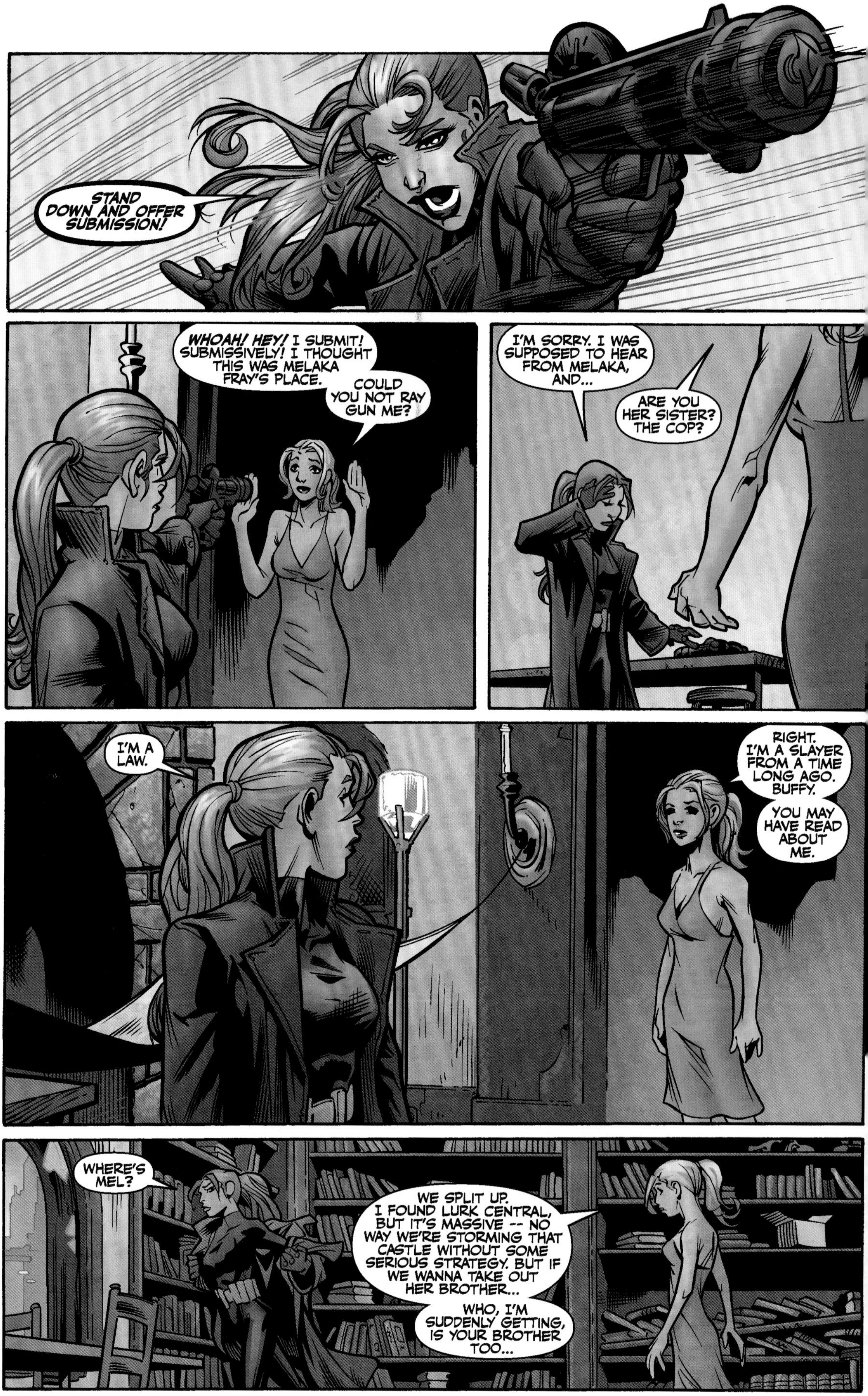
STAND DOWN AND OFFER SUBMISSION!
WHOAH! HEY! I SUBMIT! SUBMISSIVELY! I THOUGHT THIS WAS MELAKA FRAY'S PLACE.
COULD YOU NOT RAY GUN ME?
I'M SORRY. I WAS SUPPOSED TO HEAR FROM MELAKA, AND...
ARE YOU HER SISTER? THE COP?
I'M A LAW.
RIGHT. I'M A SLAYER FROM A TIME LONG AGO. BUFFY.
YOU MAY HAVE READ ABOUT ME.
WHERE'S MEL?
WE SPLIT UP. I FOUND LURK CENTRAL, BUT IT'S MASSIVE -- NO WAY WE'RE STORMING THAT CASTLE WITHOUT SOME SERIOUS STRATEGY. BUT IF WE WANNA TAKE OUT HER BROTHER...
WHO, I'M SUDDENLY GETTING, IS YOUR BROTHER TOO...

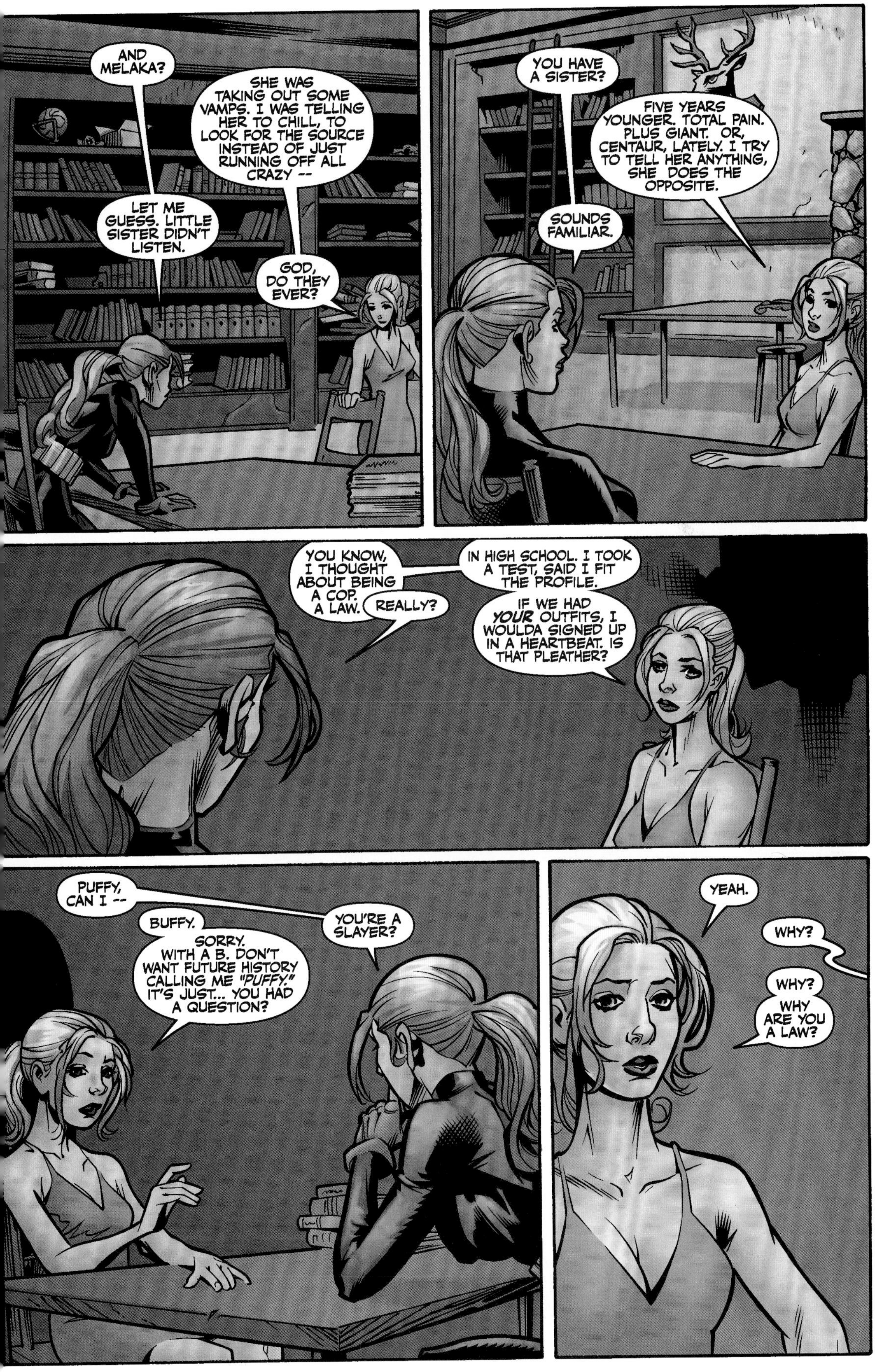
AND MELAKA?
SHE WAS TAKING OUT SOME VAMPS. I WAS TELLING HER TO CHILL, TO LOOK FOR THE SOURCE INSTEAD OF JUST RUNNING OFF ALL CRAZY --
LET ME GUESS. LITTLE SISTER DIDN'T LISTEN.
GOD, DO THEY EVER?
YOU HAVE A SISTER?
FIVE YEARS YOUNGER. TOTAL PAIN. PLUS GIANT. OR, CENTAUR, LATELY. I TRY TO TELL HER ANYTHING, SHE DOES THE OPPOSITE.
SOUNDS FAMILIAR.
YOU KNOW, I THOUGHT ABOUT BEING A COP. A LAW.
IN HIGH SCHOOL. I TOOK A TEST, SAID I FIT THE PROFILE.
REALLY?
IF WE HAD *YOUR* OUTFITS, I WOULDA SIGNED UP IN A HEARTBEAT. IS THAT PLEATHER?
PUFFY, CAN I --
YOU'RE A SLAYER?
BUFFY.
SORRY. WITH A B. DON'T WANT FUTURE HISTORY CALLING ME "PUFFY." IT'S JUST... YOU HAD A QUESTION?
YEAH.
WHY?
WHY?
WHY ARE YOU A LAW?

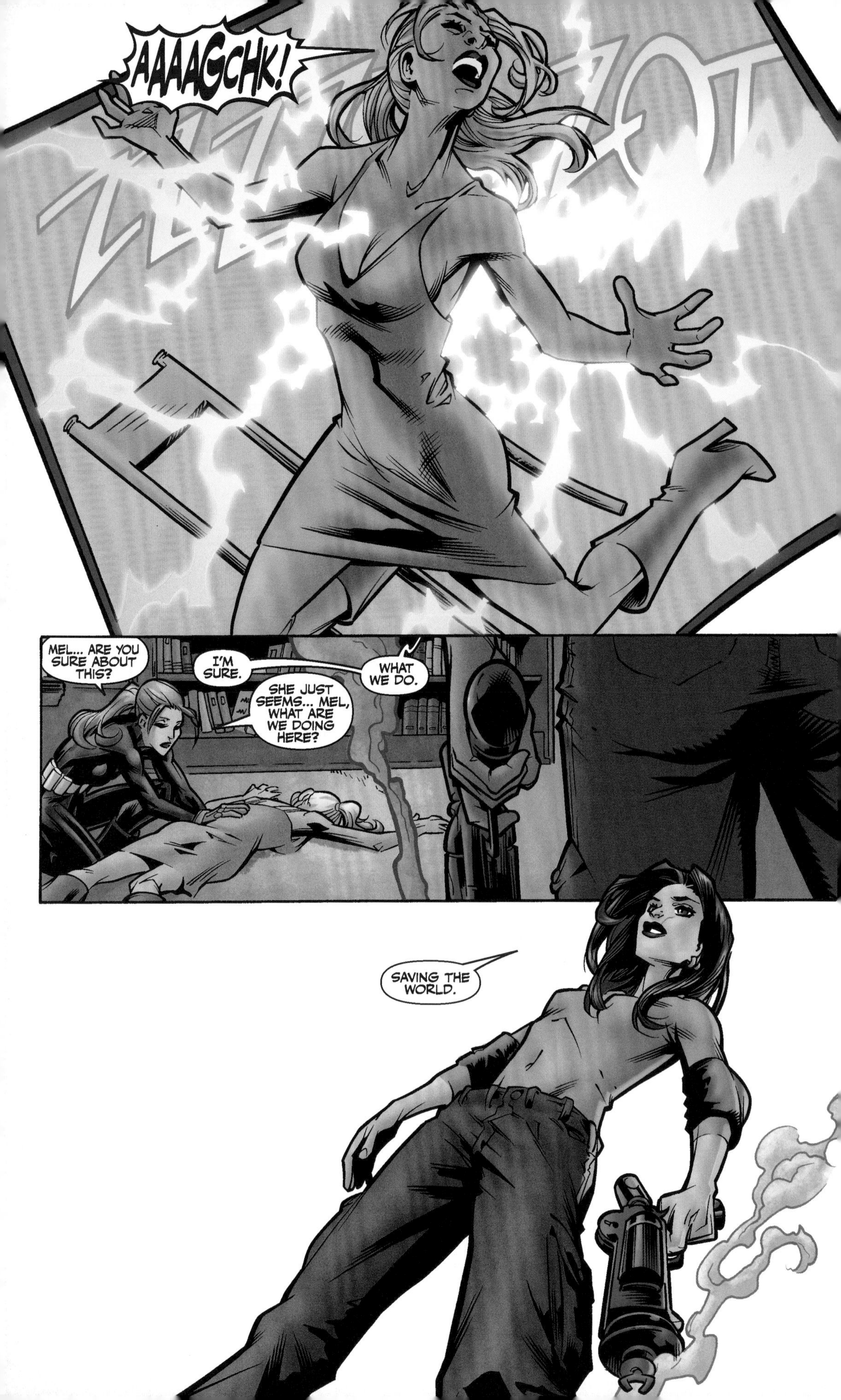
AAAAGCHK!
MEL... ARE YOU SURE ABOUT THIS?
I'M SURE.
SHE JUST SEEMS... MEL, WHAT ARE WE DOING HERE?
WHAT WE DO.
SAVING THE WORLD.

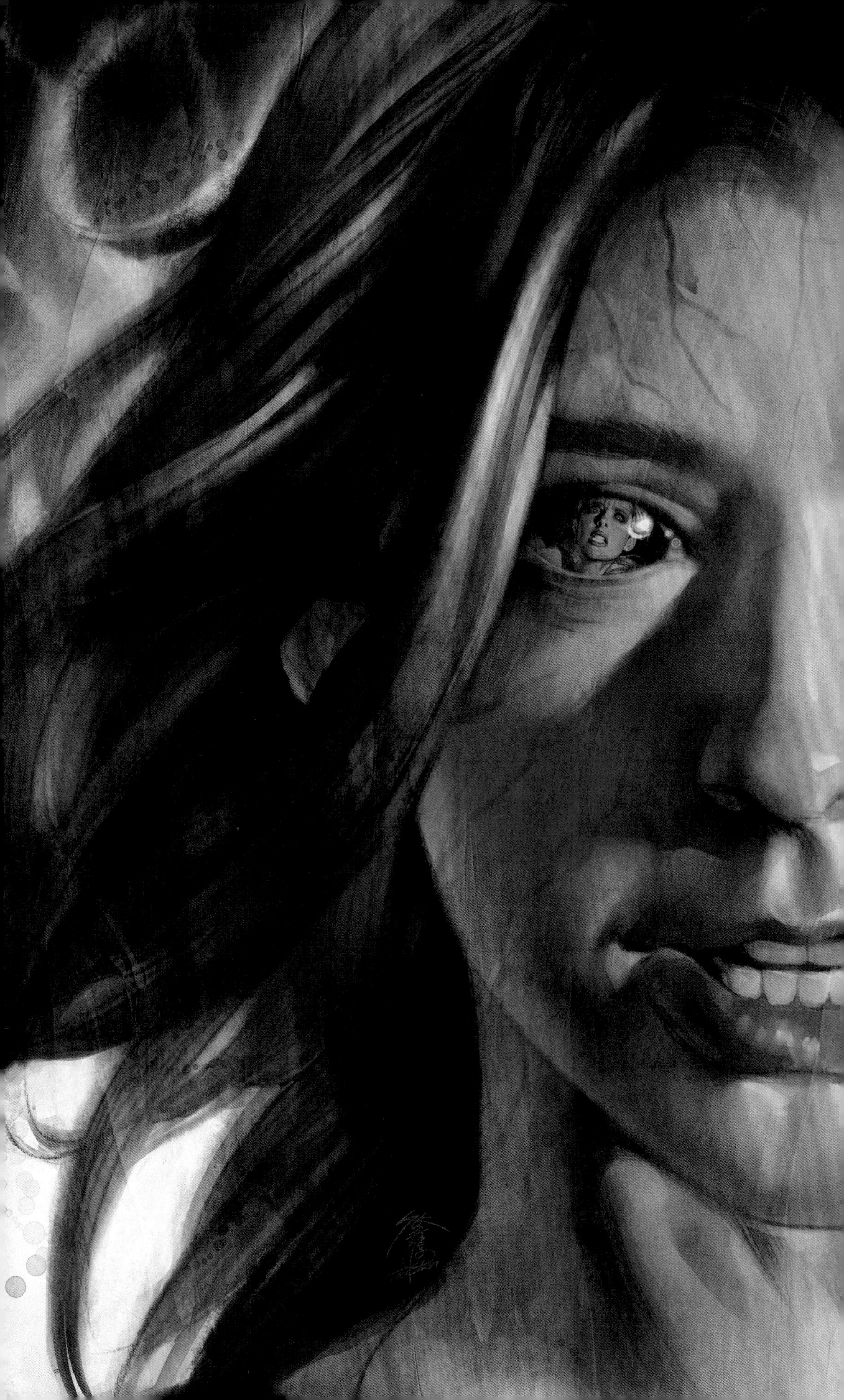

TIME OF YOUR LIFE
PART FOUR

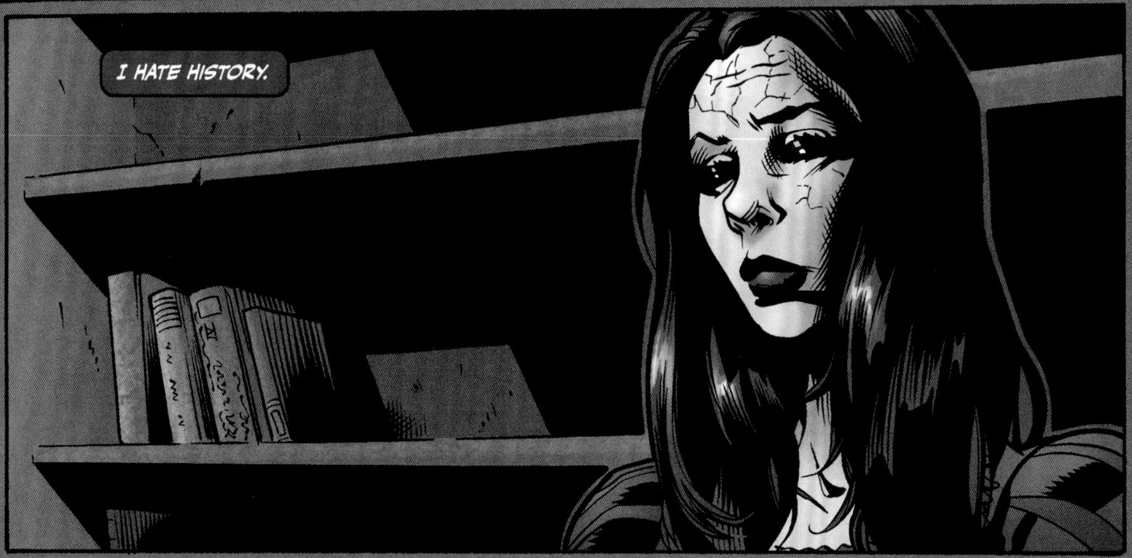

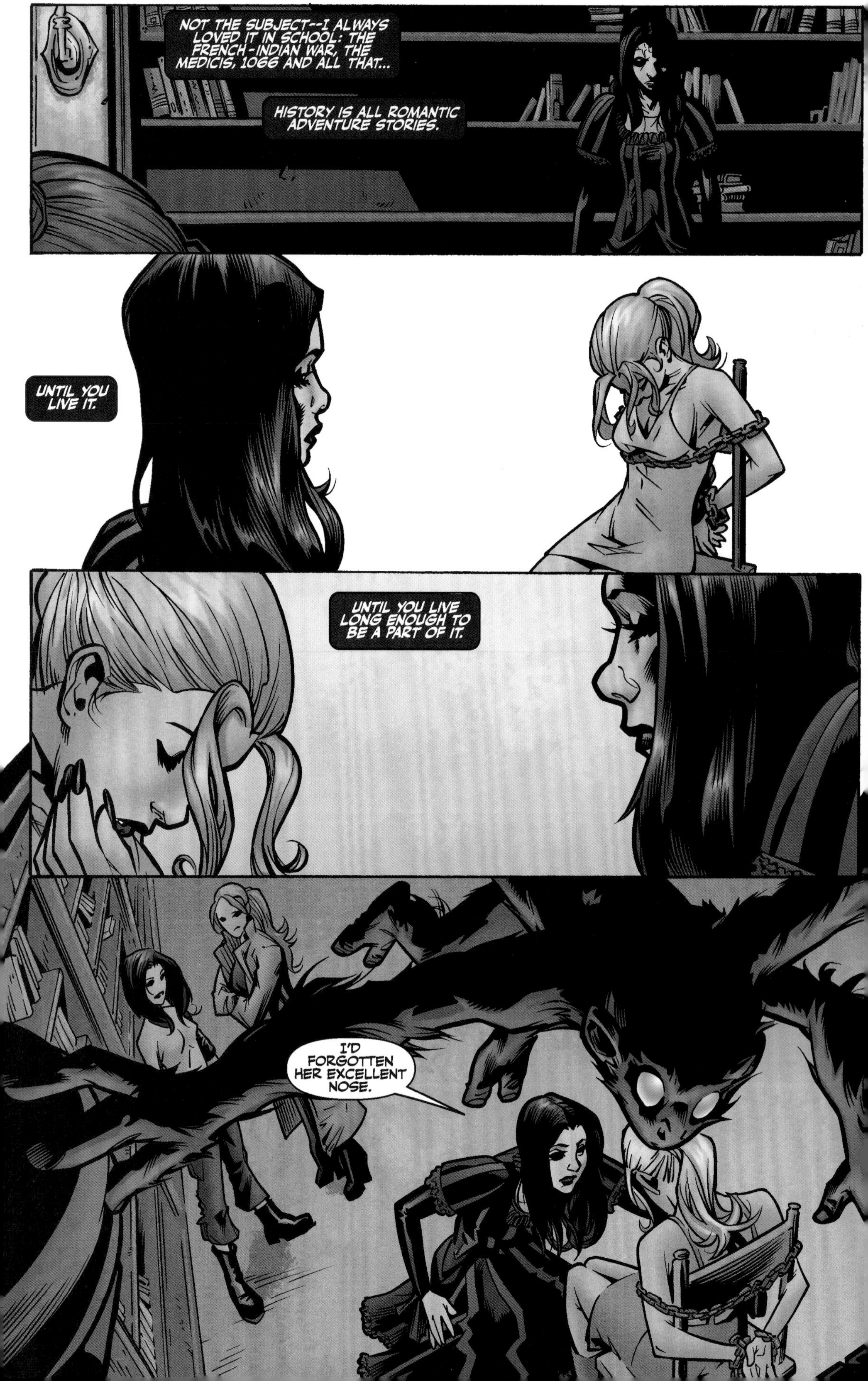
NOT THE SUBJECT--I ALWAYS LOVED IT IN SCHOOL: THE FRENCH-INDIAN WAR, THE MEDICIS, 1066 AND ALL THAT...
HISTORY IS ALL ROMANTIC ADVENTURE STORIES.
UNTIL YOU LIVE IT.
UNTIL YOU LIVE LONG ENOUGH TO BE A PART OF IT.
I'D FORGOTTEN HER EXCELLENT NOSE.

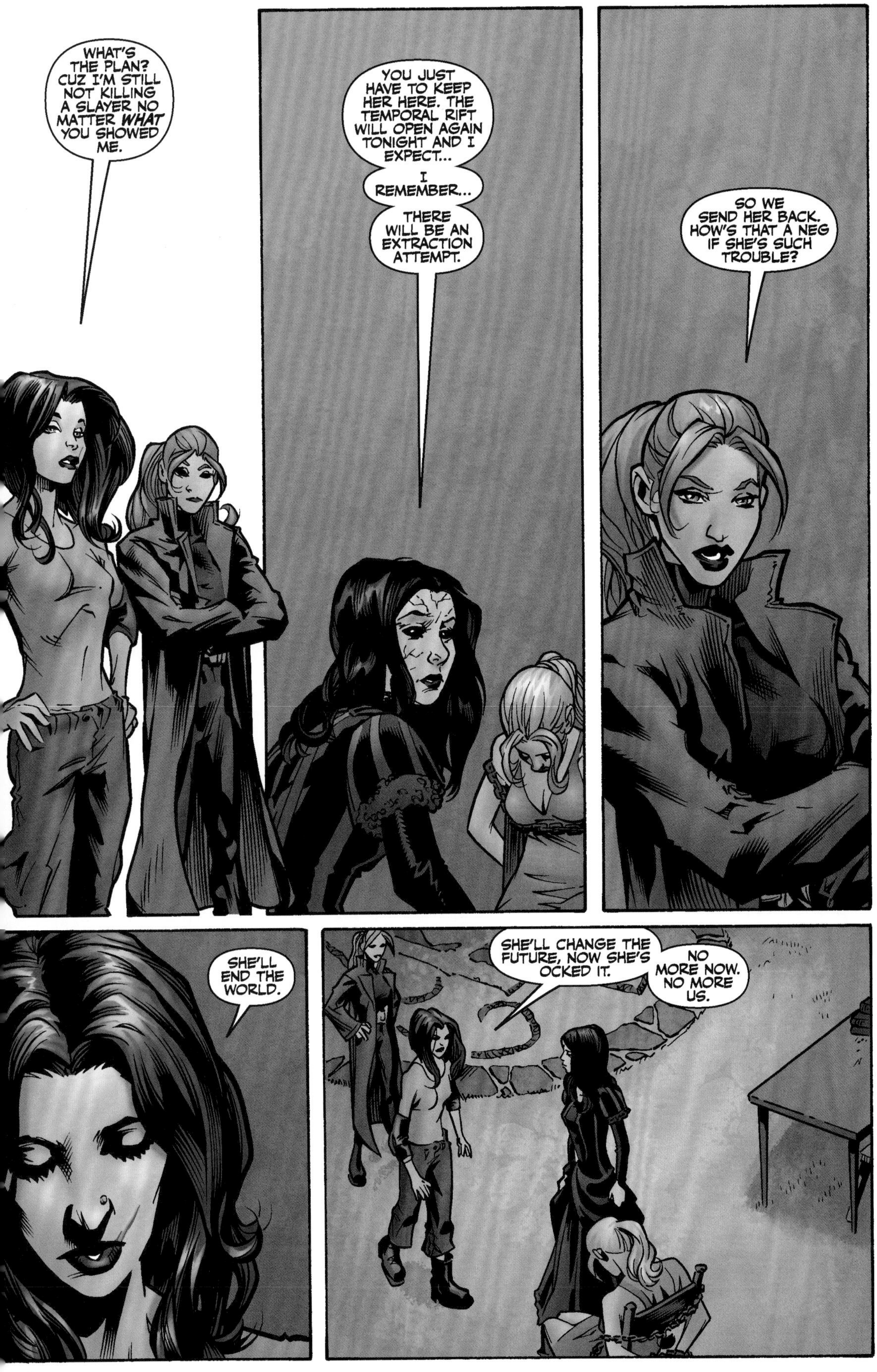
WHAT'S THE PLAN? CUZ I'M STILL NOT KILLING A SLAYER NO MATTER *WHAT* YOU SHOWED ME.
YOU JUST HAVE TO KEEP HER HERE. THE TEMPORAL RIFT WILL OPEN AGAIN TONIGHT AND I EXPECT...
I REMEMBER...
THERE WILL BE AN EXTRACTION ATTEMPT.
SO WE SEND HER BACK. HOW'S THAT A NEG IF SHE'S SUCH TROUBLE?
SHE'LL END THE WORLD.
SHE'LL CHANGE THE FUTURE, NOW SHE'S OCKED IT.
NO MORE NOW. NO MORE US.

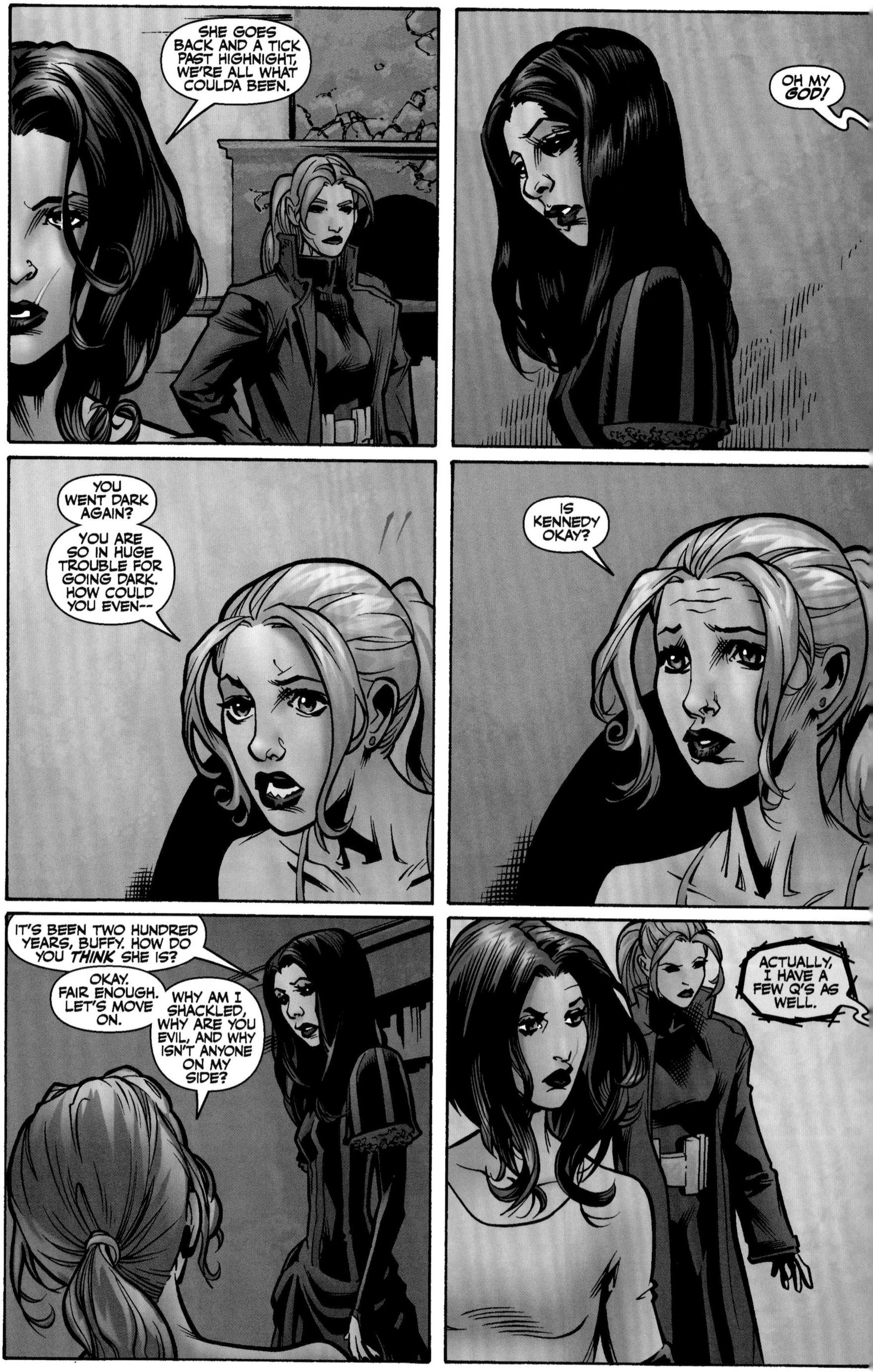
SHE GOES BACK AND A TICK PAST HIGHNIGHT, WE'RE ALL WHAT COULDA BEEN.
OH MY GOD!
YOU WENT DARK AGAIN?
YOU ARE SO IN HUGE TROUBLE FOR GOING DARK. HOW COULD YOU EVEN--
IS KENNEDY OKAY?
IT'S BEEN TWO HUNDRED YEARS, BUFFY. HOW DO YOU THINK SHE IS?
OKAY. FAIR ENOUGH. LET'S MOVE ON.
WHY AM I SHACKLED, WHY ARE YOU EVIL, AND WHY ISN'T ANYONE ON MY SIDE?
ACTUALLY, I HAVE A FEW Q'S AS WELL.

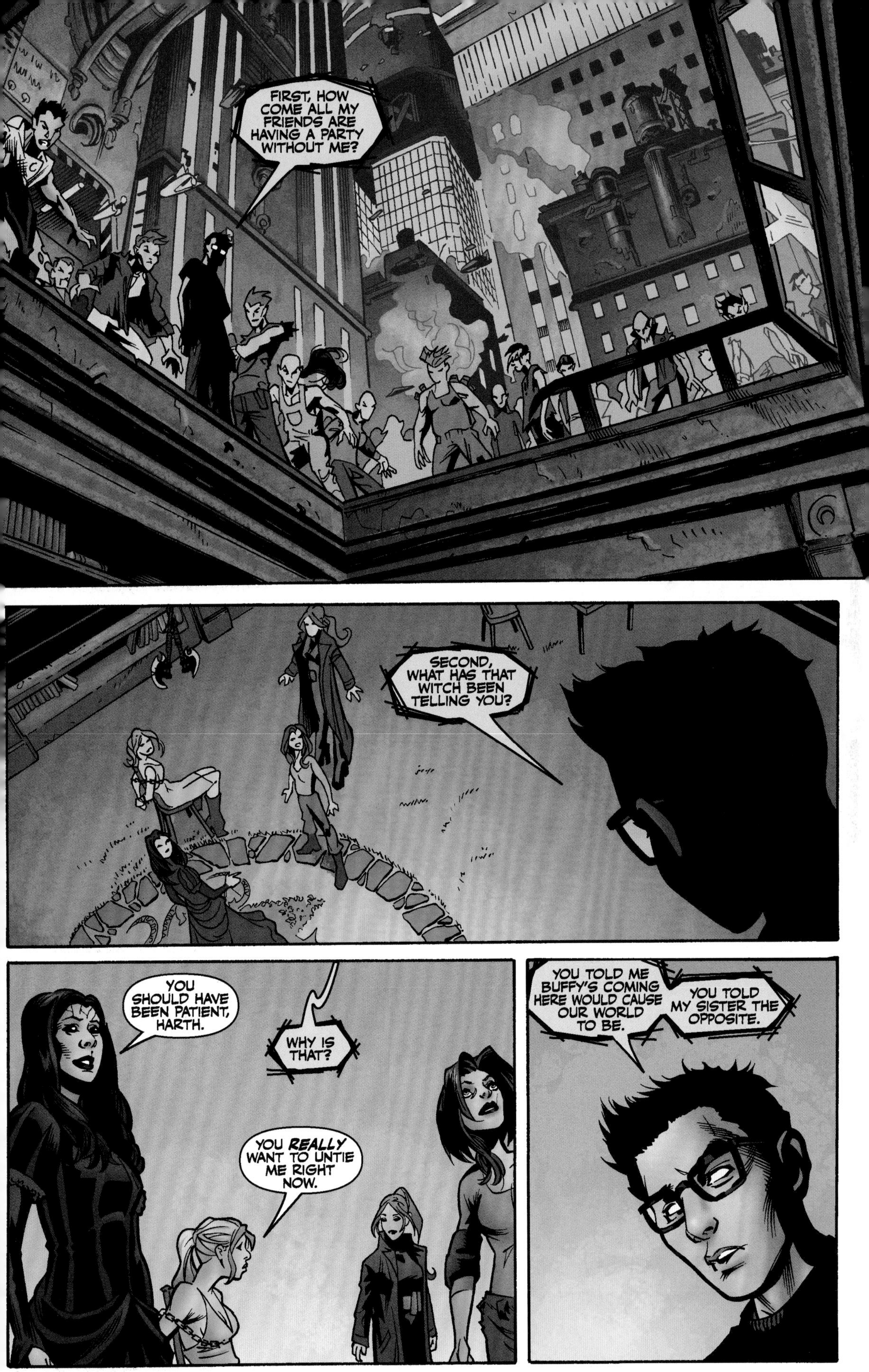
FIRST, HOW COME ALL MY FRIENDS ARE HAVING A PARTY WITHOUT ME?
SECOND, WHAT HAS THAT WITCH BEEN TELLING YOU?
YOU SHOULD HAVE BEEN PATIENT, HARTH.
WHY IS THAT?
YOU REALLY WANT TO UNTIE ME RIGHT NOW.
YOU TOLD ME BUFFY'S COMING HERE WOULD CAUSE OUR WORLD TO BE.
YOU TOLD MY SISTER THE OPPOSITE.

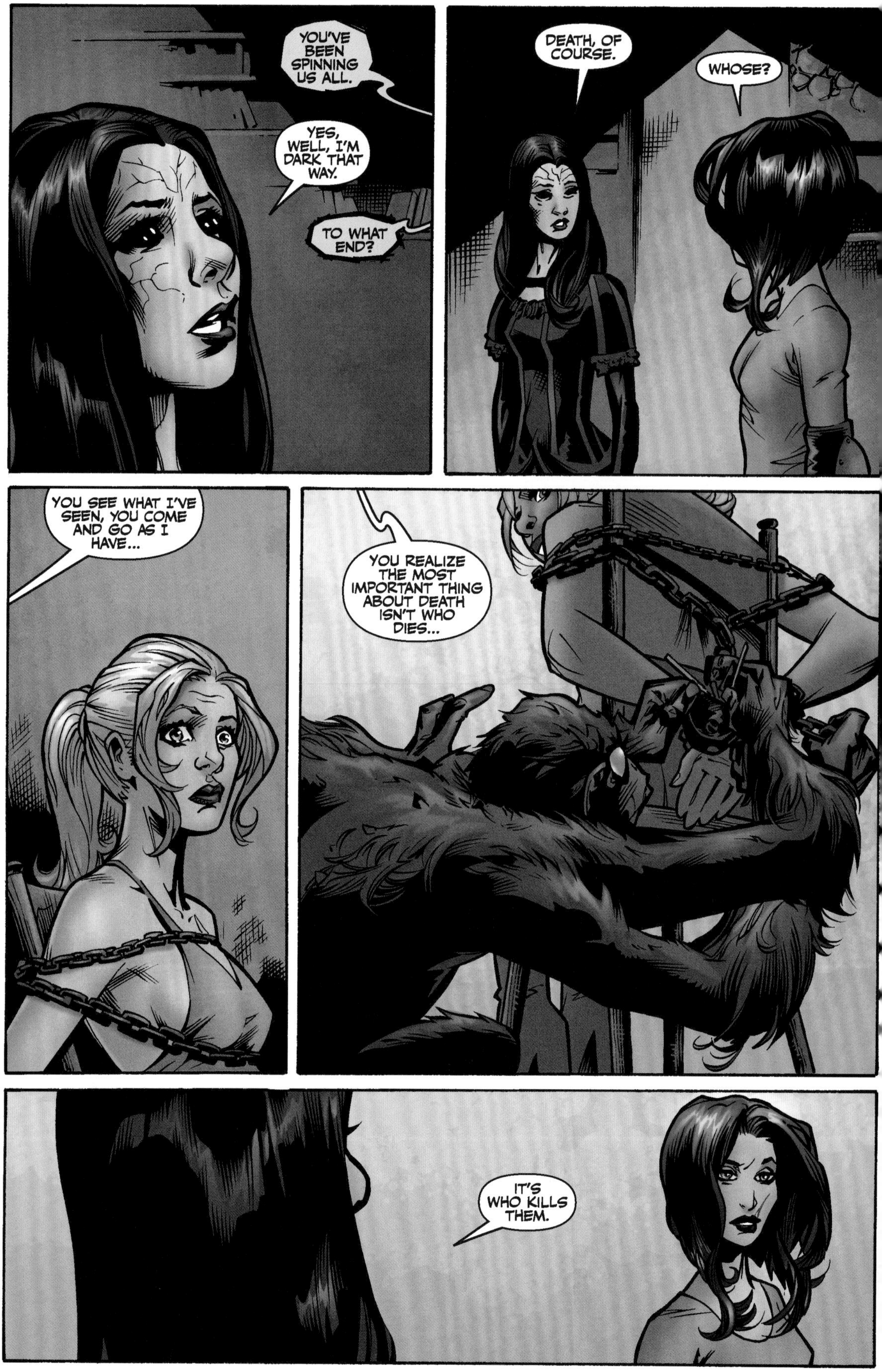
YOU'VE BEEN SPINNING US ALL.
YES, WELL, I'M DARK THAT WAY.
TO WHAT END?
DEATH, OF COURSE.
WHOSE?
YOU SEE WHAT I'VE SEEN, YOU COME AND GO AS I HAVE...
YOU REALIZE THE MOST IMPORTANT THING ABOUT DEATH ISN'T WHO DIES...
IT'S WHO KILLS THEM.

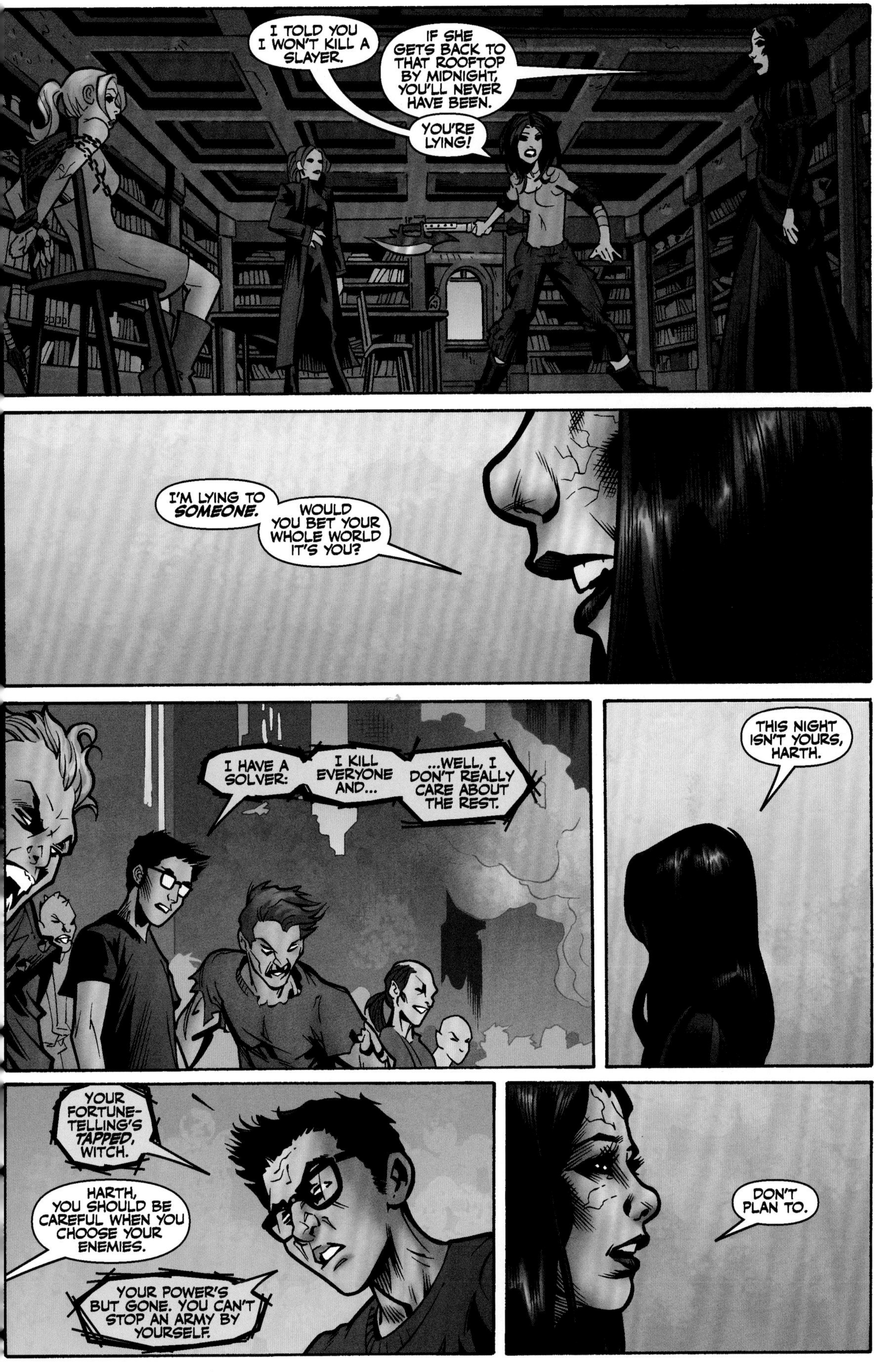

I TOLD YOU I WON'T KILL A SLAYER.
IF SHE GETS BACK TO THAT ROOFTOP BY MIDNIGHT, YOU'LL NEVER HAVE BEEN.
YOU'RE LYING!
I'M LYING TO *SOMEONE.*
WOULD YOU BET YOUR WHOLE WORLD IT'S YOU?
I HAVE A SOLVER:
I KILL EVERYONE AND...
...WELL, I DON'T REALLY CARE ABOUT THE REST.
THIS NIGHT ISN'T YOURS, HARTH.
YOUR FORTUNE-TELLING'S *TAPPED,* WITCH.
HARTH, YOU SHOULD BE CAREFUL WHEN YOU CHOOSE YOUR ENEMIES.
YOUR POWER'S BUT GONE. YOU CAN'T STOP AN ARMY BY YOURSELF.
DON'T PLAN TO.

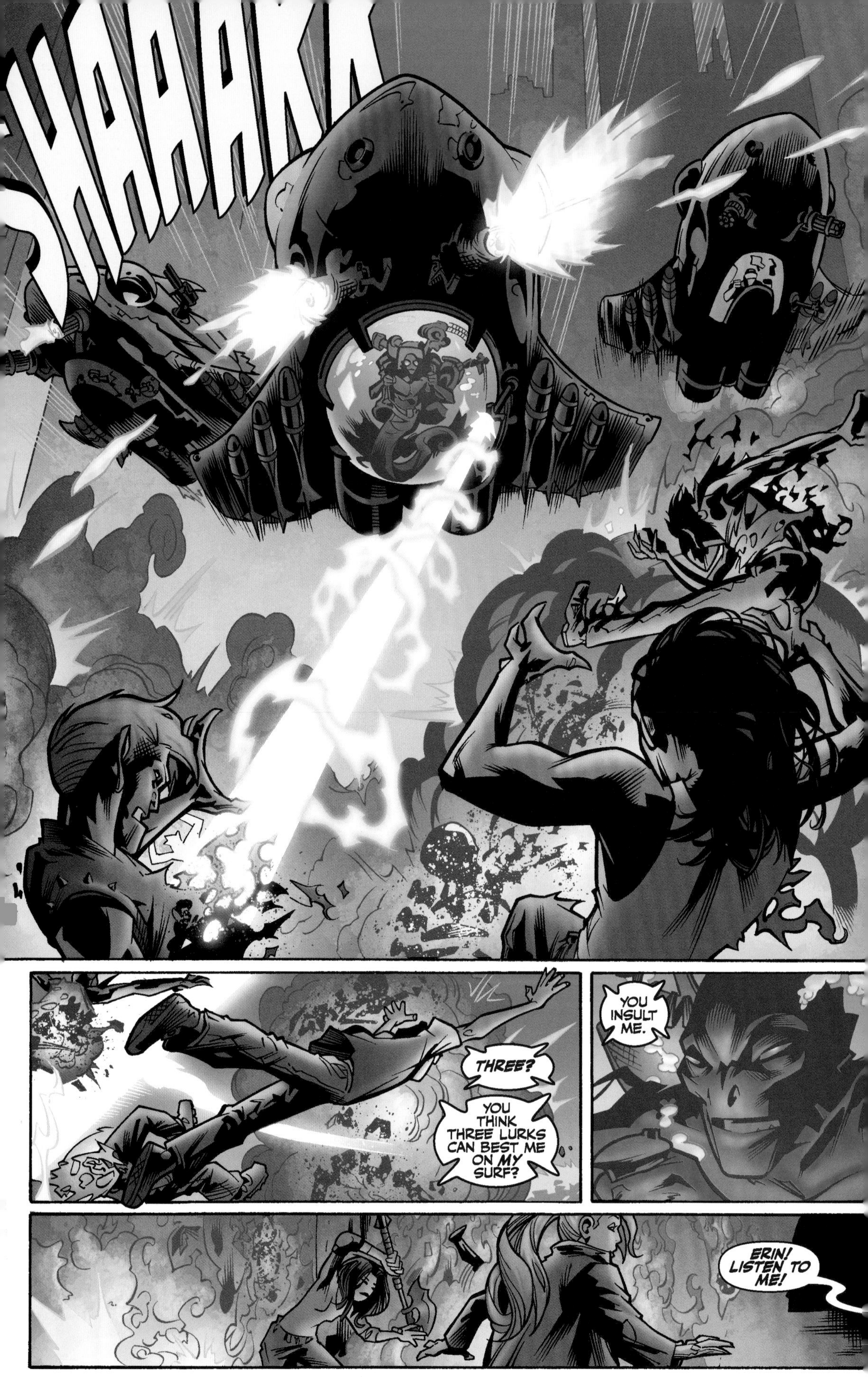
SHAAAKK
THREE?
YOU THINK THREE LURKS CAN BEST ME ON MY SURF?
YOU INSULT ME.
ERIN! LISTEN TO ME!

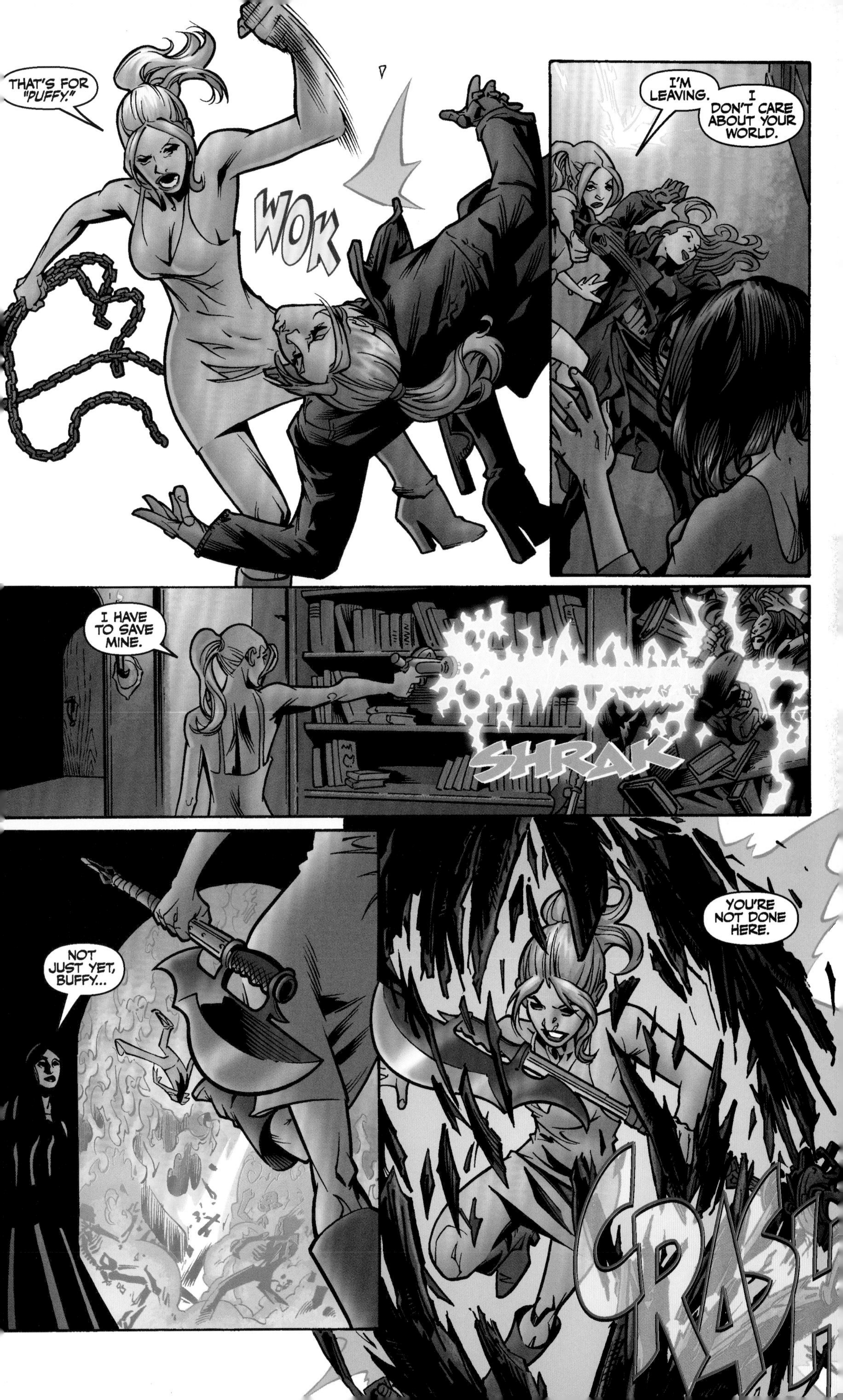
THAT'S FOR "PUFFY."
WOK
I'M LEAVING.
I DON'T CARE ABOUT YOUR WORLD.
I HAVE TO SAVE MINE.
SHRAK
NOT JUST YET, BUFFY...
YOU'RE NOT DONE HERE.
CRASH!

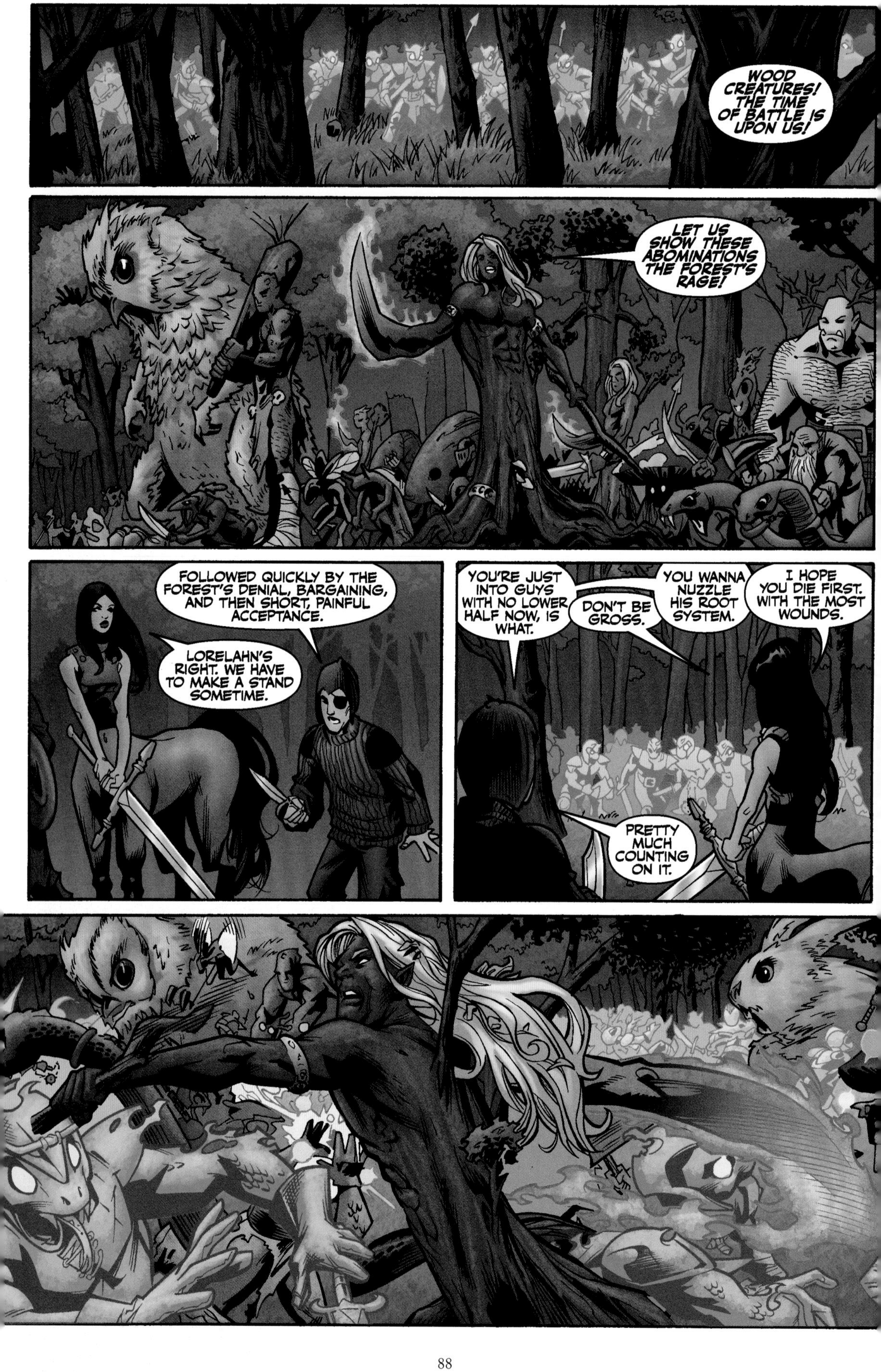
WOOD CREATURES! THE TIME OF BATTLE IS UPON US!
LET US SHOW THESE ABOMINATIONS THE FOREST'S RAGE!
FOLLOWED QUICKLY BY THE FOREST'S DENIAL, BARGAINING, AND THEN SHORT, PAINFUL ACCEPTANCE.
LORELAHN'S RIGHT. WE HAVE TO MAKE A STAND SOMETIME.
YOU'RE JUST INTO GUYS WITH NO LOWER HALF NOW, IS WHAT.
DON'T BE GROSS.
YOU WANNA NUZZLE HIS ROOT SYSTEM.
I HOPE YOU DIE FIRST. WITH THE MOST WOUNDS.
PRETTY MUCH COUNTING ON IT.

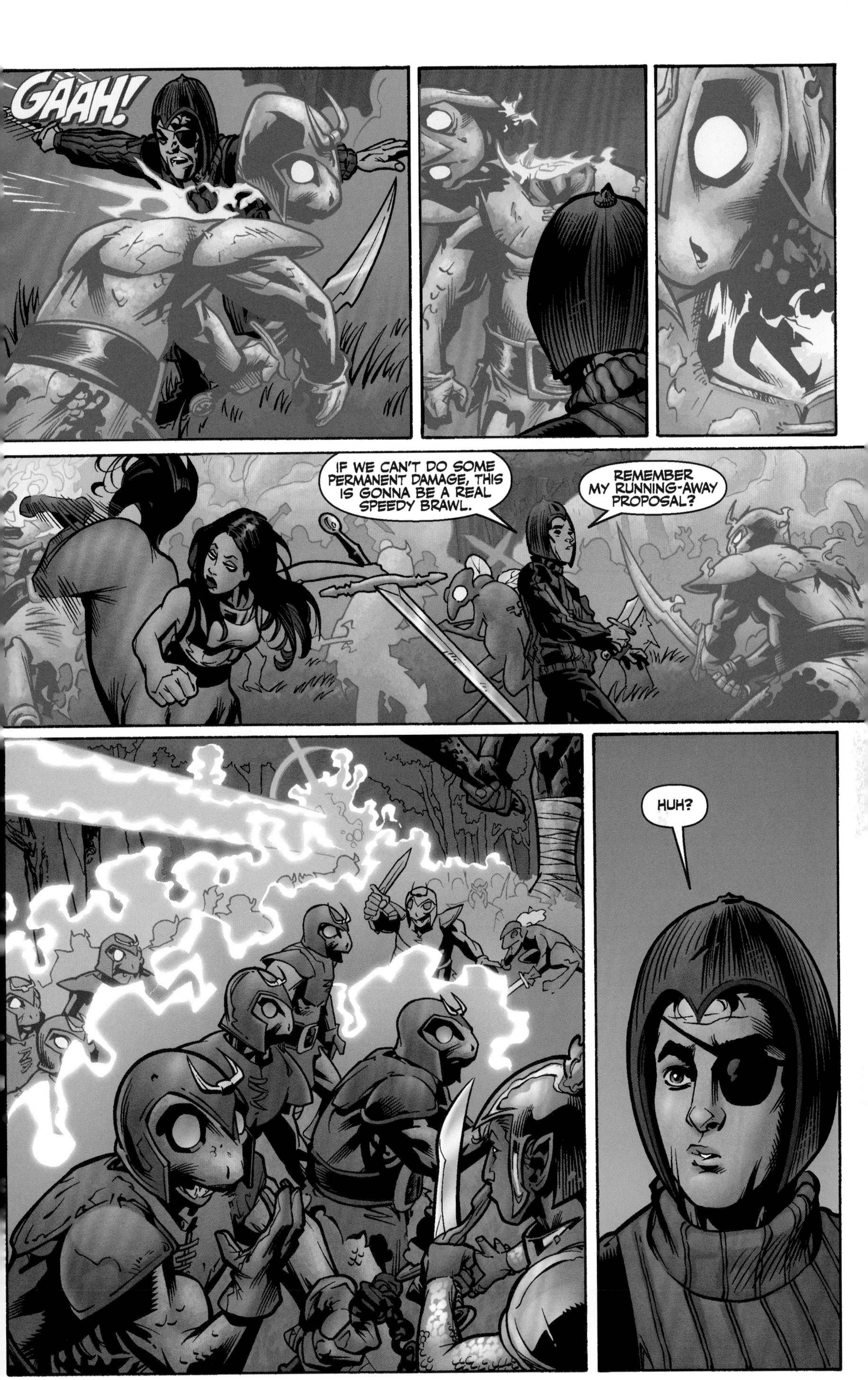
GAAH!
IF WE CAN'T DO SOME PERMANENT DAMAGE, THIS IS GONNA BE A REAL SPEEDY BRAWL.
REMEMBER MY RUNNING-AWAY PROPOSAL?
HUH?

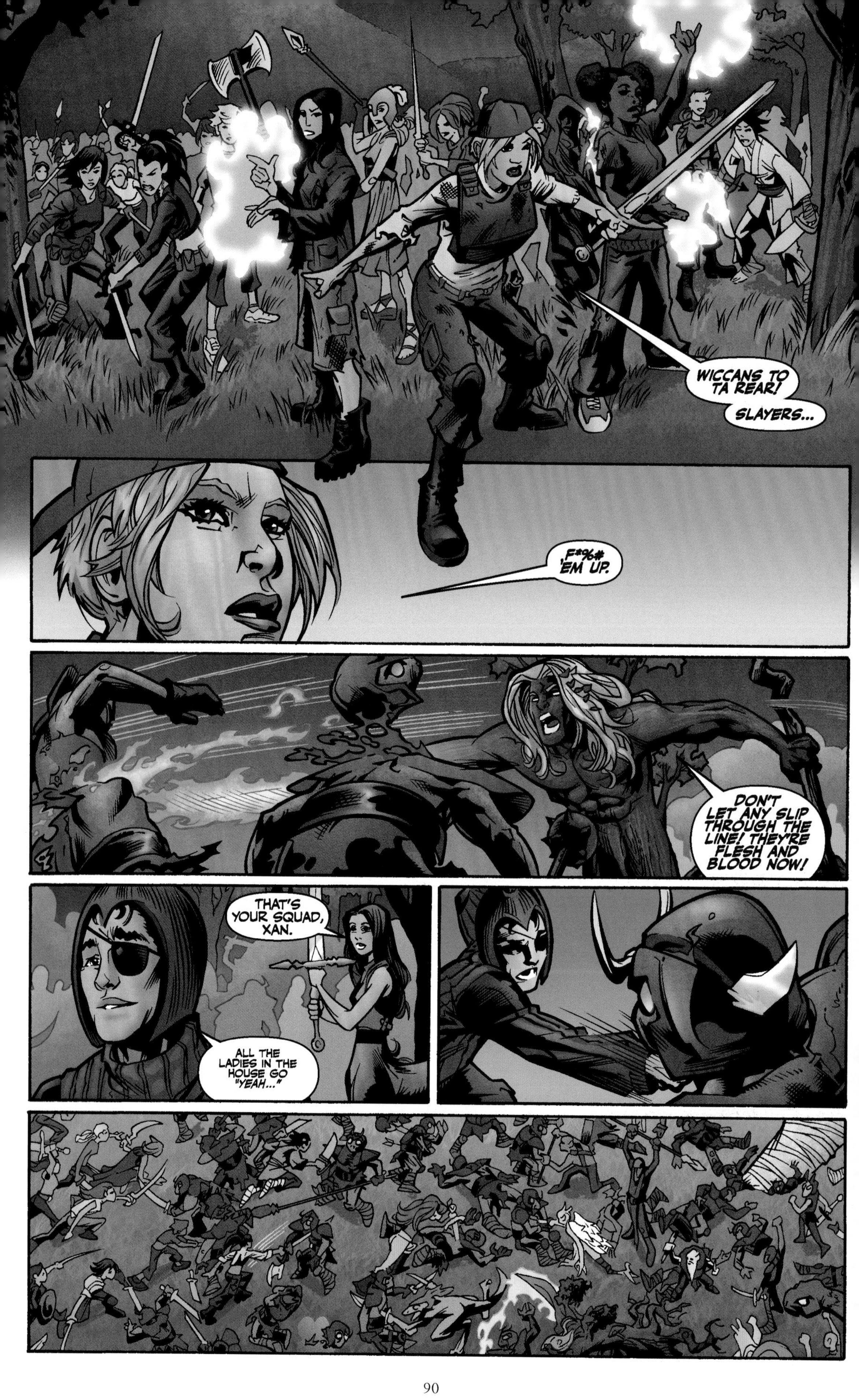
WICCANS TO TA REAR!
SLAYERS...
F*%# 'EM UP.
DON'T LET ANY SLIP THROUGH THE LINE! THEY'RE FLESH AND BLOOD NOW!
THAT'S YOUR SQUAD, XAN.
ALL THE LADIES IN THE HOUSE GO "YEAH..."

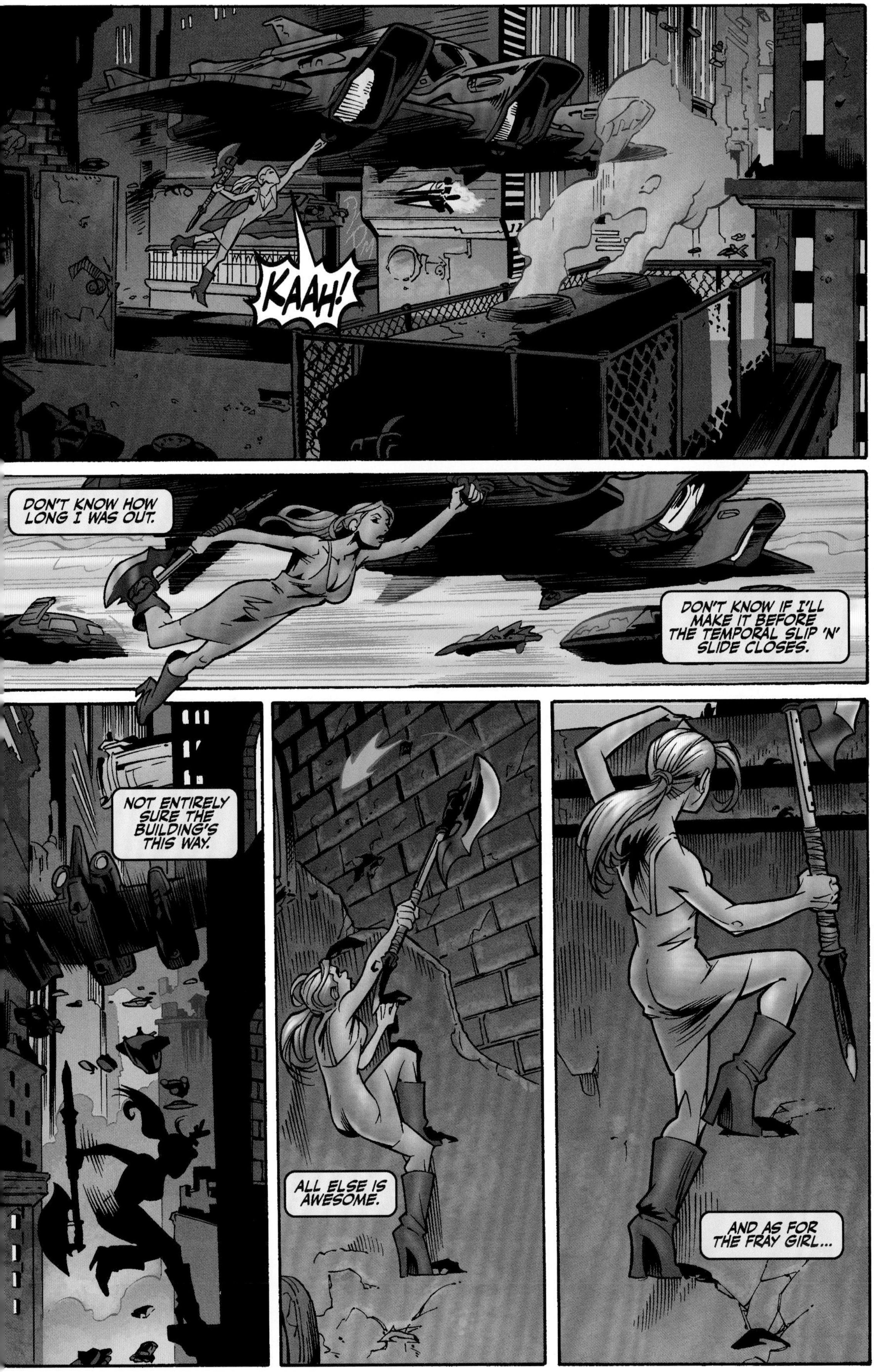
KAAH!
DON'T KNOW HOW LONG I WAS OUT.
DON'T KNOW IF I'LL MAKE IT BEFORE THE TEMPORAL SLIP 'N' SLIDE CLOSES.
NOT ENTIRELY SURE THE BUILDING'S THIS WAY.
ALL ELSE IS AWESOME.
AND AS FOR THE FRAY GIRL...

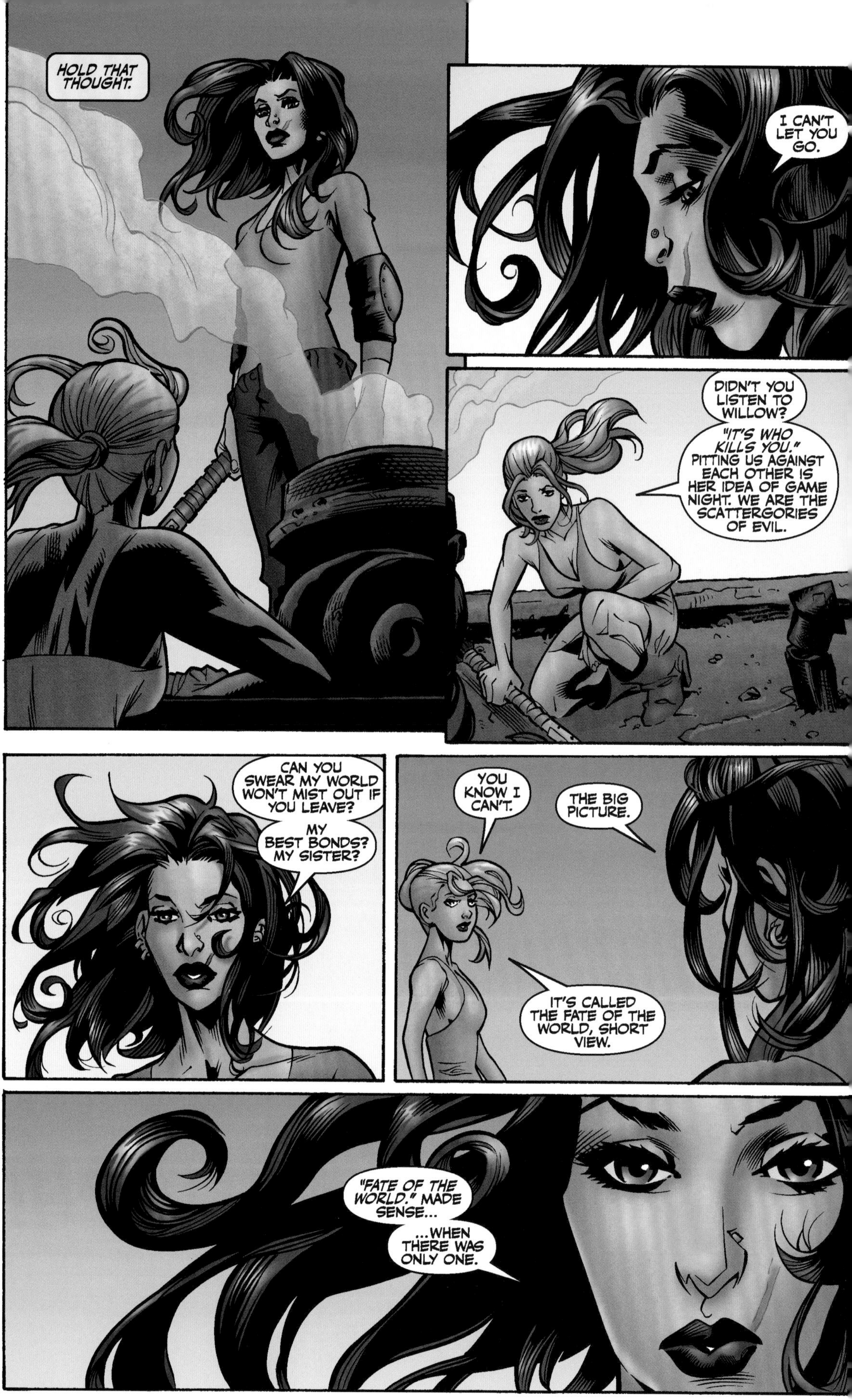
HOLD THAT THOUGHT.
I CAN'T LET YOU GO.
DIDN'T YOU LISTEN TO WILLOW?
"IT'S WHO KILLS YOU." PITTING US AGAINST EACH OTHER IS HER IDEA OF GAME NIGHT. WE ARE THE SCATTERGORIES OF EVIL.
CAN YOU SWEAR MY WORLD WON'T MIST OUT IF YOU LEAVE?
MY BEST BONDS? MY SISTER?
YOU KNOW I CAN'T.
THE BIG PICTURE.
IT'S CALLED THE FATE OF THE WORLD, SHORT VIEW.
"FATE OF THE WORLD." MADE SENSE...
...WHEN THERE WAS ONLY ONE.

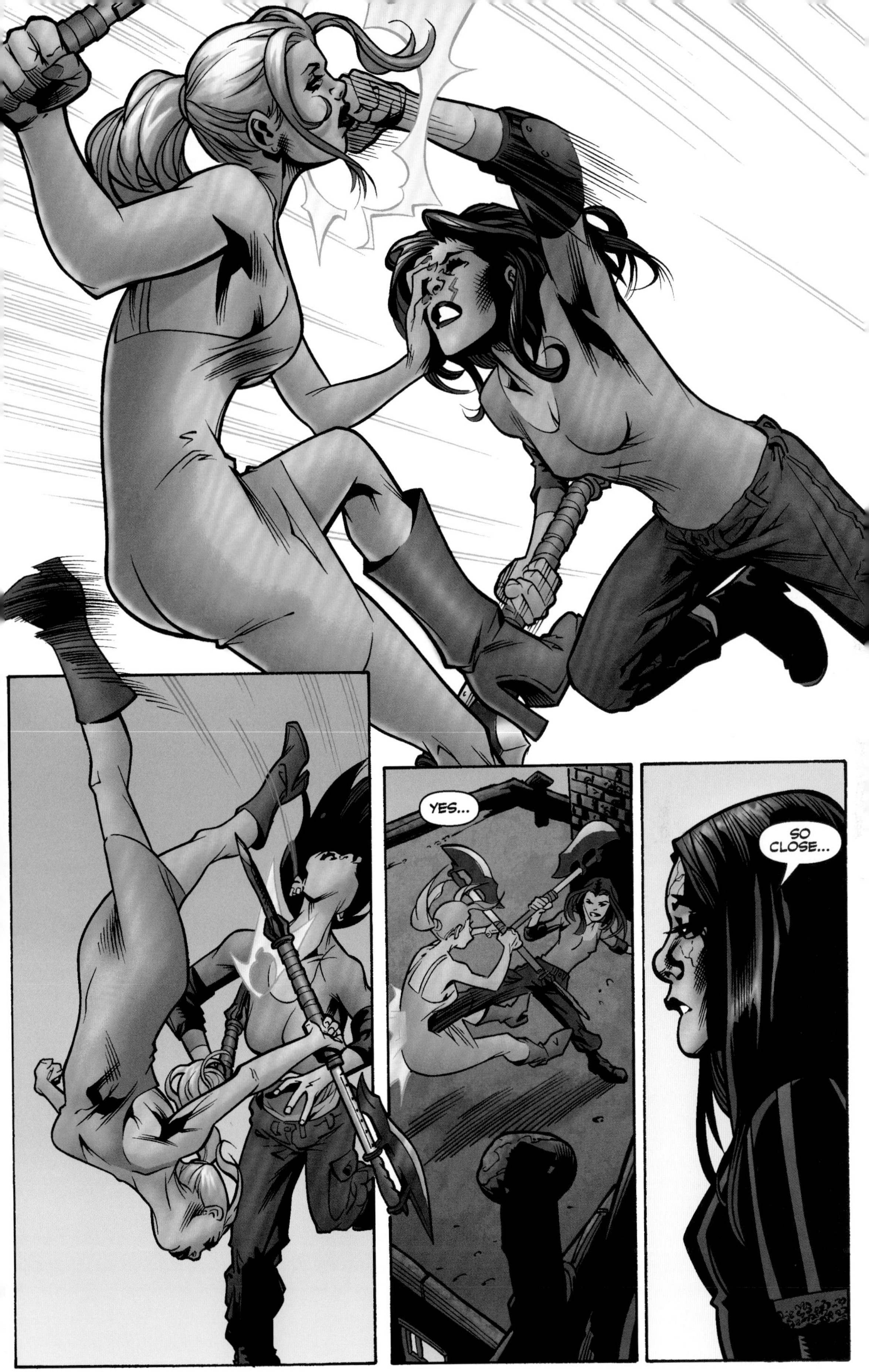
YES...
SO CLOSE...

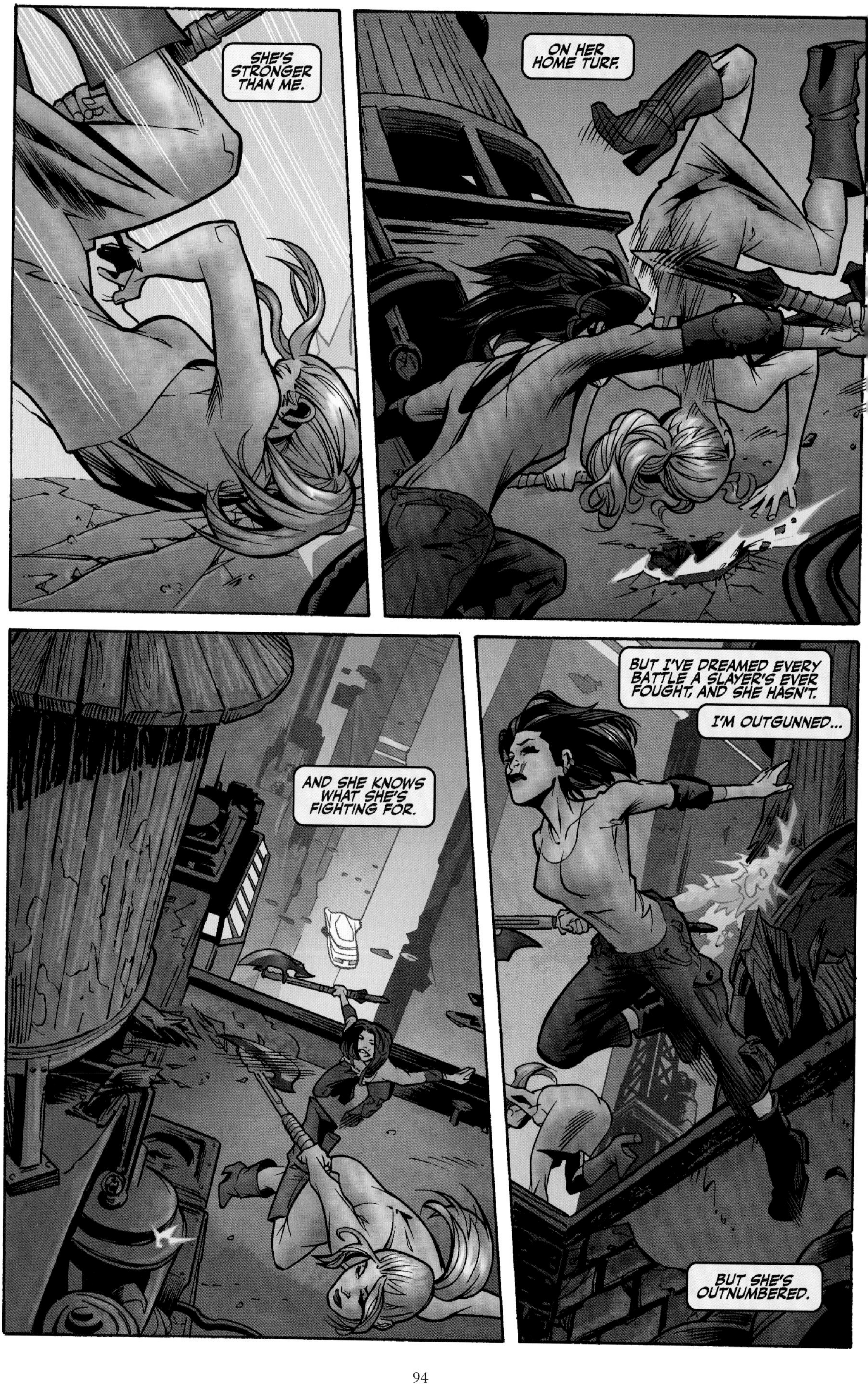
SHE'S STRONGER THAN ME.
ON HER HOME TURF.
AND SHE KNOWS WHAT SHE'S FIGHTING FOR.
BUT I'VE DREAMED EVERY BATTLE A SLAYER'S EVER FOUGHT, AND SHE HASN'T.
I'M OUTGUNNED...
BUT SHE'S OUTNUMBERED.

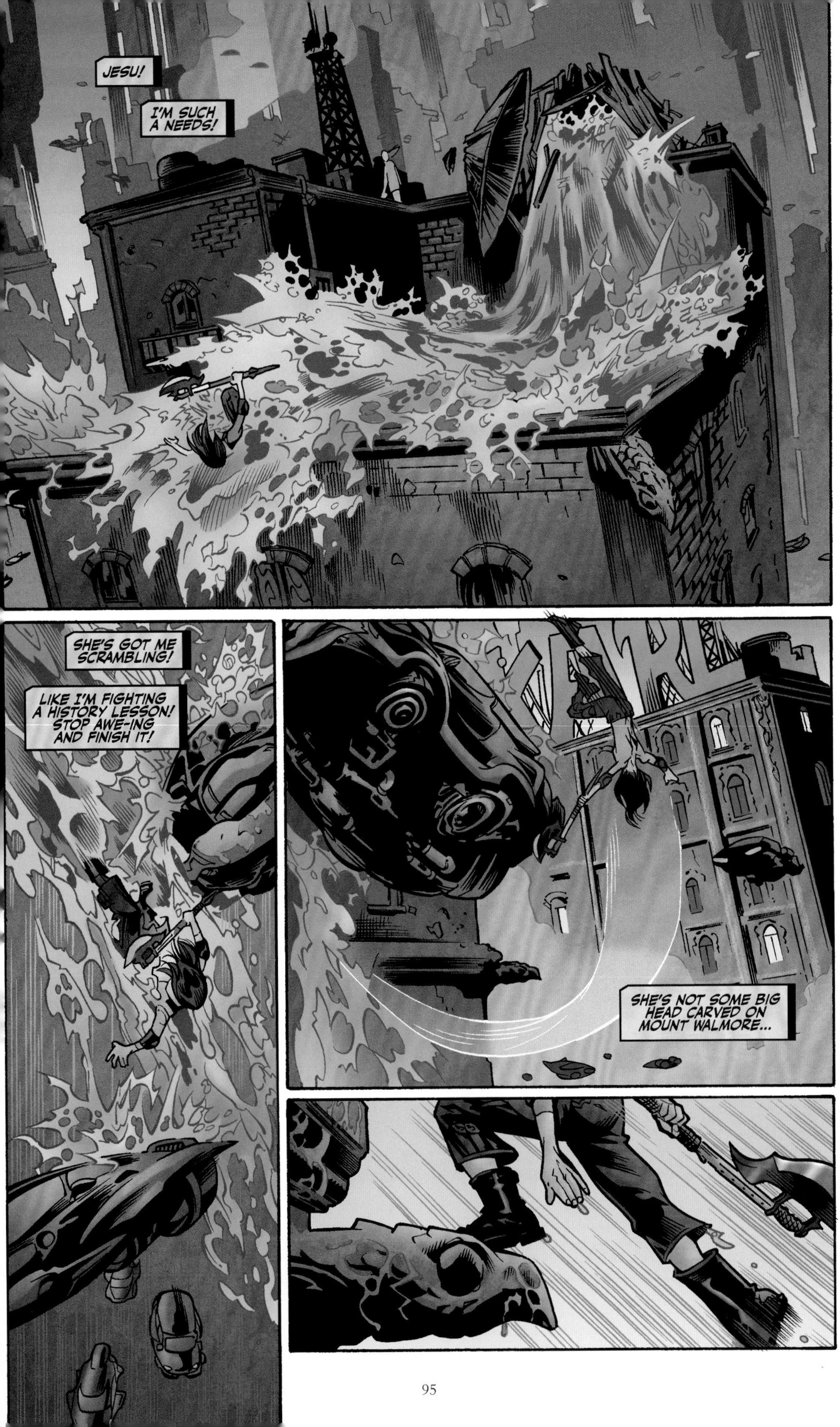
JESU!
I'M SUCH A NEEDS!
SHE'S GOT ME SCRAMBLING!
LIKE I'M FIGHTING A HISTORY LESSON! STOP AWE-ING AND FINISH IT!
SHE'S NOT SOME BIG HEAD CARVED ON MOUNT WALMORE...

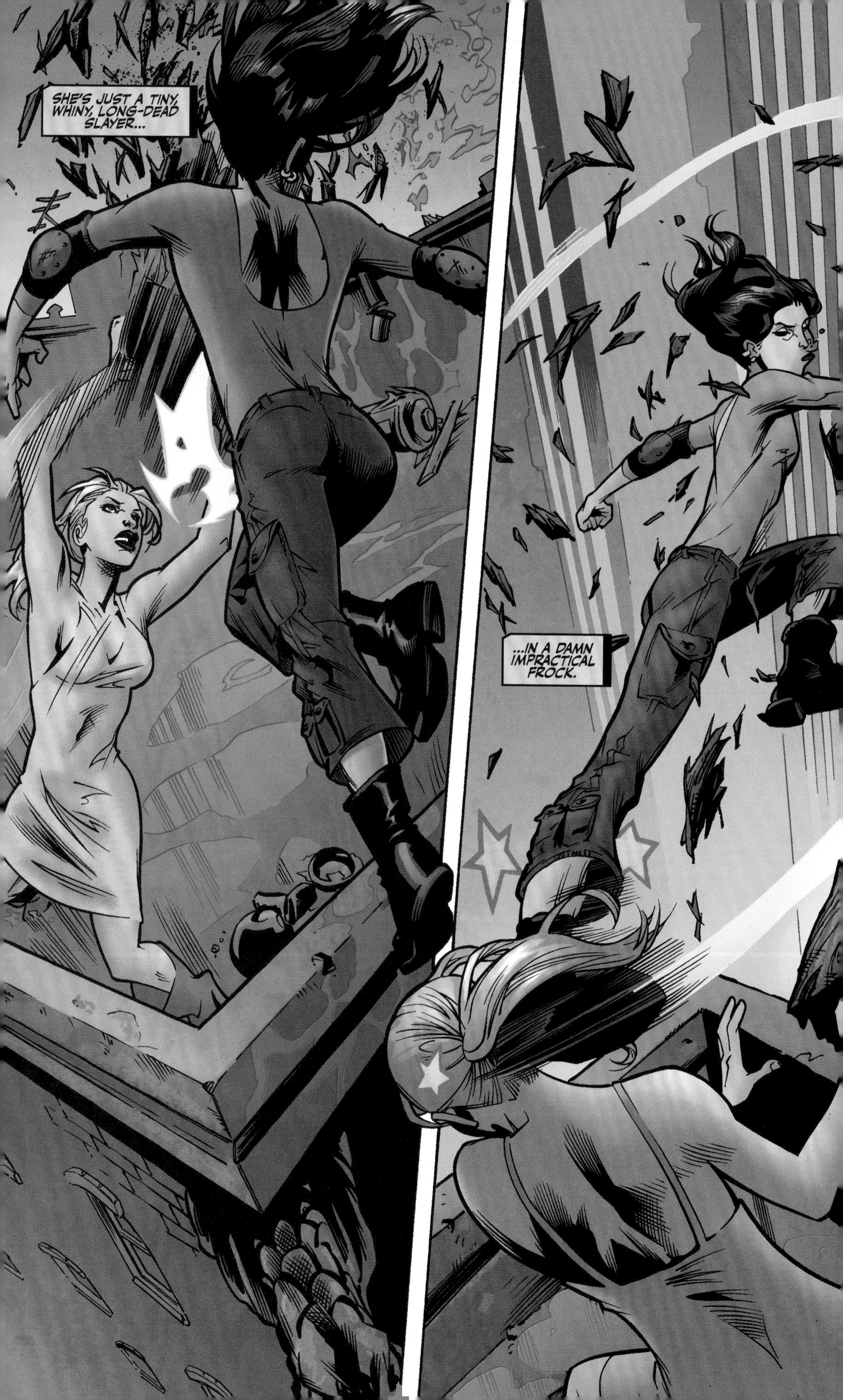
SHE'S JUST A TINY, WHINY, LONG-DEAD SLAYER...
...IN A DAMN IMPRACTICAL FROCK.

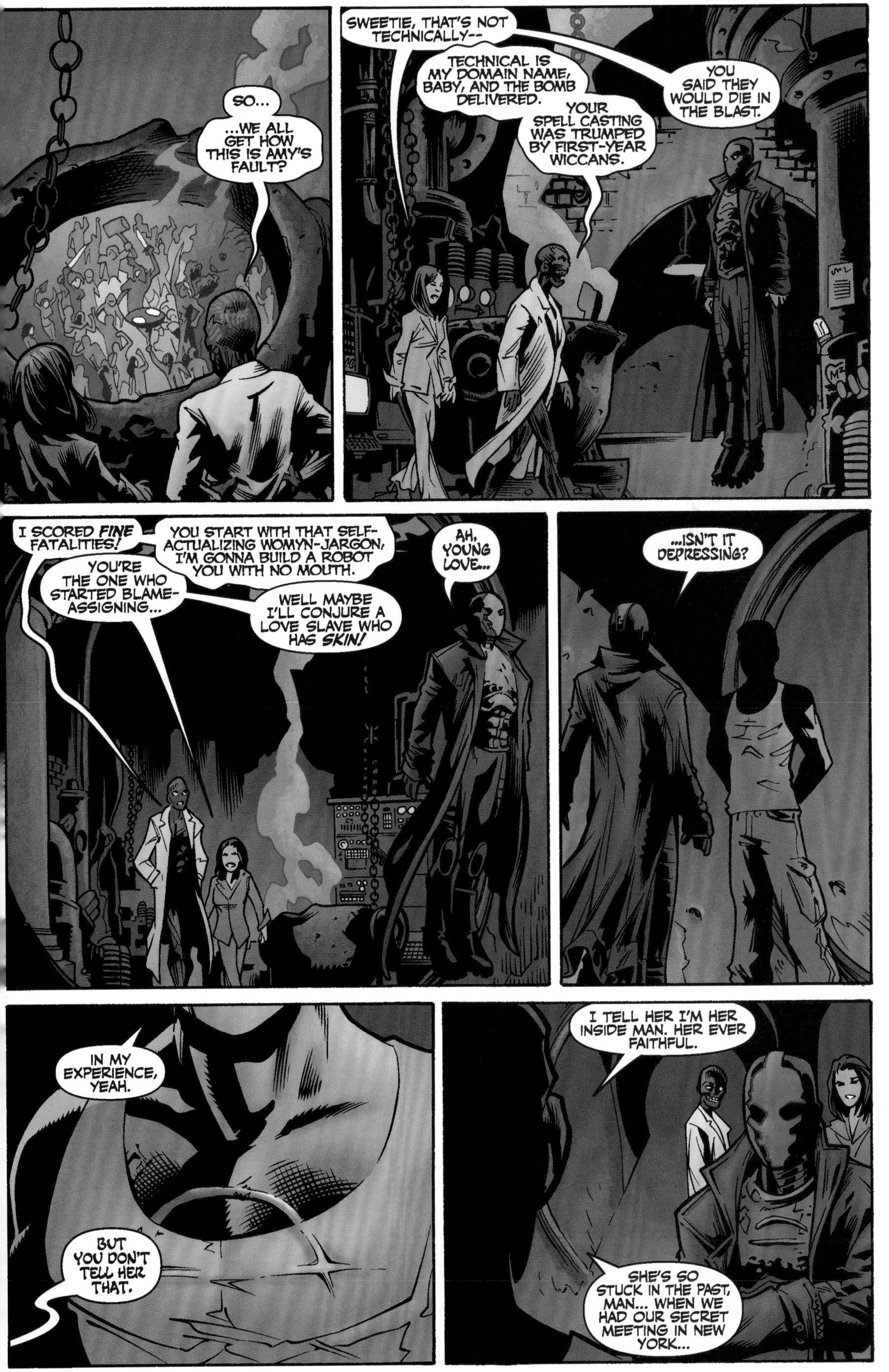
SO...
...WE ALL GET HOW THIS IS AMY'S FAULT?
SWEETIE, THAT'S NOT TECHNICALLY--
TECHNICAL IS MY DOMAIN NAME, BABY, AND THE BOMB DELIVERED.
YOUR SPELL CASTING WAS TRUMPED BY FIRST-YEAR WICCANS.
YOU SAID THEY WOULD DIE IN THE BLAST.
I SCORED FINE FATALITIES!
YOU'RE THE ONE WHO STARTED BLAME-ASSIGNING...
YOU START WITH THAT SELF-ACTUALIZING WOMYN-JARGON, I'M GONNA BUILD A ROBOT YOU WITH NO MOUTH.
WELL MAYBE I'LL CONJURE A LOVE SLAVE WHO HAS SKIN!
AH, YOUNG LOVE...
...ISN'T IT DEPRESSING?
IN MY EXPERIENCE, YEAH.
BUT YOU DON'T TELL HER THAT.
I TELL HER I'M HER INSIDE MAN. HER EVER FAITHFUL.
SHE'S SO STUCK IN THE PAST, MAN... WHEN WE HAD OUR SECRET MEETING IN NEW YORK...

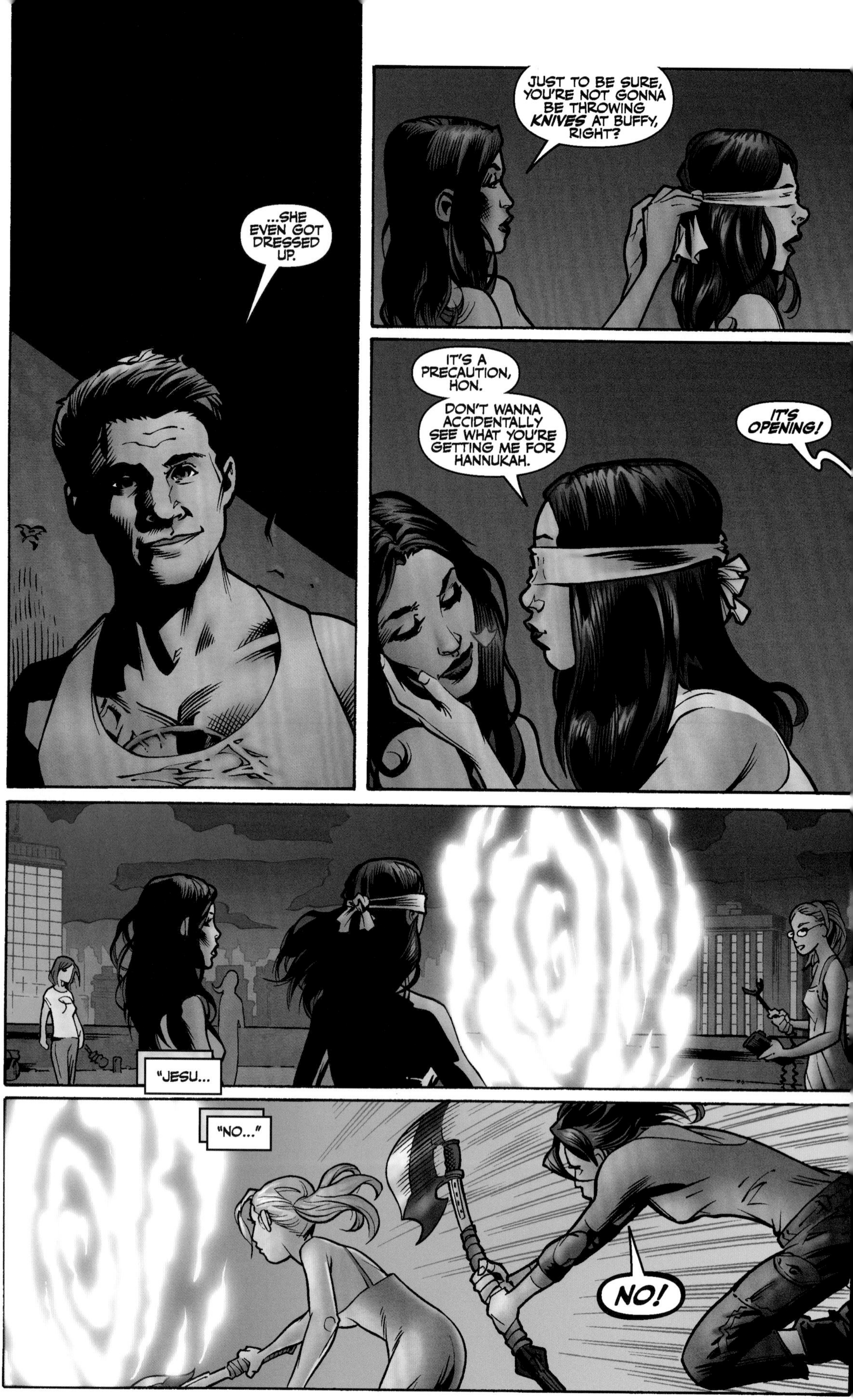
...SHE EVEN GOT DRESSED UP.
JUST TO BE SURE, YOU'RE NOT GONNA BE THROWING KNIVES AT BUFFY, RIGHT?
IT'S A PRECAUTION, HON.
DON'T WANNA ACCIDENTALLY SEE WHAT YOU'RE GETTING ME FOR HANNUKAH.
IT'S OPENING!
"JESU...
"NO..."
NO!

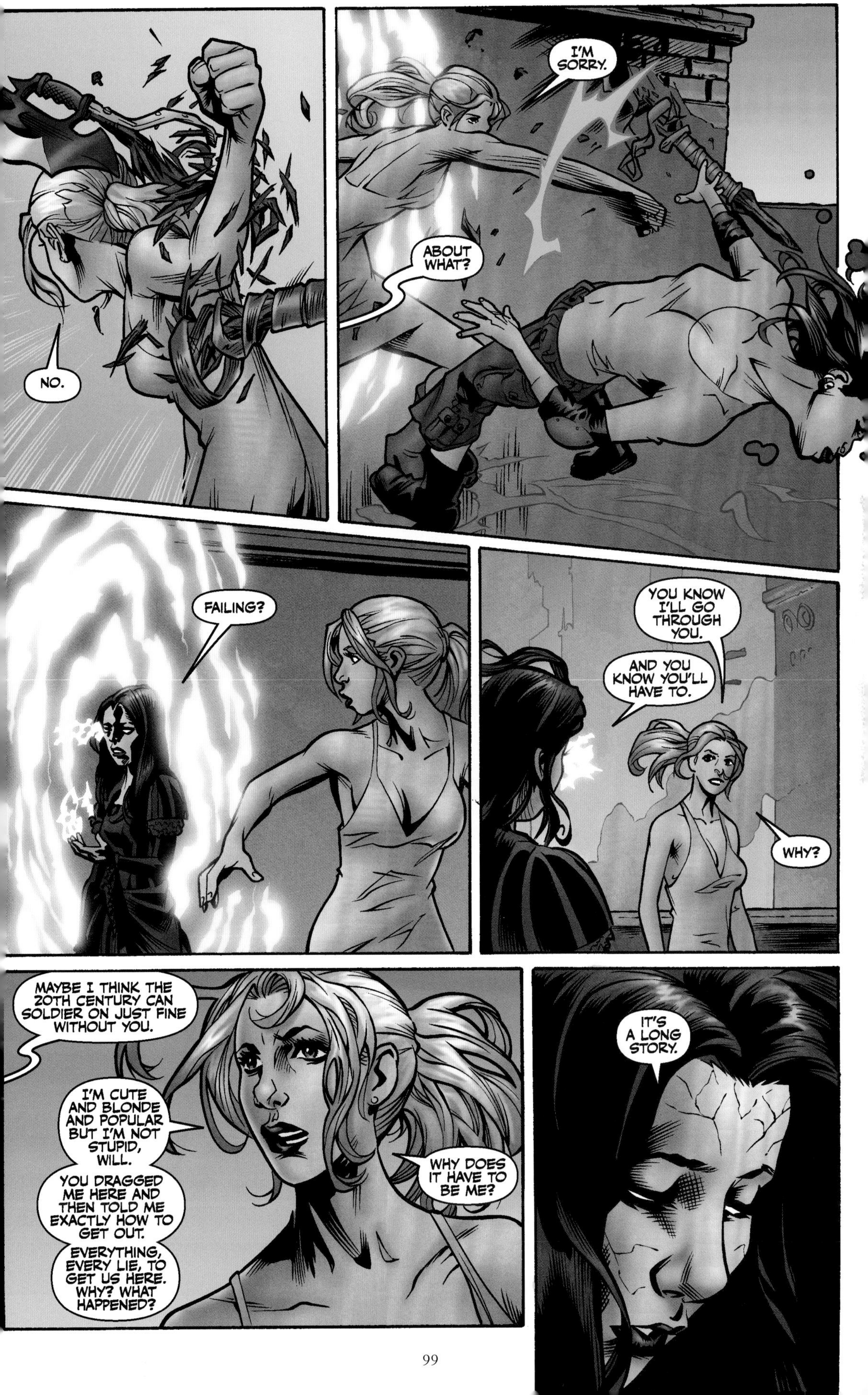
NO.
I'M SORRY.
ABOUT WHAT?
FAILING?
YOU KNOW I'LL GO THROUGH YOU.
AND YOU KNOW YOU'LL HAVE TO.
WHY?
MAYBE I THINK THE 20TH CENTURY CAN SOLDIER ON JUST FINE WITHOUT YOU.
I'M CUTE AND BLONDE AND POPULAR BUT I'M NOT STUPID, WILL.
YOU DRAGGED ME HERE AND THEN TOLD ME EXACTLY HOW TO GET OUT.
EVERYTHING, EVERY LIE, TO GET US HERE. WHY? WHAT HAPPENED?
WHY DOES IT HAVE TO BE ME?
IT'S A LONG STORY.

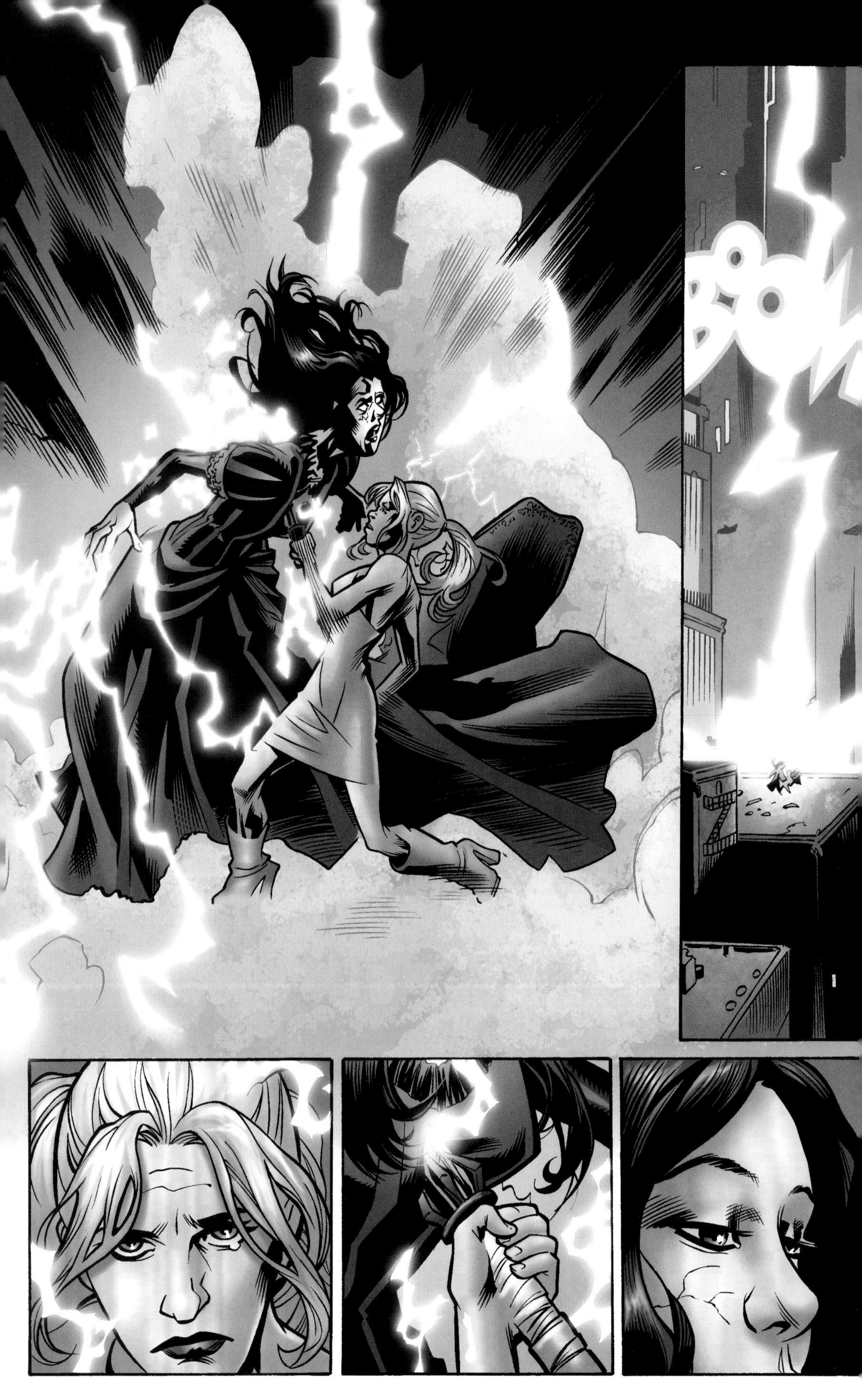

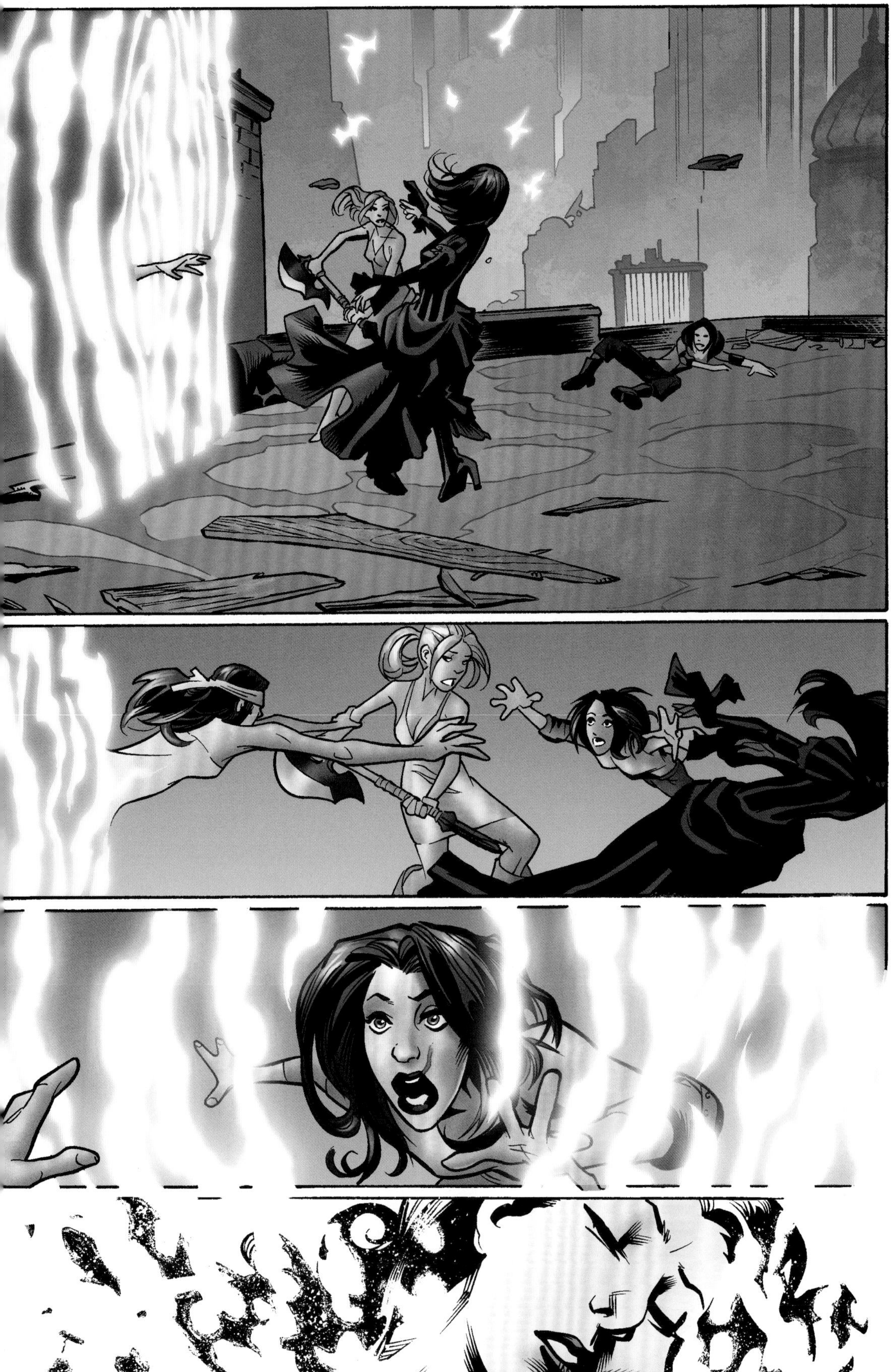

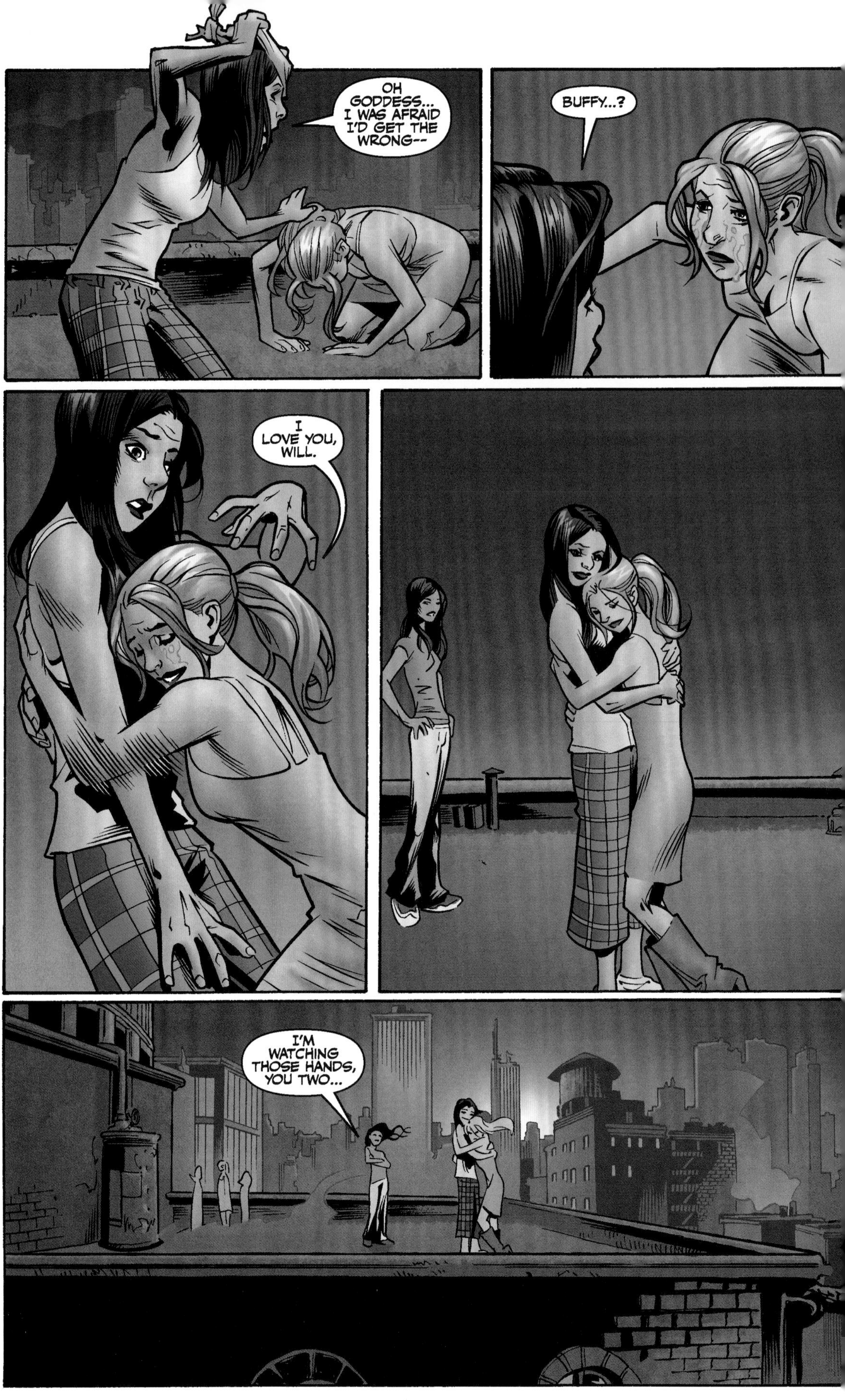
OH GODDESS... I WAS AFRAID I'D GET THE WRONG--
BUFFY...?
I LOVE YOU, WILL.
I'M WATCHING THOSE HANDS, YOU TWO...

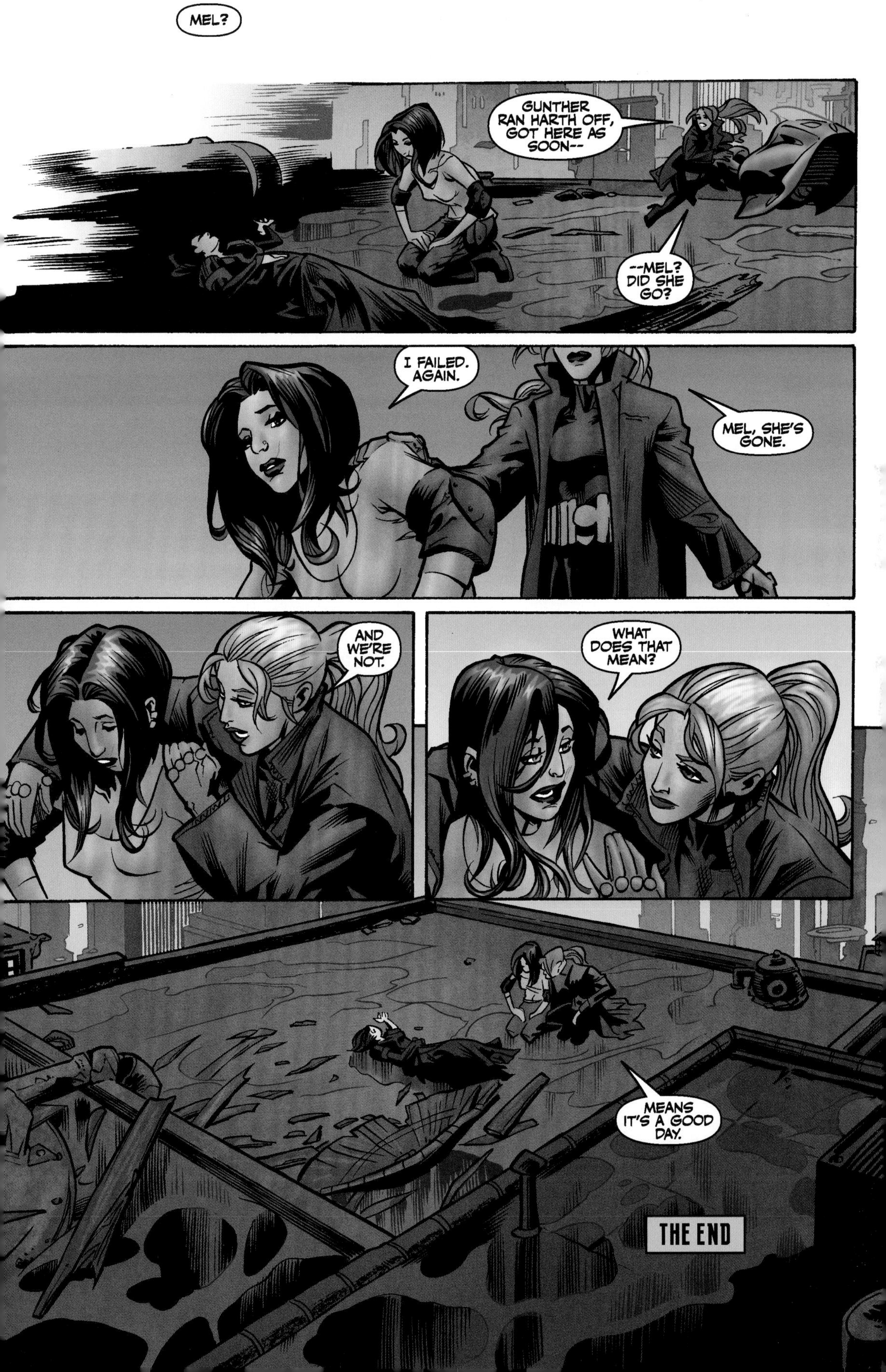
MEL?
GUNTHER RAN HARTH OFF, GOT HERE AS SOON--
--MEL? DID SHE GO?
I FAILED. AGAIN.
MEL, SHE'S GONE.
AND WE'RE NOT.
WHAT DOES THAT MEAN?
MEANS IT'S A GOOD DAY.
THE END

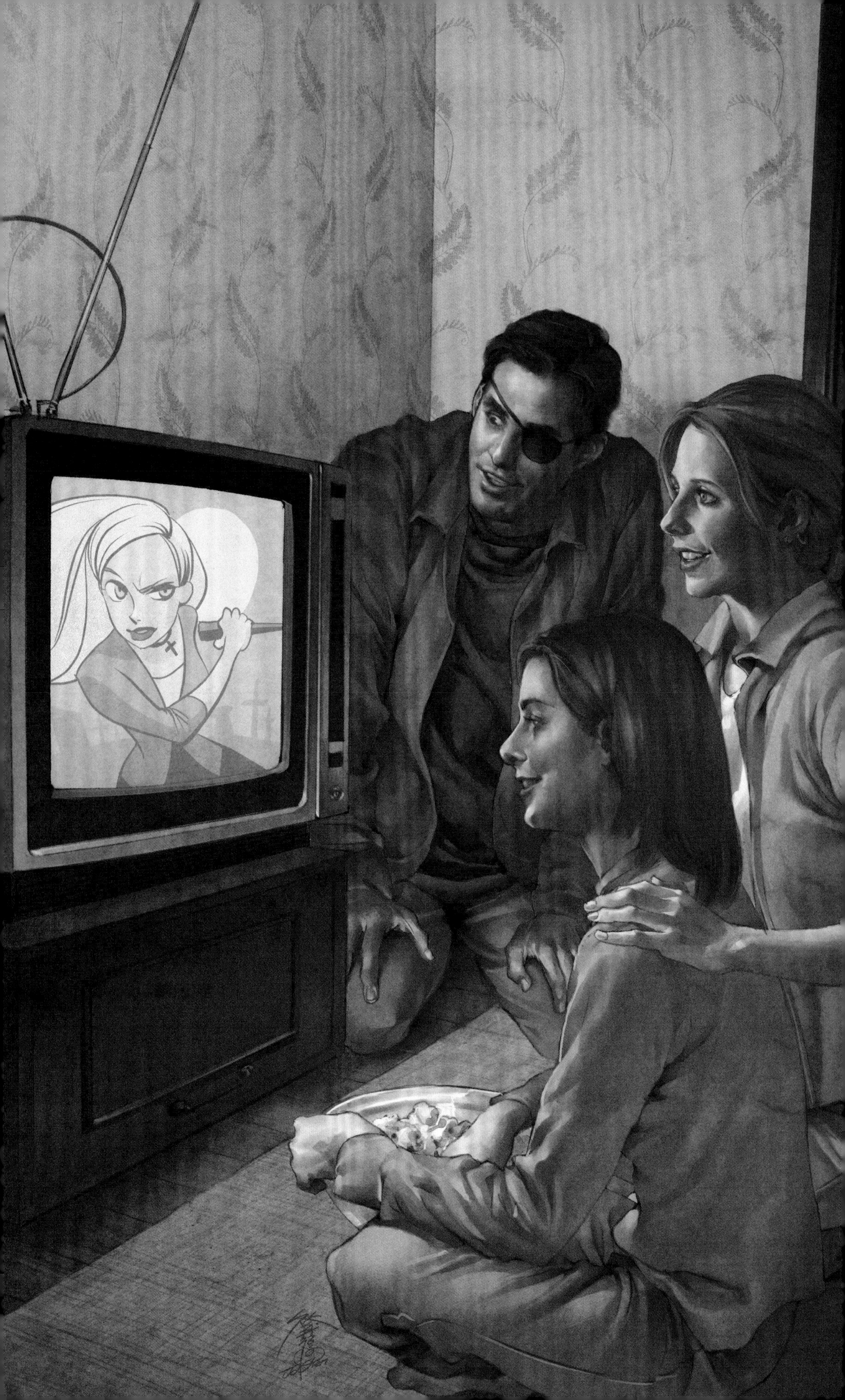

after these messages...

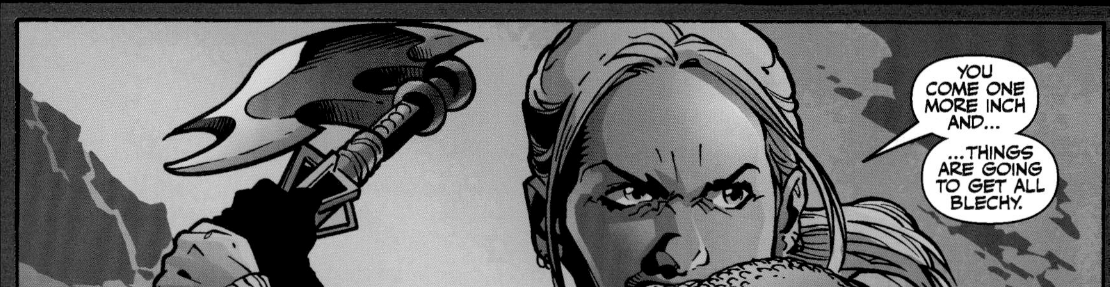
YOU COME ONE MORE INCH AND...
...THINGS ARE GOING TO GET ALL BLECHY.

...we'll be right back!

dedicated with love &
a smile to
sam loeb

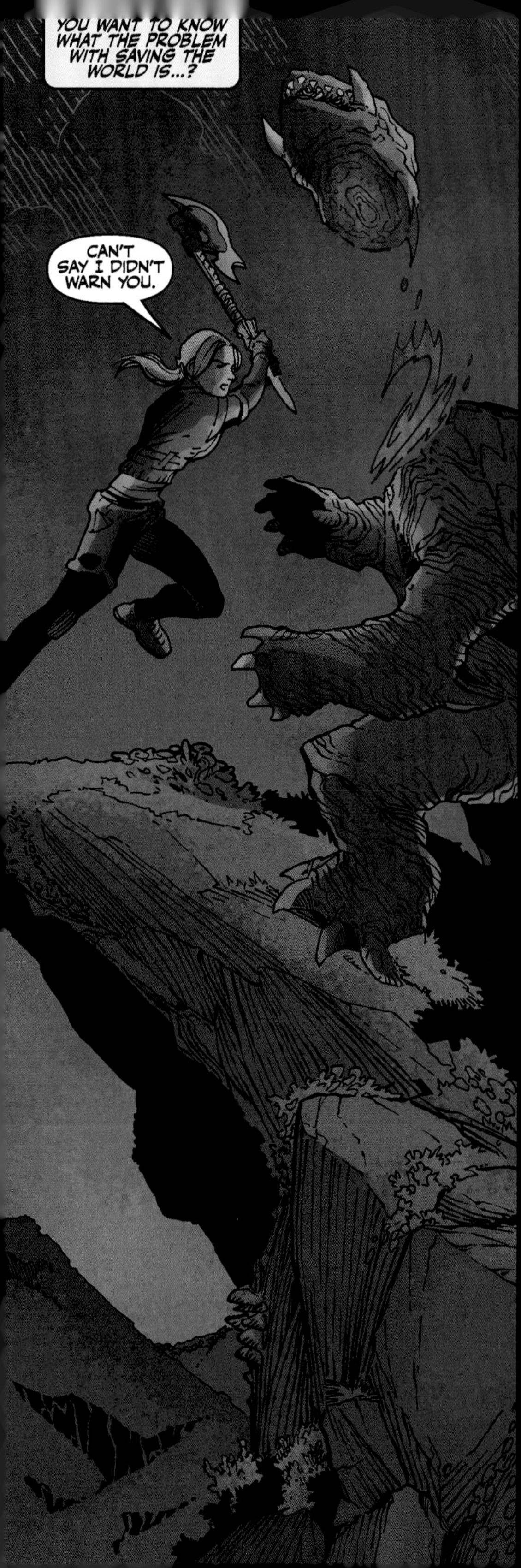
YOU WANT TO KNOW WHAT THE PROBLEM WITH SAVING THE WORLD IS...?
CAN'T SAY I DIDN'T WARN YOU.
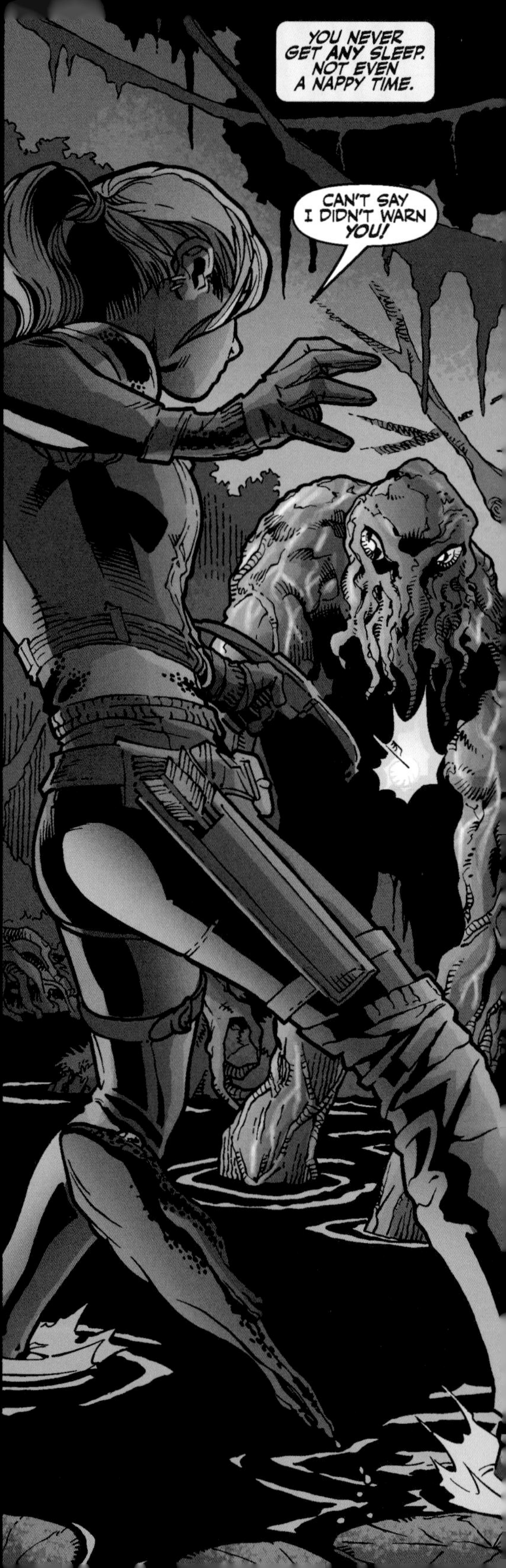
YOU NEVER GET ANY SLEEP. NOT EVEN A NAPPY TIME.
CAN'T SAY I DIDN'T WARN YOU!

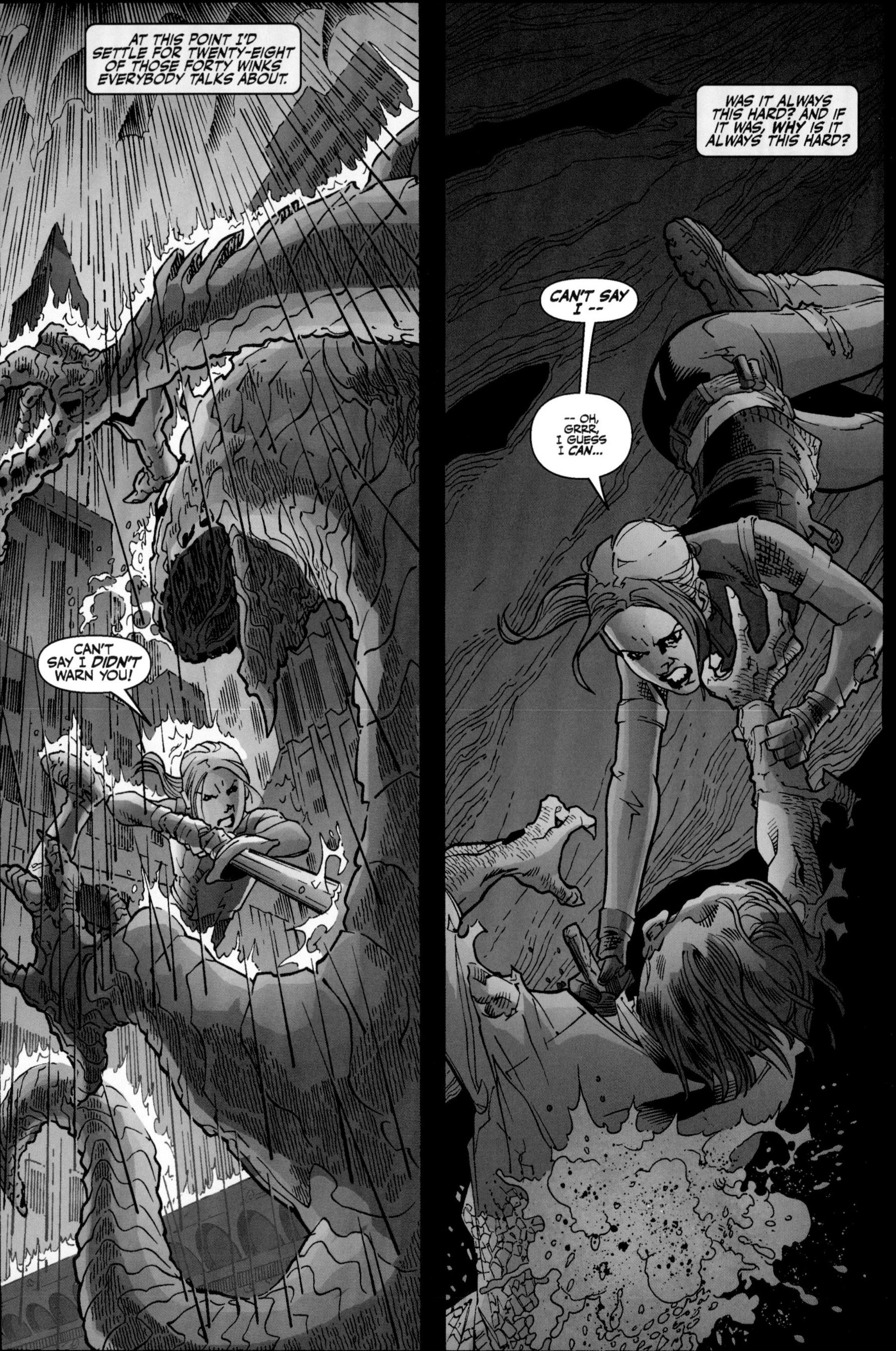
AT THIS POINT I'D SETTLE FOR TWENTY-EIGHT OF THOSE FORTY WINKS EVERYBODY TALKS ABOUT.
CAN'T SAY I *DIDN'T* WARN YOU!
WAS IT ALWAYS THIS HARD? AND IF IT WAS, **WHY** IS IT ALWAYS THIS HARD?
CAN'T SAY I --
-- OH, GRRR, I GUESS I *CAN*...

FINALLY.

XANDER!

WHAT ABOUT "DON'T WAKE ME EVEN IF THERE'S ANOTHER APOCALYPSE!" DON'T YOU GET?

NO, GOT THAT.

IT'S JUST --

WHAT?... IS IT ABOUT DAWN?

HAS SHE TURNED INTO SOMETHING ELSE?

IS SHE A GIANT MONKEY NOW?

OR A GIANT ROBOT?

OR A GIANT ROBOT MONKEY?!

NO, SHE'S NOT A GIANT ROBOT MONKEY.

BUT I'D LIKE TO SEE THAT TOO...

ALTHOUGH... DAWNY CHANGED INTO A GIANT ROBOT MONKEY I'D LIKE TO SEE...

XANDER. PUH-LEASE.

I'M ALL STINKY.

I'M STILL IN MY STINKY CLOTHES.

IN MY STINKY BED.

SO GO AWAY FROM MY STINKY BED AND I CAN GET SOME STINKY SLEEP!

BUT... THAT'S JUST IT, BUF.

THIS ISN'T YOUR BED YOU'RE MAKING ALL STINKY...

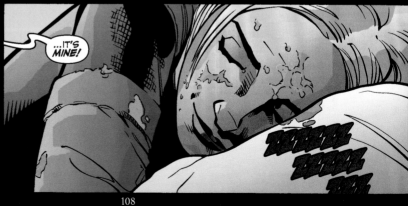

...IT'S MINE!

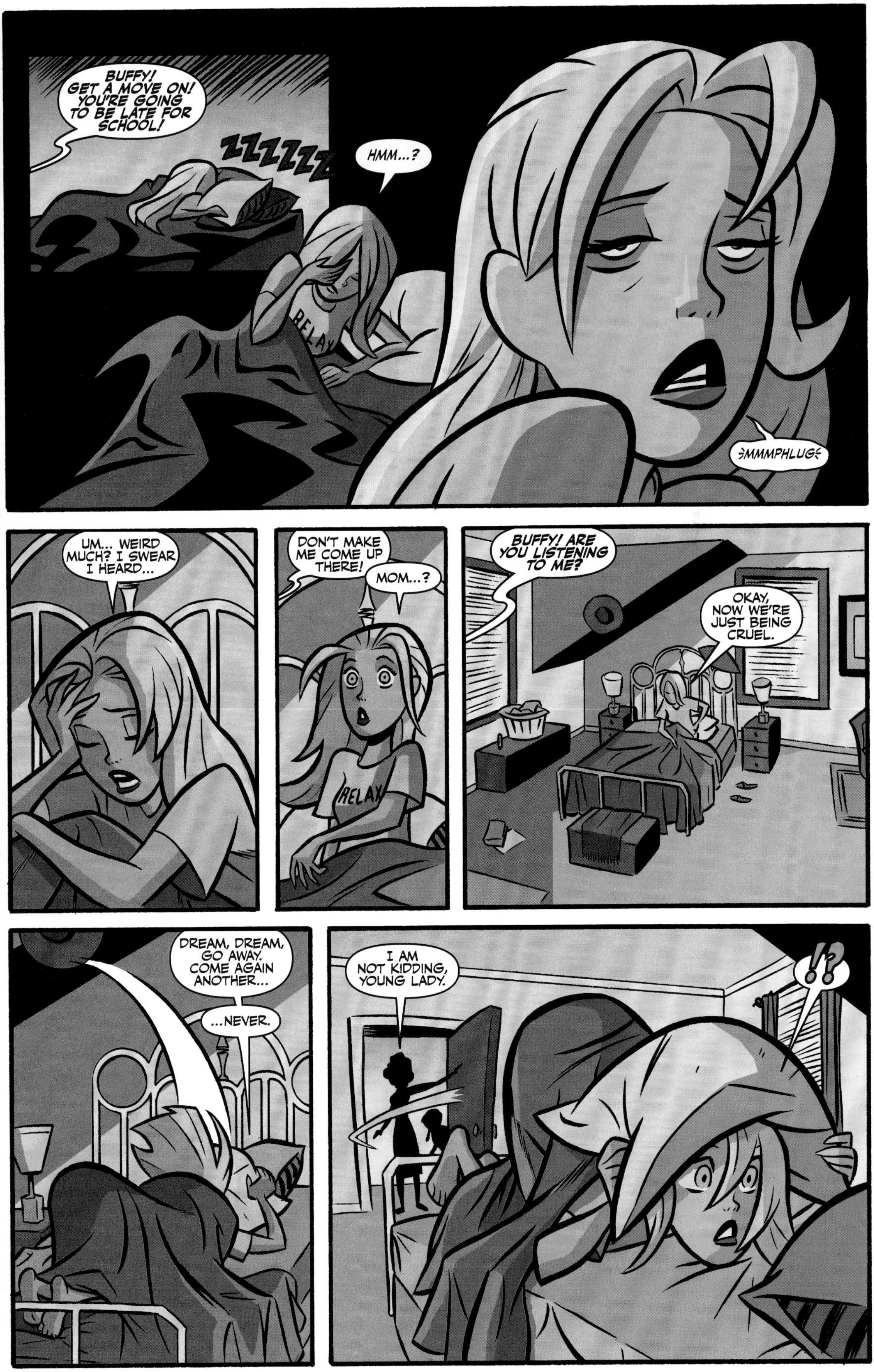
BUFFY! GET A MOVE ON! YOU'RE GOING TO BE LATE FOR SCHOOL!
ZZZZZZ
HMM...?
RELAX
MMMPHLUG
UM... WEIRD MUCH? I SWEAR I HEARD...
DON'T MAKE ME COME UP THERE!
MOM...?
RELAX
BUFFY! ARE YOU LISTENING TO ME?
OKAY, NOW WE'RE JUST BEING CRUEL.
DREAM, DREAM, GO AWAY. COME AGAIN ANOTHER...
...NEVER.
I AM NOT KIDDING, YOUNG LADY.
!?

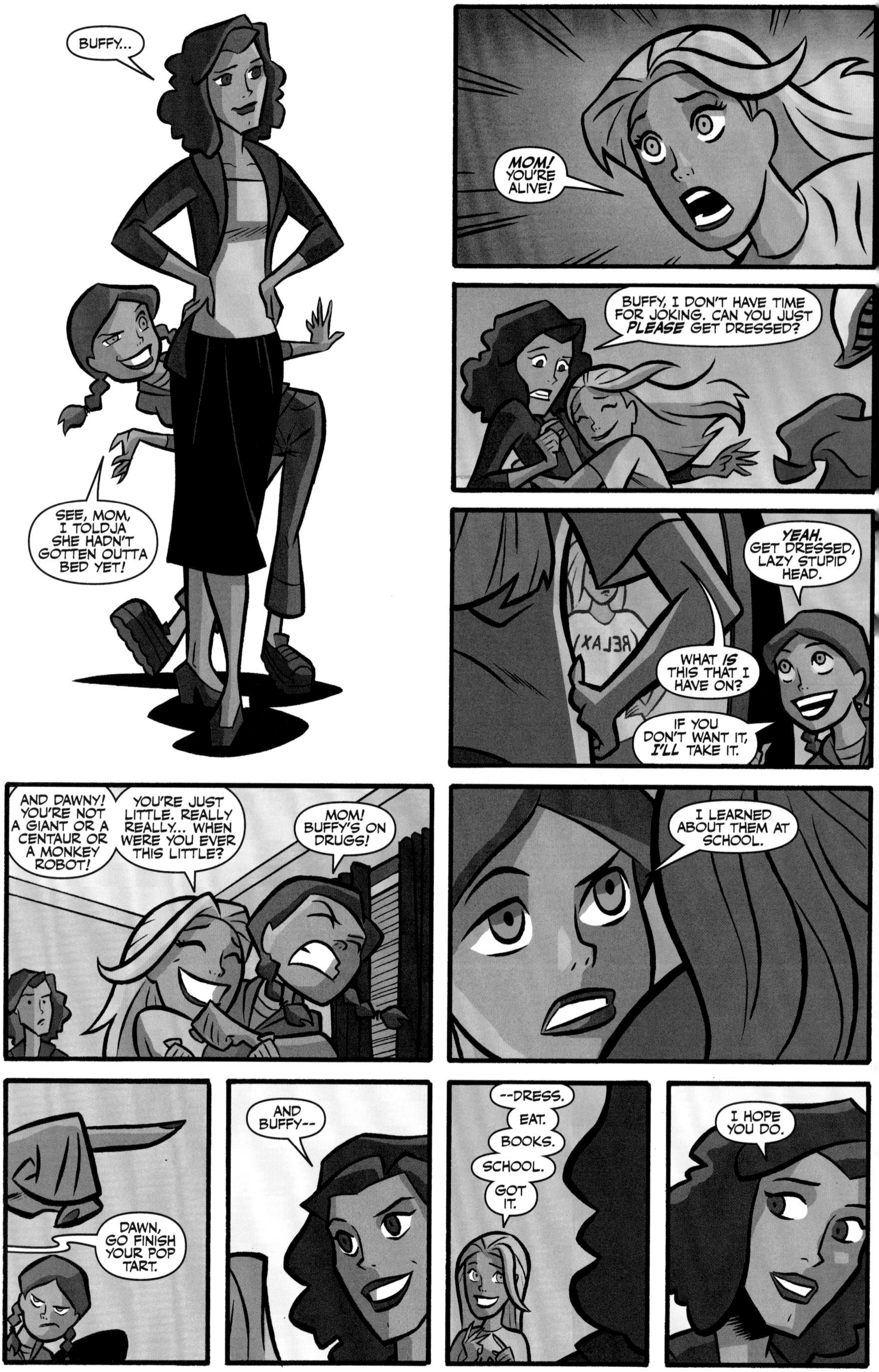
BUFFY...
SEE, MOM, I TOLDJA SHE HADN'T GOTTEN OUTTA BED YET!
MOM! YOU'RE ALIVE!
BUFFY, I DON'T HAVE TIME FOR JOKING. CAN YOU JUST PLEASE GET DRESSED?
YEAH. GET DRESSED, LAZY STUPID HEAD.
RELAX
WHAT IS THIS THAT I HAVE ON?
IF YOU DON'T WANT IT, I'LL TAKE IT.
AND DAWNY! YOU'RE NOT A GIANT OR A CENTAUR OR A MONKEY ROBOT!
YOU'RE JUST LITTLE. REALLY REALLY... WHEN WERE YOU EVER THIS LITTLE?
MOM! BUFFY'S ON DRUGS!
I LEARNED ABOUT THEM AT SCHOOL.
DAWN, GO FINISH YOUR POP TART.
AND BUFFY--
--DRESS.
EAT.
BOOKS.
SCHOOL.
GOT IT.
I HOPE YOU DO.

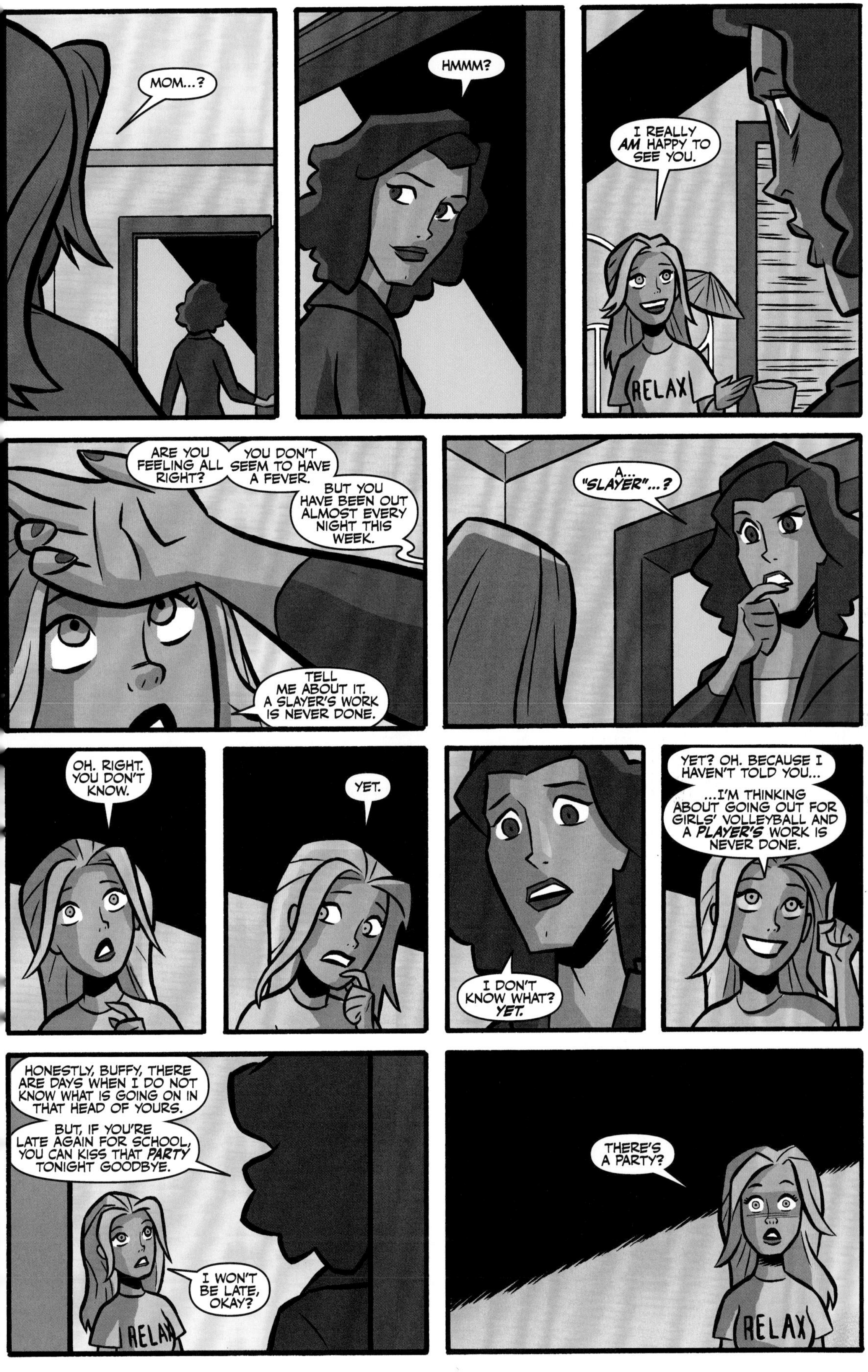
MOM...?
HMMM?
I REALLY AM HAPPY TO SEE YOU.
RELAX
ARE YOU FEELING ALL RIGHT?
YOU DON'T SEEM TO HAVE A FEVER.
BUT YOU HAVE BEEN OUT ALMOST EVERY NIGHT THIS WEEK.
TELL ME ABOUT IT. A SLAYER'S WORK IS NEVER DONE.
A... "SLAYER"...?
OH. RIGHT. YOU DON'T KNOW.
YET.
I DON'T KNOW WHAT? YET.
YET? OH. BECAUSE I HAVEN'T TOLD YOU...
...I'M THINKING ABOUT GOING OUT FOR GIRLS' VOLLEYBALL AND A PLAYER'S WORK IS NEVER DONE.
HONESTLY, BUFFY, THERE ARE DAYS WHEN I DO NOT KNOW WHAT IS GOING ON IN THAT HEAD OF YOURS.
BUT, IF YOU'RE LATE AGAIN FOR SCHOOL, YOU CAN KISS THAT PARTY TONIGHT GOODBYE.
I WON'T BE LATE, OKAY?
RELAX
THERE'S A PARTY?
RELAX

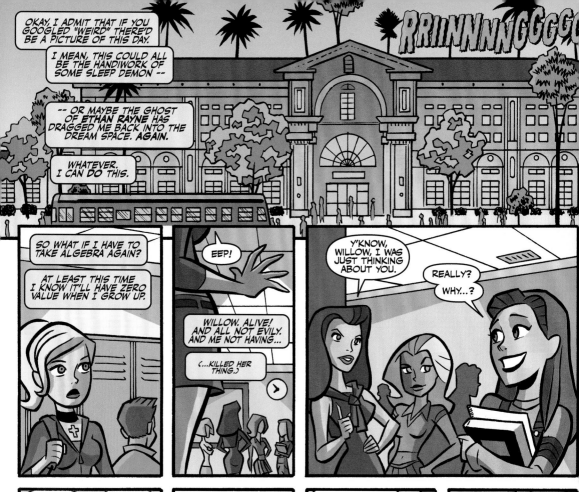

OKAY, I ADMIT THAT IF YOU GOOGLED "WEIRD" THERE'D BE A PICTURE OF THIS DAY.

I MEAN, THIS COULD ALL BE THE HANDIWORK OF SOME SLEEP DEMON --

-- OR MAYBE THE GHOST OF ETHAN RAYNE HAS DRAGGED ME BACK INTO THE DREAM SPACE. AGAIN.

WHATEVER. I CAN DO THIS.

RRIINNNNGGGGG

SO WHAT IF I HAVE TO TAKE ALGEBRA AGAIN?

AT LEAST THIS TIME I KNOW IT'LL HAVE ZERO VALUE WHEN I GROW UP.

EEP!

WILLOW. ALIVE! AND ALL NOT EVILY. AND ME NOT HAVING...

(...KILLED HER THING.)

Y'KNOW, WILLOW, I WAS JUST THINKING ABOUT YOU.

REALLY?

WHY...?

WELL, I'M SURE YOU'VE HEARD ABOUT MY BIG PARTY TONIGHT.

SH-SURE, CORDELIA. A BUNCH OF US. I MEAN, BUFFY, AND XANDER AND I WERE PLANNING--

--YES, AND I WAS TALKING.

DON'T YOU THINK IT'S TIME YOU TRIED SOMETHING WITH YOUR HAIR?

THOSE BANGS DO SO MUCH TO HIDE YOUR FACE.

JUST CUTTING IT SHORTER OR EVEN GIVING IT A PERM.

THIS WAY, WE COULD SEE MORE OF YOU.

AND...THAT WOULD BE A GOOD THING?

NO, BUT YOU'D GET A CLEARER PICTURE OF EXACTLY HOW HOPELESS YOU TRULY ARE.

HA HA HE

TEE HEE

NO BIGGIE, WILL. MAYBE SOMEDAY SHE'LL BE DEAD AND YOU'LL BE A SORCERESS SUPREME.

REALLY...?

DO I GET TO WEAR A POINTY HAT?

ONE SIDE, LADIES!

XANDER?!

YEP. XANDER.

KRASH

XANDER HARRIS. THAT WOULDN'T BE A *SKATEBOARD* YOU'D BE RIDING IN *MY* HALLWAYS, WOULD IT?

TECHNICALLY SPEAKING, *PRINCIPAL SNYDER*, "NO." I WASN'T RIDING THE SKATEBOARD AS MUCH AS IT WAS RIDING ME.

YOU'LL GET THIS BACK AT THE END OF THE SCHOOL YEAR.

BUT... IT'S A *BRAND-NEW BOARD!*

EITHER *THAT BOARD* OR *YOU YOURSELF* WILL BE LOCKED UP IN MY OFFICE --

--WHICH IS IT GOING TO BE?

...WAUGH.

LOOK AT IT THIS WAY, XANDER.

MAYBE SOMEDAY SNYDER WILL GET EATEN BY A *HUGE GINORMOUS SNAKE*--

--AND YOU'LL WEAR AN *EYE PATCH* AND BE IN CHARGE OF *LOTS OF WOMENS.*

REALLY...? LIKE A PIRATE? CAN I BE LIKE A *SPACE* PIRATE? WITH AN ALIEN DOG?

≶KOFF≶ BUFFY ≶KOFF≶!

OH. THAT'S RIGHT. YOU LIKE... AND YOU'RE NOT... WELL, YOU PROBABLY *ARE*... BUT NOT...

I'M NOT *WHAT?*

YIKES. OPEN MOUTH. INSERT WHOLE BODY.

HEY! I BET THERE'S SOMETHING *GILES* HAS FOR US TO DO...

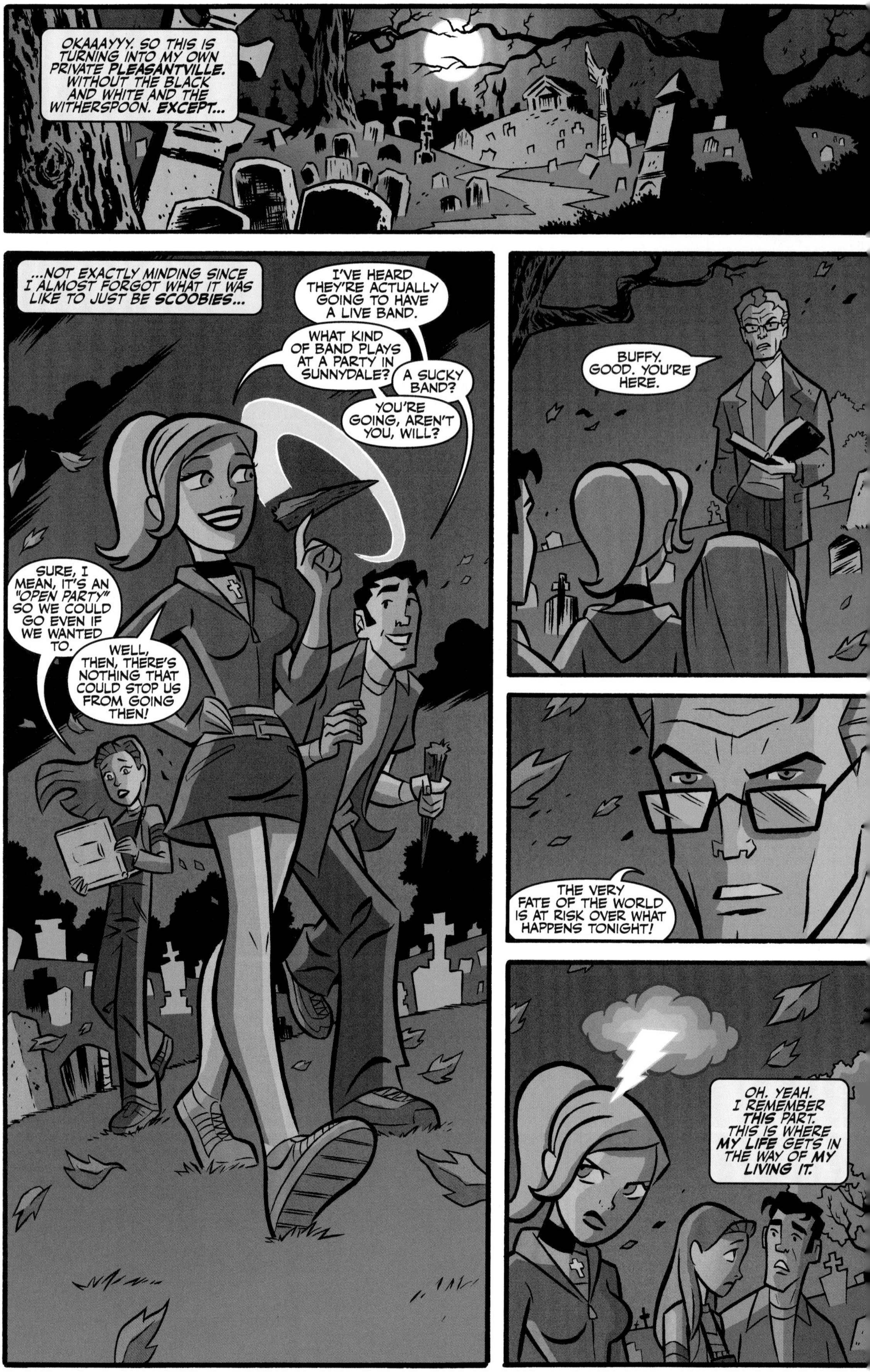
OKAAAYYY. SO THIS IS TURNING INTO MY OWN PRIVATE **PLEASANTVILLE.** WITHOUT THE BLACK AND WHITE AND THE WITHERSPOON. **EXCEPT...**
...NOT EXACTLY MINDING SINCE I ALMOST FORGOT WHAT IT WAS LIKE TO JUST BE **SCOOBIES...**
I'VE HEARD THEY'RE ACTUALLY GOING TO HAVE A LIVE BAND.
WHAT KIND OF BAND PLAYS AT A PARTY IN SUNNYDALE?
A SUCKY BAND?
YOU'RE GOING, AREN'T YOU, WILL?
SURE, I MEAN, IT'S AN *"OPEN PARTY"* SO WE COULD GO EVEN IF WE WANTED TO.
WELL, THEN, THERE'S NOTHING THAT COULD STOP US FROM GOING THEN!
BUFFY. GOOD. YOU'RE HERE.
THE VERY FATE OF THE WORLD IS AT RISK OVER WHAT HAPPENS TONIGHT!
OH. YEAH. I REMEMBER **THIS** PART. THIS IS WHERE **MY LIFE** GETS IN THE WAY OF **MY LIVING IT.**

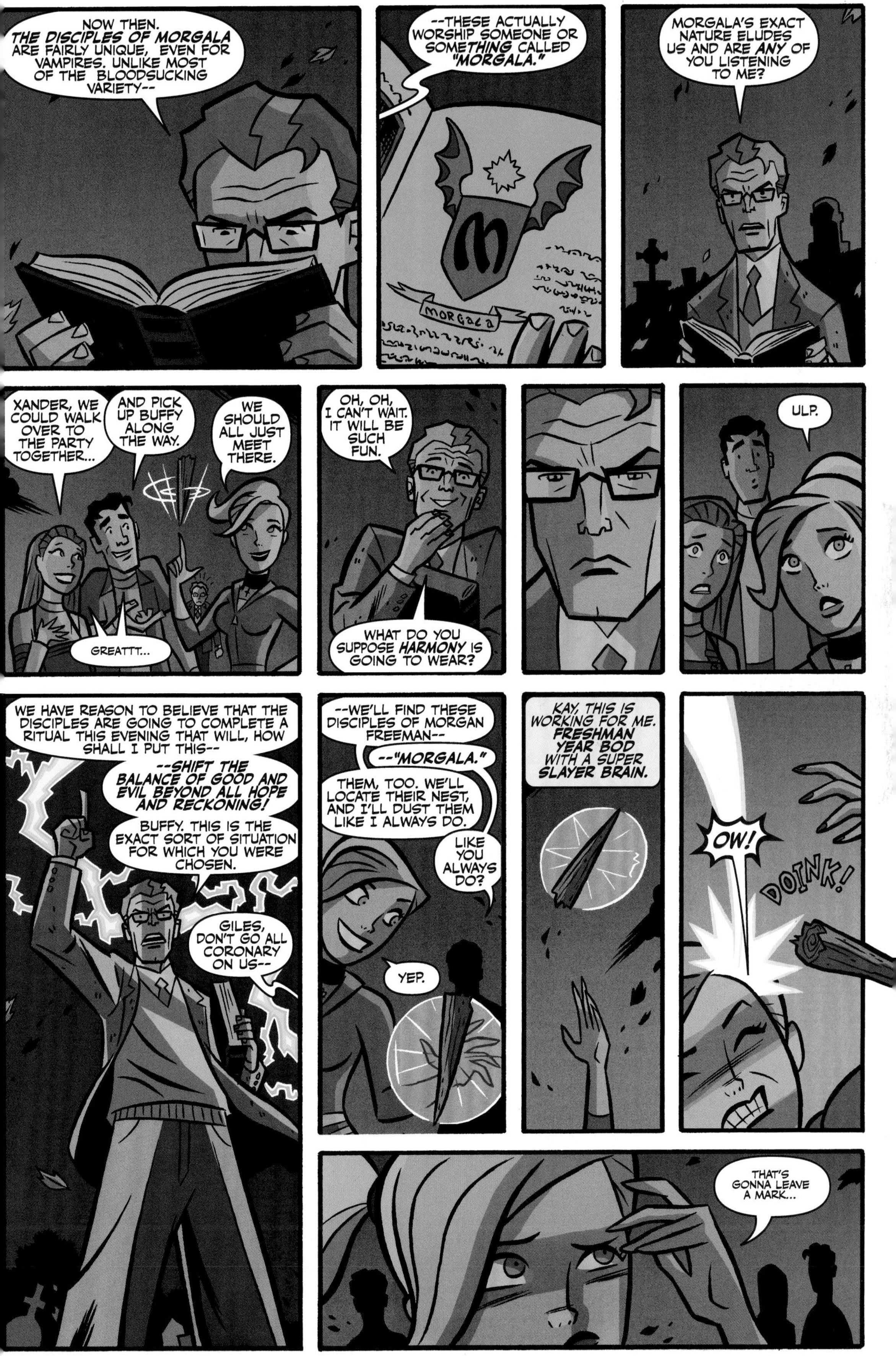

NOW THEN. THE DISCIPLES OF MORGALA ARE FAIRLY UNIQUE, EVEN FOR VAMPIRES. UNLIKE MOST OF THE BLOODSUCKING VARIETY--
--THESE ACTUALLY WORSHIP SOMEONE OR SOMETHING CALLED "MORGALA."
MORGALA
MORGALA'S EXACT NATURE ELUDES US AND ARE ANY OF YOU LISTENING TO ME?
XANDER, WE COULD WALK OVER TO THE PARTY TOGETHER...
AND PICK UP BUFFY ALONG THE WAY.
WE SHOULD ALL JUST MEET THERE.
GREATTT...
OH, OH, I CAN'T WAIT. IT WILL BE SUCH FUN.
WHAT DO YOU SUPPOSE HARMONY IS GOING TO WEAR?
ULP.
WE HAVE REASON TO BELIEVE THAT THE DISCIPLES ARE GOING TO COMPLETE A RITUAL THIS EVENING THAT WILL, HOW SHALL I PUT THIS--
--SHIFT THE BALANCE OF GOOD AND EVIL BEYOND ALL HOPE AND RECKONING!
BUFFY. THIS IS THE EXACT SORT OF SITUATION FOR WHICH YOU WERE CHOSEN.
GILES, DON'T GO ALL CORONARY ON US--
--WE'LL FIND THESE DISCIPLES OF MORGAN FREEMAN--
--"MORGALA."
THEM, TOO. WE'LL LOCATE THEIR NEST, AND I'LL DUST THEM LIKE I ALWAYS DO.
LIKE YOU ALWAYS DO?
YEP.
KAY, THIS IS WORKING FOR ME. FRESHMAN YEAR BOD WITH A SUPER SLAYER BRAIN.
OW!
DOINK!
THAT'S GONNA LEAVE A MARK...

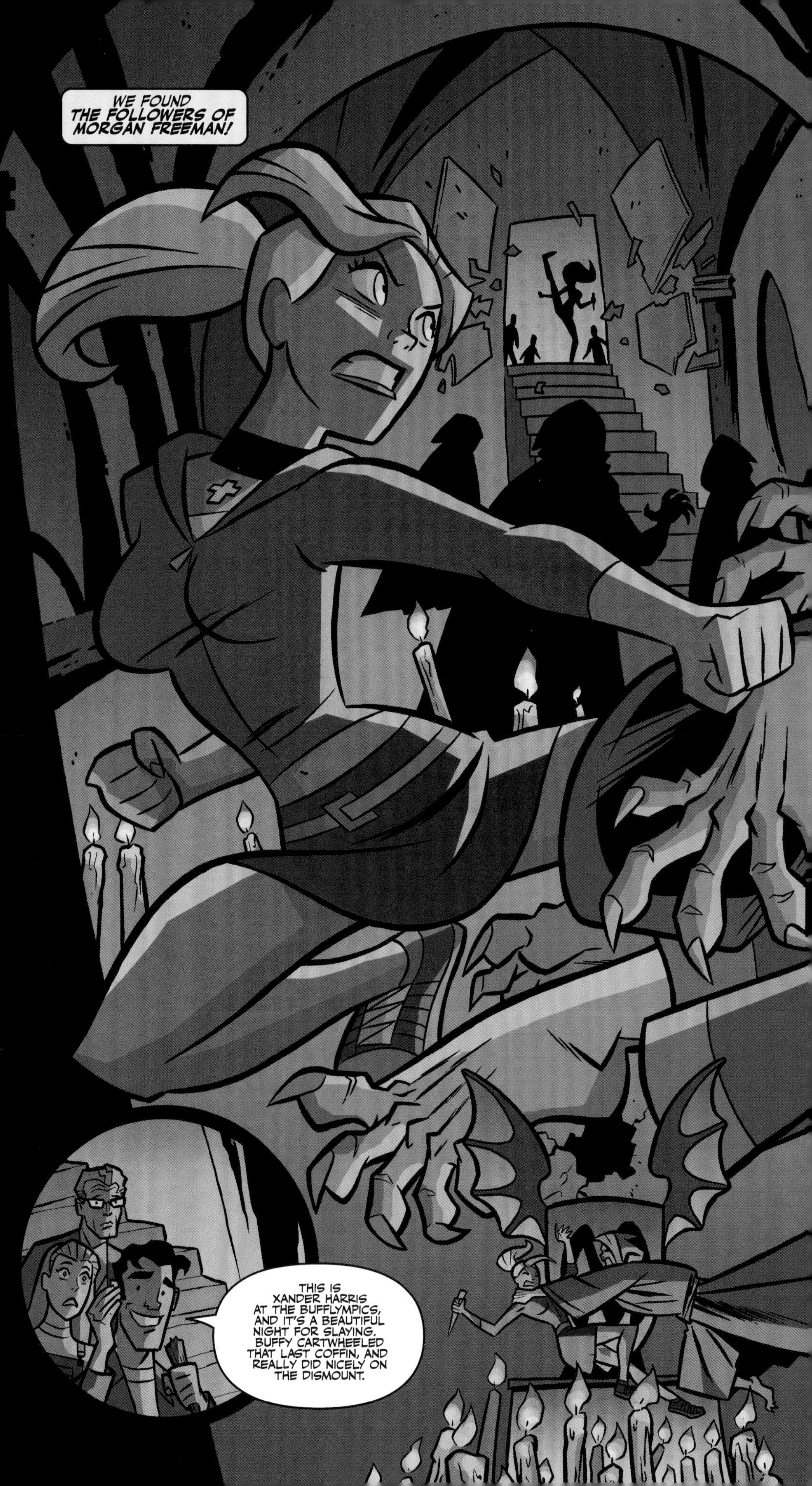
WE FOUND THE FOLLOWERS OF MORGAN FREEMAN!
THIS IS XANDER HARRIS AT THE BUFFLYMPICS, AND IT'S A BEAUTIFUL NIGHT FOR SLAYING. BUFFY CARTWHEELED THAT LAST COFFIN, AND REALLY DID NICELY ON THE DISMOUNT.

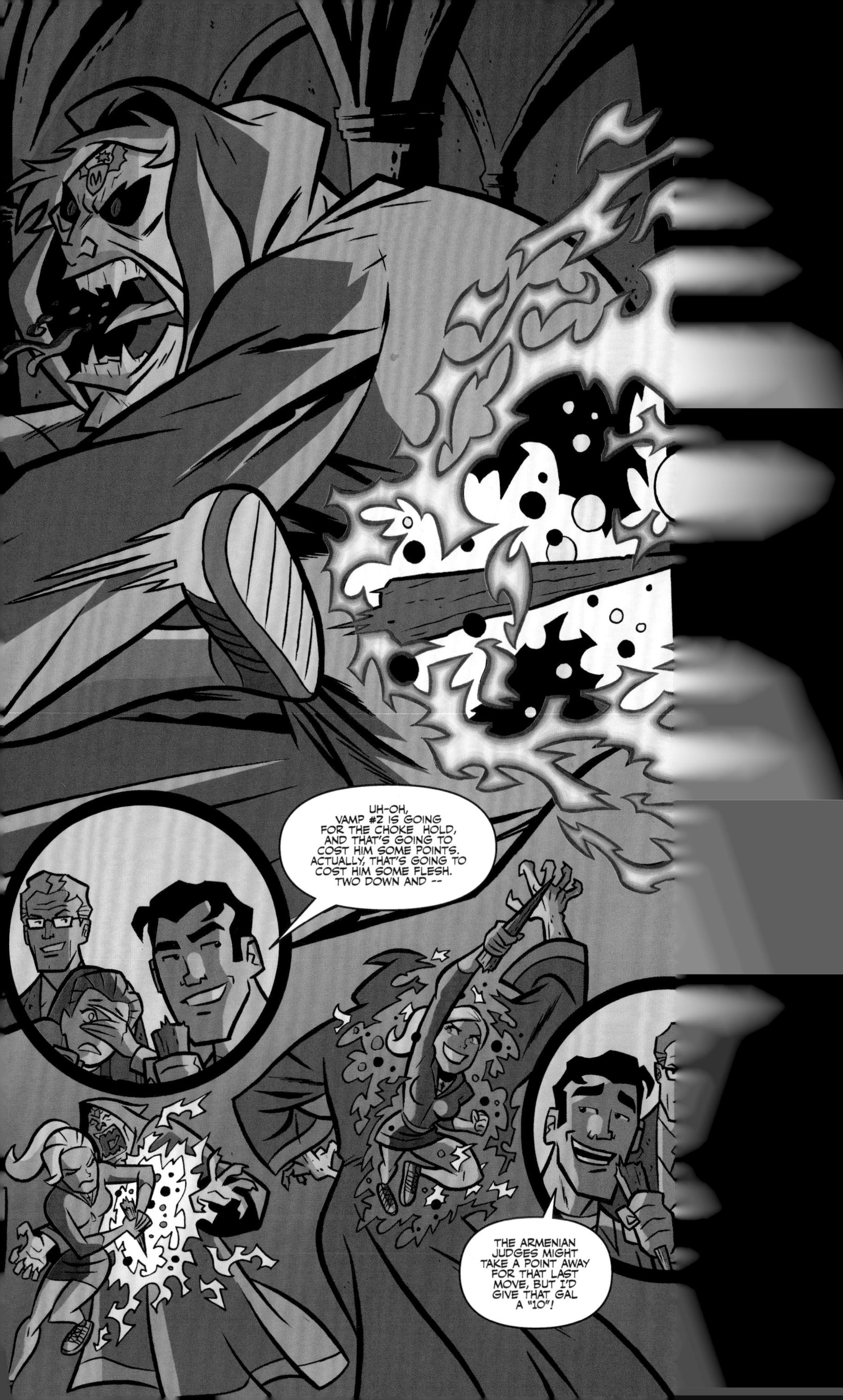
UH-OH, VAMP #2 IS GOING FOR THE CHOKE HOLD, AND THAT'S GOING TO COST HIM SOME POINTS. ACTUALLY, THAT'S GOING TO COST HIM SOME FLESH. TWO DOWN AND --
THE ARMENIAN JUDGES MIGHT TAKE A POINT AWAY FOR THAT LAST MOVE, BUT I'D GIVE THAT GAL A "10"!

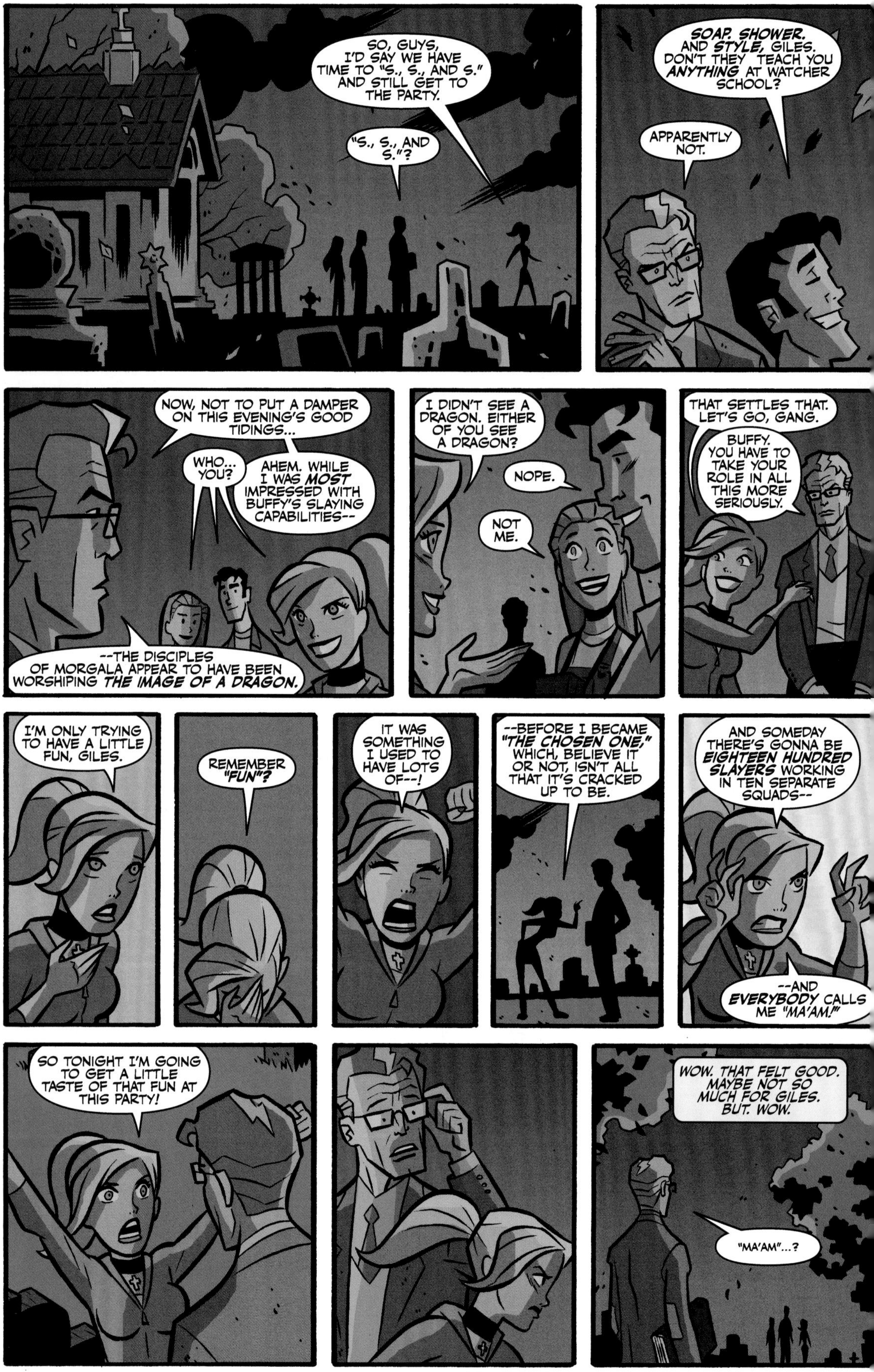

SO, GUYS, I'D SAY WE HAVE TIME TO "S., S., AND S." AND STILL GET TO THE PARTY.
"S., S., AND S."?
SOAP. SHOWER. AND STYLE, GILES. DON'T THEY TEACH YOU ANYTHING AT WATCHER SCHOOL?
APPARENTLY NOT.
NOW, NOT TO PUT A DAMPER ON THIS EVENING'S GOOD TIDINGS...
WHO... YOU?
AHEM. WHILE I WAS MOST IMPRESSED WITH BUFFY'S SLAYING CAPABILITIES--
--THE DISCIPLES OF MORGALA APPEAR TO HAVE BEEN WORSHIPING THE IMAGE OF A DRAGON.
I DIDN'T SEE A DRAGON. EITHER OF YOU SEE A DRAGON?
NOPE.
NOT ME.
THAT SETTLES THAT. LET'S GO, GANG.
BUFFY. YOU HAVE TO TAKE YOUR ROLE IN ALL THIS MORE SERIOUSLY.
I'M ONLY TRYING TO HAVE A LITTLE FUN, GILES.
REMEMBER "FUN"?
IT WAS SOMETHING I USED TO HAVE LOTS OF--!
--BEFORE I BECAME "THE CHOSEN ONE," WHICH, BELIEVE IT OR NOT, ISN'T ALL THAT IT'S CRACKED UP TO BE.
AND SOMEDAY THERE'S GONNA BE EIGHTEEN HUNDRED SLAYERS WORKING IN TEN SEPARATE SQUADS--
--AND EVERYBODY CALLS ME "MA'AM!"
SO TONIGHT I'M GOING TO GET A LITTLE TASTE OF THAT FUN AT THIS PARTY!
WOW. THAT FELT GOOD. MAYBE NOT SO MUCH FOR GILES. BUT. WOW.
"MA'AM"...?

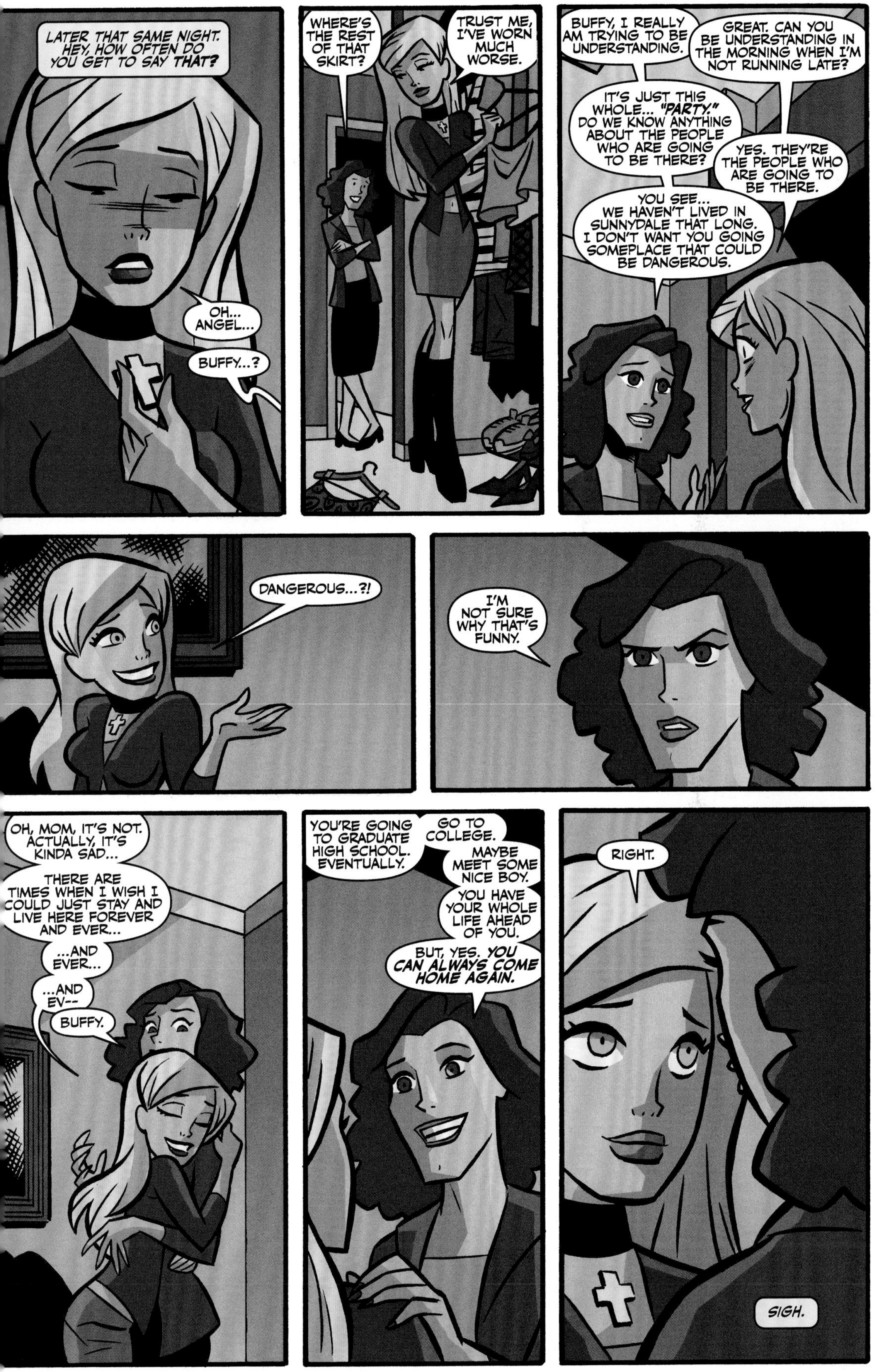

LATER THAT SAME NIGHT. HEY, HOW OFTEN DO YOU GET TO SAY THAT?
OH... ANGEL...
BUFFY...?
WHERE'S THE REST OF THAT SKIRT?
TRUST ME, I'VE WORN MUCH WORSE.
BUFFY, I REALLY AM TRYING TO BE UNDERSTANDING.
GREAT. CAN YOU BE UNDERSTANDING IN THE MORNING WHEN I'M NOT RUNNING LATE?
IT'S JUST THIS WHOLE... "PARTY." DO WE KNOW ANYTHING ABOUT THE PEOPLE WHO ARE GOING TO BE THERE?
YES. THEY'RE THE PEOPLE WHO ARE GOING TO BE THERE.
YOU SEE... WE HAVEN'T LIVED IN SUNNYDALE THAT LONG. I DON'T WANT YOU GOING SOMEPLACE THAT COULD BE DANGEROUS.
DANGEROUS...?!
I'M NOT SURE WHY THAT'S FUNNY.
OH, MOM, IT'S NOT. ACTUALLY, IT'S KINDA SAD...
THERE ARE TIMES WHEN I WISH I COULD JUST STAY AND LIVE HERE FOREVER AND EVER...
...AND EVER...
...AND EV--
BUFFY.
YOU'RE GOING TO GRADUATE HIGH SCHOOL. EVENTUALLY.
GO TO COLLEGE.
MAYBE MEET SOME NICE BOY.
YOU HAVE YOUR WHOLE LIFE AHEAD OF YOU.
BUT, YES. YOU CAN ALWAYS COME HOME AGAIN.
RIGHT.
SIGH.

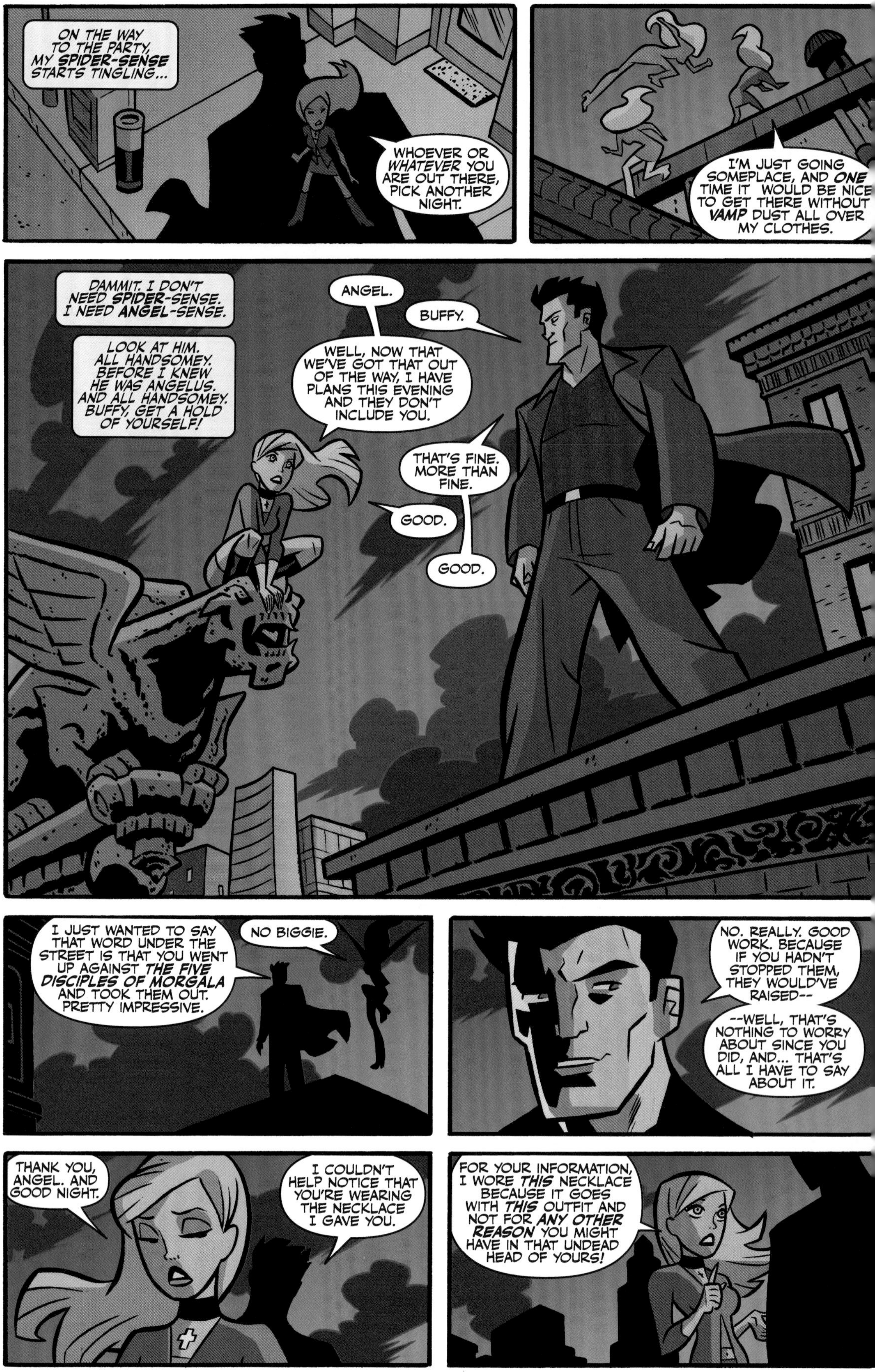
ON THE WAY TO THE PARTY, MY SPIDER-SENSE STARTS TINGLING...
WHOEVER OR WHATEVER YOU ARE OUT THERE, PICK ANOTHER NIGHT.
I'M JUST GOING SOMEPLACE, AND ONE TIME IT WOULD BE NICE TO GET THERE WITHOUT VAMP DUST ALL OVER MY CLOTHES.
DAMMIT. I DON'T NEED SPIDER-SENSE. I NEED ANGEL-SENSE.
LOOK AT HIM. ALL HANDSOMEY. BEFORE I KNEW HE WAS ANGELUS. AND ALL HANDSOMEY. BUFFY, GET A HOLD OF YOURSELF!
ANGEL.
BUFFY.
WELL, NOW THAT WE'VE GOT THAT OUT OF THE WAY, I HAVE PLANS THIS EVENING AND THEY DON'T INCLUDE YOU.
THAT'S FINE. MORE THAN FINE.
GOOD.
GOOD.
I JUST WANTED TO SAY THAT WORD UNDER THE STREET IS THAT YOU WENT UP AGAINST THE FIVE DISCIPLES OF MORGALA AND TOOK THEM OUT. PRETTY IMPRESSIVE.
NO BIGGIE.
NO. REALLY. GOOD WORK. BECAUSE IF YOU HADN'T STOPPED THEM, THEY WOULD'VE RAISED--
--WELL, THAT'S NOTHING TO WORRY ABOUT SINCE YOU DID, AND... THAT'S ALL I HAVE TO SAY ABOUT IT.
THANK YOU, ANGEL. AND GOOD NIGHT.
I COULDN'T HELP NOTICE THAT YOU'RE WEARING THE NECKLACE I GAVE YOU.
FOR YOUR INFORMATION, I WORE THIS NECKLACE BECAUSE IT GOES WITH THIS OUTFIT AND NOT FOR ANY OTHER REASON YOU MIGHT HAVE IN THAT UNDEAD HEAD OF YOURS!

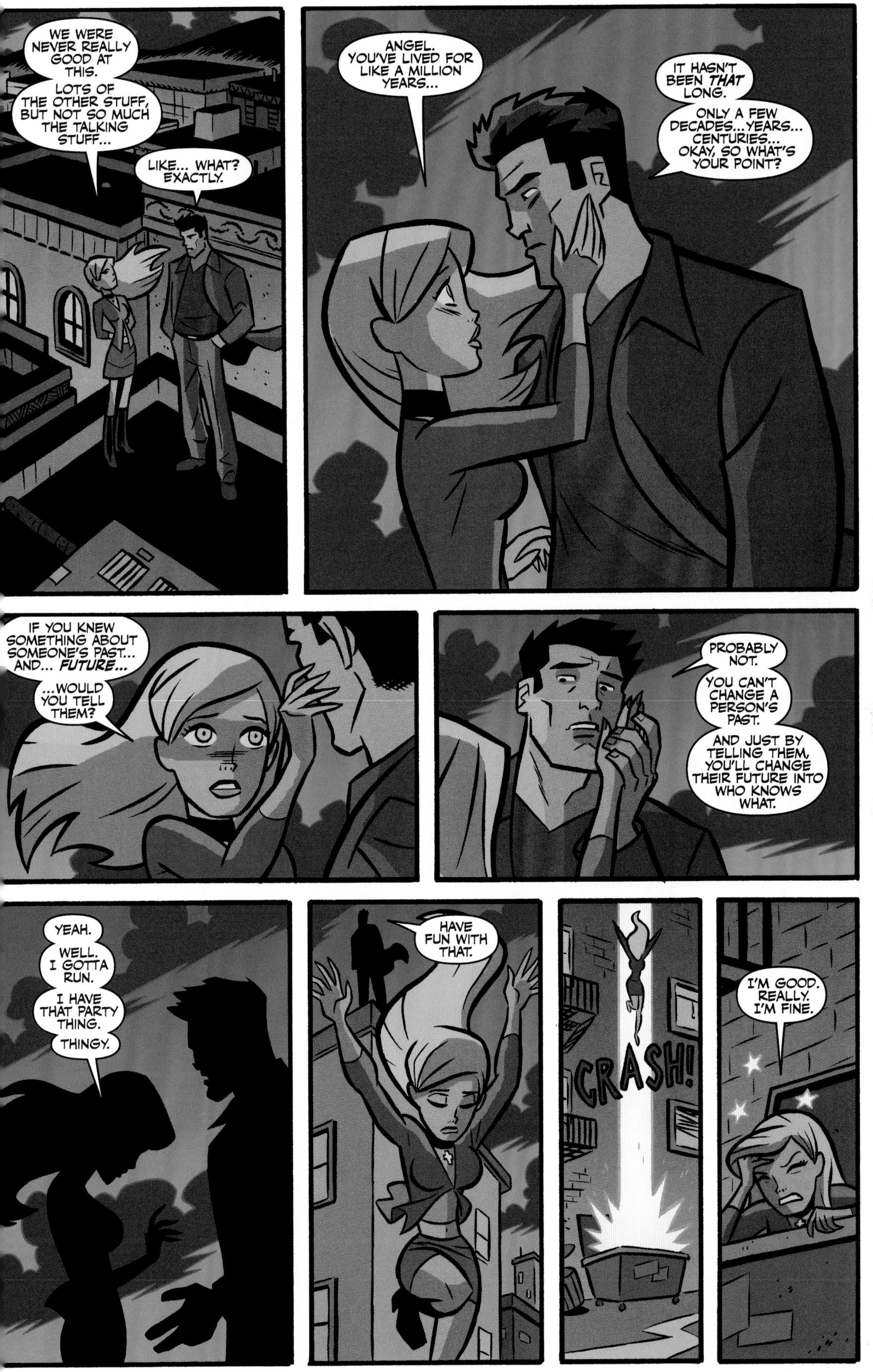

WE WERE NEVER REALLY GOOD AT THIS.
LOTS OF THE OTHER STUFF, BUT NOT SO MUCH THE TALKING STUFF...
LIKE... WHAT? EXACTLY.
ANGEL. YOU'VE LIVED FOR LIKE A MILLION YEARS...
IT HASN'T BEEN *THAT* LONG.
ONLY A FEW DECADES...YEARS... CENTURIES... OKAY, SO WHAT'S YOUR POINT?
IF YOU KNEW SOMETHING ABOUT SOMEONE'S PAST... AND... *FUTURE*...
...WOULD YOU TELL THEM?
PROBABLY NOT.
YOU CAN'T CHANGE A PERSON'S PAST.
AND JUST BY TELLING THEM, YOU'LL CHANGE THEIR FUTURE INTO WHO KNOWS WHAT.
YEAH.
WELL. I GOTTA RUN.
I HAVE THAT PARTY THING.
THINGY.
HAVE FUN WITH THAT.
CRASH!
I'M GOOD. REALLY. I'M FINE.

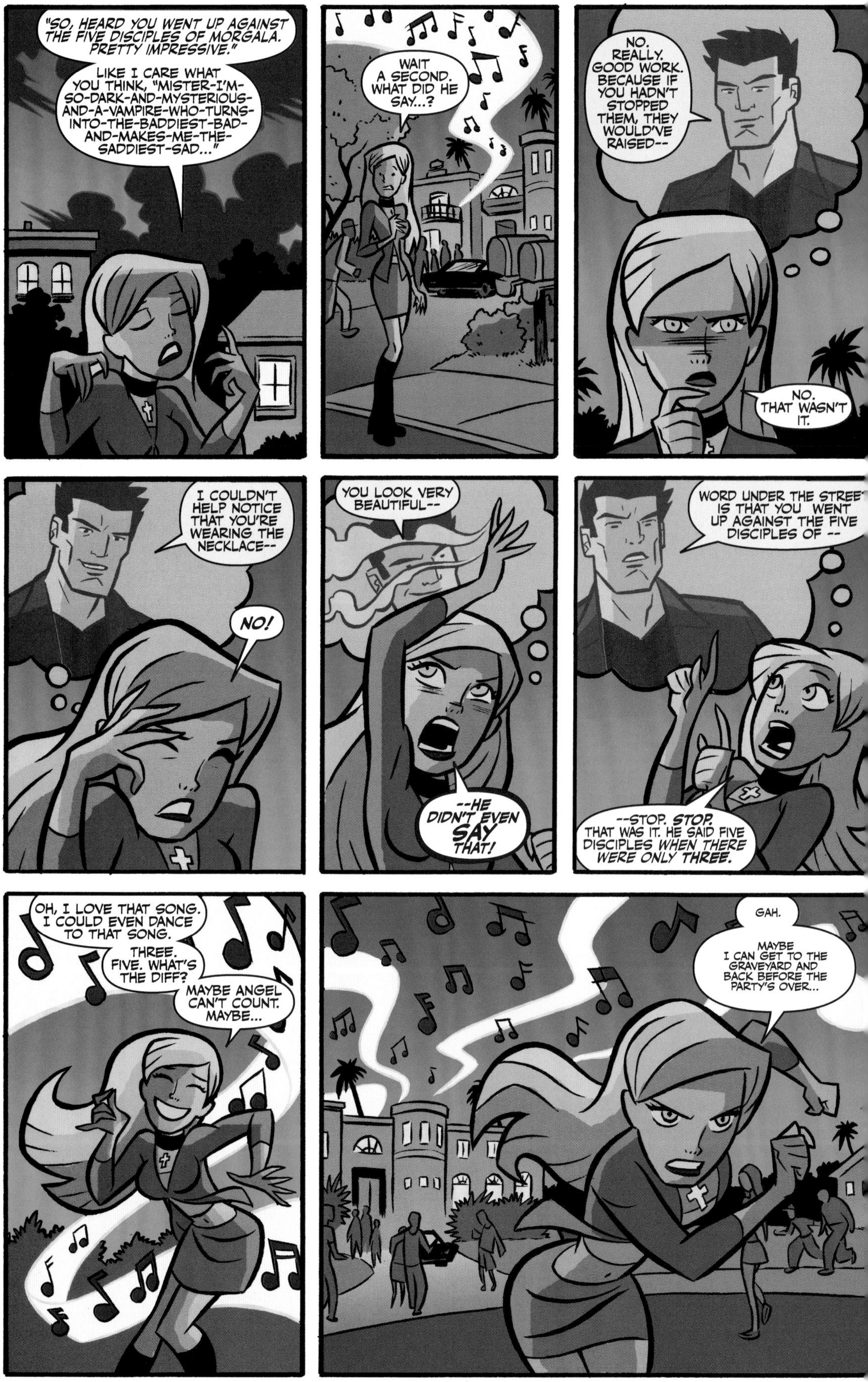
"SO, HEARD YOU WENT UP AGAINST THE FIVE DISCIPLES OF MORGALA. PRETTY IMPRESSIVE."
LIKE I CARE WHAT YOU THINK, "MISTER-I'M-SO-DARK-AND-MYSTERIOUS-AND-A-VAMPIRE-WHO-TURNS-INTO-THE-BADDIEST-BAD-AND-MAKES-ME-THE-SADDIEST-SAD..."
WAIT A SECOND. WHAT DID HE SAY...?
NO. REALLY. GOOD WORK. BECAUSE IF YOU HADN'T STOPPED THEM, THEY WOULD'VE RAISED--
NO. THAT WASN'T IT.
I COULDN'T HELP NOTICE THAT YOU'RE WEARING THE NECKLACE--
NO!
YOU LOOK VERY BEAUTIFUL--
--HE DIDN'T EVEN SAY THAT!
WORD UNDER THE STREE IS THAT YOU WENT UP AGAINST THE FIVE DISCIPLES OF --
--STOP. STOP. THAT WAS IT. HE SAID FIVE DISCIPLES WHEN THERE WERE ONLY THREE.
OH, I LOVE THAT SONG. I COULD EVEN DANCE TO THAT SONG.
THREE. FIVE. WHAT'S THE DIFF?
MAYBE ANGEL CAN'T COUNT. MAYBE...
GAH.
MAYBE I CAN GET TO THE GRAVEYARD AND BACK BEFORE THE PARTY'S OVER...

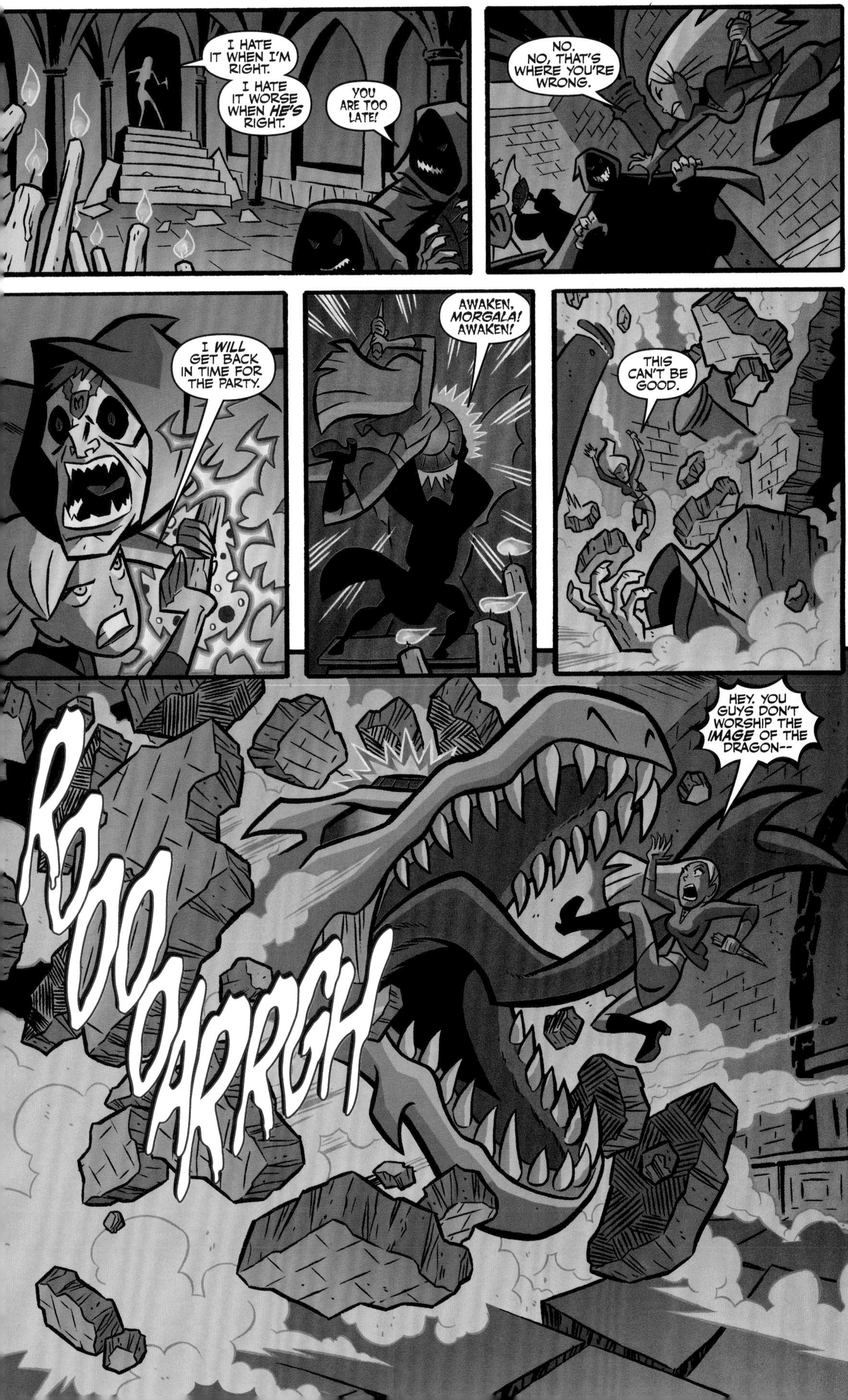

I HATE IT WHEN I'M RIGHT.
I HATE IT WORSE WHEN *HE'S* RIGHT.
YOU ARE TOO LATE!
NO. NO, THAT'S WHERE YOU'RE WRONG.
I *WILL* GET BACK IN TIME FOR THE PARTY.
AWAKEN, *MORGALA!* AWAKEN!
THIS CAN'T BE GOOD.
ROOOOARRGH
HEY. YOU GUYS DON'T WORSHIP THE *IMAGE* OF THE DRAGON--

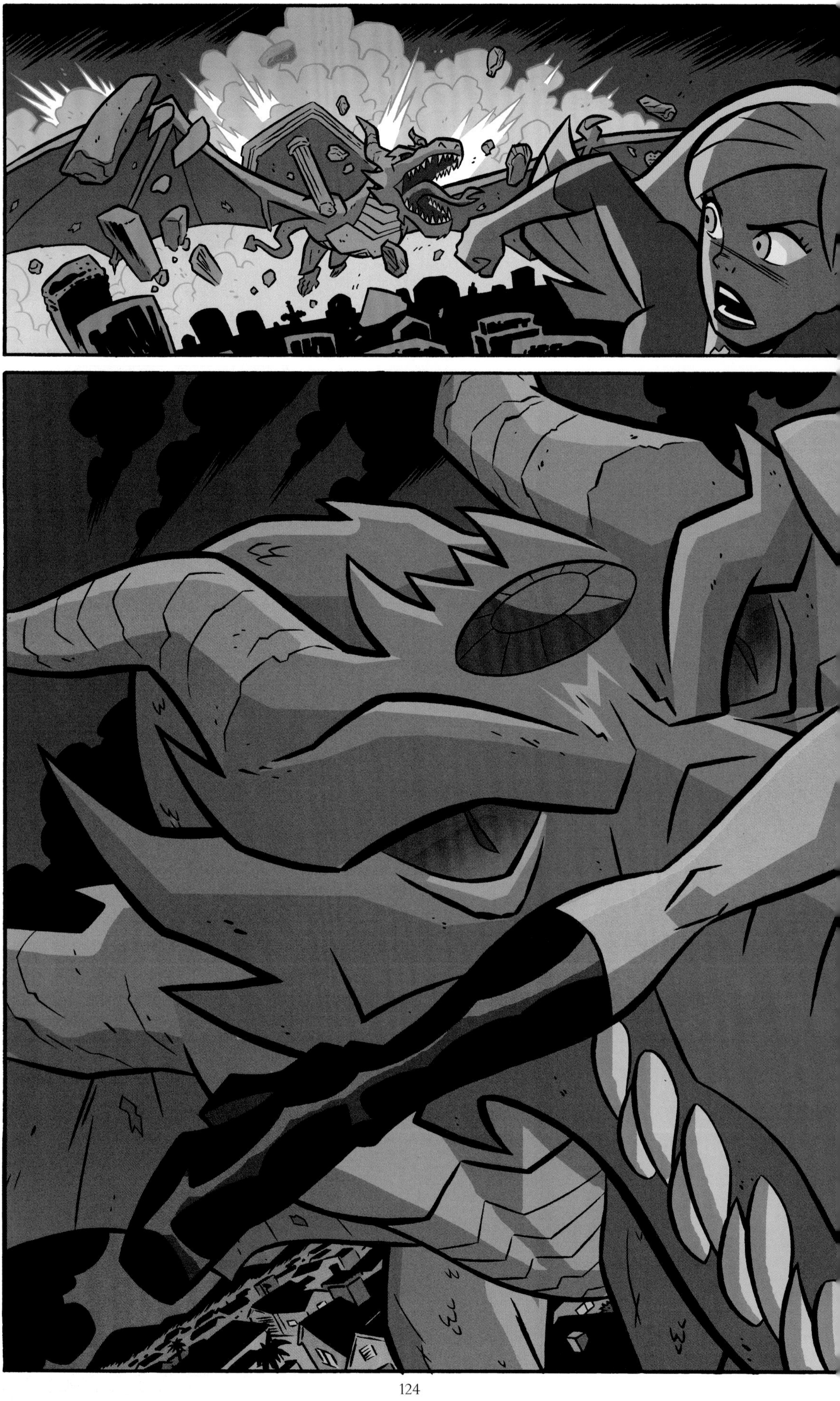

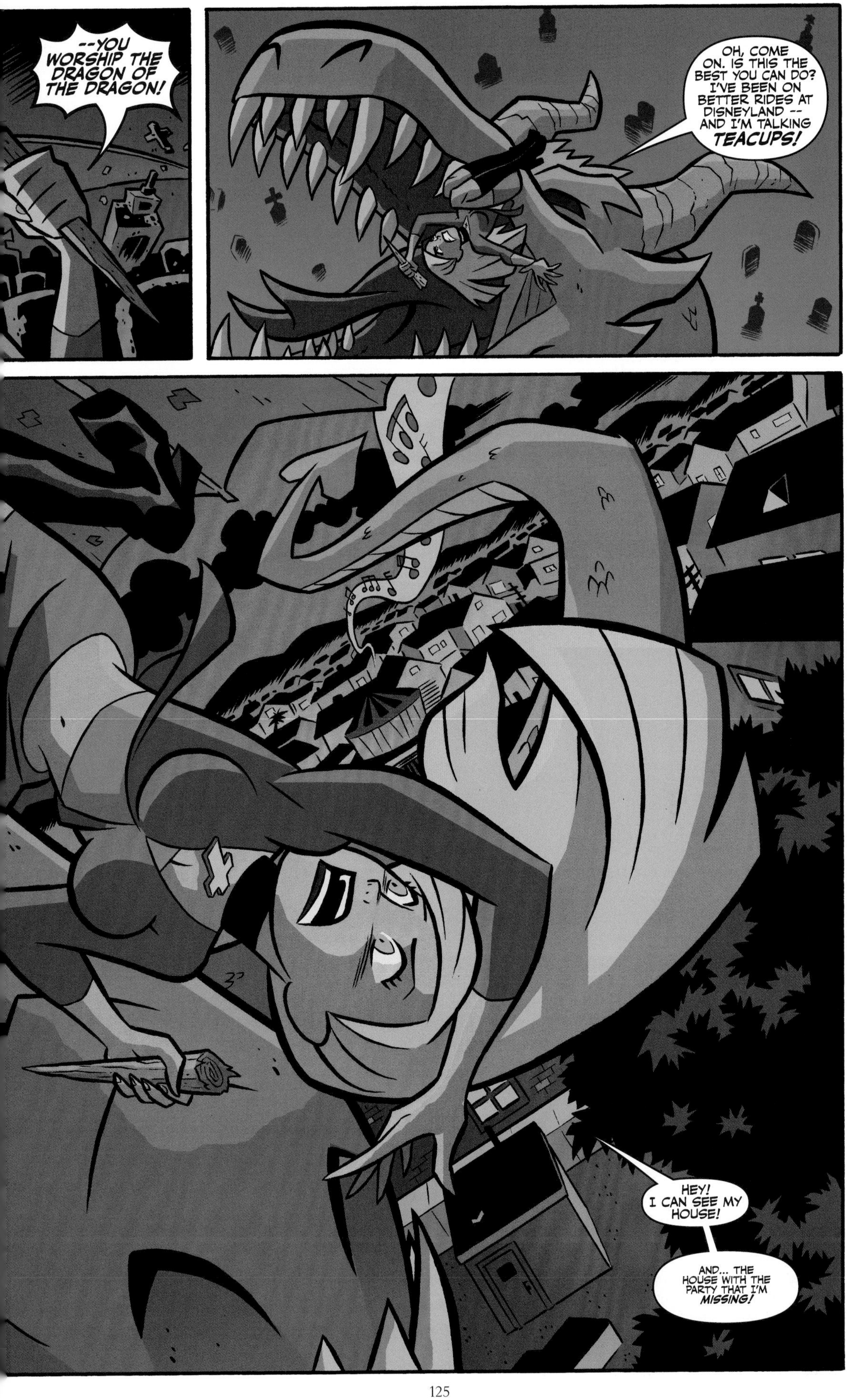
--YOU WORSHIP THE DRAGON OF THE DRAGON!
OH, COME ON. IS THIS THE BEST YOU CAN DO? I'VE BEEN ON BETTER RIDES AT DISNEYLAND -- AND I'M TALKING TEACUPS!
HEY! I CAN SEE MY HOUSE!
AND... THE HOUSE WITH THE PARTY THAT I'M MISSING!

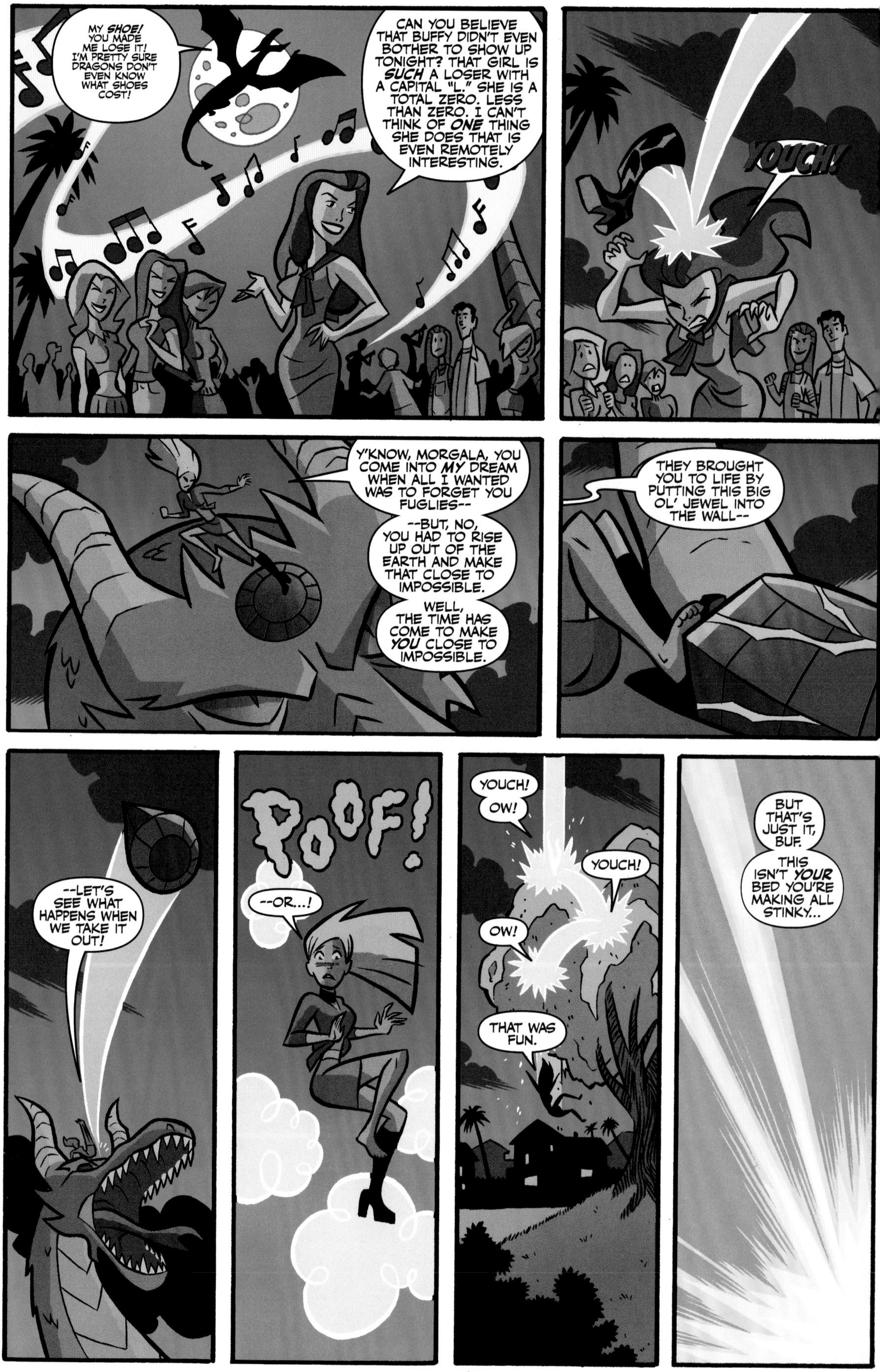
MY SHOE! YOU MADE ME LOSE IT! I'M PRETTY SURE DRAGONS DON'T EVEN KNOW WHAT SHOES COST!
CAN YOU BELIEVE THAT BUFFY DIDN'T EVEN BOTHER TO SHOW UP TONIGHT? THAT GIRL IS SUCH A LOSER WITH A CAPITAL "L." SHE IS A TOTAL ZERO. LESS THAN ZERO. I CAN'T THINK OF ONE THING SHE DOES THAT IS EVEN REMOTELY INTERESTING.
YOUCH!
Y'KNOW, MORGALA, YOU COME INTO MY DREAM WHEN ALL I WANTED WAS TO FORGET YOU FUGLIES--
--BUT, NO, YOU HAD TO RISE UP OUT OF THE EARTH AND MAKE THAT CLOSE TO IMPOSSIBLE.
WELL, THE TIME HAS COME TO MAKE YOU CLOSE TO IMPOSSIBLE.
THEY BROUGHT YOU TO LIFE BY PUTTING THIS BIG OL' JEWEL INTO THE WALL--
--LET'S SEE WHAT HAPPENS WHEN WE TAKE IT OUT!
POOF!
--OR...!
YOUCH!
OW!
YOUCH!
OW!
THAT WAS FUN.
BUT THAT'S JUST IT, BUF.
THIS ISN'T YOUR BED YOU'RE MAKING ALL STINKY...

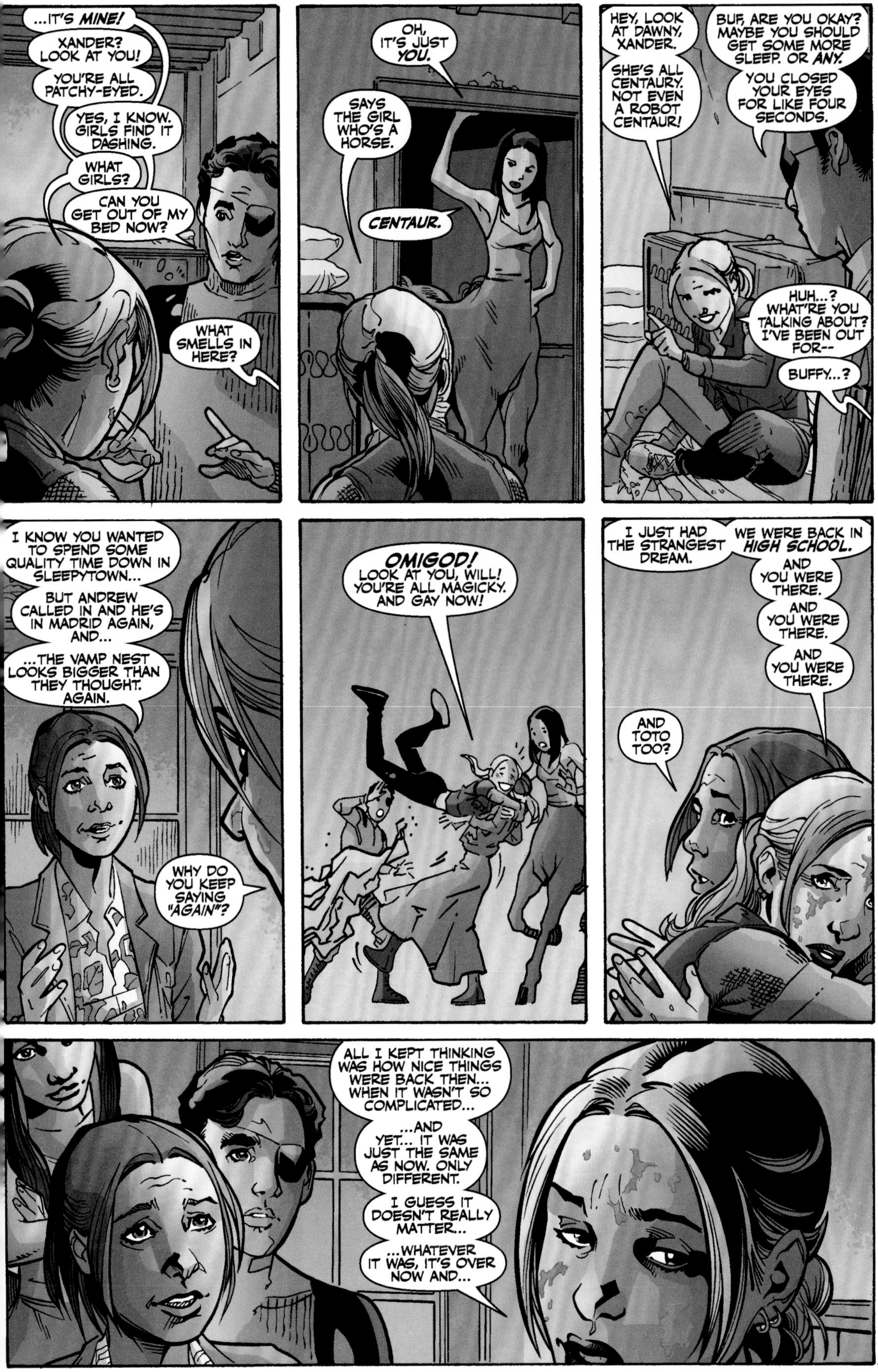
...IT'S *MINE!*
XANDER? LOOK AT YOU!
YOU'RE ALL PATCHY-EYED.
YES, I KNOW. GIRLS FIND IT DASHING.
WHAT GIRLS?
CAN YOU GET OUT OF MY BED NOW?
WHAT SMELLS IN HERE?
OH, IT'S JUST *YOU.*
SAYS THE GIRL WHO'S A HORSE.
CENTAUR.
HEY, LOOK AT DAWNY, XANDER.
SHE'S ALL CENTAURY. NOT EVEN A ROBOT CENTAUR!
BUF, ARE YOU OKAY? MAYBE YOU SHOULD GET SOME MORE SLEEP. OR *ANY.*
YOU CLOSED YOUR EYES FOR LIKE FOUR SECONDS.
HUH...? WHAT'RE YOU TALKING ABOUT? I'VE BEEN OUT FOR--
BUFFY...?
I KNOW YOU WANTED TO SPEND SOME QUALITY TIME DOWN IN SLEEPYTOWN...
BUT ANDREW CALLED IN AND HE'S IN MADRID AGAIN, AND...
...THE VAMP NEST LOOKS BIGGER THAN THEY THOUGHT. AGAIN.
WHY DO YOU KEEP SAYING *"AGAIN"*?
OMIGOD! LOOK AT YOU, WILL! YOU'RE ALL MAGICKY. AND GAY NOW!
I JUST HAD THE STRANGEST DREAM.
WE WERE BACK IN *HIGH SCHOOL.*
AND YOU WERE THERE.
AND YOU WERE THERE.
AND YOU WERE THERE.
AND TOTO TOO?
ALL I KEPT THINKING WAS HOW NICE THINGS WERE BACK THEN... WHEN IT WASN'T SO COMPLICATED...
...AND YET... IT WAS JUST THE SAME AS NOW. ONLY DIFFERENT.
I GUESS IT DOESN'T REALLY MATTER...
...WHATEVER IT WAS, IT'S OVER NOW AND...

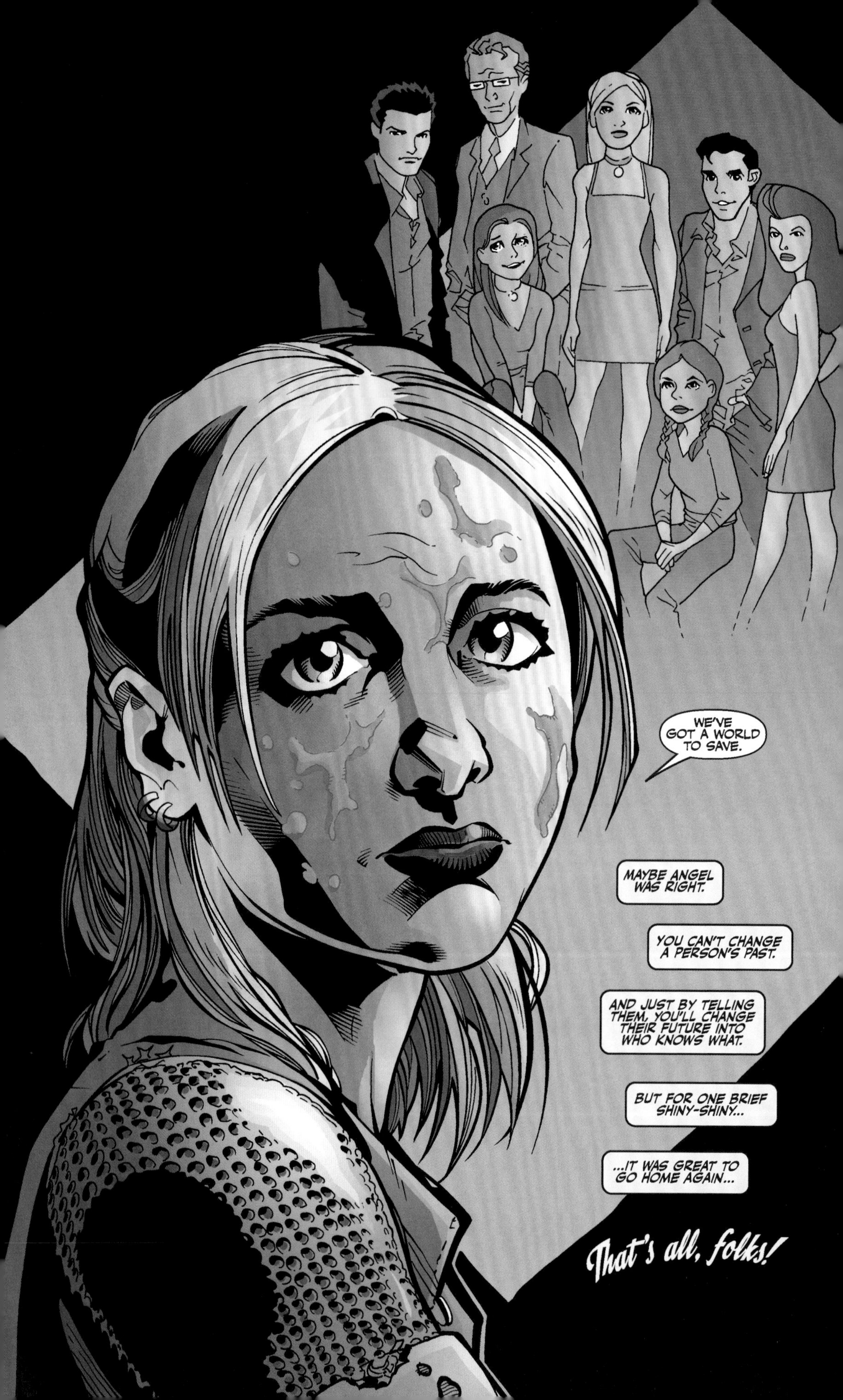
WE'VE GOT A WORLD TO SAVE.
MAYBE ANGEL WAS RIGHT.
YOU CAN'T CHANGE A PERSON'S PAST.
AND JUST BY TELLING THEM, YOU'LL CHANGE THEIR FUTURE INTO WHO KNOWS WHAT.
BUT FOR ONE BRIEF SHINY-SHINY...
...IT WAS GREAT TO GO HOME AGAIN...
That's all, folks!

COVERS FROM

BUFFY THE VAMPIRE SLAYER

ISSUES #16–#20

By

GEORGES JEANTY

with

DEXTER VINES, MICHELLE MADSEN
& MICHAEL WIGGAM

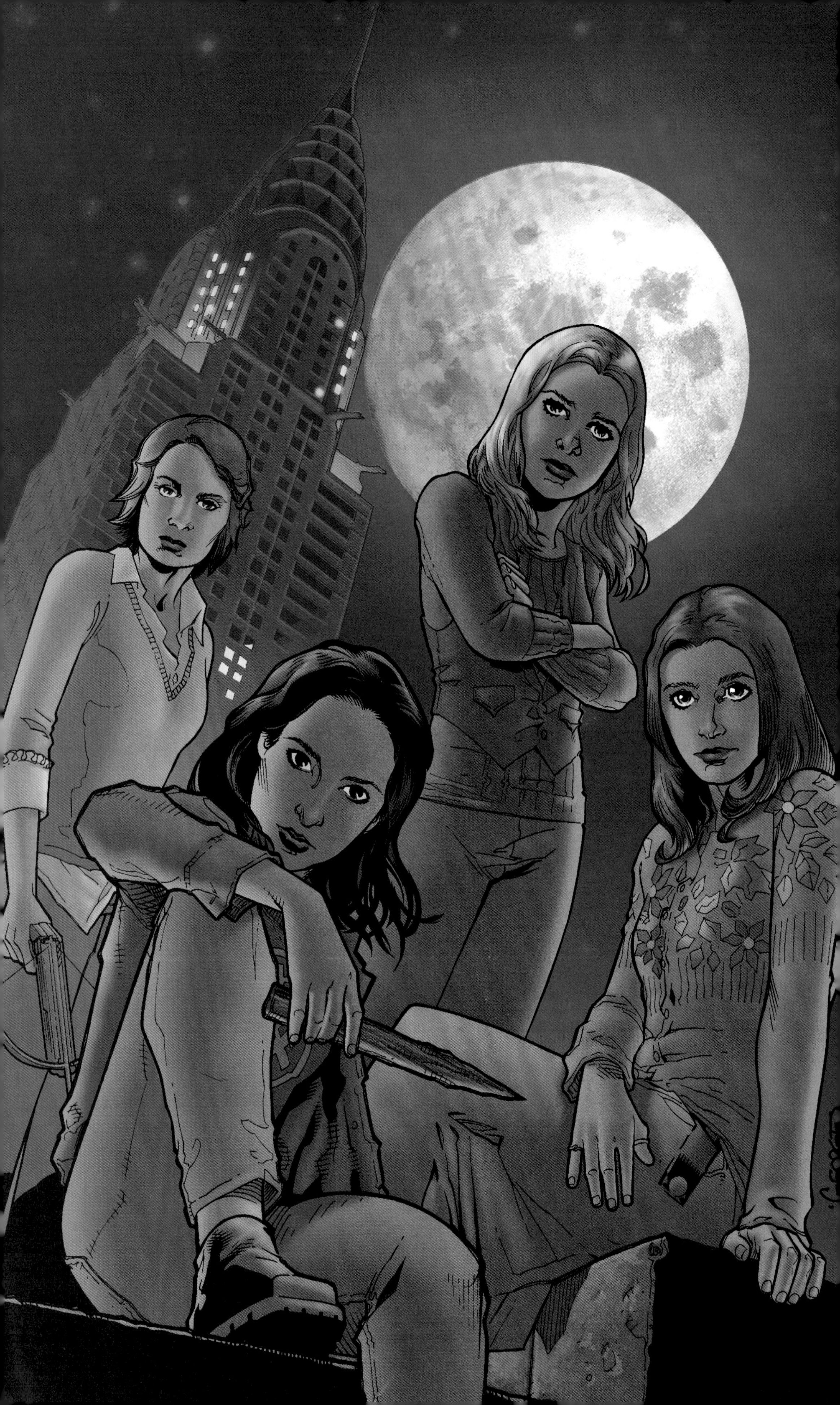

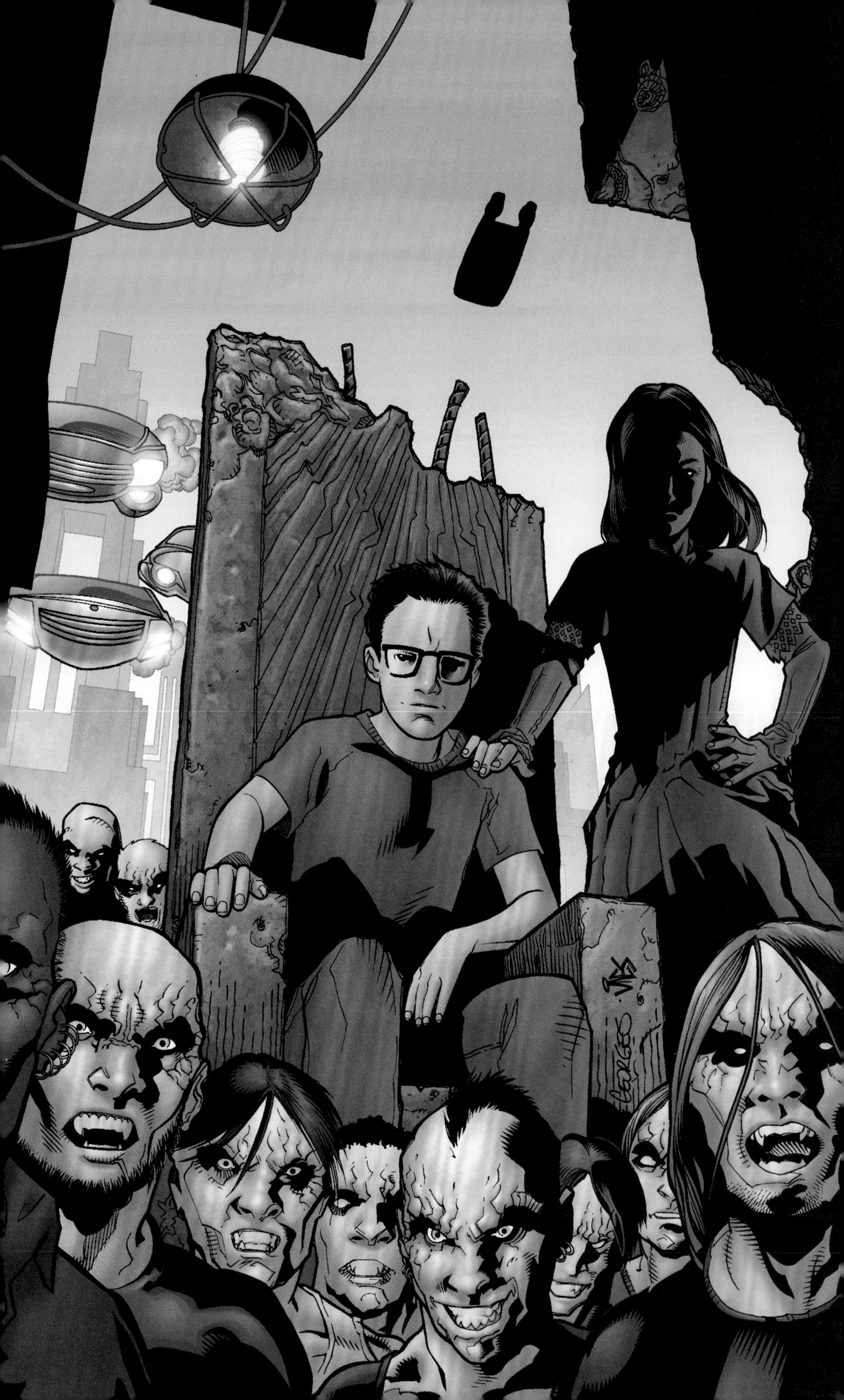

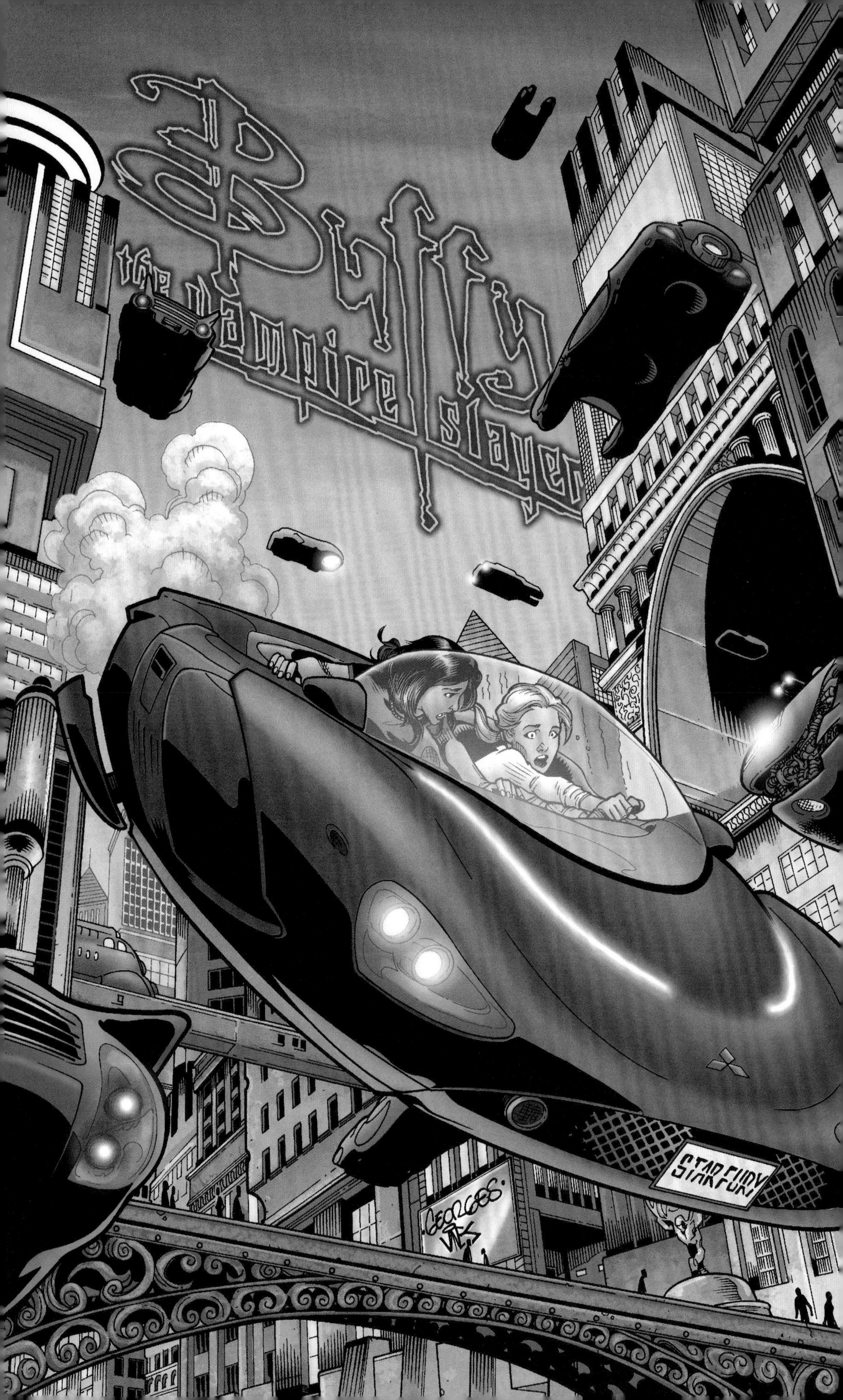
Buffy the Vampire Slayer
STAR FURY
GEORGES

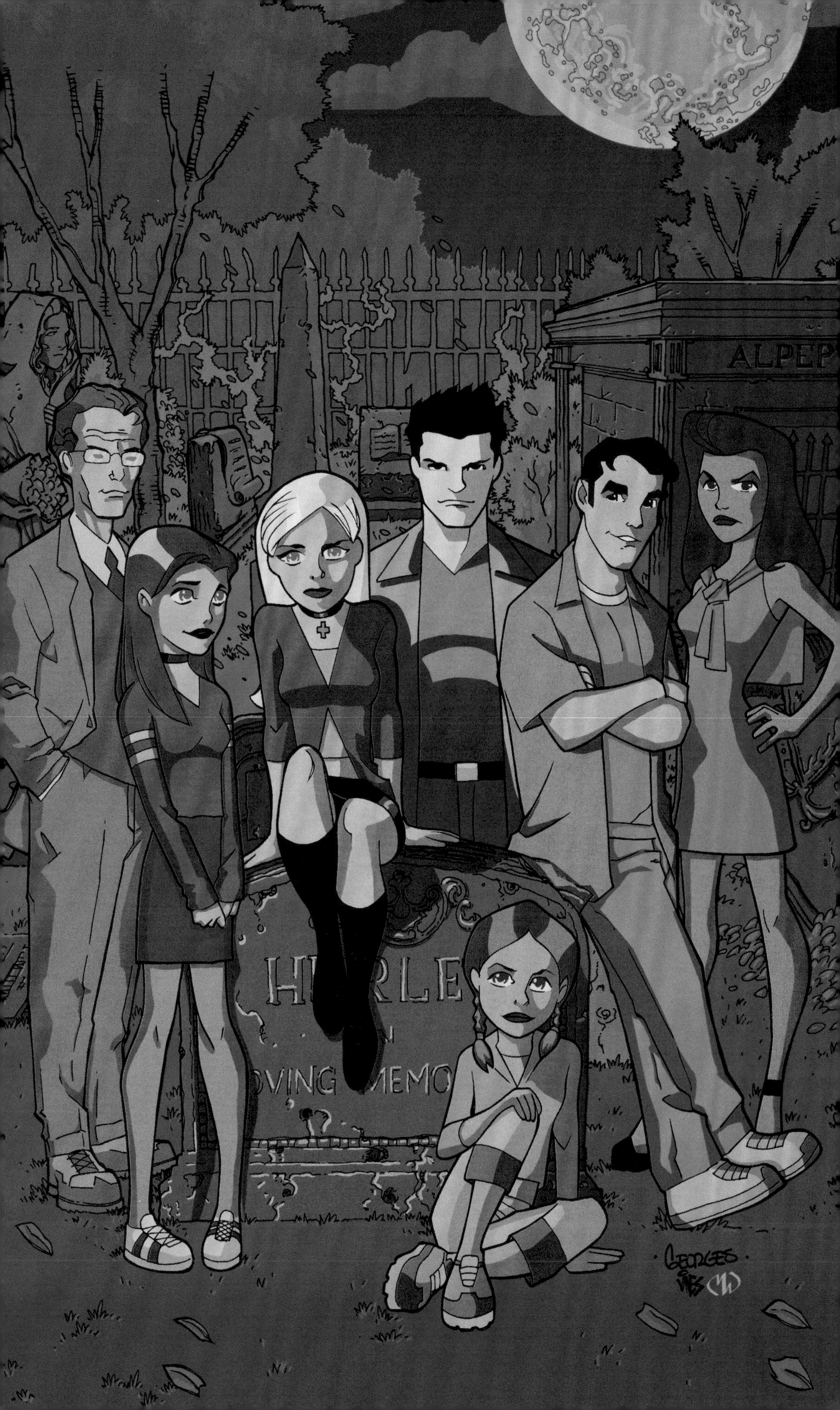

ALPEP
OVING MEMO
GEORGES

FROM JOSS WHEDON

BUFFY THE VAMPIRE SLAYER SEASON 8:

VOLUME 1: THE LONG WAY HOME
Joss Whedon and Georges Jeanty
ISBN 978-1-59307-822-5 | $15.95

VOLUME 2: NO FUTURE FOR YOU
Brian K. Vaughan, Georges Jeanty, and Joss Whedon
ISBN 978-1-59307-963-5 | $15.95

VOLUME 3: WOLVES AT THE GATE
Drew Goddard, Georges Jeanty, and Joss Whedon
ISBN 978-1-59582-165-2 | $15.95

VOLUME 4: TIME OF YOUR LIFE
Joss Whedon, Georges Jeanty, Jeph Loeb, and others
ISBN 978-1-59582-310-6 | $15.95

TALES OF THE SLAYERS
Joss Whedon, Amber Benson, Gene Colan, P. Craig Russell, Tim Sale, and others
ISBN 978-1-56971-605-2 | $14.95

TALES OF THE VAMPIRES
Joss Whedon, Brett Matthews, Cameron Stewart, and others
ISBN 978-1-56971-749-3 | $15.95

FRAY: FUTURE SLAYER
Joss Whedon and Karl Moline
ISBN 978-1-56971-751-6 | $19.95

SERENITY, VOLUME 1: THOSE LEFT BEHIND
Joss Whedon, Brett Matthews, and Will Conrad
ISBN 978-1-59307-449-4 | $9.95

ALSO FROM DARK HORSE . . .

BUFFY THE VAMPIRE SLAYER OMNIBUS

VOLUME 1
ISBN 978-1-59307-784-6 | $24.95

VOLUME 2
ISBN 978-1-59307-826-3 | $24.95

VOLUME 3
ISBN 978-1-59307-885-0 | $24.95

VOLUME 4
ISBN 978-1-59307-968-0 | $24.95

VOLUME 5
ISBN 978-1-59582-225-3 | $24.95

BUFFY THE VAMPIRE SLAYER:
PANEL TO PANEL
ISBN 978-1-59307-836-2 | $19.95

BUFFY THE VAMPIRE SLAYER:
CREATURES OF HABIT
ISBN 978-1-56971-563-5 | $17.95

MYSPACE DARK HORSE PRESENTS, VOLUME 1
Featuring "Sugarshock" by Joss Whedon and Fábio Moon
ISBN 978-1-59307-998-7 | $17.95

Buffy the Vampire Slayer™

GEORGE
OWENS

DARK HORSE BOOKS®
darkhorse.com

AVAILABLE AT YOUR LOCAL COMICS SHOP OR BOOKSTORE!
To find a comics shop in your area, call 1-888-266-4226.
For more information or to order direct: • On the web: darkhorse.com • E-mail: mailorder@darkhorse.com • Phone: 1-800-862-0052
Mon.–Fri. 9 AM to 5 PM Pacific Time. *Prices and availability subject to change without notice

ALSO FROM DARK HORSE BOOKS!

MICHAEL CHABON PRESENTS . . . THE AMAZING ADVENTURES OF THE ESCAPIST VOLUME 1

Glen David Gold, Howard Chaykin, Kyle Baker, Jim Starlin, Eric Wight, and others

This thrilling volume of *Michael Chabon Presents . . . The Amazing Adventures of the Escapist* collects the first two issues of the comic book and features an original story penned by Michael Chabon, the comics debut of novelist Glen David Gold, a new story written and drawn by Howard Chaykin, the painted artwork of Bill Sienkiewicz, and a wraparound cover by Chris Ware!

$17.95 | ISBN 978-1-59307-171-4

THE UMBRELLA ACADEMY VOLUME 1: APOCALYPSE SUITE

Gerard Way, Gabriel Bá, Dave Stewart

In an inexplicable worldwide event, forty-seven extraordinary children were spontaneously born. Millionaire inventor Reginald Hargreeves adopted seven of the children; when asked why, his only explanation was, "To save the world." These seven children form The Umbrella Academy, a dysfunctional family of superheroes with bizarre powers. Nearly a decade later, the team disbands, but when Hargreeves unexpectedly dies, these disgruntled siblings reunite just in time to save the world once again.

$17.95 | ISBN 978-1-59307-978-9

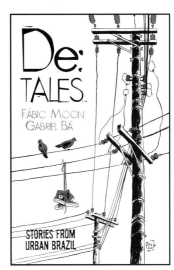

INDIANA JONES ADVENTURES VOLUME 1

Philip Gelatt, Ethen Beavers, Ronda Pattison

In the deep winter of Northern Europe, Dr. Henry Jones Jr. is about to undergo one of the most harrowing archaeological digs of his career! Amidst a deadly blizzard, he must find an ancient monument and unlock its secrets before someone with much darker intentions gets there first!

$6.95 | ISBN 978-1-59307-905-5

DE:TALES

Fábio Moon and Gabriel Bá

Brazilian twins Fábio Moon and Gabriel Bá share an award-winning talent for comics and an abiding love of the medium. This collection of short stories is brimming with all the details of human life—charming tales move from the urban reality of their home in São Paulo to the magical realism of their Latin American background.

$14.95 | ISBN 978-1-59307-485-2

AVAILABLE AT YOUR LOCAL COMICS SHOP OR BOOKSTORE
To find a comics shop in your area, call 1-888-266-4226
For more information or to order direct visit darkhorse.com or call 1-800-862-0052
Mon.–Sat. 9 AM to 5 PM Pacific Time.
*Prices and availability subject to change without notice

darkhorse.com

The Escapist™ & © 2003 Michael Chabon. All rights reserved. Indiana Jones™ & © 2008 Lucasfilm Ltd. All rights reserved. Used under authorization. The Umbrella Academy™ & © 2008 Gerard Way. De:Tales™ © 2006 Fábio Moon and Gabriel Bá.

HELLBOY™

by MIKE MIGNOLA

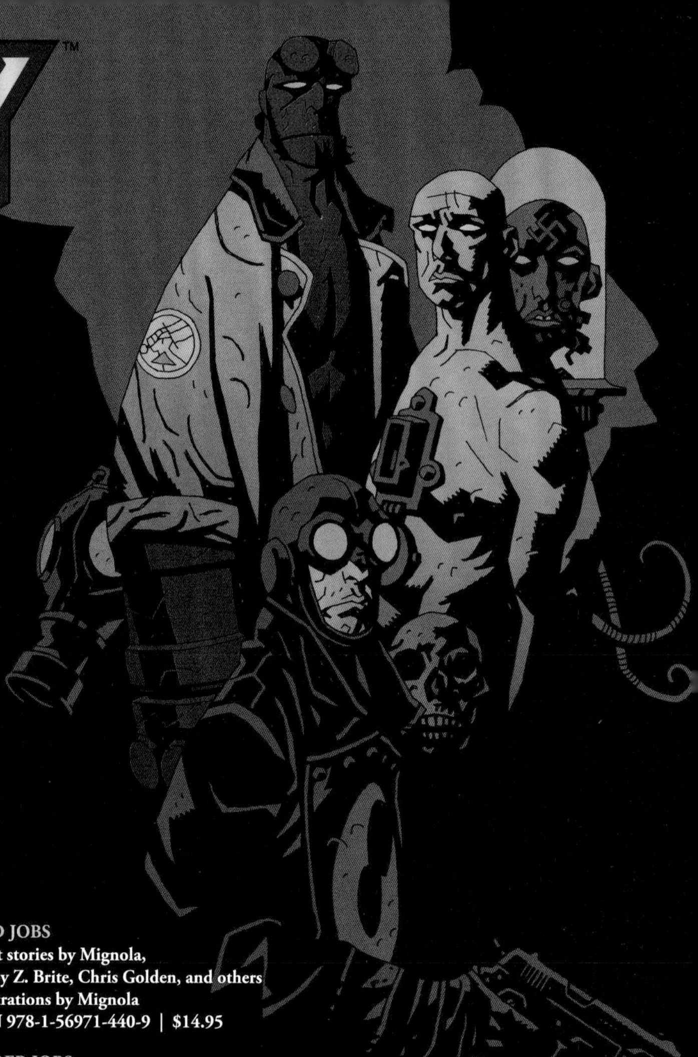

HELLBOY LIBRARY EDITION VOLUME 1:
SEED OF DESTRUCTION
AND WAKE THE DEVIL
ISBN 978-1-59307-910-9 | $49.95

HELLBOY LIBRARY EDITION VOLUME 2:
THE CHAINED COFFIN
AND THE RIGHT HAND OF DOOM
ISBN 978-1-59307-989-5 | $49.95

SEED OF DESTRUCTION
with John Byrne
ISBN 978-1-59307-094-6 | $17.95

WAKE THE DEVIL
ISBN 978-1-59307-095-3 | $17.95

THE CHAINED COFFIN
AND OTHERS
ISBN 978-1-59307-091-5 | $17.95

THE RIGHT HAND OF DOOM
ISBN 978-1-59307-093-9 | $17.95

CONQUEROR WORM
ISBN 978-1-59307-092-2 | $17.95

STRANGE PLACES
ISBN 978-1-59307-475-3 | $17.95

THE TROLL WITCH AND OTHERS
By Mignola, Corben, and Russell
ISBN 978-1-59307-860-7 | $17.95

DARKNESS CALLS
ISBN 978-1-59307-896-6 | $19.95

THE ART OF HELLBOY
ISBN 978-1-59307-089-2 | $29.95

HELLBOY II: THE ART OF THE MOVIE
ISBN 978-1-59307-964-2 | $24.95

HELLBOY: THE COMPANION
ISBN 978-1-59307-655-9 | $14.95

HELLBOY WEIRD TALES
Volume 1
ISBN 978-1-56971-622-9 | $17.95

Volume 2
ISBN 978-1-56971-953-4 | $17.95

To find a comics shop in your area,
call 1-888-266-4226
For more information or to order direct:
• On the web: darkhorse.com
• E-mail: mailorder@darkhorse.com
• Phone: 1-800-862-0052
Mon.–Fri. 9 AM to 5 PM Pacific Time

ODD JOBS
Short stories by Mignola,
Poppy Z. Brite, Chris Golden, and others
Illustrations by Mignola
ISBN 978-1-56971-440-9 | $14.95

ODDER JOBS
Short stories by Frank Darabont,
Guillermo del Toro, and others
Illustrations by Mignola
ISBN 978-1-59307-226-1 | $14.95

ODDEST JOBS
Short stories by China Miéville,
Ken Bruen, Mark Chadbourn, and others
Illustrations by Mignola
ISBN 978-1-59307-944-4 | $14.95

B.P.R.D.: HOLLOW EARTH
By Mignola, Chris Golden,
Ryan Sook, and others
ISBN 978-1-56971-862-9 | $17.95

B.P.R.D.: THE SOUL OF VENICE
By Mignola, Mike Oeming, Guy Davis,
Scott Kolins, Geoff Johns, and others
ISBN 978-1-59307-132-5 | $17.95

B.P.R.D.: PLAGUE OF FROGS
By Mignola and Guy Davis
ISBN 978-1-59307-288-9 | $17.95

B.P.R.D.: THE DEAD
By Mignola, John Arcudi, and Guy Davis
ISBN 978-1-59307-380-0 | $17.95

B.P.R.D.: THE BLACK FLAME
By Mignola, Arcudi, and Davis
ISBN 978-1-59307-550-7 | $17.95

B.P.R.D.: THE UNIVERSAL MACHINE
By Mignola, Arcudi, and Davis
ISBN 978-1-59307-710-5 | $17.95

B.P.R.D.: GARDEN OF SOULS
By Mignola, Arcudi, and Davis
ISBN 978-1-59307-882-9 | $17.95

B.P.R.D.: KILLING GROUND
By Mignola, Arcudi, and Davis
ISBN 978-1-59307-956-7 | $17.95

B.P.R.D.: 1946
By Mignola, Dysart, and Azaceta
ISBN 978-1-59582-191-1 | $17.95

B.P.R.D.: THE WARNING
By Mignola, Arcudi, and Davis
ISBN 978-1-59582-304-5 | $17.95

ABE SAPIEN: THE DROWNING
By Mignola, Jason Shawn Alexander,
and Dave Stewart
ISBN 978-1-59582-185-0 | $17.95

LOBSTER JOHNSON:
THE IRON PROMETHEUS
By Mignola, Jason Armstrong,
and Dave Stewart
ISBN 978-1-59307-975-8 | $17.95

DARK HORSE COMICS®
darkhorse.com
drawing on your nightmares™